VALLEY OF CHOICE, BOOK 2

In Plain View

Olivia Newport

THORNDIKE PRESS
A part of Gale, Cengage Learning

GALE
CENGAGE Learning·

Detroit • New York • San Francisco • New Haven, Conn • Waterville, Maine • London

30.00

GALE
CENGAGE Learning®

© 2013 by Olivia Newport.
Thorndike Press, a part of Gale, Cengage Learning.

Thorndike Press® Large Print Christian Romance.
The text of this Large Print edition is unabridged.
Other aspects of the book may vary from the original edition.
Set in 16 pt. Plantin.

LIBRARY OF CONGRESS CATALOGING-IN-PUBLICATION DATA

Newport, Olivia.
  In Plain View / By Olivia Newport. — Large Print edition.
    pages cm. — (Valley of Choice ; Book 2) (Thorndike Press Large Print Christian Romance.)
  ISBN-13: 978-1-4104-6273-2 (hardcover)
  ISBN-10: 1-4104-6273-0 (hardcover)
  1. Amish—Fiction 2. Life change events—Fiction. 3. Colorado—Fiction. 4. Large type books. I. Title.
PS3614.E686I57 2013
813'.6—dc23   2013025558

Published in 2013 by arrangement with Barbour Publishing, Inc.

Printed in the United States of America
1 2 3 4 5 6 7 17 16 15 14 13

DEDICATION

For Sonja

ACKNOWLEDGMENTS

It is hard to know how to say thank you to all the people who helped bring this book into being. My agent, Rachelle Gardner, believes in me, which probably spurs me on more than she knows. How blessed I am to call her friend as well!

I have no doubt about Barbour's commitment to make the book the best it can be. After all, they had the good sense to connect me with Traci DePree to work as editor on the Valley of Choice series.

My husband is always game to gallivant off somewhere with me, literally or cyberly, in search of information. Every writer should be so lucky.

And Sonja. What can I say?

Sometimes writing feels like a lonely enterprise, but when I lift my eyes from the screen I see a host of people cheering me on. I am thankful for each one.

ONE

Annie Friesen had a lot to learn about how to ride a bicycle in a dress that brushed her ankles.

The late-April day slushed with spring snow vacillating about whether to melt. Temperate Colorado mountain air beckoned a population sick and tired of huddling indoors all winter, Annie among them. Five miles stretched between her and the Beiler farm, five miles she was determined to traverse without depending on Rufus Beiler and his buggy to pick her up. She could walk or she could bike from her house in Westcliffe to the Beiler home, where Rufus's family expected her for supper, and she would surrender herself to their long arms of hospitality and acceptance. The moment to begin the walk and arrive on time had passed thirty minutes ago, though.

Annie turned the bicycle around in the narrow, century-old garage and assessed its

readiness for the first outing of the spring. The tires seemed acceptable, the pedals spun appropriately when she kicked at one, and the brakes squeezed when cued. She walked the bike into the sunlight and laid it down on the ground while she heaved the garage door closed. Then she situated herself on the seat, straightened the heavy wide-knit navy cardigan she wore, and hiked up the skirt of her deep purple dress as far as a good Amish girl dared.

Annie was not a good Amish girl. At least not yet. She did not even always wear Amish clothing. After eight months of friendship with the Beilers and regular attendance at the district's worship services, she would have to rate her German as pitiful. She understood more every week, but she could not get her mind and tongue to cooperate in speaking. Private lessons were some help, though she often left more frustrated than when she arrived. Singing hymns from the *Ausbund* might as well have been reading a census listing, which meant she had a lot to learn about both patience and devotion. The *Ordnung* was a mystical obscurity she wished someone would translate to bulleted points in plain English. The hairstyles seemed severe — but only when she looked in a mirror, which she did less and less these

days. The ties to her prayer *kapp* annoyed her whether she tied them or let them hang loose on her shoulders.

But she was trying. For one thing, she had given up driving her own car, which was up on blocks in her parents' garage in Colorado Springs.

Annie checked the strap on her helmet — a promise she made to her mother when she gave up driving — then put her weight on the top pedal and leaned into the bike's forward movement. The streets in town were wet but friendly enough for cycling. Once she got to the highway, though, Annie scowled at the sludge passing vehicles sprayed at her. She knew what the drivers were thinking because she used to be one of them. *What kind of idiot rides a bike on a high-speed road? If they can't go the speed limit, they should get off the road.* She was lucky if drivers moved three inches toward the center of the two-lane highway when they whizzed past her.

Rufus had offered to pick her up. All winter long he fetched her when she needed to venture beyond the confines of Westcliffe, where she worked on Main Street and lived on a side street. But Annie did not want to depend on Rufus for her every move until she learned to care for a horse

and drive a buggy of her own. The promise of spring allowed independence, as far as she was concerned. Milder weather meant she could come and go as she wished, as long as she did not mind the rigors of riding or walking at high elevation. This first ride of the season made her want to lengthen her stride and let her feet hit pavement in heart-pumping rhythm. Did good Amish girls run cross-country?

By the time Annie turned into the long Beiler driveway, she was refusing to shiver in her damp sweater, and the sodden hem of her skirt was slapping against drenched stockings. The best she could hope to do was keep her headpiece on straight. The Beilers had taken her into heart and hearth as she was, but she still wished she could arrive without looking a mess once in a while.

Seven-year-old Jacob was the first to spot her, as he always was. He loped down the wide porch steps and across the yard with one hand holding his straw hat in place and his black winter-weight wool jacket flapping open. Annie checked to be sure he was at least wearing shoes, knowing that as soon as the ground dried up he would leave his boy-sized brown work boots neatly under his bed.

"Annalise!" The boy flung himself into her arms even before she could properly dismount. The bicycle tumbled on its side and she let it go in favor of his enthusiasm against her torso. Jacob knocked her slightly off balance, and her cell phone spilled from a sweater pocket. Jacob squatted to scoop it up. "Do you ever miss your old phone? I liked your old phone."

Her iPhone had been her lifeline to another world — e-mail, texting, Internet, Facebook, Twitter. She had done it all on her phone, and she never turned it off. She ran her whole company from that phone sometimes.

"I would trade a thousand phones just to know you." Annie wrapped her hand around the simple flip-style phone. This one was not even turned on. So far, in the last six months, Annie managed to avoid any emergency calls. Otherwise she only turned it on for her weekly calls to her mother, a compromise that helped keep the peace. Her parents had the number Rufus used for his woodworking business, so if one of her parents had a true emergency, they could reach her.

Annie glanced toward the house, ready for her pulse to quicken at the sight of Rufus.

"The Stutzmans are here." Jacob took her

13

hand and tugged.

"Who?"

"The new family."

Annie managed a smile for Jacob's sake. She was expecting supper with only the Beiler family. They knew her well and patiently guided her through the path of learning Amish ways. The presence of another family, especially a new one, took the edge off her anticipation of the evening — and immediately she felt remorse at her ungenerous thought.

When Rufus Beiler heard the screen door slam behind his little brother, he lifted his eyes to the big window that looked out the front of the house. As it often was, Annalise's *kapp* was cockeyed, an unintended habit that made him smile.

"Excuse me," he said to Beth Stutzman, who hardly broke her chatter to breathe. "I'll be back shortly."

On his way out the front door, Rufus grabbed his coat off the rack. He met Annalise and Jacob halfway down the driveway.

"I told Annalise the Stutzmans are here," Jacob said.

"Thank you, Jacob." Rufus tilted his head toward the house. "Maybe *Mamm* needs your help."

"I hope she's all out of beets from the cellar."

"Jacob!"

"I'm sorry." The boy huffed. "I will be thankful for whatever is put in front of me to eat."

Rufus watched his brother start to kick the dirt beneath his boot and then think better of it. As the little boy clomped up the porch steps, Rufus laid his coat around Annalise's shoulders. She had, as she nearly always did, underdressed for the spring temperatures.

When she turned toward him and lifted her face in thanks, he wanted to kiss her right there. She was so lovely. Bits of moisture clinging to her face shimmered in waning sunlight. He barely kept himself from smoothing her blond hair back into place under her *kapp.*

"Stutzmans?" Her wide gray eyes questioned.

" 'Fraid so." He straightened the jacket around her.

"I'm not cold, you know." Her eyes smiled even if her lips were turning blue.

"So you often tell me." He would never admit he hung his coat around her so her scent would be on it when he wore it next

"Anyway, Stutzmans," she reminded him.

15

"Just moved from Pennsylvania to join the settlement here."

"Did you know them in Pennsylvania?"

"Quite well. They are second cousins of my brother Daniel's wife and had a farm only four miles from ours." He paused and put his hand on her elbow.

"Oh. That's nice."

He heard the disappointment in her tone. "If you don't feel up to meeting new people tonight, I can take you home."

"Don't be silly. I'm here. The Stutzmans are here. I'm sure we'll get along famously."

Rufus was not so sure.

Instead of making a dripping entrance through the front door, Annie asked Rufus to walk her to the back door. She could slip into the kitchen and up the back stairs to dry off and straighten herself out. When she glanced in the small mirror in the bathroom, she rolled her eyes. Why did she seem to be the only Amish woman — well, almost Amish — who could not seem to wear a prayer *kapp* properly?

Under her thick sweater, the dress was surprisingly dry. She could do little about the hem of her skirt, which had plunged through one puddle too many. It would have to dry in its own time.

Downstairs, the table was extended to its full length and Jacob was rounding up the last of the extra chairs from around the house. Eli and Franey, Rufus's parents, shared their home with five of their eight children. In between their eldest son, Rufus, and youngest son, Jacob, were Joel, Lydia, and Sophie, all teenagers.

Hospitality oozed out of Franey Beiler's bones, a trait that first brought Annie into the house last summer. Franey would not blink twice at accommodating seven extra people for dinner.

She suggested the Stutzmans sit where they pleased and the Beilers — and Annalise — would fill in. Annie's stomach heated as the tallest Stutzman daughter took the chair directly opposite Rufus. Annie pressed her lips together and took another chair. As Eli Beiler presided over the silent prayer at the beginning of the meal, Annie could not help but wonder about one empty seat. Joel Beiler was missing.

Ike and Edna Stutzman's daughters — Beth, Johanna, and Essie — seemed to Annie close enough in age that she would not be surprised to discover a set of twins among them. She guessed they were between nineteen and twenty-two. The boys — Mark and Luke — were younger, perhaps

17

recently finished with eighth-grade formal schooling.

They were loud. *Laut.* Jacob had taught Annie that word.

Annie could not summon a more polite description that remained honest. The entire family spoke as if they were addressing a deaf grandfather, and one on top of the other. They were full of news of former neighbors in Pennsylvania, and Franey and Eli lit up in gratitude for stories of people they had lived so long among, including their own two married sons.

For Annie's sake, the Beilers often spoke English. The Stutzmans, however, made no such effort, beyond initial introductions. Pennsylvania Dutch flew around the table too fast for Annie to keep up with much of the conversation. Jacob sat beside her, as he always did when she came to dinner. Occasionally, he leaned toward her and offered a brief translation, which helped Annie to smile and nod in appropriate lulls.

Annie did not need translation to see that Beth Stutzman directed many of her remarks at Rufus in a way that forced him to respond. *She must be the eldest,* Annie decided. Johanna and Essie made no effort to compete with their sister but instead sat quietly, observing the conversation and

18

smiling benignly. Beth would have been finishing the eighth grade when Rufus left Pennsylvania, when he was a grown man already. But now she was grown up — and quite pretty, Annie had to admit. Had Beth Stutzman swept into town and thought she would snag Rufus Beiler on her first evening?

Jacob leaned toward her and whispered. "The Stutzmans are going to stay with us for a while. They want to paint their house before they move in. I hope they will let me help paint."

Annie smiled. "I'm sure you're a very good painter."

"No one ever gives me a chance to try."

Annie reached over and scratched the center of his back then laid her arm across the top of his chair, angling toward Rufus as she did so.

Despite the decibel level and Beth's brazenness, the evening was drenched in friendship going back generations. Annie could see for herself that these were not like the unfamiliar families in Colorado Springs who intersected each other's routines at swim classes and soccer matches for three years until someone transferred to a new job. They shared each other's days and nights, and various branches of their families had

19

intermarried. Ike and Edna had come west for many of the same reasons Eli and Franey had come six years earlier. Unlike the Beilers, though, the newcomers had a community ready to welcome them and give them aid.

Even after six months of living as plainly as she could, and despite her dress and *kapp,* Annie felt very much the *English.* And she had been at the Beiler table enough times to feel the undercurrent that grew between Eli and Franey as conversation rose and fell and Joel failed to appear. Annie glanced at Rufus, catching his eye in a fleeting connection before Beth launched into another story meant for Rufus's benefit. The evening was nothing like what Annie craved when she had started out on her bicycle.

Eli's eyes, Annie noticed, moved between the clock and the front door.

Joel was going to have some explaining to do.

Two

Johanna Stutzman and her brother Mark sat on either side of Joel's empty seat. As the meal progressed, both seemed to absorb a share of the available space, as if they no longer expected someone would arrive to occupy the chair.

Annie regretted putting so much food on her plate. She felt left out of the rapid, reminiscent conversation in the language she still struggled to learn, and whenever she looked at Eli, her anxiety for Joel heightened. Both factors dimmed her appetite.

This was not the first time Joel had been late for dinner, she knew. That only made things worse. Had he not known the Stutzmans would be there? If he had, would he have made an effort to be present?

The creak of the front door's hinges raised eyes around the table. Joel entered and closed the door carefully behind him. A still-

growing seventeen-year-old, his trousers inched off his ankles as he turned to face the gathering at the table.

"Ah, Joel." With just two words, Eli's voice bore through the chatter.

"I'm sorry, *Daed.*" Joel moved toward the table, his back erect. He brushed a bookcase, and a cell phone clattered to the polished wood floor.

"Hey, that's just like Annalise's." Jacob clambered out of his chair and picked up the phone.

"Jacob, get back in your seat." Eli's eyes remained on Joel.

Jacob handed the phone to Joel and obeyed his father.

"It's Carter's phone." Joel took his own seat. "I forgot he gave it to me to hold."

"We'll talk later," Eli said. "Just turn it off and put it away."

Annie winced on Joel's behalf. She saw Joel reach under the table and fiddle with the phone, which was indeed on. Eli was not going to embarrass Joel in the presence of guests — even old family friends — but even if the phone was not Joel's, Eli would want to know what his son was doing with it.

"Carter is the son of Tom Reynolds." Speaking English, Rufus deftly explained.

"You'll want to meet Tom as soon as possible. He does a fair bit of taxiing and hauling for our people, and he doesn't mind the distances involved in our district."

"That's good to know." Ike Stutzman's voice was deep and commanding. "I heard that because of the distances, your district allows the use of telephones."

Oops. Annie caught Rufus's eyes and saw the flicker of dismay that his effort to deflect the conversation had been short lived.

"That's true," Eli said, "but the concern is for safety, not convenience or amusement."

His expression was not lost on Annie, so she had no doubt that Joel understood perfectly.

"Carter's dad was out looking at the new recreation area," Joel said. "He took some pictures."

Oops again. Not the best topic of conversation Joel could have introduced to take the heat off himself.

"No one has made any decisions about the use of that property," Eli said.

"What property is that?" Ike's inquiry sounded idle enough.

Annie pushed peas around on her plate. At least they were not beets. She stood in solidarity with Jacob on the beets question.

She was relieved to hear Rufus's voice again.

"The county owns a few acres not far from here," Rufus explained in English. "There is some thought to developing a park. The organizers would like volunteers to offer their labor in order to keep costs to a minimum. They have invited everyone to participate."

"Even the Amish?" Edna Stutzman asked from beside Franey. "Surely they understand that we live apart."

Rufus tilted his head. "The park would be for everyone to use. If everyone shares the load, then everyone benefits as well."

"But this is an *English* project, is it not?" Ike thumped the table as he persisted with the distinction.

"Well, yes, I suppose," Rufus said. "It was the idea of Tom Reynolds and a few others. They propose a simple shelter from rain and sun, a children's play area, and trails for families to use."

"But this is an *English* project," Edna repeated.

Annie did not need a translation for the consonants spitting from Edna's mouth when she said *English*. She reached up and tugged on the two strings of her *kapp,* a habit developed over the last six months in nervous moments. While she was living

24

largely plain until she decided whether to join the Amish officially, Annie resented Edna's inferences about the *English*.

"Do you often cooperate with the *English*?" Edna bristled as she broke open a biscuit.

"The *English* are our neighbors here," Rufus said, persisting in English. "When do you hope to move onto your farm?"

And that was it. He let it go and moved on.

Annie stifled a sigh. How did he do that? Just let things go when the tension mounted?

Relief blew out on Franey's breath, Annie noticed. She was not opposed to a park. She was not even opposed to working with the neighbors. Franey simply did not want to get involved with that particular plot of land. Annie did not know why.

It had something to do with Ruth. Annie knew that much. Annie missed Ruth. Rufus's sister would have known how to navigate the emotions in the room.

Franey's reticence about the land proposed for the park.

Joel's running around with Carter Reynolds and the boys from town.

Eli's need for order.

Even Beth Stutzman batting her eyes at Rufus.

Annie was glad that she could picture where Ruth was — the roadways of Colorado Springs bearing the buses Ruth rode to work and school, the university she attended, the small dorm room she lived in. Even though she knew Ruth was sure of her choice, Annie felt Franey's sadness.

Franey stood up. "How about dessert?" She smiled around the table. "I have peach pie, apple schnitzel, and rhubarb crisp."

Rufus's sisters Lydia and Sophie took the cue and began clearing the table. Annie did the same.

The Stutzman daughters rested comfortably in their chairs. Beth even put her elbow on the table, set her chin in her hand, and leaned toward Rufus. Annie shoved down the resentment that welled.

Humility, humility, humility, she told herself. No matter what she thought of their manners, she would serve them with a smile.

Rufus remembered the Stutzman girls differently. Perhaps it was because they were so much younger than he was that he never paid close attention to them when the families lived near each other in Lancaster County. They were taller now, more filled

out. Beth's hair was much the same color as Annalise's, he observed. He supposed that her forwardness would wear off soon enough when she saw that he did not return her feelings, and when she met some of the other families who had sons looking for wives.

He looked at Annalise across the table. Concentrating so hard to follow conversation in Pennsylvania Dutch exhausted her, he knew, and the evening's exchanges had been particularly rapid. Several times during the evening he had switched to English in an effort to include her, but clearly the Stutzmans were not used to using English at home and inevitably switched back within a few sentences. As they told stories of Lancaster County, their enthusiasm spilled out in a torrent of Pennsylvania Dutch.

Annalise smiled at him in an expression he had come to know meant, *I'm tired and I want to go home.*

Rufus pushed back his chair. "It's been good to hear so much news from home. Now I think I'd better make sure Annalise is home before it gets later."

Annalise stood. "Thank you, Rufus. I do have to open the shop early tomorrow."

"You work in a shop?" Edna asked. "What sort of shop?"

"Antiques, collectibles, odd and ends," Annalise said. "It's right on Main Street."

"They sell some of my jam," Franey said. "Weekend visitors seem to like it."

"Beth makes excellent jam," Edna said, smiling at Rufus.

Rufus nodded politely and stood up. "I'll take Annalise home now."

"Let Joel take her," Eli said.

Rufus stopped in his steps. He always took Annalise home. In fact, often the quiet ride home was the part of an evening he looked forward to most. Talking freely with Annalise, holding her hand, hearing the way she laughed when only he was around. Rufus would not counter his father, though, especially in front of guests.

Eli lifted his chin toward Joel. "Stop on your way back and return Carter's phone, please. I don't want it in the house."

The phone could have waited until the morning, Rufus thought.

"I'll walk out with you." Rufus gestured toward the front door. "It will take Joel a few minutes to bring the buggy around."

Annalise followed him to the front door, where she retrieved her half-dry sweater. He read the mixture of disappointment and gratitude in her face when they stepped out under the porch light and she turned her

face to him.

"I'm sorry," Rufus said. "I thought we would have some time to talk."

"Me too. But we must respect your father."

Rufus sighed gently. "You are learning our ways."

They descended the steps together.

"I really do have to open the shop early," Annalise said. "Mrs. Weichert is going into Cañon City to visit an old rancher's house. The family claims some of the pieces have been in the family for well over a hundred years. They may be an easy sell to the weekend antiquers."

"Will you be at the shop all day?"

She shook her head. "She promises to be back before noon."

"Then you'll be back here tomorrow?"

"My Saturday quilting lesson is the highlight of my week. Wouldn't miss it."

He nodded in satisfaction. "I'm sure I'll see you."

They walked halfway down the driveway to where her bicycle still lay on its side.

"I should check your brakes," he said.

"The brakes are fine. The tires, too."

"It can't hurt to double-check."

"It's fine, Rufus. You're sweet, but I built and sold two high-tech companies. I think I

can keep a bicycle in working order."

Joel arrived with a horse and the small cart.

"You should have brought the buggy," Rufus said. "It's getting cold."

"I thought this would be easier to put the bike in." Joel was already gripping the frame in two places and lifting the bike into the cart.

"This is fine," Annalise said. "I'm not cold, you know."

Rufus smiled. "So you often tell me."

"You two can hold your smiling contest later," Joel said. "Let's get this over with."

Rufus did not much care for his brother's attitude, but this was not the time to challenge him. He turned to Annalise and offered a hand to help her up into the cart. "I'll see you tomorrow."

"Right after lunch."

"Have you got the phone, Joel?" Rufus asked.

Joel raised the reins. "I'm not an idiot."

"I know you didn't want to do this." Annie gripped the seat. Joel was letting the horse have a little too much head.

"Don't worry about it." He did not turn an inch in her direction.

He was seventeen. Annie had never been

an Amish boy, but she did remember seventeen. She let an entire mile roll by before she spoke again.

"You and your father are going to work this out."

"Work what out?"

"This thing between you. That keeps you from talking to each other."

"I don't know what you're talking about."

Another mile.

If Joel did not choose to be baptized and join the Amish church, it might just take Franey around the bend. His older sister Ruth had already left home without joining the church, and while the relationship between mother and daughter had tenuously stitched itself back together over the last few months, Annie was sure Franey was not ready to go through that again with another child.

"I'm not Ruth, you know," Joel said.

How did he do that? "I didn't say anything."

"You don't have to. I'm not stupid. I know *Mamm* wants me to be baptized, the sooner the better."

"You have to do what is right for you."

"Look where that got Ruth."

"Still. It's true."

Another mile. Two more to go.

"I'm going to be baptized," he said. "I'm just not on a time schedule. There's no hurry unless I decide I want to get married."

"True enough."

"And I'm not getting married any time soon."

"I'm sure you know what you're doing."

"About as much as you do."

Everybody she knew back in Colorado Springs thought she needed a good shrink. Sell her business for millions of dollars and park the money where she could not touch it? Give up modern technology? Move into a decrepit house one-third the size of her custom-built condo and immediately get rid of the electricity? Take classes — in German — to learn the Amish faith?

"I stumble through one day at a time," she said.

"It seems to me you've got a pretty good grip on things."

"Smoke and mirrors, I assure you."

"I'm Amish," he said. "I'm not supposed to know about magic tricks."

Annie elbowed him and laughed. They turned off the main highway and onto Main Street heading east. A few blocks later, Joel turned the horse north.

"Lights are on in your house," he said.

ł you leave them burning?"

nnie leaned forward. "No."

Well, somebody did."

The living room was well lit. Annie wondered if there were such a thing as an Amish thief. Who else would know not to reach for a wall switch?

Joel slowed the horse and reached to extinguish the lantern hanging from the front of the cart.

"I guess I forgot," she said.

"You don't forget, Annalise. Even I know that."

They stopped in front of the house. "Should we call 911?" Annie pulled her phone out of her sweater pocket and flipped it open. Westcliffe was the seat of Custer County. A county sheriff's car would be just minutes away.

"I can't just leave you here." Joel put a hand on Annie's arm.

They watched the house for a few silent seconds.

"I'm going in with you," Joel finally said. "But turn on the phone just in case."

THREE

Joel looped the reins around the mailbox at the curb. Staying in the shadow of the house, Annie led the way up the driveway and around the back of the house.

"How do you think they got in?" Joel's whisper might as well have been a megaphone.

Annie put a finger to her lips and stepped onto the small porch outside her back door. With one hand still gripping her cell phone, she slowly lowered the handle on the screen door. Ready to wince if the contrary spring at the top betrayed them, she opened the door inch by inch and slipped into the opening. Joel was right behind her when she tested the knob on the main door. She was sure she had locked it when she left, but it turned easily now.

Inside, her fingers found the edge of the counter and she felt her way along it across the small dark kitchen. A shadow crossed

the light seeping around the edges of the swinging door between the kitchen and dining room. Someone was definitely on the other side — and moving around.

"I can't see anything." Joel's feet dragged on the floor.

"Put your hand on my shoulder. Watch out for the trash —"

But Annie's hushed warning was too late. Joel stumbled and sent the metal can clanging across the floor. She halted and froze. Joel's tumbling weight against her back nearly knocked her over.

The door from the dining room opened. "Annie, is that you?"

The air went out of Annie so fast she almost whistled like a balloon. "Mom!"

Annie reached for the small propane lamp she knew was at the end of the counter and turned the switch. Her father now stood behind her mother in the doorway. Myra Friesen looked from her daughter to the young man behind her.

"This is Joel," Annie said. "Rufus's brother. Joel, these are my parents, Myra and Brad Friesen."

"Hello, Joel," Myra said.

"It's nice to meet you." Joel nudged Annie. "Everything's okay, *ya*?"

She nodded. Whatever brought her parents

to her home without prior arrangement was nothing she needed Joel for. "Thank you for seeing me in."

"I'll leave the bike on the side of the house."

"Danki." Thank you.

The screen door slammed behind him, and Annie closed the solid inner door. Then she righted the trash can, grateful she chose the covered model when she outfitted her kitchen.

Myra glanced around the kitchen. "You've done a nice job making something of this room . . . with its limitations."

"Thank you. Mom, what's going on? How did you even get in?"

"You've got a tree in the backyard just like the one at home. It even has the same low branch — good for climbing. It was simple enough to think you'd hide a key there like we do at home."

"Busted. Where did you stash your car?" If she had seen their sedan, she might have spared a few extra heartbeats moments ago.

Myra set the house key on the counter. "We figured your garage was empty, considering your car is in our garage at home."

Home. Was her mother going to work that word into every sentence? Annie let the comment pass and instead gestured to the

36

dining room. "Why don't I make some coffee and you can tell me why you're here?"

Along with the coffee, Annie produced
half a chocolate cake. They sat at the oval
table up against the window in the dining
room.

"Mmm. Delicious!" Myra jabbed her fork
in for a second bite of cake. "Is this from a
bakery in town?"

"No. I made it."

"You made this? You never used to like to
bake."

"I'm trying a lot of new things these days."
Annie nudged a small pitcher of cream
toward her dad, who she knew would want
a generous portion.

"Well, I miss some of your old habits."
Myra licked chocolate off her top lip. "Like
calling your mother."

"I call you every Saturday and we yak the
charge out of my phone." Annie twirled her
fork, balancing a piece of cake. "I would
have called you tomorrow like always." So
why were they here?

Brad cleared his throat. "We're here on a
special mission."

"Which is?"

"Penny is coming home." Myra looked at
Annie hopefully.

Annie had not seen her sister in almost a

year and a half. Though Annie had gone to Colorado Springs for Christmas, at the last minute Penny had to cancel her flight from Seattle and missed the holiday.

"When does she arrive?"

"Tomorrow night."

"Tomorrow!" Annie set her mug down. "Why didn't we find out sooner?"

"We found out last Saturday. She called right after I got off the phone with you. I meant to send you a note, but I never got to it. I'm just not used to communicating the old-fashioned way, I guess."

Annie wondered how many times she and her mother would have to go around this loop.

"I wanted to leave a message on your phone," Myra said, "but you have all these rules about what is a true emergency."

"It seemed the simplest thing to drive out here," Brad said.

"I'm sorry I wasn't home." Annie reached for the pot and warmed up her coffee.

"We can take you back with us in the morning," Myra said.

"You're staying the night?"

"Certainly. Not here, of course. We've already checked in at Mo's."

Annie nodded. Mo's motel. Where they had electricity. And complimentary Wi-Fi.

"I'm sure you'll be comfortable there." She paused. "I'm not sure about going back with you, though."

Myra's fork hit the bare plate. "But you have to. I told you. Penny's coming. It's hard for her to get away."

"It might be hard for me to get away on short notice, too, Mom."

"But Penny's only going to be here for a few days. She's coming all the way from Seattle. Can't you come seventy-five miles? I'd like to have you both home at the same time."

"I know, Mom. I'm not sure about tomorrow, that's all. I'll have to figure out my work schedule."

Myra waved a hand. "You don't even need that job."

"I need work for reasons other than money."

"If you need something," Brad said, "you let me know."

"Don't be silly, Brad." Myra pushed her empty plate away. "She has more money than you and I can ever dream of."

Annie groaned. "Mom, we've been through this. I only have what I made when I sold my condo. I have to be careful. It has to last me indefinitely. All the profits from the sale of the business went into a charity

foundation. I can't touch it."

"Your compassionate humanitarianism is admirable, but why you left yourself in need, I'll never understand."

"I'm not in need," Annie said. "I'm just living more simply, and it's good to have work."

"But in an antiques store? Why don't the Amish rules let you make money with what you know how to do — technology?"

"This is what I want, Mom. You have to accept it."

"But they put such value on family. We're your family. Surely they would want you to see your sister."

"I do want to see Penny." Annie missed her sister, who had not written so much as a thank-you note in at least five years. They used to communicate by texting most of the time. Annie had written two letters explaining the changes in her life, but she heard Penny's reaction only through their mother on the phone. "How long will she be here?"

"Just until Thursday. It's a short visit. You must come home."

"Please come," Brad said. "We can have dinner together a few times and catch up."

As determined as Annie had been over the winter to live without electricity and a car, and to learn to cook her own food instead

of ordering takeout every night, she would be lying if she said she did not miss her family. But Mrs. Weichert was counting on her to look after the shop in the morning, and Franey Beiler was expecting her tomorrow afternoon.

"I'll figure something out." Annie's eyes suddenly ached to close, and she clamped her jaw against the urge to yawn.

Brad stood up and started stacking dishes, a habit Annie had always admired in her father. If she did not stop him, he would take the dishes into the kitchen and insist on washing them.

"That's a beautiful shelf." Brad glanced at a white oak shelf fixed to the wall beside the dining room window.

"Thank you. Rufus made it."

Brad inspected the carved pattern along the front ledge. "He's quite skilled."

"I know." Pride flushed through Annie, and she reminded herself. *Humility, humility, humility.*

"And these books?" her father asked. A dozen or so volumes in various colors and thicknesses populated the shelf.

"Various genealogy books," Annie said. "Several have come from Amish families, but the rest have come through the antiques

41

shop. Mrs. Weichert doesn't mind if I take them."

"Are they all about the Beilers?"

Annie shook her head. "Most of them are not. I've gotten interested in the whole idea of tracing the generations back in any family."

Brad pulled a slim black binder off the shelf and opened it. "Is this the book you found in our basement?"

"Yep. That's your Byler roots, going all the way back to Jakob Bcyeler in 1737."

"I thought it had a spiral binding," Myra said.

"I figured it would hold up better in a notebook with page protectors."

"That's a nice thought."

"That red volume is all about the Bylers of North Carolina."

"Are we related?"

"I'm pretty sure. I'd like to spend more time studying the family lines than I have."

Brad chuckled. "I'll let you give me the abbreviated version, but I admit I find it fascinating that my mother's family may be related to the very people you've become so attached to here."

"Me, too." Annie covered a yawn. "Sorry."

"We're all tired." Myra stood and picked up the coffeepot and creamer. She dis-

appeared into the kitchen, still talking. "We'll pick you up for breakfast. Not too early, though. How about eight thirty?"

"Sorry, Mom. Mrs. Weichert is going to an estate sale in the morning. I have to be in the shop."

"Will it matter if you're late? How many customers do you get, anyway?"

Annie had to admit traffic was slow most days, but Saturday was likely to bring weekend lookers. "I promised her, Mom. She's counting on me."

"Well all right, then. We can have lunch in that quaint bakery down the street before we head back to town."

"Let's figure that out tomorrow." Annie stifled another yawn.

"Will you have your phone on?" Myra looked as if she already knew the answer.

Annie wondered why her mother insisted on pressing the question. "I'm sure I can get a message to you at Mo's. I'll use the phone in the shop."

"But you'll definitely go home with us as soon as you're free?"

"Mom, I do want to see Penny. I'm just not sure about tomorrow."

FOUR

October 1774

"Push!"

At her mother-in-law's command, Katie Byler grunted and bore down.

In the other room, Jacob heard the urgency in his mother's voice and the resolve in his wife's guttural response. It would not be long now.

Jacob soothed one of the twins by jiggling the child on his knee. He welcomed the other to lean against his leg. At two, the twins were too young to know what caused their *mamm* to make those sounds, and he saw terror in their round, ruddy, silent faces. At seven and five, their older brothers, Jacob Franklin and Abraham, remembered the twins' arrival and were less concerned about the event.

Four boys, all of them sturdy and healthy. Katie wanted a girl this time. A little sister.

Jacob's own sister was supposed to come

from Philadelphia to help, but Katie had gone from uneventfully stirring the morning porridge to digging fingernails into his arm in the space of four minutes — three weeks earlier than anyone imagined. All the boys had been tediously late, even the twins. So with or without Sarah's presence, this baby was coming. It was all Jacob could do to send seven-year-old Jacob Franklin sprinting across the acres to fetch his grandmother from the big house. Soon after her arrival, Elizabeth Byler pronounced the child would appear before lunch. Jacob could not see how it was going to take even that long. Katie's scream melded into the wail of the new baby protesting an abrupt arrival into the chilly room.

"A girl!" Jacob's mother called.

Jacob stood and thrust the reluctant twins toward Jacob Franklin. He had to see for himself that Katie was all right.

At the bedroom door, he stopped and smiled. Katie was already grinning. She eagerly caught his eye.

"A girl," she said.

"A girl!" Jacob softened in satisfaction. Their daughter continued her objections while her grandmother wrapped her in a towel and placed her on Katie's chest. Katie counted fingers and toes as she had with all

their children. Jacob moved closer to the bed.

"She has your forehead, Elizabeth." Katie gently rotated the child to get a good look at both sides of her face.

"Perhaps not my best feature." Elizabeth discreetly positioned a clean rag under Katie to await the afterbirth.

Jacob soaked up his wife's pleasure, glimpsing the depth of her yearning for a girl after four boys.

"Her aunt Sarah has four brothers," Katie said. "Your sister will have to teach this little one how she survived."

Jacob put his massive hand around the back of the baby's head. "For starters, Sarah never once let us take advantage of her."

His mother laughed as long-past years lit her eyes. She had borne five children but mothered ten, taking into her heart Jacob's older Amish half siblings.

He knew the story well. Both his parents had told it often. More than thirty-five years ago, after surviving a treacherous sea journey without losing anyone in their family, his five older siblings were abruptly left motherless in Philadelphia, their father crushed in loss. And then Lisbetli found Elizabeth's heart in a stationer's shop, and Elizabeth found his father's heart. The

bookish woman of the city married the homesteader and moved to the wilderness, where she labored with five children she could call her own no matter what.

No matter what.

His Amish siblings loved her. Jacob believed that. Who could not love Elizabeth Kallen Byler and her gentle, self-sacrificing ways? Yet she refused to convert to the Amish faith, and for that the Amish siblings put on her the weight of luring their father away from the church.

And now this woman who had loved them all moved about the room cleaning up and delicately setting aside a bucket and soiled cloths. Her movements were swift and efficient, as she made sure Katie was as comfortable as possible. She stepped to the other side of the bed and pulled a quilt up over her daughter-in-law then paused to lay one last damp cloth across Katie's forehead.

His father had made his own choice. Jacob had no doubt. And his mother made hers.

The others were gone now. Lisbetli was in her grave, and Maria disappeared years ago, run away to who knew where. Unwilling to raise arms in skirmishes with Indians or the French, Christian sold his land and moved to the Conestoga Valley, farther from the frontier. Land the Amish had labored to

clear and make farms of was now quite valuable, so other Amish families followed Christian, including Jacob's half-sisters Barbara and Anna. Eventually many of the Amish settled in a reconfigured Lancaster County, while Jacob remained on land that became part of Berks County.

"We should write to them." Katie looked up at Jacob, reading her husband's mind as she always had. "Your sisters will want to know about the babe."

Jacob nodded. "What would you like to call her?"

Katie shifted the infant into Jacob's arms. "Her name is Catherine."

"That's a big name for a little one."

"She'll grow into it. They all do."

A wail from the front room reminded them that Catherine's four older brothers were unattended.

"I'll go, Jacobli. You should be here now." Elizabeth laid a small quilt over the child nestled in his arms, quieted now. Jacob recognized it. All his children had slumbered under it in newness, warmed by a token of their grandmother's love.

Elizabeth left the room, and Jacob handed the baby back to Katie.

"I'll stoke the fire," he said. "It's too chilly in here for a babe."

48

Katie pulled the bedding up to where she held the child against her chest.

"Then I'll get you some food," Jacob said. "And tea."

"Your brothers will be along soon, I suppose," Katie said.

Jacob nodded. "By now John will have noticed I'm not at the tannery today. He'll call Joseph and David in from the fields."

"Your family does rally around a new babe. I have to say that about them."

"You might say a great deal more about them, but God has graced you with forbearance."

She laughed. "They are my family, too," she said. "Send them in as soon as they come. Sarah should be here tomorrow."

Tomorrow. Jacob was relieved it was not next week after all.

Magdalena Byler stood at the end of the lane, shading her eyes with one hand. Nathanael was late. If pressed, she would have to admit he was late habitually, but no matter when he turned up her heart quickened. He was twenty-two to her seventeen years. If they spoke to the bishop soon, they might yet marry before this year's wedding season passed.

The approaching cart stirred up dust

49

before she heard the clatter of horses' hooves and wagon wheels. Nathanael would have come on foot. This must be Nicholas, the *English* who carried mail from Lancaster to the outlying farms twice a week. Magdalena raised one corner of her shawl to spare her lungs the whirling dust.

Nicholas waited till the last moment to pull on the reins, just as he always did.

"*Guder mariye,* Nicholas. Good morning. What do you have for us today?"

He passed her a bundle of envelopes tied together with string. "One is from Berks County."

"My *onkel.*" Magdalena pulled the knot out of the string and began to flip through the stack. She paused when she recognized the blockish lettering of Jacob, her father's younger half brother. "It must be news of the baby."

"You can tell me all about it next time," Nicholas said. "Nothing going out?"

"Not today. *Danki,* Nicholas."

The horse resumed its trot. Magdalena scanned the road again, looking for any sign of Nathanael. Nothing stirred on the horizon. She was tempted to tear the end of the envelope, but it was addressed to her father and his wife. After one more glance around, she chose to take the letters to her father.

Nathan could find her there.

Her parents had brought the family to the Conestoga Valley several years earlier. Her mother's death, just two years ago, stunned them all. But Christian Byler, her father, lost little time in marrying again to another Yoder daughter. Now he and Babsi coddled a baby of their own. With three brothers and three sisters, Magdalena had thought herself too old to become a sister again, but of course no one could resist baby Antje's blond curls and violet-blue eyes.

Magdalena decided to go to the barn rather than the house. Her father was sure to be there. She was curious enough about *Onkel* Jacob's news to want her *daed* to open that letter, even if he read the rest when he was sitting comfortably in his chair by the fire. Magdalena found him right where she expected, standing in the hayloft with a pitchfork in his hands. When he saw her, he thrust the implement upright into the hay and leaned on it to look at her.

"*Onkel* Jacobli has sent a letter." Magdalena waved the entire mail packet up for her father to see.

Christian Byler wiped his hands on his pants then carefully maneuvered down the sturdy ladder to the main floor. At forty-five, he still seemed robust to Magdalena.

He did not ask younger men to do what he was not willing to do himself. The end of his brown curly beard rested against his chest as he took the stack of mail from Magdalena.

She had laid Jacob's letter on top. Her father now carefully broke through the end of the envelope and extracted a single sheet of paper.

"*Maedel*. A girl," Christian said a moment later. "They're calling her Catherine."

Magdalena smiled. "A pretty name. When did she come?"

"Nearly three weeks ago. Sarah is there now. All is well." Christian looked up. "I thought you were to walk with Nathanael Buerki this morning."

"I am."

"He's late."

"I know."

"Are you sure you want to spend your life waiting on this man?"

Magdalena nodded. Nathanael's perpetual tardiness bothered her father more than it did her. "He is worth it."

"You had better be sure."

"I am."

"You could have been married last year. He has his own land with a cabin. It's not the house you're used to, but it would serve

you well for now."

"The cabin is fine. We'll marry when the time is right." Magdalena hoped it would be soon. "I'd better go back up to the road to wait for him."

Nathan was there when Magdalena reached the end of the lane again. He looked over his shoulder as he hustled her down the road.

"What's wrong, Nathan?"

"Patriots," he said. "I saw a gang of them on the ridge."

"They could be there for any number of reasons," Magdalena said. "One of their meetings, perhaps."

"I had a bad feeling, Maggie. From up there they can see the road in both directions. You never know when they will drop down."

"I don't understand why they cannot leave us alone. Is it so terrible that the Amish want to be neutral and peaceful?"

"Ever since the Patriots dumped tea in the Boston Harbor, there is no such thing as neutral in their minds." Nathanael slowed his steps and reached for Magdalena's arm when she got a few steps ahead of him.

"You said they were on the ridge," Magdalena said.

"I think they've moved," Nathan whispered.

Magdalena gasped and clutched Nathanael's hand as four young men lunged from bushes beside the road.

One of the men broke from the others and sliced between Magdalena and Nathanael, knocking her down at the side of the road and pinning her shoulders there. She stared into his gray eyes. He was Stephen Blackburn. His family had arrived in the Conestoga Valley the same year hers had. They were hardly more than children when they first met. He was *English,* but he had never threatened harm.

"Don't try anything." He gave her shoulder an extra shove; then he stood up.

What did he think she would try? She was Amish. She would not strike him or purposefully cause him harm. And neither would Nathan.

The foursome now circled a frozen Nathanael.

"Have you considered the hypocrisy of your position?" Stephen taunted. "Your people came to America seeking freedom, but now that the British threaten the freedom of all the colonies, you will not stand up against persecution."

Magdalena watched Nathanael's Adam's

apple descend in a slow swallow.

"We are peaceful people," Nathanael said. "We would be hypocrites if we were suddenly to take up arms."

"There will be a war, you know," Stephen said. "You will have to decide whether your allegiance belongs to Britain or America."

"My allegiance belongs to God alone."

"But you live in Pennsylvania. You must have some sense of patriotism."

Nathanael did not answer. Still tasting dirt, Magdalena was afraid to move.

Stephen slapped Nathanael sharply on one side of his face. "Are you going to turn the other cheek to me?"

Nathanael did not move. Stephen slapped him again, this time with the back of his hand. Nathanael stumbled back a few steps but did not lose his balance.

"How does that feel?" Stephen jeered. "Are you holier now because you turned the other cheek?"

A sob shuddered through Magdalena. She was on one knee now, trying to stand on rubber legs.

"Take him," Stephen said, and two others twisted Nathanael's arms behind his back.

"Where are you taking him?" Magdalena tried to catch Nathanael's downcast eyes.

"Hypocrites need to learn a few lessons in

basic loyalty. Let's just say we're taking him to a school where he can learn."

"Please, we mean no harm to anyone." She stood firm on her feet now, her stomach turning itself inside out.

Stephen shoved Nathanael in the back, sending him stumbling into the bushes. He rotated toward Magdalena. "Don't try to follow. It will only make things worse."

FIVE

October 1774

At the pounding on the front door, Magdalena sprang to her feet. Across the room, her father stiffened.

"It's the men who took Nathan," Magdalena said.

"Let's not jump to conclusions," Christian answered. "Stay out of sight."

"*Daed,* they'll hurt you, too."

Christian turned from the mantel toward the door. "Maggie, take your little sisters and go into the kitchen. Babsi is there."

Magdalena shepherded Lizzie and Mary to the kitchen, grateful her other siblings were away from the house.

Her stepmother looked up from rolling a piecrust. "What's wrong?"

Magdalena shook her head. "Nothing."

"Somebody's at the door." Little Mary climbed up onto the bench at the table.

"*Daed* thought you might like some com-

57

pany." Magdalena took an apple from the basket on the table and handed it to Mary, hoping it would keep her quiet.

Babsi looked at Magdalena, doubt written across her face, but she said nothing. Avoiding Babsi's gaze, Magdalena glanced across the room to see baby Antje nestled in her cradle. The latch was off the back door. If they had to, they could all get out quickly.

"Magdalena!" Her father's voice boomed from the other room. "Magdalena! Come!"

She raced across the kitchen, pushed open the door, and launched into the spacious main room. Her brother Hans, at thirteen still growing into his man's body, was lowering Nathanael into a chair.

"I found him up the road," Hans said. "He's beaten up pretty badly."

Magdalena collapsed at Nathanael's feet, grateful he was back even if he was wounded. She had whispered prayers from her bed through the watches of the night. God had been gracious to answer her pleas, and she now murmured words of gratitude.

"Hans," her father said, "you'd better ride to tell his family. Magdalena, get some rags and a basin of water. Let's see how bad it is."

Magdalena forced down the knot in her throat. Babsi and the girls watched wide-

eyed from the other end of the room. She pushed past them to the water barrel in the kitchen and filled a basin then grabbed some clean cloths.

"It's not so bad," she heard Nathanael say when she neared him again. But she did not believe him. The strain in his voice told her that even breathing pained him. Outside the house, Hansli's horse gathered a gallop.

Magdalena knelt on the floor and dipped a rag into the water then gently pressed it to the cuts on one side of Nathan's face. His eye was black and swollen. Dried blood traced its path from his cheekbone down the side of his neck. She moved the rag, moistened again, to his swollen lips. A ragged tear in his shirt — the kind created only in violence — exposed the bruises that had already formed. Hardly more than a few square inches remained untouched across his abdomen.

When she leaned back on her haunches, covering her mouth in horror at what he had been through, her father moved in and gently began peeling Nathanael's shirt off.

"Mary," Christian said, "go get a clean shirt from my wardrobe. Magdalena, see if there is *kaffi* in the kitchen."

Babsi took over cleaning Nathanael's wounds. Magdalena roused herself and

59

went in search of coffee, though when she returned she could see that the cuts in Nathanael's lips made it impossible to know how to offer it to him. He managed a swallow and allowed Christian to lean him forward and put a fresh garment on him. In time, Nathanael put his head back on the chair and was asleep.

"Nathanael may be chronically tardy," Christian said, "but he is a good man. He does not deserve this."

Magdalena's tears came now. "What can we do, *Daed*? Is this what it means to be peaceful people?"

"I will ride to Berks County," her father said, "and talk to Jacobli."

"What can *Onkel* Jacob do?"

"He is surprisingly well connected. He might know who is behind these attacks."

"And then?"

Christian rotated his wrists and held his palms up. "We try to have a peaceful conversation."

"With the men who did this?" Magdalena could hardly believe her father would suggest an encounter.

"With their leaders," Christian said. "With men who know the difference between a British officer and an Amish farmer."

"I'm going with you." Magdalena saw in

60

her father's face the understanding that she was not asking permission.

"The cows are milked, the boys are asleep, and the fires are stoked at *Mamm*'s." Jacob rubbed his hands together over the flame in his own kitchen. He looked from his wife to his sister.

"You look pretty pleased with yourself." Katie was nursing the baby in the only comfortable chair in the kitchen.

"And why should I not be?"

"Sarah, are you sure you wouldn't rather stay up in the big house with your mother?" Katie asked. "There is more room there, and it is so much more comfortable. You've been a great help, but the baby has settled into a routine, and I can manage through the night."

"*Mamm* seems to like her own routine," Sarah said from the table, where she was writing labels for the next day's canning efforts. "But I will see about spending a few nights with her before I go home to Philadelphia. I worry about her rumbling around that big house all by herself so much."

"We see her every day," Jacob reminded her. "And David is still living there. She's not alone."

"I just worry," Sarah said. "She hasn't

been the same since *Daed* died. It's been four years."

"What is four years after all the years they had together?" Katie said quietly.

"You're right. I can't help feeling anxious for her sometimes." At the neighing of a horse, Sarah looked up. "Are you expecting someone?"

Jacob shook his head.

Katie smiled at her cooing babe. "Perhaps it's just one of your brothers coming for another look at my beautiful Catherine."

Sarah scooted her chair back and went to the window. Jacob joined her. Shadows from the end of day lay across the yard between the house and Jacob's tannery. Jacob pushed the curtain out of the way for a better look.

"Well, I'll be," Sarah said.

"What is it?" Katie moved the baby to her shoulder to burp.

"It's Christian." Sarah turned wide eyed to Katie. "And I think that's Magdalena with him, though of course I haven't seen either of them in years."

Katie stood to peer out the window for herself.

"Someone had better open the front door," Jacob said.

62

Jacob bought the family property when their father died, expanded the tannery Christian had detested as a boy, and built his own small home nearby. Christian had not been to Irish Creek since Jacobli put on the addition to shelter his growing family. The profile of the house in the shadows was pleasing.

Christian supposed it would have been easier to go to his stepmother's house. She certainly had more space to accommodate unexpected houseguests, and she would welcome them. Perhaps he and Magdalena would still end up there, but he would not sleep tonight until he laid before Jacob the injustice his associates had done.

What Christian did not expect was to see Sarah framed in light when the front door opened. Guilt stabbed his gut. He had business in Philadelphia from time to time, but he had never taken the time to see what had become of his younger half sister. He told himself he was not sure of her address since her marriage, but at the moment that excuse sounded thin even to him.

When Sarah opened the door wide, Jacob and Katie were there as well. They all

63

seemed to stare past him, and their jaws dropped.

"May we come in?" Christian asked.

Sarah inhaled sharply then said, "Of course. We're surprised to see you, that's all. Both of you."

"Yes, welcome," Katie was quick to add. "We're eager to hear your news." Her face was turned toward Christian, but her eyes fixed on the young woman behind him.

Christian followed Katie's line of sight. "You remember Magdalena," he said. "She has some interest in the matter that brings me to Irish Creek without the courtesy of a letter first."

"You're welcome anytime." Jacob laid a hand on his brother's shoulder. "Magdalena, you've grown since we last saw you."

Christian looked quizzically at their three hosts.

"Do you not see it, Christian?" Sarah finally said as she gathered their wraps.

"See what?"

"Magdalena is a striking young woman," Jacob said. "She looks just like Maria at that age."

Maria. Christian had not let himself think about his missing sister for years. Had she really run off with that young *English* trapper as everyone supposed, or had she fallen

victim to foul play? Had they given up looking for her too soon? If she had come to harm, he would not forgive himself for failing to protect her. And yet if she had run off, it was surely because of his pressure for her to be baptized and join the Amish church. Neither alternative was comforting.

Christian found his words. "I suppose to a father, a daughter's face is her own, but of course I see the resemblance."

Sarah stepped forward and embraced her niece. "You were just a girl when I saw you last. I'm so glad you've come."

"Would you like to see the baby?" Katie held her daughter out to Magdalena, who accepted the squirming, cooing bundle.

"I'll make some coffee," Sarah said. "Have you eaten? Sit down and tell us why you've come so urgently."

Sarah and Katie went into the kitchen, but the door between the rooms remained propped open.

"It's the Patriots," Christian said. "Of late they make it exceedingly difficult to remain people of peace. The British are not much better, but it's the Patriots who have just beaten up Magdalena's young man."

Katie gasped. "I'm sorry to hear that."

"I am, too," Jacob said. "I've been warning you for years that there will be a war."

"I have come to see that you are right," Christian said, "but I do not see how berating Amish young men will resolve the tensions between the Crown and the colonies. Are the Patriots any closer to their goal because they have attacked Nathanael Buerki?"

"War seems to blur the lines of morality," Jacob said.

"If war comes, the Amish will not be part of it. Why should we be pressured — with such extreme means — to take up sides?"

Sarah and Katie returned with a pot of coffee and a platter of bread and cheese. Sarah put some on a plate and offered it to Magdalena.

"Magdalena," Sarah said, "you have barely said a word."

"My father speaks for me," the young woman finally said. "I have been baptized and hope to wed in the Amish church. I want only to live plainly and at peace with everyone."

"I don't know what to say," Jacob said. "Neutrality is going to be virtually impossible." He turned to his sister. "Sarah lives in Philadelphia. The talk is in the streets all the time. Philadelphia is to be the capital of a new nation."

"The General Assembly's official position

is for Pennsylvania to oppose indepen-dence," Sarah said. "The representatives are mostly Quakers who oppose violence. But few expect that position will hold. When you walk the streets, you can feel the energy for revolt. It flows through all the colonies."

"You must know someone you can talk to, Jacob." Christian's tone grew insistent. "Do what you must. Our father raised us both to listen to our consciences. This would not be the first time you've acted in good conscience when we have not agreed. But violence toward innocent young men? How can Patriots object to the Crown forc-ing them to pay unjust taxes, yet turn around and attempt to coerce Amish men to betray their beliefs?"

Silence fell over the room. Katie poured coffee.

"They shouldn't," Jacob finally said. "Such actions are contrary to the very no-tion of freedom."

"Then talk to somebody. I know you have influence here that extends into Lancaster County." Christian gestured at Magdalena. "We will not raise a hand against our at-tackers, but there must be a peaceable solu-tion."

Jacob and Sarah looked at each other.

"Perhaps between the two of us," Sarah

said, "and my husband, of course, we may make some inroads regarding the plain peoples."

Several windows glowed with lamplight as Magdalena approached the big house with her father. She had warm memories of this place.

She remembered Elizabeth, who was not her grandmother but loved her as if she were.

She remembered the broad pleasure on her grandfather Jakob's face when her father brought his children to visit — briefly.

She remembered that her parents were always ready to go home before she was. Magdalena's own mother was kind to Elizabeth, but in a stiff way that Magdalena did not understand even as a child. Her stepmother had never met Elizabeth and was not likely to.

"It's not too late," her father used to say to *Dawdi* Jakob. "If you repent, the church will forgive."

Older now, Magdalena saw that her father had never given up hope that *Dawdi* Jakob would return to the Amish church and bring Elizabeth with him. He loved them both so deeply.

But it did not happen. And now the By-

lers who were Amish wanted only peace, while the Bylers who were not Amish were close to the center of the Patriots' revolution.

Six

"I should at least stop by and explain." Annie wiped her hands on her jeans on Saturday morning then picked dust left by her half day's work out of her T-shirt.

"Isn't this the opposite direction than we want to go?" Myra raised an eyebrow.

Seeing her mother standing in Mrs. Weichert's eclectic shop took some getting used to for Annie. Myra wore lightweight designer slacks in a hard-to-match shade of blue that she nevertheless managed to match. With the casual shirt and sweater, she looked as if she had idly thrown the outfit together on a Saturday morning. Annie knew the skill that level of shopping required.

Six months earlier, Annie gave away a walk-in closet full of clothes like that. Now she wore jeans to work because Mrs. Weichert counted on her for lifting and shoving and keeping some order in the storeroom.

Her small collection of dressy tees and polo shirts rotated with her work schedule and her new simple life in a hundred-year-old house a few blocks away. The only two dresses hanging in her wardrobe were Amish dresses. She wore them when she visited an Amish family or gathered with the Amish congregation. Annie was determined to sew the next dress herself.

Business in the shop was brisk enough to pass three hours easily. Mrs. Weichert had returned from the estate sale with a tall dresser, a writing desk, and three lamps. Annie had helped unload them and situate them in the storeroom for closer inspection later, finishing just as her parents arrived.

"Franey is expecting me," she said now. "I told you about the quilt. We work on it every Saturday."

"You could call her."

"Mom. Please." Her mother knew the guidelines for using telephones.

"It seems to me this simple life of yours is a little complicated."

"It's only five miles." Annie searched her mental files seeking a route to the Springs that did not require backtracking and making the detour total ten miles.

"I suppose we have no choice. We'll swing by your place to get your things, make this

71

one stop, then we'll be on the road. You'll have time to relax before Penny arrives."

Annie did not remember agreeing to go. But she had not said she wouldn't, so thirty minutes later she sat in the back of her parents' Toyota — new over the winter — and rested her arm on a small canvas bag containing a couple changes of clothing.

She really wanted to spend the afternoon quilting. Penny's plane was still six hours away from touching down.

And there was Rufus. Almost two weeks had passed since their last real conversation, and she missed him.

Outside the car window, trees hastened toward blooms while snow still whitened the slopes of the Sangre de Cristo Mountains. Annie sometimes rode in someone else's car on this road, but her winter in the valley had taught her the rewards of patient observance. Even as the Toyota bore down on the road, something in Annie wanted to scream for her father to slow down even though he was not going all that fast. It was just too fast for the moment.

Inside the car, Myra Friesen listed more possibilities for family fun than the chamber of commerce. Penny was only staying five days. And if Annie knew her sister, Penny was already filling her calendar with

catch-up coffee meetings with old friends.

Everything was changing with her parents' sudden personal intersection into Annie's simple life. The whole day. The next week.

Memories stirred. Two successful companies. Technology that set new industry standards. Seizing change and using it for her own advantage. Life in the fast lane.

The choice she made six months ago after she stumbled onto the Beiler family farm to give it all up. The choice her own family did not understand. They might never, she realized.

Annie leaned forward, gripping her father's seat in one hand and pointing with the other. "See the lane? Turn left. It's a long driveway."

Brad Friesen slowed the car and made the turn. Gravel ground under the tires as he let the natural grade of the lane draw the vehicle toward the house.

Annie spotted Franey in the garden. She put her window down and waved. Franey returned the wave then let her hoe drop into the dirt. She made her way toward the vehicle, arriving just as the car came to a stop and wiping her hands on a flour-sack apron.

"You remember my parents? You met once last summer, out at Mo's."

"Yes, of course." Franey leaned in the window and gave the welcoming smile that greeted all guests to her home. "You must come in for some refreshment."

"Thank you. That would be lovely." Annie was out of the car before her mother could protest, though she saw the way her parents looked at each other and slowly exited the car. "Don't you want to see the quilt, Mom? You gave me some scraps for it, remember?"

"Why, yes, that would nice." Myra turned to Franey. "We just have a moment, though, so please don't put yourself out."

"It's no bother. We have a houseful right now anyway." Franey waved an open hand toward her home. "Please come inside."

Annie scanned the wide yard for any sign of Rufus. Even just a moment alone would bolster her. He was nowhere in sight, though. The door to the workshop was shut tight with no lights showing in the windows. The barn was closed, but Annie realized two horses were missing from the pasture where they usually grazed while they were not out pulling buggies.

"The men are out looking at the work that needs to be done on the Stutzmans' house," Franey said.

Annie held her breath against the urge to sigh and stepped toward the house. "Sorry,

Dad. Guess you're stuck with girl talk."

Brad Friesen took his daughter's hand, and Annie returned the squeeze that had always been their secret reassurance.

Inside, Franey said, "Please make yourselves comfortable. I'll clean up a bit and get some iced tea." She disappeared into the kitchen.

Annie watched her mother's eyes move around the room. She knew the questions behind her gaze. The first time she came into the Beilers' home Annie whipped out her iPhone and tapped in an Internet search on Amish bathrooms. Even though her mother had been in Annie's home, which used alternate sources of energy rather than electricity, the curiosity factor was sure to be high in an authentic Amish home.

"It seems quite comfortable." Myra tentatively selected a seat on a sofa and signaled to Brad that he should sit beside her.

"Relax, Mom. I'll get the quilt."

Annie went to the cedar chest under the wide window framing a view of the Sangre de Cristos. Though she grew up in the foothills of the Rockies and had barely noticed them when she lived in the Springs, Annie did not tire of the peaks she now saw every day. She snuck a look while she lifted the lid of the chest and gathered a bundle

of Amish hues into her arms. Leaning up against one end of the chest was the lap quilting frame she used each week. Annie picked it up, still reluctant to concede that she could not spend the afternoon quilting.

Across the room Annie dropped the frame into a chair and used both hands to spread the quilt out in the open space, making sure one corner landed in her mother's lap.

"You made this?" Myra slipped one hand under the blue corner and let the fingers of the other hand graze the stitching.

Annie nodded. "It's just nine-patch squares. Nothing fancy to start with. Franey said I could use a treadle machine, but I wanted my first quilt to be handmade."

"The colors are lovely." Myra's expression softened.

"Do you see the brown?" Annie smiled. "That's the dress you made for Penny when she was in the play her senior year."

"I remember. And the dark green is the curtains we used to have in the kitchen. You and Penny were so little then."

Annie pointed to a patch. "There wasn't much of this pink, but I wanted to use it somehow. It was Franey's idea to put it at the center of each nine-patch."

"Did I hear my name?" Franey entered with four glasses of tea on an unadorned

wooden tray. She bent slightly for the Friesens to get hold of the drinks then set the tray on a side table and picked up a corner of the quilt still held together with long, evenly spaced basting stitches. "Our Annalise is learning quickly."

Annie sucked on her bottom lip as she watched her mother's reaction to the endearment in Franey's words.

"Annie masters everything she puts her mind to," Myra said, her smile fading and brow furrowing. "It started when she was three and a half and decided to do handstands."

"It is an admirable quality," Franey said. "God blessed us richly when He sent her into our lives. But I'm sure you feel the same way."

Myra reached and covered Annie's hand. "And we hope to have her with us for many more years."

Now Annie sucked her top lip.

"We would love to have you visit us any time you come to Westcliffe to see Annalise," Franey said.

No one but Annie and Penny would recognize the miniscule straightening of Myra's spine, the movement that came just before her mama bear roar.

Annie stood quickly. "My parents sur-

prised me with the news that my sister is coming home for a few days. They are hoping to have us all together."

Franey raised her eyebrows and turned her lips up. "Yes, you should do that."

The sound of rapid steps brought Edna Stutzman and her three daughters down the front stairs.

"Whose quilt is that?" Beth took the corner of the quilt from Myra's lap.

"These are our houseguests," Franey said. She made introductions quickly. "Annalise was showing her mother the work she has done on her quilt."

"That it explains it then," Beth said. "It is the work of a beginner. At least she's trying hard."

Annie swallowed a retort. *Humble, humble, humble.* "Franey is teaching me every Saturday."

Beth pulled the yardage through her hands in three swift tugs. "I could work on this in the evenings for you. It has potential."

Franey gently lifted the quilt from Beth's hands and folded it properly. "It can wait until Annalise has time. After she spends a few days with her family."

Annie met Franey's eyes. On the sofa, her mother shifted in agitation.

■ ■ ■ ■

Ike Stutzman put his finger to a chin buried in beard.

Rufus remembered that Ike had been doing that since he was a young man with neither wife nor beard. Ike had a pronounced cleft in his chin and his finger fit there nicely. Rufus was not the only boy to imitate the gesture with a snicker when he was Jacob's age. Doing it once in the presence of his father, though, halted the fun. A month doing the chores of three boys persuaded Rufus that imitation was not all that amusing. But he smiled now at the thought that Ike still put his finger in his chin when he was thinking.

"It sounds like fine land, of course." Ike nodded. "And you make a good point about participating in community decisions if we are to also benefit from the outcomes."

"I'm glad you see it that way." Rufus nudged the team to a brisker pace. Annalise should be at the house by now, working on her quilt.

"However, in this case it seems a frivolous matter, and I would have to advise against it."

Eli's voice from the bench behind them

saved Rufus from having to respond. "Ike, you just got here. You have plenty of other things on your mind."

"It seems like a simple enough matter," Ike said. "We have an abundance of God's handiwork here. Our people do not need hiking trails to see that."

Eli nudged Ike's shoulder. "Perhaps you would get to know some of your neighbors in the process."

Ike's sons also were in the back of the wagon. Rufus wondered where Joel was — again. Joel could at least extend friendship to Mark and Luke while the Stutzmans were their houseguests. Joel's new habit of disappearing from his work in the family fields had reached disconcerting frequency. His father was sure to step in soon.

The horses knew to turn into the lane.

"We have visitors," Eli said when the house came into view.

Ike huffed. *"English."*

"Our neighbors nevertheless."

Rufus took in the scene. A late-model silver Toyota, spanking clean, parked close to the house. If Annalise was there, she was not alone.

Franey laid the quilt on top of the chest and looked out the window. "The men are

back. I should pour more iced tea."

"I'll help you." Annie ignored her mother's helpless gaze, picked up the tray Franey had set aside earlier, and followed Franey into the kitchen. If Rufus put the horses away and came in through the back door she could see him, even if for just a moment.

Franey moved swiftly around the kitchen, setting out glasses, filling them with ice, and pouring cold tea. Annie dawdled with a stack of cloth napkins, running thumb and forefinger over the folded edge of each one before laying it on the tray.

"Don't worry. Rufus will be along." Franey lifted the tray and held it out to Annie.

Annie let out a sigh and returned to the front room to serve the men. Her mother still sat on the sofa, looking unsure of where to let her eyes settle. She was trying not to stare. Annie gave her credit for that much. Her father stood to shake the hands of Eli and Ike, comfortably meeting their gazes.

Ice clinked in glasses as conversation turned to work the Stutzmans needed to do on their new house to make it suitable for an Amish family. Talk of painting made Annie realize she had not seen Rufus yet. While she mentally speculated about where he might be and half listened to talk of propane

81

appliances, she cocked her head for the sound of steps in the kitchen. As long as Annie did not meet her mother's eyes, Myra would not interrupt to urge their departure.

Finally she heard the screen door chink into its framed notch. Excusing herself, Annie picked up several empty tea glasses and headed for the kitchen. Rufus was at the sink washing his hands.

"You've had a busy morning." Annie moved to the sink and set the glasses down. Standing beside him, she looked up.

He rewarded her with a smile. "Looks to me like you've had a change of plans yourself."

Her shoulders sank.

"What is it? Aren't you happy to see your parents?"

"I should be happy. My sister is coming home. My mother wants me to stay with them for a few days."

"Well, that's good. You haven't seen your sister in a long time."

"Not since before . . . all this."

"Last summer, you were the one who persuaded me that I should see my sister Ruth after a year and a half of silence." Rufus reached for a dish towel and dried his hands. "I hate to see you fall into the same trap. You should go."

"I don't know why I'm so nervous. I made a choice. Once we see each other face-to-face, I know Penny will understand." She wanted him to raise his hand to her cheek. Or cover her hand with his. Or smile again. Or something.

He reached into a cupboard for a glass and poured the last of the tea into it. And yet he said nothing more.

"Well," Annie finally said. "They're waiting. I guess I should go."

He nodded then dumped the cold drink down his gullet.

When she heard the swish of skirts, Annie turned to see Beth standing in the doorway to the dining room. She crossed her arms on her chest, suddenly self-conscious that she was wearing jeans and a tee.

Beth smiled, her eyes fixed on Rufus. "I'm glad you're back. But don't get too comfortable. Your *mamm* and my *mamm* suggest that you give me a tour of the area this afternoon. Once I know my way around, I'll be able to help with errands."

Annie glanced at Rufus, who caught her eye. "I've just put the horses away," he said.

"But it's a fine day for a ride in an open cart. Little Jacob would love to go with us. He's such a beautiful boy." Beth smoothed her rich blue dress.

"Perhaps Lydia and Sophie would like to take you," Rufus said.

"They seem to be busy today." Beth tugged one prayer *kapp* string.

Rufus shifted his weight.

He was going to do it. Annie heard it in the way he softly cleared his throat. Rufus was going to take Beth Stutzman on a tour.

She broke her pose. "I should see how my parents are getting along."

SEVEN

Ruth Beiler let her overstuffed dark green backpack plop onto her narrow bed. She rolled her shoulders, trying to urge out the hunch of nine hours in the university library staring at textbooks and computer screens.

The corner of the letter stuck out of the tall zippered compartment on the side of the bag. Looking at it, Ruth pressed her lips together. Then she turned her back on it, going instead to the narrow counter where she kept an electric kettle. She rattled the kettle.

Empty.

Ruth walked across the four-room suite to a sink and filled the kettle.

"Hey, Beiler!"

Ruth looked up to see the young woman who had moved into the suite in the middle of the spring term. Lauren sat on the love seat in the common area with her booted feet propped up on the coffee table. As

usual, she wore fatigues. Though the brown T-shirt fit snugly, the camouflage pants generally were baggy and held in place by a belt.

"Hi, Lauren. Did you hear from your brother today?"

Lauren tipped her blond head in a practiced gesture. "Yep. He has a month's leave before being reassigned for his new tour. I'll see him next weekend."

"I'm so glad for you."

Lauren stood, and Ruth saw once again the uneven gait that had resulted from a fractured kneecap — and which kept Lauren out of the army herself. Her father, an officer stationed at Fort Carson in Colorado Springs, had served three tours in Iraq. Her brother, stationed out of North Carolina, had been abroad for most of the last two years.

Despite Lauren's enthusiasm for all things military, she was Ruth's favorite suitemate. Neither of them dressed to fit in. Lauren favored her army clothes, and Ruth dressed in long skirts and modest blouses.

Ruth lifted the full kettle. "I was about to make tea. Want some?"

Lauren shook her head and let her feet thud to the floor. "My study group is meeting in a few minutes. I should get my junk

together and go."

"Another time, then." Ruth stepped toward her room. "It would be good to chat."

"Tomorrow night."

Ruth looked up again. "Tea tomorrow?"

Lauren shook her head. "Let's go out. Dinner will be my treat."

"Oh." Ruth could not find a place to fix her eyes, except on the kettle in one hand. "I probably should stay in. I have an exam on Tuesday morning."

"You need to let loose, Beiler. Just relax for a change. Between your classes and your job at the nursing home, you never take a minute for yourself. Let's get a decent meal."

"Maybe we should decide tomorrow." Ruth had never been out on a Sunday night, except for the singings at home. Going to a restaurant did not seem like keeping the Sabbath.

Lauren laughed. "When my parents say something like that, they mean no. But I'm not going to let you get away with that, Beiler."

Ruth rubbed the end of a sleeve between thumb and forefinger. "We'll talk about it tomorrow."

Back in her room, she plugged in the kettle, took a tea bag out of the box, and

dropped it in a mug.

The letter tugged at her.

Elijah's tight, meticulous script had brushed her heart when she removed the envelope from her student mailbox. It was not his first. In the last six months, he had written four times and he lost no opportunity to make plain his undimmed affection for her. More than affection. Love. The difference was that this letter was the first since she replied to one of his.

Almost as soon as she pushed her letter through the slot in the sidewalk mailbox, Ruth regretted it. She had not written anything particularly personal, certainly not a true expression of her own feelings. But writing at all would encourage Elijah, and that was wrong. He was a baptized member of the Amish church, and she had run out on her baptism.

Run out on Elijah. Run out on the future they dreamed of.

How he could still feel anything for her after that, she would never understand. There was no going back. While she still felt plain at heart and lived simply, she would never go back to the Amish church. God had made her to be a nurse, and she intended to answer the call. She refused to be the reason for Elijah to break his vows to

the church.

The kettle whistled, and Ruth once again turned away from the unopened letter.

Penny's flight was fourteen minutes early.

Annie stood between her parents just beyond the security line on the main level of the twelve-gate Colorado Springs airport. Her mother had been tracking Penny's flights on her phone since before she left Seattle. In front of them, an eager three-year-old sighted his grandmother among the disgorgement of plane passengers. Calling and running toward her, he violated the security zone. Though his father snatched him back, it was too late. The alarm blared, startling everyone. The boy wailed briefly but instantly settled when his grandmother reached for him.

Business travelers looking for drivers holding signs with their names.

Families dragging strollers and diaper bags.

Solo passengers looking lost and weary.

And people like Penny, who strode at a confident clip pulling pilot cases behind them and knowing exactly where they were going.

In the moment that she hugged her sister, Annie was glad she had come home with

89

her parents. She did not often admit to herself that she missed Penny — especially since she had given up using a cell phone and e-mail — but she did.

"Did you check a bag?" Brad Friesen asked his eldest daughter.

Penny tapped her carry-on. "Everything's in here."

Brad took over towing the bag. Myra had one arm around Penny's shoulder as they stepped side by side onto the escalator that went down to the exit. Annie pulled up the rear, feasting her eyes on this family she loved. Her throat thickened with the thought that her choices might well separate her from them.

Sumptuous. That was the only word Annie could think of to describe dinner at the downtown restaurant. In the candlelight, her mother's face lit with the bliss of having her family together. Myra had raised two daughters to be independent and take care of themselves. When she shared a table with them once again, though, a newness flushed across her face. Sitting across from Myra, Annie realized how much she loved seeing her mother look this way.

"I have presents," Penny said as soon as they passed, satiated, through the front door of their home.

Annie smiled. Penny never came home without gifts. Annie used to think it was because Penny felt guilty for living so far away. Over the years, though, she came to see that generosity spilled out of most of what Penny did. Why she had not realized this as a child, Annie did not know. She supposed she was too busy being the competitive little sister.

Penny unzipped a front pocket of her bag and extracted several small packages. To her father she presented a soft leather e-reader cover case.

"We both know you want it," Penny said.

While Brad turned the cover over in his hands, Penny handed Myra a small bottle of perfume.

Annie knew the bottle had not come cheap. She used to buy the same scent herself. Myra raised her eyebrows and flashed Penny a smile.

Then Penny turned to Annie. "I saw this and thought of you. You're the only one I know who has the figure for this dress."

Annie gulped. A dress? She had not worn any dress but Amish dresses in so long she hardly knew what it felt like. Her hands trembling slightly, Annie took the light-weight flat package from Penny. How could

she possibly wear anything Penny gave her now?

A gasp shot past Annie's best intentions as she raised the dress by the shoulders and saw how it shook out and found its drape. It was silk. Good quality silk. A rich red in color, the dress had a modest V neckline and cap sleeves. At the waist, the fabric overlapped itself and gathered to one side, where a small gold buckle was the only adornment.

"Oh, Penny!"

Myra slid a careful hand against the back of the dress, and Annie watched her mother's face. Was it only a few hours ago that she had laid her clumsy quilt in her mother's lap? Suddenly everything about Annie's new life seemed frumpy and unskilled.

"It's spectacular, Penny." Annie handled the dress gently, cautious to keep it on the white paper it had been wrapped in rather than let it brush against the roughness of her jeans. If she snagged it, Penny could not take it back.

"It will look spectacular on you," Penny said.

"Penny, it's so generous! And gorgeous. But I don't see . . . well, under the circumstances, it would not be practical for me to keep it."

"It won't hurt to try it on."

Penny raised her eyebrows. Annie knew that look.

"Just try it on," her mother urged. "Those black heels you used to love are still in the closet of your bedroom."

"I'll help you put your hair up," Penny said.

Annie closed her eyes briefly before saying, "Okay." For a few minutes she could go back in time to the sisterly habits of fifteen years ago. What harm would it do?

Thirty minutes later, Annie stood in front of the full-length mirror attached to the closet door of her childhood closet. She hardly recognized herself.

For the last eight months, she had let her hair grow uncut. She wore it either in a ponytail or braided and twisted back in the disciplined Amish style Franey taught her. Penny had swept it high on her head, leaving tendrils to frame her face. The dress fit as though Annie had been the model for the pattern. Cool, sleek silk against her skin set off sensory reactions she thought were long gone. The bodice covered well, yet left no doubt of the form beneath it. The skirt fell just above her knees. When she stepped into the black heels, the muscles in her calves found old memories.

"You. Look. Fantastic." Penny grinned.

Annie grimaced but said, "I do, don't I?"

"You have to show Mom."

"You go ahead. I'll be right out."

Penny left, and Annie tried out several angles in the mirror. If only Rufus could see her now.

Annie had never had trouble getting a man to kiss her if she wanted him to — until Rufus. She waited weeks — even months — between kisses, then afterward, invariably, he seemed sorry. He did not say he was sorry, but why else would he wait so long before doing it again? If he saw her now, he would come close and brush a tendril from her face and bring his lips close to hers. His hands would go to her waist as his mouth found hers.

Annie shuddered, ashamed. The image in her mind was everything Rufus was not. How could she even consider trying to make him kiss her like that? She pulled one pin, and then another. Her hair tumbled free around her shoulders.

"What's taking so long?" Penny stood in the doorway. "Wow. I think I like your hair down even better."

Annie did, too. Setting her hair loose only made her miss Rufus more sharply.

"Come show Mom."

Annie complied, feeling every bit as beautiful as her family told her she was. What she had not expected was to love the feeling.

Her father had been the first to fade, and her mother soon followed after securing agreement from everyone to attend church in the morning. They had not been to church together as a family in — Annie was not sure how many years.

After their parents turned in, Penny ensconced herself on Annie's bed and leaned against the wall with a bowl of popcorn.

Annie straightened the red dress on the hanger and put it in the closet. She rummaged through the old clothes. "I didn't think we'd be going to church. I didn't bring anything to wear."

"Excuse me! Did you not just hang up a smokin' hot dress?"

"For church?"

"Why not? No plunging neckline. No bare shoulders."

Annie moved a few more hangers before admitting that everything in the closet was, well, too high school. Why hadn't her mother given this stuff away years ago? "I could probably wear nice jeans."

"You're wearing the dress, girl. It will turn a few heads."

"Maybe I don't want to turn heads." Annie let her hand drift over the red silk one more time before closing the door.

Penny tilted her head back and dropped several popped kernels into her mouth. "So how serious are you about this Amish thing?"

"I'm figuring that out."

"I don't think Mom is taking it all that well."

"No kidding."

"Is it Rufus? Is that it? You can't be with him if you're not Amish?"

Heat crept up the back of Annie's neck. "Well, that's part of it." With more notice that she would see her sister face-to-face, she might have prepared her words better. "But it's more."

Penny shifted on the bed, meeting Annie's eyes.

"I was wired into everything before I met the Beilers," Annie continued. "Technology, having it all. Lots of money. But was I happy?"

"I guess I've been gone too long," Penny said. "I didn't know you were unhappy."

"I didn't know myself." Annie picked up a throw pillow left from her adolescent purple phase and sat on the bed. "It hasn't been easy to unplug, but most of the time I think

it's worth it."

"Most of the time?"

Annie licked her lips. "I have moments. But simplicity has more moments."

"Can't you just live a simpler life without giving everything up? No law requires you to own a big-screen TV. What's so evil about electricity?"

"No one says it's evil. But electricity — or texting constantly or owning a car — means you can escape to another place at a whim. The thing that makes the Amish strong is the community that brings them together, because they can't leave at a whim."

"Dad doesn't seem too rattled, but I don't know how you'll ever persuade Mom."

"I know." Annie fiddled with mementos from college that still lay on the dresser. "If I do become Amish, I don't want it to be just on the outside. I have to find out if I can really see the world as the Amish do."

"And if you can? Then you can be with Rufus?"

EIGHT

No matter how old she got, Magdalena never got used to the feel of a *kapp* on her head at the height of summer. Once she got clear of the house, she stopped to set the basket of quilt remnants on the ground and remove her *kapp*. If corn had eyes instead of ears, perhaps the hearty crop would tattle on her. As it was, Magdalena could brush undetected through rows of her father's corn almost as tall as she was. After she crossed the creek onto the land that belonged to Nathanael's family, she would put the *kapp* back in place.

The quilt fabrics were a ruse. Magdalena did not even enjoy quilting. It was a fact of life. Somebody had to piece together a family's bedding, and no Amish woman would think to marry without at least rudimentary skill. Magdalena had learned early and well from her mother before she

98

passed. Only last year Magdalena was hard at work on the quilt she hoped would cover the bed she and Nathanael would share as man and wife. She finished it, stored it carefully in a cedar chest, and waited for his proposal.

Yet, after the attack, the wedding season passed with no further mention of marriage from Nathan's lips. In another couple of months, this year's couples would begin having their banns read at the close of worship. No doubt every other Sunday would herald some new pair. Everyone acted as if they did not know who would become engaged, but of course the banns were seldom a true surprise.

Magdalena stopped in the middle of the cornfield and rubbed the heels of her hands into her eye sockets. Hard. She had hoped for last year — or this year at the latest. Nathan had his own land and was a wise farmer who learned well from the experience of his father and uncles. His farm was not large by standards of the Conestoga Valley, but it was a solid start. Everyone said he had a gift for the land, just as Magdalena's father did. Their families cared for each other. No one would stand in the way of their marriage.

Except the Patriots.

Nathan never talked about what happened that day. At first, Magdalena told herself he needed more time. When he was ready, he would tell her what happened, what they had done to him, how awful it had been, how he had refused to retaliate, how he stood strong as a peaceful man of God. She would comfort him and be proud of him.

No. Not proud. *Ordnung* did not allow pride in any form.

She could care for him and tell him he did the right thing.

But Nathanael never talked about the experience, not to Magdalena and not to anyone. Rather than looking forward to marriage and living in his own house, Nathanael seemed increasingly content with the room he had shared with his brothers growing up. As the youngest, he was the only one left living under their parents' roof, and he showed no restlessness with the arrangement.

Magdalena bunched up her *kapp* in her hand and threw it against the ground. With the ties splayed in two directions, it looked pitifully innocent, and Magdalena instantly filled with regret. Repenting, she snatched it out of the dirt and put it back on her head.

She did not know how to pray anymore.

She straightened her dress, took several

deep breaths, and adjusted the basket of cloth on her hip. Nathanael's mother would appreciate the gift of the scraps. Magdalena made up her mind right then that even if she did not get to see Nathanael, she would not regret bringing the gift. It was not too late to make it a sincere offering.

"How is he?" Magdalena asked when Nathan's mother welcomed her into the summer kitchen half an hour later.

The older woman shrugged. "He's been out to the fields this morning, but he's back now. I heard him talking to his father about the extra help they will need to get the harvest in."

"Surely they still have a few weeks to sort that out."

"Between the two farms, it's a great deal of work," Mrs. Buerki said.

What she did not say was that her youngest son did not always carry his share of the load anymore, but Magdalena understood. In the summer kitchen, they were far enough from the main house to speak freely, but after ten months, little remained to be said about Nathanael.

Despite the heat of the hearth, the summer kitchen's limestone walls kept the structure reasonably cool — for which Magdalena was grateful after her walk in the

sun. A door propped open at each end allowed the air to move.

She set the basket of fabrics on the worktable. "I thought you might want to go through these and see if you can use anything."

Mrs. Buerki's eyes brightened. "Did I tell you I'm to be *grootmoeder* again?"

Magdalena's eyes widened as her heart sank. Another of Nathanael's brothers was having *kinner* before she and Nathanael were even married. It was probably Obadiah and Esther, but she could not bring herself to ask. "Then you'll need to start a new quilt," she managed to say. "There's plenty here for a babe."

The gray-haired woman smiled briefly. "Go on in the house, Maggie. He'll be pleased to see you today, I think."

Magdalena nodded and stepped out into bright sunlight again. She crossed the yard and tapped lightly on the open door at the back of the main house. "Is anyone home?"

"In here." Nathan's voice sounded bright, but she knew that his tone was not always a promise of his mood.

She loved him. She could not imagine not loving him. Though Nathanael usually seemed glad to see her, he had not asked her to ride with him to a singing since

before the attack. Whatever hope for the future they held between them last year had weakened like coals spread too thin. Nathanael was jumpy and wild eyed at times, sparking the nickname Nutty Nathan 1. No one ever called him that to his face, of course, but Magdalena fumed nevertheless.

Nathan sat at the table beside a cold hearth, and Magdalena took a seat opposite him.

She could not stay long. She wished she could sit all day with him even if he did not speak to her again, but her chores would not allow such indulgence. Her older brother and sister were married now and in their own homes, leaving Magdalena to help with the younger children. Babsi was with child again, though so ill that the midwife feared the child would come far too early to survive.

For now, she decided to give herself half an hour to sit with the man she loved.

"Are you hungry?" Magdalena asked. "I am sure your *mamm* would not mind if I fixed you something to eat."

He shook his head then turned to gaze out the window.

"You must be tired from being in the fields in the sun." Magdalena searched his face for any encouragement.

Nathan crossed his arms and cradled his own elbows. "You are kind to come."

"Of course I came."

"I know I disappoint you, Maggie."

"No, you don't. You couldn't." She reached across the table, but he did not grasp her hand.

"Are you sure you want to do this?"

Jacob met Sarah's gaze and answered evenly, "Yes."

"It could be dangerous," she said. "Your movements may come under scrutiny."

"I am aware."

"My husband will help you however he can."

"Emerson is a fine man, Sarah."

"I've always thought so. But there's *Mamm* to think of."

"I'll be careful. *Mamm* will be in no danger."

"You may be overstating your case." Sarah tugged at the canvas covering the load in Jacob's wagon. "I hate to think what might happen if you get stopped."

"Who would stop me? The British have their hands full trying to keep their grip on Boston. That only makes our work more imperative. We must move while we have opportunity."

" 'Our work'? Is that what it is now?"

Jacob leaned forward and kissed Sarah's cheek. "We're in this together, you and I."

"Christian will be horrified."

Jacob's jaw hardened. "Last year he came here with Magdalena and asked me to do something."

"I hardly think this was what he had in mind."

"The question must be resolved so we can get on with our lives. Boston is only the beginning. If we let the British have Boston, we're done for." Jacob swung himself up into the wagon's seat and picked up the reins. As he pulled away from Sarah's stately Philadelphia home, he resolved to return to his own land the long way — by way of the Conestoga Valley. It was better to stay off the main thoroughfare between Philadelphia and Berks County anyway, and honesty was the best route with his brother as well.

Christian flipped back the canvas and flicked his eyes toward Jacob. "That is a great deal of saltpeter."

Jacob nodded.

"You can only have one end in mind for such a load."

Again, Jacob nodded.

"Jacobli, this saltpeter will produce far

more gunpowder than your household requires. Remember that I once hunted the hills of Berks County alongside you."

"If you want me to state my intentions, I will." Jacob cleared his throat. "Though we differ in our acts of conscience, I don't intend to deceive you."

"You're making gunpowder for the Patriots." Christian slapped the canvas back in place then caught himself. He would not allow Jacobli's choices to provoke his temper.

"The colonists *are* going to fight the Crown," Jacob said. "But they can't hope to be successful if they must continue to depend on the French for gunpowder. We must have our own supply."

Christian's belly heated. He prayed regularly and fervently for Jacobli and all his siblings to find the way of peace. Would God never answer?

"The land behind the tannery is more than suitable for a powder mill," Jacob said. "It's a good distance away from any other families, and it will be easy to hide the operation if need be. Having the creek so near is an advantage as well."

Christian could hardly bear the thought. Beautiful Irish Creek, once a thriving Amish settlement, was reduced to this.

"*Daed* swore an oath to the Crown you

now defy," Christian said. "I was there that day. I heard it for myself."

"*Daed* could not have foreseen the events of the last thirty-five years." Jacob was unbending. "I thought you were not taking sides."

"I'm not." Christian swallowed his frustration. Jacob had always had a way of using Christian's own words to provoke him. "Of course I shall remain neutral."

"Christian, this is the best way to put an end to the kind of danger your Maggie's young man faced."

"By arming the perpetrators? I fail to see the logic."

"We will put an end to this war before it can spread beyond Boston. The Patriots will have what they want. Establishing a new nation will leave them little time to harass peaceful Amish farmers about their lack of loyalty."

"Peaceful Amish farmers are very loyal, Jacob. It's only that we seek to serve a higher power."

"My gunpowder will ensure that you can continue to do so." Jacob stared at Christian, unmoved.

"You'd better go, Jacob. I don't want Magdalena to see what you have in your wagon."

NINE

Annie wore the red dress to church.

She scrounged up a pair of shoes with lower heels and tamed her hair demurely with a silver clip at the base of her neck, but she wore the dress.

The Friesens sat together in a pew about halfway back in the sanctuary. When Annie was young, the family attended church a couple of times a month. During high school, her training program and track competitions almost always interfered with church events aimed at teenagers. She had a few friends who had gone to the same church, and they had stayed in touch in a general way. But since she had given up Facebook and Twitter, she no longer tracked the path of their lives. And explaining her new life to anyone? Complicated.

The lively contemporary music, with a six-piece band and a concert-quality sound system, made Annie feel out of practice. She

tried to sing the unfamiliar songs, but she could not bring herself to clap as others around her did. Her months of worshipping with the Amish had left their mark. The time to sit for the sermon came as some relief. And at least the sermon would be in English. She would not have to strain to follow High German.

This was a church week for the Amish in the hills around Westcliffe. Annie wished she had missed an off weekend instead. The congregation would sing hymns. Long hymns. Slow hymns. Time-to-think hymns. And then two of the men would give sermons.

Brushing aside the image of Rufus sitting among the men, Annie reached for a Bible in the rack in front of her and found the passage listed in the bulletin. Wedged between her mother and her sister, she felt both of them looking at her out of the side of their eyes. Annie did not give them the satisfaction of turning her head. She had a lot to learn about the Bible, and she might as well take advantage of an English service. Rufus often referred to a Bible verse and Annie hardly ever knew what he was talking about. She could change that if she tried.

They stood for one last song, and that was when Annie saw him. Randy Sawyer. What

was he doing here? Across the aisle, he turned his head toward her and smiled. Annie jerked her head back to the large screen displaying the words of the song. When the music ended, and the pastor gave a final blessing, Annie stretched out the process of returning the borrowed Bible to its place. If she had been alone, she would have exited the pew at the far end, but with no escape from the path her family was taking toward the center aisle, she was face-to-face with her college boyfriend ninety seconds later.

"Are you visiting Colorado Springs?" She shook Randy's hand awkwardly and stepped away from her family. Thankfully, they continued greeting other people down the aisle, and would not hear her awkward fumbling.

"I live here now," he said. "New job." He named a technology firm she knew well and pulled out a business card.

"Oh. The Springs is a beautiful place to live." She could not help looking at the fingers of his left hand. No ring. She hated that she did that.

He nodded. "You look beautiful yourself."

Annie flushed and moved one hand down the silky skirt. Randy Sawyer had never needed a silk dress to want to kiss her — and much more. She moistened her lips,

unsure what to say next. The crowd thinned around them.

"I've heard that you've done quite well since college." Randy put one hand in a pocket.

Annie nodded. Randy did not seem nearly as unnerved by this encounter as she was. Had he selectively forgotten their frequent furtive quests to find some place on campus to be alone, and what they had done when they found those places?

"I read that you sold your business last year," he said, "but I lost track of what you went on to next."

She lifted her shoulders slightly. "I'm slowing down. Trying to enjoy life."

He smiled. "If the reports I heard are anywhere close to true, you should be able to enjoy life quite comfortably."

She had no response. What was she supposed to say? *I gave away my fortune and despite what this dress might imply, I'm thinking of becoming Amish?*

"Annie," he said, "I want you to know that I've grown up since college. I know we didn't always make the best choices in our relationship, and I'm sorry."

She put her hands up, palms out. "We made those choices together."

He nodded. "It's good to see you, Annie.

Be happy." He leaned in and kissed her cheek.

Buried sensations stirred. Annie's breath caught as she watched her first love turn and walk up the aisle of the church. She closed her fingers over his card.

Rufus sank into the Adirondack chair on the front porch, closed his eyes, and inhaled deeply. The spring mountain air heralded late-afternoon rain. If a storm rolled through, Rufus wanted to be right in that spot to watch it. The porch was deep enough and the overhang broad enough to keep storm watchers dry.

He opened his eyes to conduct his daily study of vegetation on the slopes of the Sangre de Cristos. Evergreens and snow kept shifting colors on the mountains all winter long, but rushing weeks of spring left pale green hues that Rufus waited for all year. On the Sabbath, with the worship service and shared meal finished, he could sit as long as he liked breathing in the fragrance of a new season.

Rufus grimaced slightly at the sound of the front door opening behind him. Clattering footsteps meant at least some Stutzmans were among the entourage about to burst into his peace. Rufus was still getting used

112

to the added commotion in the house.

His mother appeared — and right behind her Beth and Johanna Stutzman.

"There is a singing tonight, *ya?*" Franey looked at her son expectantly.

"*Ya, Mamm.* At the Millers'."

"*Gut.* It will be a good time for the Stutzmans to get to know other young people."

Beth pushed past her sister. "I would love to go. It would be the first singing in our new community."

"I'm sure you would be welcome," Rufus said.

"Then it's settled," Franey said. "Rufus will take you in the big buggy."

Rufus startled and sat up a little straighter. He felt too old for the biweekly singings and seldom went. His mother knew that. More than a year had passed since his last time.

Before Annalise.

Franey began to count on her fingers. "Rufus, Beth, Johanna, Essie, Lydia, Sophie, Joel, Mark, Luke. You'll need both buggies. Joel can drive the smaller one with the boys and you can take the larger one with the girls."

Rufus blinked blandly, seeing no gracious way out of this. "I suppose we should plan to leave about five."

113

Franey and Johanna withdrew into the house. Beth settled into the chair beside Rufus. "This will be the first singing ever for Mark and Luke. Perhaps they are too young to think of pairing off, but they can at least meet some of the other boys."

Rufus refrained from pointing out that the other boys would be older than Beth's brothers, as would the girls. He supposed it could not hurt for all the Stutzman children to at least learn the names of others they would worship with every two weeks.

"I didn't know it would be so beautiful in Colorado." Beth's eyes were on the mountains.

"It's a different kind of beautiful than Pennsylvania."

"I think it's spectacular. It's a wonderful place for a new settlement."

Beth's face glowed with enthusiasm. Rufus wondered whether to believe her.

"We've had to learn to farm differently," he said.

"Of course it will be hard work." Beth nodded earnestly. "But the land is beautiful, and my parents are so pleased that they will be able to help Mark and Luke have property of their own when the time comes. I hope my brothers can find something half as beautiful as your land."

Rufus was not blind. Beth was the prettiest of the Stutzman sisters. Not a hair was out of place on Beth's head. Her *kapp* perched perfectly, and her clear eyes and rosy complexion brightened any room she entered. She also was an expert quilter and had prepared last night's dinner for fourteen all on her own. More than once his mother had mentioned in Rufus's hearing how helpful Beth was around the house while her family stayed there, which was high praise for only two days' time.

He knew his mother liked Annalise, but did she think he did not have it in him to choose her over an Amish girl? Whatever she was afraid of, pushing Beth Stutzman on him was not the answer.

A vocalist and a four-piece band all crowded onto a small performance stage in one corner of the restaurant.

Ruth Beiler's heart pounded harder than the beat of the music. She was in a restaurant on the Sabbath.

Lauren took her to a small artsy restaurant downtown, which somehow increased Ruth's sense of guilt. Twice already Lauren had been mistaken for a soldier by people eager to thank her for her service to their country. Lauren was quick to explain that

wearing fatigues was her way of showing support for her father and her brother, but she basked in conversation about the military with anyone. Ruth hoped Lauren's family members would be safe, but beyond that she hardly knew what to say. Her family never spoke of the military, and Lauren seemed to speak a language foreign to Ruth. Munitions and weaponry and incendiaries and military acronyms and abbreviations.

"See? Isn't this better than being stuck in the dorm?" Lauren stabbed her blackened trout and moved an ambitious bite toward her mouth.

Ruth let out her breath and smiled. Sabbath or not, she was here. She might as well enjoy it.

When Ruth ordered a salad, she expected a modest bowl of greens. Instead she faced a plate heaped with fresh spinach, red peppers, feta cheese, and grilled salmon.

And she liked it. Her fork crunched through a pepper slice and into four spinach leaves. As Ruth lifted it to her mouth, she wondered how difficult it was to grow spinach in Colorado. Ruth knew she could buy fresh spinach at dozens of grocery stores or farmers' markets in Colorado Springs. Still, the ingrained question of growing her own food, as her family always

had, popped up at odd moments. Perhaps someday she would live in a place where she could serve as a nurse and still grow vegetables. She missed her mother's garden.

"I know you take the bus around town," Lauren said. "You could borrow my car if you ever get in a jam."

Ruth swallowed hard. "Thank you, but I don't have a license."

"No license?"

"I do have a permit." Ruth savored the tang of vinaigrette on her tongue. "A friend at work was teaching me, but her husband got transferred to Kansas City."

"Well, we'll work on that starting tonight. You can drive home."

Ruth inhaled. "No. I would be too nervous. I've never driven in the dark."

"Everyone has to learn to drive at night." Lauren maneuvered her fork with one hand and tapped the other on the tabletop in rhythm with the band's beat.

Their conversation dangled as the music's presence filled the room. Ruth realized she was tapping a foot. The music, a ballad of lost love, tugged its soft beat out of her. She watched the drummer, and her foot met his tempo. The vocalist sang with her eyes closed and a fist over her heart, as if she were singing her own heartbreak.

Ruth thought of the words in Elijah's letter, the most candid of all the letters so far. *So far.* How could she consider continuing this correspondence? She would surely break his heart.

Again.

TEN

"You're going out?" Two days later, Annie set the last of the lunch dishes in the sink and looked at her sister.

"I'll be back before dinner." Penny took a set of keys off a hook. "Mom said she couldn't get out of her committee meeting, but Mrs. Metzger is picking her up. I figure I can use her car."

"To do what?"

"Gonna catch up with Mahalia. She has the scoop on everybody from high school."

"Oh. Okay." Annie had not thought she would find a moment alone during this visit. Suddenly the afternoon yawned wide.

"It's already Tuesday. My visit will be over before I blink twice. I'd better grab the chance while I have it." The keys jangled in Penny's hand. "Did you want to go somewhere? There's always your car."

"I don't drive it. You know that. It's up on blocks."

119

"Nope. It's in the garage right next to Mom's."

"But the tires are probably low on air."

"They looked fine to me."

Penny led the way into the garage, pressed the button to lift the garage door, and got in the new silver Toyota. Annie waved as Penny backed out. Annie's blue Prius was indeed in the garage. When had her father taken it off the lifts and filled the tires?

Back in the kitchen, Annie stared at the lone key still on its hook.

Rufus dipped his brush in the paint and stroked a muted seafoam shade onto the trim around an interior door.

"Did anybody talk to Elijah Capp?"

The sonorous voice of the bishop rose above the hum of people working to get the house ready for the Stutzmans to inhabit. Rufus glanced around the dining room, where three young Amish men were painting walls. They did not interrupt their rhythms. Rufus leaned around a ladder to see Bishop Troyer standing in the living room with his sleeves rolled up and his thumbs hooked in his suspenders.

"Elijah is coming this afternoon," someone finally said. "He doesn't think it will take very long to do the conversions. Not more

than two days."

The bishop nodded. Rufus dipped his brush again. With a crew of a dozen Amish men, the painting progressed swiftly. Rufus had set aside his own work for the day, as had all the others. This sacrifice meant the Stutzmans would be in their own home soon and not living among a deluge of paint cans, ladders, and spackle tools.

Rufus glanced around. Where was Joel? he wondered. Joel was supposed to come down as soon as he and Jacob looked after the animals.

And what about Mark and Luke? This was to be their home, but they were nowhere in sight.

Neither Eli nor Ike had said anything about their missing sons, but Rufus could not help watching the pair of fathers closely for signs that they noticed the absence of the boys as the morning wore on. The women would come with lunch soon.

"I hear Elijah is eager to take up with the *English* on their project to make a park."

On the surface, Old Ezra's words were a simple remark, but Rufus heard their meaning.

"The project has merit." Eli Beiler wiped paint off the side of his hand.

"Bah!" Ike had his mind made up. "Ezra

is right. It is an *English* project."

"It doesn't have to be."

Rufus smiled slightly at his father's persistence. Eli could be every bit as stubborn as Ike.

Gideon and Joshua stopped their brushes and turned toward the conversation. From across the room, Samuel and Levi did the same. Opinions rushed through the discussion.

"We should mind our own business."

"They invited us to help. We will offend if we don't."

"They do not yet understand what it means that we live apart and have nothing to do with the *English* ways."

"We'll be using the land. Why should we not help care for it?"

"We use it only if we choose to. We can choose not to."

"I still say we should mind our own business. That is our way."

"That land is right between several Amish farms. Of course they want our cooperation."

"No need to be uncharitable."

"Who is in charge, anyway?"

"So far, it is just talk. No one is named as leader."

Rufus dipped his brush yet again and

continued working on the trim.

"The word in town is that Karl Kramer wants to have a hand in it," Old Ezra said.

"Karl Kramer! He hasn't had a kind word to say about any of us since we got here. I cannot believe he wants us to share in the work."

"All the more reason to mind our own business. I don't trust Karl Kramer."

"I've never even met the man."

"Don't think he wants to meet us. Don't forget what he did to our Rufus last year."

Rufus stiffened.

Ike moved toward Rufus. "What is this business about?"

"It's nothing," Rufus said.

"He tried to kill you," Old Ezra said.

Ike raised his eyebrows.

Rufus dabbed at the wall. "He is just uncertain about us because he does not know us."

"And if we live apart as we should, we don't have to know him."

"Rufus," the bishop said, "I'd like to hear what you think about this."

Rufus set his paintbrush down and turned toward the center of the room. Every eye was on him.

"I think," he said, "that undoubtedly we will use the land. Our young people, in

particular, look for recreation — a picnic, a hike, a safe place for outings or courting. Even if a new park were not situated between several of our farms, we would use it. Many of the people in town are happy to have us here. Almost everyone in this room hires Tom Reynolds for taxiing and hauling, and he is one of the people who would like to see a new park. Since they have invited us, I see no harm in responding to the gesture of friendship."

For a few minutes, the room was still and silent. Then a few boots shuffled. The bishop cleared his throat but did not speak.

"If Rufus were in charge, I would do it," Gideon said.

Around the room, murmurs of agreement buzzed. Rufus stifled a sigh. He had no intention of leading anything.

"There's an enormous boulder smack in the middle of that land," Samuel observed. "Are they planning to move it?"

"It's too big to yank out with a tractor."

"There's always dynamite."

"Or leave it alone."

"It's a mistake to get involved." Ike crossed his arms.

Rufus dipped his brush and reached for the trim above the door.

Old Ezra gripped a ladder and moved it

to a new spot. "Where is that younger boy of yours, Eli? He's tall enough that he could be of some help around here."

Annie spun on her heel and left the kitchen. No point standing there staring at the key. She had not driven her Prius in six months. The only reason she still owned it was to placate her mother's hope that her lifestyle change was temporary.

The house was empty. Even the cat was nowhere in sight. Her mother's committee meeting would consume the afternoon. Her father seldom was home from work before six. Penny would gab the afternoon away with her childhood best friend.

For the last three days, Annie had used electricity freely. When she walked into a room, she flipped the light switch without thinking about where the power came from. When the dishwasher was full, she turned it on. When the telephone rang and she was nearest to it, she answered. She stayed up late and watched two movies with Penny, complete with microwave popcorn. When her mother's computer froze, Annie knew just what to do to get it going again. Her hair hung freely around her face and shoulders, and she was glad for the furnace that fired up when the overnight temperatures

dipped below forty. She did not think twice about the photos her mother snapped constantly. Annie wore comfortable jeans — except for the red dress — and not once did she have to stumble over choosing the right German word or get hopelessly lost in a dinner conversation.

It was surprisingly easy to be at home. Comfortable. Automatic. And in this situation, being *English* was the most peaceful option.

Annie could find something to read and pass a quiet afternoon until her family returned.

Or she could do what she most wanted to do. See Ruth Beiler. At least she could try.

Annie pulled a finger across the spines of books on the third shelf in the family room. She turned off lights where no one was sitting and straightened the pillows on the sofa, which she and Penny had left in disarray during their morning sister talk. But Annie was simply passing through the family room, and she knew it. Her cell phone, with Ruth's number in it, was in the canvas bag she packed when she left Westcliffe. Now she went to the closet, opened the bag, and removed the phone.

Then she sat on the bed. As automatic as so many things felt in the last few days, this

was different. She lived the *English* life for the sake of peaceful hours with her family, not expecting them to adjust their lives to her choices.

But this. This was a different sort of choice. She knew Ruth Beiler now used a cell phone daily — even texting.

Ruth might not answer, though. She might be at work or in a class or studying in the library with her phone silenced.

And if she did answer — and had some free time — Annie would be making her next choice simply by turning on her phone now.

She would take the Prius's key off the hook, get in the car, and drive to Ruth's dorm across from the main university campus.

Annie sat for ten minutes with the phone in her hand, still turned off, and her lips pressed together. This was not an emergency by any stretch of the imagination. But she'd had no warning she was going to come home, so she could not arrange a visit by mail. Ruth was so close, yet so far.

Finally, Annie flipped the phone open and composed a short text. AM IN TOWN. FREE THIS AFT?

She pushed SEND then held the phone in

her hand, unsure whether she wanted it to vibrate.

It did. YES! WOULD LOVE TO SEE YOU. HOW?

BE RIGHT THERE. *SEND.* Turn the phone off. Flip it closed.

Annie jammed the phone in a back pocket just in case she had a true emergency in the course of the afternoon. She stuck her driver's license and some cash in another pocket and moved swiftly toward the kitchen. If she slowed down, she might feel the guilt.

The car key fit into her hand in a familiar mold.

ELEVEN

"I'm a failure at being Amish!" Annie flopped onto Ruth Beiler's dorm bed, landing on her back with her arms splayed over her head. "I sent you a text when it was not an emergency, just because I wanted to see you. And I drove over here in a car I still own." She did not want to admit aloud to wearing the red dress or the number of movies she had seen in the last three days. Or her reaction to Randy Sawyer.

Ruth nudged Annie's feet over to make space to sit on the end of the bed. "I ran out on my own baptism. I win the Rotten Amish contest."

Annie laughed and sat up. "Maybe I'm not meant to be Amish. I love my simpler life — most of the time — but three days at home with my parents and look what I've done. Is that all it takes to break my resolve?"

"Your family is *English,* Annalise. You are

not baptized Amish. You have done nothing wrong."

"Are you sure?"

"Yes, I'm sure."

"Good. Because I'm not. How can I expect my family to honor my choices if I can't honor them myself?"

"We all choose every day." Ruth leaned her shoulder against Annie's. "I made a huge choice when I left home. Outwardly, leaving meant I was choosing not to be Amish. On the inside, though, I have to choose every day to stay here and stay in school. Even after two years I have trouble belonging in this world."

"I think you've done very well." Annie raised her hands to tick off her points. "You're a good student, you use a computer, you have a job, you found a church, you're getting along with your mother."

Ruth got up and began to tidy the university-supplied desk next to her bed. "And I dress like a nerd, I still braid my hair, I don't see the point of reality TV, and other students don't know what to make of me other than helping them in a study group."

"I assure you, reality TV is no great loss." Annie leaned forward with her elbows on her knees.

"It would be something to talk about, that's all." Ruth snapped closed the rings of an open binder. "When are you going back to Westcliffe?"

"I'm ready to go now, but I have to get a ride." Annie put both hands up. "I drove here, so I have to drive back to my parents' house, but after that I'm hanging up my keys again. I repent!"

Ruth smiled and laughed softly.

"What's so funny?"

"You're beating yourself up about driving, and I'm learning to drive."

"What!" Annie sat up straight.

Ruth nodded. "I've had a permit for a long time. I have to carry some kind of ID that *English* will accept. A couple of friends have given me a few lessons."

"See! You do have friends. Someone who will teach you to drive and still speak to you afterward is the truest friend of all."

"The first one moved away." Ruth laughed. "Maybe that was her way of saying the lessons were not working out."

Annie swatted Ruth's shoulder.

"The second one is from a military family and is a woman on a mission."

"I like her already."

"Mostly I've steered away from any busy streets and have only driven in broad day-

light, but Lauren let me drive her car home from downtown at night."

"Lauren?"

"My new suitemate. She wears army clothes all the time, but she looks at me like I'm a regular person."

"You *are* a regular person."

"I don't understand half the stuff she says. Body armor and assault weapons and explosives. Apparently in her family, that's dinner table conversation."

"I'd like to meet her."

"I wish she were here now. Another time."

"Let's go driving." Annie jangled the key to her Prius. "We'll go out on the interstate."

Ruth shook her head. "I'm too nervous. I'm used to the speed of a horse."

"Just picture a *lot* of horses. Galloping. We'll stay in the slow lane, I promise."

Annie met Ruth's eyes and saw the gleam of desire. With a grin, Ruth clutched the key in her hand and slung her purse over her shoulder.

Ruth gripped the steering wheel at nine and three, amazed yet again at the sensation of freedom. The car was not hers, and she did not have a license. But in that moment she could choose where to go, and getting ready did not involve the tedious process of

harnessing horses or checking their shoes.

"It's not so different from driving a buggy," Annalise said. "You have to be aware of everything happening around you on the road. React appropriately with your feet rather than reining in the horses or pulling on the buggy's brakes."

Ruth nodded. Annalise was right. Even on the bus or in someone else's car, Ruth found her body reacting slightly to what she saw around her. She knew what it felt like when a driver took a fraction of a second longer to slow than she would have liked. Pedestrians ready to step off a curb put her on full alert even as a passenger. She recognized when a driver did not slow down enough for a turn and her own body fought the centrifugal force that pressed her against the inside of the passenger door.

Still. Driving. What would her mother think? Even Rufus did not drive a car, not even to haul what he needed for his work. He hired Tom Reynolds for that.

She negotiated out of the dorm parking lot and onto Austin Bluffs, heading west toward the mountains. Annalise murmured encouragement as Ruth adjusted to the speed limit and moved her eyes frequently between mirrors and the view out the windshield.

"You're enjoying this, aren't you?" Annalise answered Ruth's smile with one of her own. "It's a cultural milestone, Ruth! You're driving!"

"Yes, I am." Ruth pressed her lips together in focus. They crossed over Nevada Avenue, and she saw the signs for I-25. Choosing north would take them toward Monument. Choosing south would take them toward Pueblo. And toward Westcliffe.

"We can go where you want to go," Annalise said.

Ruth smoothly entered the interchange that would glide the car into the northbound traffic.

"Don't slow down," Annalise said. "Accelerate to enter traffic at a steady speed."

Ruth nodded, blew out her breath, and checked mirrors. Even she knew that her first experience of merging onto the interstate was perfect. Sitting back in the seat, she let out her breath.

"How far shall we go?" Annalise asked. "Monument? Castle Rock? Denver?"

Ruth shook her head. "Not Denver. That's too far." *Too far from what,* she asked herself. Too far from her dorm room? Too far from the valley where her heart longed to be?

They went past the exits, many of them marking places Ruth had never visited in a

134

routine that alternated between classes and work shifts, punctuated on Sundays by attending a nearby church. Though she had left the San Luis Valley region, her world was contained in a simple framework.

The sky shone blue and broad and bright before her. The Rockies rose bronze and unyielding on her left. The car rumbled softy forward over gray wideness.

Ruth liked the immediate response to even slight pressure on the accelerator.

She liked the effortlessness of steering a vehicle, compared to the slow, awkward maneuverings of a team of horses.

She liked adjusting the seat to fit her.

She liked being enclosed and keeping the temperature comfortable.

She liked the speed.

Ruth glanced at her passenger. "Annalise, I'm going to say something I've never said before in my entire life."

Annalise smiled slowly. "Can't wait."

"Wheeee!"

TWELVE

May 1776

Christian heard the rustle of the corn and looked up, alarmed. The sound came too fast, the steps too heavy and too many. Instinctively he turned his head toward the house, though it was too distant to see from his western field. Despite his first impulse at the breakfast table that morning, he had agreed Magdalena could take the small cart for a half day to visit her friend Rebekah. No doubt she would also drop by Nathanael's family farm. That meant Babsi was home alone with the smallest children — and heavily pregnant.

Christian dropped the knife he was using for digging out weeds and stood up straight. A moment later, three men drew their three horses to a halt in front of him.

"Good morning, gentlemen." Unafraid to look them straight in the eye, Christian assessed them in turn.

"Which way did they go?" One of the riders had trouble stilling his mount.

"They? I assure you I have been alone in my field all morning." Though he refused to look at the path they had taken, Christian knew the intruders had flattened countless ears of corn. These men were British sympathizers. He had seen them before.

"Four treasonous Patriots came this way," the man said. "We saw where they turned off the road. They cannot have gone anywhere else."

Christian shook his head. "I have not seen them."

"They turned into your field not four minutes ago. You are hiding them."

Christian made a wide sweep with one arm. "I'm growing corn, gentlemen, as I do every year. That is all. I hardly think I would be able to disguise four beasts and their riders in a half-grown cornfield."

"How do we know you would not give them aid?" As the man's horse continued to strain against the reins, the hilt of his sword glinted in the sun.

"I have nothing to do with your dispute."

"Dispute! Man, do you not understand that this is war?"

"I have nothing to do with your war,

either. I only wish to live at peace with all men."

"You delude yourself, good sir. If you are not for us, you are against us."

"I am against no man." Christian spoke with calm. "If I might be permitted, I ask you to kindly take care of my crop on your way back to the road. It may provide your sustenance one day."

"We are not going anywhere until we find the traitors."

Christian stepped to one side. "Then I will not detain you further."

"If we find these men in your field, we will be back for you. Your Amish pretensions do not deceive us."

"It is not my intention to deceive you. I speak truth when I tell you I have seen no Patriots come through my land."

The man snorted. "Soon enough you will have to choose a side. If you don't choose wisely, you will be as traitorous as they."

Christian said nothing. What good could come from antagonizing them?

At the crack of a whip, the horses thundered through the corn.

Jacob had had enough of the rain for one day. No doubt the farmers of Pennsylvania were happy for some moisture in their

fields, but once he left the stone-paved streets of Philadelphia, the risk of a wagon wheel bogging down in muddy country roads would make the trip home to Berks County tedious.

For the moment, though, Jacob did not want to be anywhere else but in the city where his parents had met.

He had come to Philadelphia on a routine supply trip, with lists from a few of his neighbors and plenty of space in his wagon for any saltpeter that might have found its way to the city in an unrecorded manner. Only a few hours ago he was eating breakfast in his sister's kitchen. The simple note from his brother-in-law came by messenger. Nearly giggling, Sarah read it aloud. *Come to the State House. We will make history today.*

When Jacob and Sarah arrived at the brick-towered State House, they could not get anywhere near the building, nor catch any sight of Sarah's husband. Drays, coaches, and chaises congested the streets around the State House. Pedestrians from every neighborhood of the city swarmed the flat brick sidewalks. Despite the steady rain, hundreds — then thousands — pressed in to plant their feet in the yard behind the State House.

"There's Emerson." Sarah pointed, and Jacob saw her relief at the sight of her husband in the throng.

Even in her layers of petticoats, slender Sarah was nimble enough to twist among the crowd and devise her own path to the other side of the yard. Jacob, requiring more space to maneuver respectfully, kept his eye on the crimson dress his sister sported that day. Her feathered hat made her easy to spot. A step or two at a time, he crossed the yard politely, catching snatches of conversation in the process.

"Pennsylvania needs an assembly that represents the will of the people."

"We're here to show we mean business. We're through being bullied by the British or our own Assembly."

"By the end of the day, the Assembly will be out on their ears. We'll have men of vision running Pennsylvania."

"Is it true?" Jacob asked as soon as he reached Emerson and Sarah. "Is the Assembly to be ousted?" He wiped rain from his eyes and strained to bring into focus the scene unfolding before him.

Emerson nodded. "How fortuitous that you are in Philadelphia just now. I knew you wouldn't want to miss this, not after all the risks you've been taking for the cause."

Sarah glanced around. "Are you sure you ought to speak so forthrightly, Emerson?"

Her husband threw his head back and laughed freely. "This is a Patriot crowd if ever there was one. We are among like-minded souls."

"Can they really throw out the Assembly?" Jacob asked.

"The Assembly did themselves in. Clearly the people want them to vote for independence at the new Continental Congress. Since they refuse to commit themselves to such a path, the people will take matters into their own hands."

"I hope there will be no violence here today," Sarah said.

Emerson shook his head. "Let's hope it is only the noise of a determined crowd."

The chanting started then. "Independence now! Independence now!"

"There must be three thousand people here." Despite the sheltering brim of his hat, rain once again streaked Jacob's face.

"My guess is closer to four thousand," Emerson said. "I could hear the chanting from my office three blocks over."

"Imagine what it might have been if the weather were fair." Sarah gripped her brother's forearm. "Look! One of the assembly-men is trying to speak."

From their position across the yard, they could not make out the man's words, but the booing that followed left no doubt of the crowd's sentiment. Nothing he said placated the throng, and nothing short of mass resignations would satisfy. Jacob opened his mouth to speak again then abruptly took in breath and held it.

Was it even possible that he saw what his mind registered?

He squinted against the drizzle and wiped his eyes on his coat sleeve. The crowd swallowed the figure that had caught his eye just a moment ago. What had he seen? A woman. No, a man. If it was a woman, it seemed unlikely, and if it was a man, it was impossible. It had been so long, and she — or he — was far enough away to make Jacob distrust his own vision.

Jacob stepped away from Sarah and Emerson — as much as the crowd would allow — and tried to follow what he had seen, but the shifting mob obscured his view at every step. When he found a clear break in the multitude, whatever he had seen was no longer there. He squeezed his way back to Sarah and Emerson.

"Jacob, what is it?" Sarah asked.

He turned to her, uncertain whether to put into words what made no sense as it

flashed through his mind.

"Jacob," Sarah said again. "You look as if you've seen a ghost."

"I just may have," Jacob said.

"Someone you know? You do business with a lot of people in Philadelphia now."

He shook his head slowly. "Not business. And someone you know as well." He turned to lock eyes with his sister.

"Oh?"

"Maria." Jacob exhaled the name. "I think I saw Maria."

"How can that be?" Emerson asked. "You've always said she disappeared when she was barely grown."

"She did," Sarah said. "We never knew what happened. No one knew she was unhappy, if that's what she was. I was only seven or eight myself. Jacob, you can't have been more than ten. Christian was not married yet. Are you certain?"

"No. It was someone in men's clothing. Drab, ordinary fabrics. A hat pulled down low. But the face! It was like looking at Magdalena, only twenty years older."

Sarah's eyes locked on his. "Jacob, do you know what it would mean to *Mamm* to find Maria?"

Jacob nodded.

"What can we do to find out if it is Ma-

143

ria?" Sarah turned to her husband. "Emerson, you must help."

Emerson turned his palms up. "How? I never met Maria. I've never even met Magdalena. And I certainly did not see whoever Jacob thinks he saw — which may have been a complete stranger."

"But if it was Maria —"

Jacob put a hand on his sister's shoulder. "Emerson's right. I'm not even sure what I saw. The rain distorts many things."

"But if it was Maria, then she is here in Philadelphia. We can ask around. You have connections. Emerson knows a lot of people. We could at least try for a few days."

Jacob shook his head. "Katie is due to have the new baby in a few weeks. I promised this would be the last trip for a while. This is no time for me to linger in Philadelphia. No, it couldn't have been her."

The crowd thundered again.

"That's it," Emerson said. "They're demanding a new government, and I believe we're going to get it. The Assembly will have no choice but to vote themselves out of existence because of their own incompetence. When the Continental Congress meets next month, Pennsylvania will vote for independence."

■ ■ ■ ■

From where Magdalena sat, she could see Nathanael clearly. He always sat in the same place during church. No matter whose home the congregation met in, Nathanael managed to put himself along the outside edge among the unmarried men. Magdalena learned long ago that she could sit on the same outside edge, in the facing women's section, and see Nathanael clearly during most services.

Nathan helped his father work both their farms, but he had never moved into his own cabin. Just last week Magdalena had stopped in at the cabin and saw that someone was squatting there. Though Nathan's mother had outfitted the cabin with basic supplies when he acquired the land, anyone passing through now could see it was untended. What was to stop someone from taking up occupancy?

Mrs. Buerki often invited Magdalena to supper, where she sat next to Nathan and smiled as she passed dishes around the table. Nathan was polite and ate well. He seemed to find some pleasure in her silent company after meals. As far as anyone knew, he slept well at night. His family said he

145

was the first one to wake in the morning and out to the barn to tend the animals. If asked a question, he answered as simply as possible, but never discourteously.

But he was not *her* Nathanael any longer. Magdalena wondered if it would be worse to give up hope that he would return to her, or worse to be certain he never would.

It had been a year and a half. In a few weeks another wedding season would begin — the third since she and Nathan talked of marriage. Magdalena was tempted to stop stitching linens for her chest. What was the point?

She sang the last hymn with half a heart, feeling as if it were moving at half the usual ponderous pace of the hymns from the *Ausbund.* This one had fourteen stanzas, and they would sing them all. Once it had been one of Nathanael's favorites, and whenever they sang it she would catch his eye with a shy smile.

This time, as soon as the final phrase of the hymn dissipated into the air, Magdalena stood and swiftly moved out of the congregation, out of the house, out of the close air that was strangling her next breath.

She ran, and she did not answer the voices calling her back.

THIRTEEN

"If you do what I ask, you can see for yourself." Annie, with her feet up on an ottoman in the living room, tilted her head and snared her sister's eyes.

"I don't know, Annie." Penny tossed a pillow at Annie.

"Please." Annie caught the pillow. She intended to milk her little-sister status for as much as she could get. "You could see my house. Meet my friends."

"You mean meet Rufus."

"Well, yes, but others in his family as well, if we catch them at home."

"I'm afraid I'll stare."

"You won't. I know you have a lot of questions about what I've been doing the last few months. If you come and stay overnight —"

"Whoa. Overnight?"

"Yes, overnight. You can see what my house is really like, even at night. You always

147

say you like to visit people where they live so you can imagine them in their own homes."

"By 'always' you mean I said that once when I was thirteen."

"And maybe one other time when you were seventeen. Pretty please?"

"It's Wednesday. It's my last full day here, Annie. I fly out tomorrow afternoon."

"Come on, Penny, you've seen all your friends. We've had family meals coming out our ears. Frankly, I think Dad would like his peace and quiet back."

"You're the noisy one."

"Am not."

"Are too." Penny sighed. "If I'm back in time to have lunch with Mom before my flight tomorrow, it might work."

Annie swung her feet from the ottoman to the hardwood floor with a thud. "Perfect. I'll go pack."

"We can't take Mom's car, you know," Penny said.

"I know. We'll take the Prius, but you drive. I'll send Ruth a text."

"Ruth?"

"Ruth Beiler. If we're just going overnight, she'd probably like the chance to see her mother."

"Are you even supposed to be texting her?"

"So now you're the Amish police?" Annie laughed and opened her phone. "Last time. I promise."

"Why did Ruth Beiler leave if the Amish are so phenomenal that you're trying to get in?"

"It's not a question of 'getting in,' Penny." Annie nimbly thumbed in the text message to Ruth. "It's following a calling. It's choosing something, rather than being run over by the stampede of everybody else."

"Are you sure you're not just choosing Rufus?"

Annie set her phone down on the cushion next to her to await Ruth's response. "Would it be so terrible if I were?"

"Since I haven't met him, I reserve judgment."

"Thank you for being fair. But no, I don't think it's just about Rufus. Maybe I belong with the plain people even if I don't belong with Rufus."

"Annie, if you join the Amish, am I even ever going to see you again?"

"Of course you will." Annie answered quickly, but the color was gone from Penny's face. "They're not some kind of cult that brainwashes kids and cuts them off from

their families."

Annie watched as her sister swallowed hard. Then Penny sucked in a ragged breath.

"It will be all right, Penny," Annie said. "We'll still be sisters. We may just have to get better at writing letters."

"Won't they ask you to believe a bunch of crazy stuff?"

"What do I believe now, Penny? That's the bigger question. What kind of faith do I have? Do I make choices that have anything to do with Jesus, or do I buy into thinking I deserve everything at my fingertips?"

"Surely those aren't the only two choices."

"Perhaps not. I'm still asking a lot of questions."

"I go to church," Penny said. "There's plenty to believe without being so drastic about it. Why can't you join a normal church?"

"Who decides what's normal?"

Penny pushed the pillow off her lap. "Never mind. Let's just do this."

A couple of hours later, Ruth opened a rear door of the Prius and settled into the backseat. Annie made the introductions. Penny was polite, but she made no effort to strike up a conversation with Ruth. Every minute or two, Annie saw Penny glance in the rearview mirror and she wondered if

Ruth were looking back, inspecting her sister at regular intervals. Ruth and Annie's occasional murmurs softly infused the awkwardness that settled over the car. *One step at a time,* Annie told herself. Penny did not have to love Ruth today. But Annie did wonder what tomorrow's drive back would be like, when Penny and Ruth would be alone in the car.

Rufus knelt and fished through his open wooden toolbox, not finding what he wanted.

"What have you lost now?" Mo, owner of the motel, put one hand on her hip and gazed down at Rufus.

Rufus looked up, pushed his hat out of his eyes, and gave a halfhearted smile. "Does it seem to you that losing things has become a habit?"

"Yes, I seem to hear you rummaging in that toolbox more often these days."

"I prefer to believe I haven't lost anything. It's a matter of not anticipating what to bring with me from my shop. I did not anticipate needing a small corner chisel."

"I can offer you an ice pick."

Rufus smiled and shook his head. "I'll manage somehow. Thank you again for the new project."

She waved him off. "This place is a perpetual remodeling effort. I'm lucky you're available." Mo picked up a pile of fresh towels and headed down the hall.

The only chisels Rufus had with him were too large and awkward for the fine corner work he needed to do. The task would have to wait for another day. He doubted anyone would notice if he did not tap off the barely visible overhang at the end of the closet, but he wanted the work to be right.

He stood up and wiped his hands on a rag then swished the rag over the trim he had been bent over. Another doorway across the hall was waiting for its custom trim installation. Spring air gusted through the propped-open front door of the motel and threatened to take his hat. As Rufus picked up his toolbox, he heard a horse whinny — and it was not his. He grimaced as he craned around a corner to see what other Amish person had business at the motel.

Beth Stutzman. Driving her family's brand-new buggy.

She did not have business at the motel, he knew, except to find him. The temptation to step quietly out of sight flitted through his head. Instead, he stepped into view. "Hello, Beth."

Beth grinned, making her seem a little too

enthusiastic to see him. She carried a thermos.

"I thought you might like something cold to drink." Beth unscrewed the lid, which doubled as a cup, filled it with the liquid, and handed it to Rufus.

"That's kind of you." He took a swift swallow — lemonade, it turned out to be — and handed it back to her. "What brings you out this way?"

"I wanted to see if I could be any help to you."

"You would not happen to have a small corner chisel in your apron?"

"No, but I'll be happy to go fetch it for you." Beth's face lit up. "Did you leave it on your workbench?"

He had not expected that response. "Do you know what one looks like?"

"Of course. My father uses a corner chisel all the time."

That answer made sense. Ike Stutzman was the first person to demonstrate how to use a corner chisel to Rufus two decades ago.

"Mine is part of a set of small tools wrapped in a leather pouch," Rufus said. "But it's not urgent. I'll bring it the next time I come."

"Nonsense. You're here now. You might as

153

well get the job done. I'll be back before you know it." She thrust the thermos at him and swished her skirts back through the lobby and out the front door.

Round-trip, the errand was eight miles. Then she would have to scour his workbench to find the packet of chisels. Most of an hour would pass before she returned.

It was too late to stop her now.

Franey was sitting on the front porch of her home when they drove up. Her face lit when her daughter stepped out of the Prius, and Annie saw the curiosity that piqued when she and the driver emerged as well.

"What do we have here?" Franey asked as her daughter kissed her cheek.

"*Mamm,* this is Annalise's sister, Penny."

"Welcome to our home," Franey said. "I am so glad Annalise took the opportunity to visit with you."

Penny flashed Annie an unsettled look before saying, "Thank you. Me, too."

"When Annalise left on Saturday, I had not imagined I would have the pleasure of meeting you. Your sister has been a delight to our family."

"She seems very glad to know you as well." Penny looked around the yard. "It's beautiful here."

"Won't you come inside?"

Penny's eyes widened, and Annie took the cue. "No thanks. I just wanted you and Penny to meet. I'm going to show her my house and where I work."

"Annalise has a lovely little house," Franey said.

"I am only here overnight, *Mamm,*" Ruth said. "Penny will drive me back tomorrow."

"The Stutzman sisters are sleeping in your room, but I can put up a cot in Lydia and Sophie's room for you."

A few minutes later, Annie was back in the passenger seat of the car. She rolled her gaze toward Penny. "Isn't Franey great?"

"She seems very nice."

"Of course she's nice. And she would not have bitten you if you had accepted her hospitality."

"Hey. I'm being a good sport. Don't push it." Penny put the car in reverse and looked back over her shoulder at the lengthy Beiler driveway.

"It's easier to just turn around," Annie said, "and drive out going forward."

Penny glanced at her then put the car in DRIVE. "I suppose you've had a lot of experience figuring this out." She twisted the steering wheel sharply to the left.

"I'm here a lot. Of course, I'm not usually

in a car."

"I'm not sure who Franey was happier to see, Ruth or you."

"Ruth is her daughter."

"And you might be . . . well, you know." Penny pulled out onto the highway and headed toward town.

"Just drive."

"Are we really going to drive all over tarnation hunting for Rufus?"

"He's probably at the motel. It's four miles."

"That's one of their buggies, isn't it?" Penny carefully steered around an enclosed black buggy headed in the same direction.

"Yes. I'm not sure who." Annie twisted in her seat, but she could not see the driver.

A few minutes later they parked in front of the motel. Annie saw Rufus's buggy off to one side. The horse was unhitched and wandering on a generous tether, so Rufus must have been there a long time.

As she slammed the passenger door, Annie looked over the top of the car at her sister. "You behave yourself."

Penny smiled in that way that Annie did not quite trust.

They entered the motel. From behind the desk, Mo looked up. "Who do we have here?"

"This is my sister, Penny."

Mo's eyebrows went up a notch. "Bringing her to meet Rufus?"

"Maybe." Annie tilted her head.

Mo waved them on through. "I won't tell anyone! He's just down the hall."

"Thanks, Mo."

Penny elbowed Annie. "She treats you like a couple already."

Annie pushed back with her own elbow. "Behave."

And there he was, his white shirt stretched across his broad back as he expertly placed pieces of trim he had crafted in his workshop on the Beiler land. Annie slowed her steps, wanting just to watch him and breathe in the fragrance of his artistry as it took form.

Penny stubbed her toe on a stray chair, and when it scraped the floor Rufus turned.

His face brightened.

"Rufus, I want you to meet my sister. This is Penny."

Rufus brushed a hand against his trousers before offering it to Penny. She took it then glanced at Annie with upturned lips. Annie allowed herself a slow breath of relief.

"It's a pleasure to meet you," Penny said with perfect manners. With one finger, she traced the carved pattern in a piece of trim.

"Your work is beautiful — everything Annie said it was."

"I trust you had a relaxing drive down." Rufus caught Annie's eye before dipping his hat at Penny.

"I had no idea this part of the state was so gorgeous," Penny said.

Annie felt as if she were watching from the outside. Her *English* sister was chatting with the Amish man who had made her rethink her life. She had harassed Penny into coming. Now, though, her blood pulsed faster. Annie wanted Penny to like Rufus. She wanted Penny to see everything wonderful that she saw in him. She wanted Rufus to see past Penny's *English* exterior and believe she was a wonderful sister. When she met Rufus's gaze, and the familiar warmth flushed through her, she saw delight in his violet-blue eyes.

The lobby door clattered open, and Annie turned toward steps that progressed firmly in her direction.

Beth Stutzman stood there, and Rufus's eyes moved to her expectantly.

"It's not there. I looked everywhere." Beth Stutzman's gaze moved to Annie. "Oh, hello. Annalise, is it? I almost didn't recognize you dressed like . . ."

Annie swallowed and moistened her lips

before responding, but Rufus broke in. "Beth, this is Annalise's sister, Penny Friesen. And Penny, this is Beth Stutzman, an old family friend. She was kind enough to go look for a tool I neglected to bring today."

Annie felt her sister's eyes on her, as if saying, *Old family friend? Sure.*

"It's the oddest thing, though," Beth said. "I definitely know what a corner chisel looks like, and I promise you, it is nowhere in your workshop. The whole set is missing."

"I'm sure it will turn up," Rufus said.

"I'll help you look again later," Beth said. "But I wanted you to know right away that it's lost."

Annie's brow furrowed. Since when would Rufus send Beth Stutzman to look for tools? She caught Rufus's eye then looked away quickly at the slight paling of his complexion. The concern — and the triumph — in Beth's face were unconvincing, but Annie preferred to sort out her questions with Rufus later. In private.

"Why don't we go?" Annie nudged Penny. "We don't want to get in the way here."

FOURTEEN

Ruth knelt in the garden. Late afternoon was her favorite time to fill her hands with the mystery of the earth. The garden was dormant now, still readying for its summer yield. In a few weeks, when her sisters worked the soil and planted, the family would see the promise of nourishment for a new year. Weeds were already pressing their way to the sun, though. One by one Ruth picked them out, being sure to get the roots, and tossed them into a wheelbarrow.

A few feet away, her mother wielded a hoe, splitting clots that had formed over the winter and pounding the fragments into smooth soil. The rhythm was familiar to both of them. Whether in Pennsylvania when Ruth was young or during the last six years in Colorado, Ruth and her mother had chased out the evidence of winter and prepared to feed the family. Until two years ago. Ruth pushed the thought out of her

mind and imagined her sisters working in the garden. They would do the weeding and watering as the vegetables grew. For yet another year, she would not be there to see the plants sprout.

Ruth watched her mother work, envying the contentment she saw and the simple companionship of silence. Finding a ride from Colorado Springs was worth the trouble to see these simple moments of pleasure in her mother's face.

"Annalise wants to have a garden," Franey said. "She has never had a vegetable garden."

"She'll enjoy it. She's so curious about everything."

"Plenty of the *English* grow vegetables." Franey raised the hoe several feet before thudding it through a stubborn clot repeatedly. "But gardening will have special meaning to Annalise. For her, it's part of learning our ways."

"Yes, I suppose so." Ruth wrapped her fingers around a weed already six inches high and yanked.

"Annalise is persistent about her quilt, too. I suggested she start with a lap quilt, but she was determined to make something she could put on a bed."

"She is used to aiming high."

"As long as success does not lead to pride, doing your best is an excellent quality."

"*Demut.* Humility. This is not always easy for Annalise."

"*Demut* is not always easy for any of us." Franey winked. "After all, no one makes a better schnitzel than I do."

"*Mamm!*" Ruth laughed at her mother's pride. *Hochmut.*

"I'm teaching Annalise to cook our traditional foods. She never cooked much at all, you know, before moving here."

"She was too busy running a company."

"She's trying hard to change and understand our ways. And she learns so quickly."

Ruth stuffed weeds deeper into the wheelbarrow. She loved Annalise, too, but she had not expected the garden conversation to be all about her. Where was the contented silence she used to share with her mother, or the soft humming of hymns from the *Ausbund*?

"Rufus says Annalise has room on her land for a small barn," Franey said. "I think she should learn to drive a buggy soon."

Ruth hid a smile at the memory, just a few days old, of Annalise teaching her to drive a car. Would Annalise think managing a horse and buggy was as easy as driving a car?

"She wants to begin making her own clothes. I told her perhaps over the winter."

"But it's only spring now," Ruth said.

"Gardening, cooking, quilting, driving — she has plenty to learn for now."

"She won't want to wait that long."

Her mother never asked Ruth about what she was learning. Pharmacology, pathology, health care ethics. Franey had made her peace that Ruth was pursing higher education, but apparently even talking about her courses was too *English.*

But Annalise, it seemed, could do no wrong. Jealousy warmed Ruth's chest.

"Canning." Franey stood still and looked over the garden plot. "When we're just planting, I seem to forget how much will grow. I'll need all the help I can get canning everything for the winter."

"Well, you won't miss me because you'll have Annalise." Ruth tossed an entire clump of dirt instead of knocking the small weed loose from it.

"Ruth Beiler, what has gotten into you?" Franey leaned on her hoe and stared wide eyed at her daughter.

"I'm sorry, *Mamm.*" And she was. Ruth had chosen to leave. She had chosen to miss the rhythm of planting and growing and harvesting the family's vegetables. She had

chosen to surrender the closeness of her family to her own future, away from them.

Franey slowly resumed slicing into the soil with her hoe, but her vigor had dissipated.

"Forgive me, *Mamm.* I should not have said that. I should not even have thought it."

"We should go and see how Lydia and Sophie and the Stutzman girls are coming along with supper." Franey grasped her hoe and carried it toward the house, where she leaned it against the back porch railing and disappeared through the door.

Ruth slowly stood, brushed dirt from her skirt and gripped the handles of the wheelbarrow.

After dinner at a small restaurant on Main Street, Annie put her key in the lock of her back door and turned it. She stepped aside to let Penny enter first. They each carried an overnight bag.

"Maybe I should have taken you in through the front door," Annie said, "but this is how I usually come and go." She turned a knob on a lamp at one end of the counter and a clean light illuminated the simple kitchen.

Penny looked around. "It's . . . quaint."

"The house is a hundred years old, Penny.

So yes, the kitchen is small. It's all small, and I've come to love it."

"Do you cook much?"

"All the time now. Not the kind of cooking you do, of course. But you'll be glad to know I'm going to have a garden this year. I know how strongly you feel about fresh food."

"Amish or not, a garden is a great idea. I may make a foodie out of you yet."

"Rufus has drawn it all out. He's going to come and turn the soil for me." Soon, Annie hoped. "Let me show you the rest of the house."

Annie led the way into her small dining room, which opened into the living room. She paused several times to turn on lamps.

Penny inspected the cabinet beneath one of the living room lamps. "That's beautiful." She opened the door. "A propane tank?"

Annie stoked the tabletop. "Rufus's handiwork. Propane is a common way to provide light."

"Among the Amish, you mean. It's sort of like camping."

A fire started in Annie's stomach and burned its way up. "Look, Penny, I asked you here to show you my home, my life. Don't make fun."

Penny laid three fingers across her mouth and stared at Annie, silent. But Annie knew what her sister's expression meant.

"Ever since we picked up Ruth today," Annie said, "you've been acting weird."

Penny put a finger to her own chest. "I'm acting weird? You're the one who gives up electricity and moves to the boonies, and I'm acting weird?"

Annie exhaled. "I understand you need some time to take it all in."

"This man had better be worth it," Penny said. "You might tell yourself being Amish is not just for him, but you'd better be sure. You're changing everything. I mean, hey, Annie, just because you found we had one Amish ancestor doesn't mean you have to go back in time."

"I'm not going back in time, Penny. I'm just choosing a simpler way to live. Simpler values. A faith that asks me to measure my decisions more carefully."

"In the end, you're still choosing Rufus Beiler. So you'd better be sure. Don't think I didn't notice your reaction when Beth Stutzman showed up. You're not sure."

Penny was right, of course. Annie was not sure she was the right wife for Rufus. Someone like Beth Stutzman would know how to be an Amish wife who brought no

disgrace or embarrassment to her husband. Annie moved to the stairs.

"I'll go get your room ready," she said. "Make yourself comfortable for a few minutes."

Upstairs, Annie opened a chair that unfolded into a twin-size bed and stretched sheets across it. She moved to the small desk and stacked up the papers there, clearing a surface for Penny to use. While her hands were busy, her mind also whirled. Sitting in the desk chair, she pulled open the bottom drawer and riffled through file folders. Her fingers settled on one folder, and she paused to think.

When Annie heard Penny's footsteps on the stairs, she made a rapid decision.

FIFTEEN

The night was deep when Ruth left the sleepy house. Even the Stutzman girls, who seemed to giggle behind their teeth more than Ruth remembered, had settled in for the night. She had taken a flashlight from the kitchen drawer, and now she turned it on and aimed at the path. Even without a light, though, her feet knew the way. Clouds hung low, a curtain hiding the stars. Her frame ached to lie against the solidity of the broad rock and stare into forever.

She wore her brother Joel's warm jacket because it was handy on the hook next to the back door. The flashlight beam bobbed ahead of her steps. Ruth moved swiftly, remembering the tree root she once tripped over and the low branches of an evergreen, the depression in the ground that often collected water, and the bushes with hidden spurs. Ruth's parents had no idea how many times over the years she had escaped to the

rock, whether by light of sun or moon.

With two families under the roof, fragmented conversation had bounced around the rooms during dinner and games. If she was hearing right, this might be the last time she could find solitude at the rock. At the very least, because of the park improvement project, the acres around the rock would be more populated. And at the very worst, the rock would be blasted. Its pieces could be used to outline a footpath with no hint that they had stood united and unmoved for eons.

If she walked briskly, Ruth could reach the rock in twelve minutes. On a cloudy night, Ruth estimated fifteen. She moved through trees to a clearing, and there, even under a dull, dim sky, the rock beckoned. The boulder stood more than five feet high and spread six feet long and nine feet across. Ruth knew where to put her foot on the rear side of it in order to heft herself to the top in two wide climbing steps. The flashlight turned off, she lay flat on her back and stared up.

Without the ornamentation of stars, the view lacked the unfathomable sense of infinity. Instead, clouds veiled the secrets of the sky, leaving Ruth to ponder the shroud around her own life.

On this rock she had imagined her future as a public health nurse. On this rock she plotted to escape her own baptism and go to college. On this rock, she chose to break Elijah's heart.

Now she lived in the in-between, sure of her life calling to nursing, but not yet qualified to carry it out. Sure that leaving the church was the right decision, but not truly finding her place among the *English*. Sure that she could not drag Elijah away from his promises, but not able to keep him out of her heart. She should not have answered his last letter. She should not even have read the last letter. He was getting brazen.

A glimpse of one star would reassure her that it was not for nothing.

The rock was cold, as it always was. Eventually the chill seeped through Joel's jacket, through Ruth's sweater, through her skin. Ruth gripped the front panels of the coat and held them tightly around her, but in truth she did not mind the cold. Inhaling, she took in the fragrance of spring, the murkiness of apple blossoms carried on a breeze jumbled with the smell of mud in the damp earth below. Surely rain would come before the night was over.

Ruth flinched at the sound of a cracking branch. The night was too cloudy to cast a

shadow, but she knew someone was there. She sat up and turned her head in the direction the sound had come from.

"Ruth? Are you here?" The voice was a solid sort of whisper.

Ruth fumbled for the flashlight and pointed it toward the voice. "Elijah?"

He emerged from the nearest tree.

"What are you doing here?" Adrenaline surged into Ruth.

"I might ask you the same question." Elijah found the footholds and climbed onto the rock. "Turn off that light."

She clicked the flashlight off and lay flat again. "I don't get many chances to come here anymore. I hear they may blast this rock to smithereens."

"Not if I have anything to say about it." Elijah lay down beside her.

The hammer in Ruth's chest pounded harder, faster. More than two years had passed since she and Elijah used to meet at the rock in daytime innocence — and night-time guilt.

"Elijah," she said staring into the gray again, "how did you know I was here?"

"I didn't."

"Do you come often?"

The length of his silence confounded her.

"I feel you close when I come here," he

171

said. "This is where I first knew I loved you."

Ruth's pent-up lungs deflated. "Elijah, I'm sorry I answered your letters. I was thinking of myself and not what is good for you."

"My feelings are the same, Ruth. *You* are what is good for me."

"We can't keep going around this circle, Elijah. We can't be together."

"You made your choice. I could make mine."

"No! Not because of me. You've been baptized. They would shun you. I would always know what I took from you."

"I hope," he said, his voice low as he turned his face toward hers, "that you would always know what I gave willingly."

They were not more than twelve inches apart. A familiar tremble began when she felt his breath, warm against the cold, mingling with her halting respiration. He raised a hand and grazed her cheek and neck then settled on her shoulder. Ruth could barely feel his touch through her layers of clothing, but memories roused, and she closed her eyes and breathed in his smell.

Ruth heard Elijah shift his weight, putting himself up on one elbow and turning his whole body toward her. He shielded her

now from the chilled breeze, casting a stillness between them. When she opened her eyes, his face was right where she thought it would be, so close to hers that she could barely focus on his features. He was going to kiss her. It would be sweet and ardent and complete. She moistened her lips and swallowed in anticipation.

A star glimmered through the fog above them. Ruth rolled away from Elijah and sat up out of his reach.

Sixteen

June 1776

"General Washington has fallen back time and again." Joseph moved mashed potatoes around on his plate. "If he doesn't have a victory soon, we're going to lose Philadelphia."

John reached toward the basket in the center of the table and helped himself to a thick wedge of bread. "Washington has had his share of victories."

Joseph let his fork clatter against his plate. "Not lately. I don't think you appreciate how precarious our position is."

Jacob observed that while one brother's analysis of military realities caused him to leave food on his plate meal after a meal, the other's unflagging enthusiasm for the cause fed his appetite. He glanced at his mother and winced. At least their wives had already taken most of the dishes to the kitchen to wash up.

"I think I'll go help the girls." The Byler matriarch rose from her chair. "I never know where I'll find things when someone else cleans up."

Jacob waited until the broad door closed between the main room and the kitchen. "You know *Mamm* does not like when you talk about the war at the dinner table."

"I cannot help it," Joseph said. "I must do more."

"Your crops help feed the militia. You play an important role."

"You and John could look after my land."

"We have our own fields, and the tannery and the powder mill."

"I know. But all the powder in the world will not matter if Washington does not have enough soldiers."

"Washington is a better general than you give him credit for," John said.

"We are all trying to do our part, Joseph." Jacob tapped his fingers on the tabletop. "You cannot take the weight of winning the war on your own shoulders."

They heard the wagon and sat alert.

"That will be David," Jacob said. He crossed the room to open the front door in time to see David sling down from the wagon seat and hitch the horses to a post. He raised his eyebrows in question as his

175

youngest brother stomped the dust off his boots before entering.

David shook his head. "I delivered the load just as we planned, but I did not find much to haul back."

"How much?"

"More coal and brimstone than saltpeter."

Jacob tilted his head and sighed. "I have some saltpeter left from May. Perhaps we will be better off than we think."

David reached inside his shirt. "I have this as well."

"From Sarah?" Jacob took the envelope.

"I did not get to see her, but she left the letter with her maid."

Jacob laughed. "She's using her maid for subterfuge. There is no telling what Sarah would do right under the nose of a British officer if she had the chance." He opened the envelope and scanned the note. "Thomas Jefferson, eh? She says he is the best man for the job."

"Apparently he has a knack for word-smithing," David said. "I'm sure the rest of the Congress will hack his effort to pieces, but somebody has to get something on paper."

Jacob could not help but wonder if Sarah had made any inquiries that might lead to

Maria. If she had, she did not mention them.

"Is there any food?" David asked.

"There's bread on the table. I'll see what else is left."

As David sank into a chair, Jacob pushed through the door to the kitchen and scanned the room. "Where's Katie?"

"I sent her to lie down on my bed," his mother answered. "The poor thing is worn out. The new *boppli* will be here soon. I sent all the children upstairs."

"David is home."

"And hungry, I suppose." Elizabeth held out a hand, and John's wife put a plate in it.

"Of course." David always wanted food.

Elizabeth moved to the pie cabinet, where the leftover food sat, and began to fill the plate.

"I think I'll go check on Katie," Jacob said.

On his mother's bed, Jacob found his wife turned on one side with a hand on her swollen belly. She smiled when he appeared in the door frame.

"I noticed you did not eat much." Jacob sat and massaged Katie's arm from elbow to wrist.

"Indigestion."

"That's what you said before Catherine, and before the twins. It went on for days."

"I know. It won't be much longer."

"Catherine needs a sister."

Katie nodded. "I want to name her Elizabeth. Do you think your mother would mind if we called her Lisbet?"

He leaned over and kissed her forehead. "She would be honored to share her name, and pleased that you want to remember my sister." He stroked the back side of her hand. "Would you like to go home to your own bed?"

"After I have a nap. Do you mind waiting?" Katie snuggled her face into a pillow.

In the end, his mother insisted on putting the children to bed upstairs so Jacob would not have to disturb Katie to take her home. She would need her rest before hard labor began.

John and Joseph collected their families and rumbled off the homestead, which had become a productive farm in the last thirty years. Jacob's mother occupied a widow's seat — the house and a few acres around it, where she kept chickens and sometimes a pig, and had a couple of cherry trees. Though he built his own house near the tannery after his father died and Jacob owned the rest of the land that had once been his father's, he would provide for his mother as long as she lived. David still

resided in the big house, hesitant to buy his own land because he dreamed of North Carolina.

"After independence," David said often, "America will open wide." It would not be long now, Jacob hoped.

Mother and son sat on the front porch together admiring the stars.

"I'm sorry the boys are not more careful about their war talk," Jacob said.

Elizabeth let a long moment lapse. "Until the day your father died, Christian hoped he would return to the Amish church and peaceful ways."

"*Daed* was a peaceful man, but he would do whatever was necessary to protect his family."

"I am not Amish," Elizabeth said, "but that does not mean I love war."

"I know. I hope you do not think any of us loves war."

"I am a mother of four able-bodied sons. Of course the thought of war distresses me. And do not think I cannot guess what is really in those wagons you send David out with. You could not possibly be tanning that many hides."

Jacob chuckled. "No, *Mamm.*"

"Just remember that the British soldiers are sons and husbands and fathers as well."

■ ■ ■ ■

"What does this mean?" Magdalena wanted to know. "Are we citizens of this new nation whether we want to be or not?"

"It does not change our lives," her father answered. Gently he took the newspaper from her hands and folded it. "Why are you reading this? We have nothing to do with any of that. You know this, Magdalena." Where did she even get this newspaper? News of the Declaration of Independence had reached the countryside outside Philadelphia within a day. He could not shield her from that, but she had no business reading an *English* newspaper. Calmly, Christian sat on the top step leading up to the broad front porch of his home.

"How can you say it has nothing to do with us, *Daed*? These people took Nathanael from me. And now they want to force me to be a part of their new nation?" Magdalena paced in the dirt at the bottom of the steps. Her youngest siblings tumbled in the grass beyond her.

"We live separate, Magdalena," Christian said. "Apart. Peacefully. We give our allegiance to God. Force is not a part of our lives."

180

"Tell that to Nathan."

"Magdalena!"

She stopped pacing, crossed her arms, and turned to face him. "I'm sorry, *Daed*. I mean no disrespect. They attacked Nathanael and he has never been the same. I know the men who did it."

"One of them was shot in the battle at Lexington. The ways of force did not help him."

"You know Nathanael was not the only one they bullied," Magdalena said.

"The Patriots bully anyone who is not a Patriot." It was simple fact, Christian thought.

"But they *especially* bully the Amish."

"They understand an enemy," Christian said. "The British are an enemy, and they believe they must fight an enemy. But they do not understand neutrality. They do not understand loving their enemies."

"The British are not much better. Look what they did to your corn."

"They harmed only a small fraction of the crop."

"Were you really there when your father swore allegiance to King George?"

Magdalena seemed to be calming, he was glad to see. "I was not supposed to be. I was a disobedient little boy who snuck off a

181

ship and into a strange city. I put myself and my family at risk because I wanted to see my *daed* take the oath. But yes, I was there."

"He promised allegiance to the Crown. Did that duty die with him? Or are we bound by it as well?"

"Magdalena, you are full of questions tonight." Christian was not surprised. Of all his children, Magdalena was the most spirited. She had grown into the image of her missing *aunti* Maria in more ways than one.

"If I have to choose a side, I choose the British," Magdalena said.

"But we will not choose a side. You understand this, *ya*?"

She did not answer.

"Take the little ones inside to clean up for bed, please," Christian said.

Magdalena called the children, and they rambled up the steps, pausing to kiss their *daed* on their way into the house.

In a month or so Babsi would bear their second child. After two miscarriages following Antje's birth, Babsi was particularly anxious to hold this child in her arms. When he was a boy, Christian's parents left Europe because of the proliferation of wars. They did not want their only son to grow up and

182

be forced to serve in an army. That was why his father swore allegiance to the king of England. Pennsylvania was a free land. But could it now remain free and be peaceful while his own children grew up?

A few days later, Jacob held his own declaration of independence. Lisbet lived up to her name and even looked like his mother. This squalling bundle was the first of his children — the first of his family — to be born in the United States of America, rather than a British colony.

Jacob kissed his new daughter's cheek, grateful she would grow up in a free nation.

SEVENTEEN

"Did you sleep?" Annie handed Penny her largest mug filled with hot coffee.

Eyes closed, Penny inhaled the steam. "I didn't think I would, but I did."

"Must be the mountain air." Annie gestured to the dining room table. "I made blueberry muffins."

"From scratch?"

"From scratch."

"I'm impressed."

"You should be." Annie picked up a muffin and bit into it.

"You have hot water in this joint? I need a shower."

"We are a five-star camping facility. But me first. I know how you dawdle."

Upstairs, Annie showered and dressed. Then half listening to the sounds of Penny's progress, she opened the folder she had retrieved the night before and stuck an envelope in the bag she always carried. An

hour later, with Penny at the wheel, they rolled into the Beiler driveway.

Ruth was ready, sitting on the porch with her small bag and her head back against the top of the Adirondack chair. She looked weary to Annie. When Ruth spotted the car, she leaned forward and lifted herself out of the seat.

Annie got out of the car and met Ruth coming down the porch steps. "Excuse my bluntness, but you look like a truck hit you."

Ruth rubbed one hand over an eye. "I didn't sleep."

"Your next visit will be more restful. The Stutzmans will move out and you'll get your room back."

Ruth shook her head. "There's just so much to think about when I come here."

Annie considered probing, but Ruth moved toward the Prius and did not meet her eyes. A car door slammed, and Annie saw that Penny had gotten out and was walking toward them.

Annie pulled an envelope out of her bag. "Ruth, before you go, I have something for you."

Ruth twisted at the waist to look at Annie. "You do so much for me as it is."

"I want to give you some papers." Annie slipped a form out of the envelope and

unfolded it. "This is the title to the Prius. I've signed it over to you."

"What?" Ruth's sluggish steps froze.

Penny came near. "Yes, what she said. What?" She took the paper from Annie's hands. "You really did sign over the title to Ruth Beiler."

"You have to take it back," Ruth said.

Annie shook her head. "Nope. I already put your name in and signed."

Penny handed the paper to Ruth. "Looks legal to me."

"It may be legal," Ruth said, "but it's crazy."

"Why?" Annie set her jaw in challenge. "You need a car."

"I've been getting along without one."

"It's stressful to get around in Colorado Springs without a car. You can't do that indefinitely. You have a permit, after all."

"For ID purposes," Ruth said.

"Then why have you been learning to drive?"

Penny's eyebrows went up. "You've been learning to drive?"

"Shh. Not so loud." Ruth glanced toward the house. "My mother doesn't know and this is not the way to tell her."

"Of course not." Penny lowered her voice. She turned to Annie. "But what about

insurance? Repairs?"

"It's still under warranty for two more years." Annie handed the envelope to Ruth. "The papers are in here, along with enough cash to put insurance in your name for the next six months."

"But your *car,*" Ruth said.

"*Your* car." Annie blew out a breath. "I've been thinking about this constantly the last few days. And about what I did on Saturday. I can't have the car sitting there, tempting me, making it so easy. I would always know I could get it whenever I want. You need it. I don't."

Penny looked from Annie to Ruth. "You really have a permit?"

Ruth nodded.

"Then this is yours." Penny dangled the Prius key in front of Ruth.

Ruth softened. "I don't know what to say, Annalise."

"Just drive carefully."

"I will," Ruth said. She looked back toward the house. "But not until we're out of town. I don't need to rub it in *Mamm*'s face."

"Then let's hit the road," Penny said. "We'll drop Annie off and get going."

Annie shook her head. "I don't have to be at the shop until two o'clock. I'm going to

187

hang around here awhile. Maybe work on my quilt."

"I'm sure *Mamm* would love that," Ruth said.

Something in Ruth's tone sounded off to Annie, but Ruth was already putting her bag in the car so the moment for conversation passed. Annie hugged her sister then waved good-bye as Penny turned the car around and aimed for the road. What would Penny and Ruth find to talk about? she wondered. Or would they be content with silence? She hoped not.

Annie turned, went up the steps, and crossed the porch. Tapping lightly on the front door, she turned the knob with the other hand. She glanced over her shoulder and across the clearing to Rufus's workshop. Franey would know if Rufus was around.

No one was in the front room. Jacob would be in school, and Joel should be out in the fields with his father. *Franey, Lydia, and Sophie must be scattered in the house,* Annie thought, *or perhaps in the barn.* She heard no sound of any of the Stutzmans, either. Perhaps they were busy readying their own home.

Annie moved to the cedar chest under the window. If she had a few minutes alone, she could surprise Franey by making some

progress. Her palms stroked the polished finish of the chest. She imagined Rufus's hands insisting on perfection in his craft. The touch of the solid chest that he had labored over started a tremble in her fingers. She wished Rufus would feel that way about the quilt she labored over. Annie knew it was far from perfect, though. Perhaps this would not be the quilt he admired, but the next one, or the one after that. Her throat thickened. How long would it take before she could offer Rufus what he deserved in a wife?

Maybe never. Even if she could learn to be perfectly Amish, she had done things in her past she was not sure she would ever want to admit to Rufus.

Penny's words knocked around in Annie's head. Was she sure becoming Amish was not just for Rufus? She could be wrong. With a sigh, she lifted her eyes to the ceiling. *Lord, make me sure. I'll go or I'll stay. Just make me sure.* But at the thought of a future without Rufus her chest heaved in protest.

She had begun to lift the lid when she heard the familiar weight on the outside steps.

Rufus opened the front door, an empty

189

tumbler in his hand that he intended to refill in the kitchen.

The cedar chest's lid thumped closed. Annalise spun around and smiled at him. He loved her smile. Today, though, it left him doubting her state of mind.

"So our sisters are off together," Rufus said.

Annalise nodded. "They may spill all our secrets to each other."

"More likely they'll stare at each other for an hour or so."

"No doubt." Annalise moved toward him and reached for the glass. "Let me pour you a cold drink."

He let go of the glass but did not miss the tremor in her hand. "Just finishing a few odd jobs." He looked around. "Is no one home?"

"Not that I can tell," Annalise said.

She turned toward the kitchen, but he touched her wrist then held her hand. "I don't really care about the drink. We haven't talked in ages. I want to know how you are."

She was trembling. He was sure of it. And her eyes were puddles.

"How was your visit home?" He nudged her gently to the sofa and sat down beside her.

Her lips moved through about twenty

poses without settling on words.

"Complicated, eh?" he said.

She nodded and put her hands up to the sides of her head, squeezing. "My family doesn't understand what I'm doing. Sometimes I think I don't understand what I'm doing myself."

Now the tremble was in her voice. He took her hands in his and lowered them to her lap, holding them there. Under his fingers, he felt the resistance slide away. He waited a few more seconds, holding her with his eyes, urging the tension from her.

"You're listening," he said, "and trying to obey."

She took a deep breath and exhaled heavily. Her hands, still under his, relaxed.

Rufus raised a finger to her lips. "You don't have to explain everything now." He traced her lips, lightly, barely touching them. In the months he had known her, he could count on one hand the times he had kissed her. But he had lost track of the number of times he wanted to kiss her. If he gave in every time he wanted to — every time she wanted him to — he would not be thinking of her good, but only his pleasure.

The tremble was in her face now, and he knew he should stop. If he did not, he would move his hand to her hair, and his face close

to hers. This woman, this *English* who dared to take up Amish ways, turned him inside out.

He brushed the back of his hand across her cheek and moved away from her. "I can take some time away from my work," he said. "Let's go for a walk."

Her eyes brightened, the puddles cleared. "Yes, I would like that."

He heard the faint rattle of a buggy turning down their lane, and his mind rapidly indexed who it might be. The horse's steps were solid, the trot steady. The axle of the buggy creaked. Ike Stutzman almost had not bought the buggy because of that creak.

When the front door opened, Annalise stood up. Rufus rose and turned to see Beth come through the door.

"Oh, good," Beth said, "you're not busy. *Daed* asked me to come fetch you. He wants your advice about some cabinets in the new house. He wonders if you might be able to repair them."

"Perhaps I could come by later in the afternoon."

Annalise moved out of his peripheral vision, but Rufus forced himself not to glance at her in Beth's presence.

"He was hoping you could come now. If you don't think you can fix them, then he'll

tear them out today. He doesn't want any more delay in making the house ready for us to move in."

"*Ya,* I suppose every day matters. You go on, though. I'll get my tools and bring my own buggy."

"I would be happy to take you." Beth took a step toward him and smiled. "I'd love the company."

"I may need my buggy to go on to a job site anyway." Rufus stepped back. "Let your *daed* know I'm coming and I'll be right there."

"If you insist."

He let out a sigh when she retreated through the door. When he turned, though, Annalise was not in the room.

Rufus went through the house to the kitchen, where Annalise was washing the tumbler he had carried in.

"I'll come right back," he said. "We'll take that walk."

She shook her head. "I'll just walk back to town. I have some thinking to do." She set the glass in the dish rack.

Rufus regretted not kissing her when he had the chance.

Eighteen

If he had just kissed her, she would feel better. Annie had not expected Rufus to kiss her, though, because he hardly ever did. Still, if only he had.

Annie hit the button on the cash register and the change drawer kicked open, nudging her just below the ribs. She counted back change to a customer who left happily with a small silver-framed mirror Annie had priced and set out only two hours ago. When Mrs. Weichert returned, she would be pleased to hear of several sales that made the day profitable. Two other couples still lingered in the shop, unusual for a Thursday afternoon. Annie picked up a rag to wipe down an empty shelf before she began bringing knickknacks from the back room to fill it.

Of course Rufus was not interested in Beth. Annie knew that, even if Beth did not. But the undefined nature of her own rela-

tionship with Rufus left her feeling uncomfortably exposed. She did not have to be Amish to see that the community would love to see him married — to an Amish woman. Beth Stutzman would be a better Amish wife than Annie could ever hope to be.

Annie blew out her breath and rattled her lips. A buzzing sound escaped. Oops.

"Pardon me," she said to a startled customer who was approaching the counter. "May I help you?"

The customer led her to the back of the shop where yellow-paged tomes stood in formation in trim uniforms on neat shelves. The books the shop carried did not qualify as rare, but they were anywhere from forty to eighty years old. Novels, biographies, histories, and genealogies beckoned from decades past. Annie sometimes got distracted with them herself, pausing to read when she was supposed to be organizing. Certainly they were more noteworthy than the unsorted hardbacks in the several thrift stores in town. The customer already had three books in his hands. Annie focused on helping him find the final volume he sought then returned to the front of the store to ring up yet another sale.

She needed to stop thinking about Rufus.

That was all there was to it. She had work to do.

The bell on the door jangled as the remaining customers left the shop without purchasing anything. Annie pulled a clipboard from a shelf below the cash register and traced a finger down the task list Mrs. Weichert had created for the week. Alone in the shop, Annie could not disappear to the back room longer than it took to bring items to the front. She went back and forth a few times, wiping down each item as she put it on a shelf, always listening for the bell.

And she was not thinking about Rufus. Not much, anyway. But he still owed her a walk, and she intended to collect.

When the door opened next, a medley of tenor and bass voices drowned the bell. Annie looked up. A mass of gangly teenage appendages stampeded as a herd through the door. Out of the center of the creature they had become, three crates emerged and hit the floor in thuds.

"Hello, Annalise."

Joel Beiler came into focus. Mark and Luke Stutzman stood on either side of him, and behind them were Carter Reynolds and Duncan Spangler. Somebody thumped fingers rhythmically against a denim-leg drum, but Annie could not see who. It had

to be one of the *English*. At the random thought that Amish cloth did not make that sound, Annie blinked twice.

She tossed her dust rag on the front counter. "Hello, boys." She glanced at each one in turn. "What do we have here?"

"Amish stuff." Carter Reynolds peered at his phone and moved his thumbs into action on its buttons.

"Mrs. Weichert said Mrs. Stutzman could sell things on commission." Joel pointed a foot toward a crate. "Carved boxes, small wooden buggies. Some quilting."

"I see." Annie bent and lifted a lap quilt off the top of one crate. Rich colors in a complex pattern with small pieces, exquisite stitching. "It's beautiful."

"My sister Beth made that one," Mark Stutzman said.

Of course she did. Annie dropped the quilt, unfolded, back onto the crate. "We'll have to go through and price everything individually."

Mark produced a sheet of paper folded down to a square. "*Mamm* put on here what she would like to sell them for."

"I see." Annie unfolded and inspected the page. Mrs. Weichert would likely add another 20 percent, but the items would still be priced attractively. The word *Amish* on

the labels would raise the curiosity factor. Amish items tended to move quickly on the weekends.

Carter elbowed his way past the Amish boys. "I'll help you carry them to the back." He set his phone on the counter and bent down.

"Thank you, Carter." Annie squatted, briefly riffling through the contents of a crate before grasping its sides. She felt her own cell phone escape her back pocket just as she stood again. It hit the floor. "Can someone grab that? Just set it on the counter."

She followed Carter into the back room, and Joel trailed with the last of the crates. Annie wondered about the motley assortment of boys who had arrived together. Joel was slightly older than the others, with responsibilities of his own. How did he come to have a free afternoon to spend with *English* boys? Carter's father often provided taxi service for Amish families. From what Annie observed a few days ago, though, she did not think Joel was interested in befriending the Stutzman brothers. Yet here they were, all together. Joel's face was as blank as a whiteboard. She could discern nothing from watching him. And Duncan? The Spanglers were neighbors not too far from

her house off Main Street, but she knew little about them. Annie supposed Duncan and Carter went to school together.

"Did you bring a buggy into town?" Annie picked up a carved wooden buggy.

"We came in the back of my dad's truck," Carter offered.

"How will you get home, then?" Her eyes turned to Joel.

Joel glanced out the shop's window. "Tom said he might have to run back our way later. Or we can walk."

Annie nodded. It was not as if she could offer them a ride, by car or by buggy.

"Let's go," Mark called from the front room.

Annie wondered what they could be in such a hurry about, but the boys, once again silhouetted by the afternoon sunlight, morphed into one creature with entangled legs that managed to amble out of the shop. She watched them for a moment through the display window as they traversed Main Street in a black huddle. They did not pause to examine any windows but rather moved purposefully, leaving Annie pondering again what united the five of them.

Ten minutes passed before Annie encountered the cell phone on the counter. She knew immediately it was not hers — the

scratches on the front cover were not right. It had to be Carter's.

She flipped the phone open just to be sure. It lit immediately with a hideous screen saver no doubt hacked from a video game Carter was not technically old enough to purchase.

With the phone in her hand, Annie stepped out to the sidewalk and looked up and down the street. The boys could be anywhere by now. Surely Carter would try to use his phone and realize the mistake. She needed to close the shop in twenty minutes. Would they come back by then? Even if she could justify the situation as an emergency — which it was not — calling her phone to alert Carter was pointless. Her phone was not turned on.

Annie went back inside the shop and sat on the stool behind the counter. The phone buzzed with a text message. Out of long instinct she flipped it open again. MOM SAYS BE HOME FOR DINNER. The message must be from one of Carter's sisters.

Sometimes Annie thought giving up her cell phone was harder than surrendering her computer. Her iPhone had been such an easy connection to any information she wanted. The phone she had now, identical to Carter's, was capable of connecting to

the Internet but she did not carry the service. Did Carter's parents let him have an Internet package on his phone? she wondered. Pressing her thumb in a quick sequence answered her question.

His Internet history twisted her gut. She was being nosy, she knew. Not an admirable quality in an Amish woman. But she saw what she saw, and now she would not be able to ignore it. Why was a fifteen-year-old boy from a small town looking for that kind of information?

Annie cleared her throat. She powered the phone off, slapped it closed, and jammed it in a back pocket. Her lips worked in and out six times.

She had faced temptation and lost — again. Just for a moment she remembered running her life from her phone.

Temptation led to knowledge, though.

To seek help for the boy, she would have to admit she poked around in Carter's private business.

Maybe it was nothing. She had searched for stranger topics herself, just out of curiosity.

But maybe it was something.

Nosy or not, and almost Amish or not, Annie was going to find out what those boys were up to.

The hands on the clock ticked slowly toward four thirty, when Annie could close the shop. The boys would have almost thirty minutes' head start. She would sprint the four blocks home, grab her bicycle, and start asking questions around town. Five teenage boys on foot could not disappear without leaving a trail.

One thought made Annie press her fingers against closed eyes. If Joel was involved in this, Franey would tremble to her core.

NINETEEN

Rufus hitched up the lightweight open cart to Dolly, his favorite horse among the three the Beilers kept. Under the cart's seat, as always, a basket held apples. Rufus grabbed one and pressed it against Dolly's lips, smiling as she snatched it with her teeth and crunched. He swung up into the driver's seat and took the reins in his hands.

The front screen door thwacked closed. Joel was supposed to fix the broken spring three days ago. Someone was sure to get hurt if it went unattended much longer. Before turning his head toward the porch, Rufus knew the footsteps crossing it were his mother's.

"I'm looking for Joel." Franey stood at the base of the steps, one hand on a hip and the other shading her eyes. "He should have been in from the fields by now. They've only just planted the alfalfa. How much weeding could there be to do? If he'd said he was ir-

rigating I might believe he is still out there."

"Would you like me to ride out to the field to find him?" Rufus's stomach sank at the thought of chasing after his wayward brother rather than accomplishing his errand.

"No. You have things to do. I think I should ask your *daed* to speak to Joel. But if you see your brother, bring him home with you."

"Yes, *Mamm*. I will see you for supper with or without Joel." Rufus nudged the horse forward.

Dolly found her trotting rhythm as soon as he turned out onto the highway. Time was tight. Rufus clicked his tongue to see if Dolly had any canter in her.

When he pulled up in front of the construction trailer that served as the office of Kramer Construction, Rufus tied Dolly securely to the closest tree, climbed the three narrow makeshift steps up to the trailer, and opened the door. Just inside, a young woman lifted her eyes without moving her head. Her fingers held their place above the keyboard.

"I would like to see Mr. Kramer, please." Rufus looked her in the eyes. Her frown made clear she knew who he was. And she knew how the man who signed her paycheck felt about him.

"He's on the phone." The woman's fingers resumed their patter.

"I'll wait."

There was no place to sit. File cabinets and stacks of blueprints cluttered the space. Rufus spread his feet apart slightly and crossed his hands in front of him. The thin walls of the trailer did little to disguise the animation in Karl Kramer's voice behind a closed door. Whatever the deal was, Karl intended to have his way. His price. His schedule. His crew. Rufus focused his eyes on the back of the woman's computer monitor and tried to hear more of her soft keys clacking than the voice in the other room.

When the voice fell silent, he thought she might look up. Because she did not, he cleared his throat.

"Just a moment." She leaned toward the monitor, squinted, and made two quick corrections. "I'll ask Mr. Kramer if he is available to see you."

Not, *I'll tell Mr. Kramer you're here.* The difference was not lost on Rufus as she slipped through the office door and closed it behind her. On the other side the voices were low, indistinct.

She returned perhaps ten seconds later. "Mr. Kramer is unavailable. He has a number of matters to attend to before the

town meeting tonight. Perhaps another time."

Rufus was not surprised in the least, though he was fairly certain that these were not the same words Karl Kramer used to express his decision. "My business is *about* the meeting tonight," Rufus said. "It is important that I see him."

Her smile was vacant. "I'm afraid that's not possible." She took her chair again. "Can I help you with anything else?"

"No. Nothing else, thank you. Only this one thing." Rufus did not move.

"Perhaps if you were to make an appointment for some time next week."

He shifted his weight to one leg. "The afternoon is nearly over. I will just wait and have a word with him on his way out."

"I'm afraid he was quite specific that he did not want to see you, Mr. Beiler." She turned over a stack of papers and moved her fingers back to the keyboard.

Rufus counted to ten.

Then he counted back from ten.

Then he turned, took two steps, rapped three times, and opened Karl Kramer's office door himself.

At home, Annie changed into a sturdy pair of tennis shoes and made sure she wore a

sweatshirt with a hood. April afternoons could turn chilly without notice. She zipped up, rolled the bike forward, and jumped on. The boys had headed east on Main Street, which meant they could have crossed the vague line between Westcliffe and Silver Cliff.

It was probably nothing. She hoped it was nothing. Just a teenage boy curious about a question in the news. But even what she scanned before shutting down the phone seemed like more than idle curiosity to Annie, and she wanted to be sure. After all, it could be dangerous. She pedaled down Main Street, stopping at a few of the shops to duck her head in and ask if anyone had seen the boys. One of the perks of living in a small town was that people were likely to know the boys and whether they had been around. Sometimes it seemed to Annie that the town had all-seeing eyes.

She traced them for most of a mile before information petered out. Her last stop was a gas station.

"Hello, Hank." Annie pulled up to the air pump alongside a service bay and fiddled with it. She pushed a couple of squirts of air into her rear tire. "I wonder if you've seen some boys. Kind of a strange bunch. Amish and *English* together."

Hank laughed. "Dressed in black?"

"Last time I looked."

"They were here." Hank wiped oil off his hands onto a cloth. "They were hanging around the diesel pumps."

Annie's stomach tightened. Diesel fuel?

"The only one who looked old enough to drive was Amish," Hank said. "If they had bothered to bring a can, I might believe somebody needed gas for a tractor. But it wouldn't take five guys to carry a can. They're getting nothing from me. I shooed them off."

Annie swallowed. "Did you happen to see which way they went?"

Hank waved his rag down a side street. Annie hopped back on her bike.

Even though they had a half hour's jump, they were still on foot when they left the gas station.

Annie pedaled into the wind, scanning the flat acres of the valley between the Wet Mountains and the Sangre de Cristos as she moved from town streets, around aging buildings at the edge of town, to broken asphalt and gravel stretches. Every now and then, someone stepped outside to check a mailbox or fill a garbage can or rake a flower bed.

Across a field, she spotted a mass of black

that seemed to shapeshift, first a stretched line, then a compact ball, then a straggling string. She pedaled harder. They were cutting across open field — easier on foot than on a bike. Twice Annie lost her balance when she hit a stubborn rise of earth with insufficient momentum, her ankle taking the impact of catching herself on one foot. Annie debated abandoning her bicycle to move more quickly on foot, but she dreaded the thought of having to find her way back to retrieve it from under a random scrub oak. Annie rode when she could and walked beside the bike when she could not pedal safely. Keeping the boys in view while lugging the bike pushed her heart rate up higher than it had been in a long time.

Finally she was close enough to call out. "Joel!"

The black mass thinned as one figure paused and turned. The others slumped along, unperturbed. Annie resolved to succeed at keeping her balance on the old bike and swung a leg over its seat. She forced the top pedal down and threw her slight weight into making it rotate.

Joel heard her, she was sure of it. He paused, after all, and looked back across the field at the sound of his name. But he had turned back to follow the others. Annie saw

them disappear one by one, at random intervals, but because of the rise in the hill and the distance she could not see where. She pedaled yet harder — and tumbled to the ground. Splayed in the dirt with the bike three feet away, Annie gobbled air. When she managed to get upright again and assure herself that it did not hurt to move, Joel was out of sight.

Annie kicked the bike's front tire and left it lying in the dirt. Then she muttered, "Humble, humble, humble."

On foot, she scrambled to where she had last seen the boys. Without the eye-bending rise and fall of terrain, she saw now where they disappeared. A slight slope hid their final steps, but only one destination was possible.

A construction site. Or at least some kind of storage site.

It was fenced and surrounded by a tent of thick plastic. Annie sidestepped along the fence line looking for an interruption to the boundary, any place they might have slipped under a loose flap of plastic sheeting or squeezed around a post.

"Hey!"

The booming voice nearly stopped her heart. "What are you doing here?"

Annie expelled breath then allowed a

measured amount of air back into her lungs as she turned around. She did not recognize the tall, deeply tanned man. "Just out enjoying the countryside."

"This is a hard hat zone." He knocked his knuckles against his own head covering. "And it's private property."

Annie raised her hands, palms out. "Not looking for trouble."

TWENTY

Hard Hat Guy gestured with one thumb that the conversation was over. He pointed Annie back the way she had come.

Annie smiled pleasantly. "Have a nice evening."

She backtracked to where her bicycle had betrayed her and yanked it upright. Scanning the view once more, she saw for the first time the tracks of mashed weeds. Twenty feet away were the twin ruts trucks must have used. Following the boys earlier, she had descended the knoll at the wrong angle. The truck route would have been doable on the bike. She heard an engine catch and watched the man in the hard hat steer his truck onto the makeshift road and head in the other direction.

Good. The coast was clear. It took more than a guy in a hard hat to deter Annie Friesen.

On her bike again, Annie rode in the

tracks down to the fenced area and around to the other side. If a construction site had a front, this was it. She approached and held still, certain that if the boys were inside she would hear them. Nothing. No shuffle. No murmur. A cat brushed her leg as it emerged through the fence. It shot off in a typical feline manner, but Annie figured the cat saved her some time looking for an opening. She laid her bike down and squatted to peer through the tear in the plastic sheeting.

Stacks of bricks. Bags of cement. Piles of lumber neatly arranged by size. Twin green wheelbarrows. Rolled rubber edging.

What was so secretive about that? Annie did not see what Carter might have been looking for, but other than some odd storage she did not see any sign of actual construction, either. She might have been strolling the aisles of a home improvement store. Relieved not to find anything more sinister, she straddled her bike again.

She still had Carter's phone.

Rufus closed the trailer door behind him, having come to a fragile agreement with Karl Kramer. He would do everything he could to prove he meant what he said.

Next he would have to persuade a few

213

more people that he had not lost the good sense God gave him. He untied Dolly, led her in a half circle to get turned around, and headed the cart toward home. He needed a good meal before the evening meeting.

Annie spotted Joel, perhaps a mile later, his lanky height in relief to his surroundings. He was on a footpath that ran parallel to the highway in stretches and disappeared at other times. This time she did not call his name. She just pedaled harder.

He was alone when she reached him and cut him off by riding just past him, then bringing the bicycle to an abrupt halt in his path.

He met her eyes but said nothing.

"I know you heard me." Annie planted her feet on either side of the bike and removed her helmet.

"I wasn't sure you were calling me," he mumbled.

Yes, he was. Annie let it pass. "Where is everyone else?"

"Heading home for supper, I guess. Carter and Duncan have homework."

"And Mark and Luke?" Why wouldn't the Stutzman boys be with Joel if they were all

returning to the Beiler home for the evening meal?

"Not sure. I think they went to find their *daed* for a ride. I decided to walk."

At that rate, he would be late for supper again. Annie reminded herself she was not his mother. Joel was seventeen. He knew what he was choosing.

"What were you all doing at that storage site?"

"We weren't." Joel answered quickly. "It's just a shortcut."

That was the longest shortcut to nowhere Annie had ever seen.

She pulled Carter's phone from her back pocket. "Carter picked up the wrong phone."

"No wonder it wasn't ringing constantly." Joel put out an open hand. "I'll get yours back for you."

Annie swung her arm back, moving the phone beyond Joel's reach. "That's all right. I'll hang on to this one for now. I know how your father feels about having cell phones in the house."

She watched him, looking for a sign that he knew what was on the phone. The wobble in Joel's nod was unconvincing.

"By now Carter has probably figured out the mistake," Joel said. "I'm sure he'll want

to trade back as soon as he can."

"No doubt. He can come by the shop."

Joel scuffed a step away from Annie. "I should probably get going."

Annie did not move. "What's going on, Joel?"

"Excuse me?"

Joel did not have the same wide violet-blue eyes several of his siblings had. His were brown. Annie never could read brown eyes. She stared into them and found no hint of anything amiss, but she did not believe it.

"How is Carter getting along these days?"

Joel spread his feet and stood solid. "The *English* make everything so complicated."

Who was he talking about?

"Joel, I looked at Carter's phone. At his Internet history. I saw what he was looking up."

"Carter is always looking at his phone. He sends texts and plays games. I don't pay attention."

"So you don't know what he was looking up today?"

He moved to get around her. Annie let the bike roll forward to block him again, relieved that he was reluctant to lie outright.

"Joel," Annie said, "if Carter's in trouble, you want to help him, don't you?"

"Carter is just *English*. They don't know how to let things be."

Again with the doublespeak about the *English*.

"I think you know what's on his phone."

"You make too much of it."

"Do I?"

Brown eyes or not, Annie was ready to stare down Joel.

Rufus slowed the cart, looking for a safe place to pull over and be out of traffic. His tug on the reins halted Dolly.

"Joel!"

Joel and Annalise both answered his call with their glances. Though Joel was on foot and Annalise had her bicycle, Rufus suspected he had interrupted more than a random encounter between friends.

"Joel, *Mamm* was looking for you. She'll be wondering where you were. I'll take you home."

"She does not have to worry about me." Joel gripped the side of the cart's seat and prepared to heft himself up.

"It's a matter of simple respect to tell her if you need to leave the farm."

"I'm not a child, Rufus."

Rufus turned away from his sulking brother and took in the sight of Annalise.

Dirt smudges on her jeans. The gray sweat-shirt, unzipped, falling off one shoulder. A haphazard elastic band slipping out of her hair. Disheveled. Annalise at her best, in Rufus's opinion. "You look like you could use a ride home."

Annalise sat on the bike, her hands grip-ping the handlebars, one foot on a pedal, the other ready to push off. "I'll be fine."

She always said that. So independent.

"It will only take me a few minutes to ride a couple of miles," Annalise said. "You should take Joel home."

She would manage, Rufus knew. And it was better if he did not imply that she needed his help. Still, he wished he had time to take her home.

"Are you going to the town meeting tonight?" Annalise asked.

"Yes." Rufus perked up. "And you?"

She nodded. "At the elementary school, right?"

"Yes, I believe so."

"Then I'll see you there." Annalise smiled.

"I'm sorry we did not have our walk, Annalise."

"There will be other days."

Joel swung himself into the seat. "We'd better go or we'll both be late for supper."

Rufus turned back to Annalise. "May I

pick you up for the meeting this evening?"

Her eyes flickered bright. "That would be lovely."

Again, she glanced at Joel. Rufus followed her eyes. What was going on between those two?

"Then I'll see you in a couple of hours," Rufus said.

Annalise nodded and shoved off. Rufus watched her pedal in the opposite direction; then he nudged Dolly forward.

"Joel," he said, "is there something going on that I should know about?"

"Just drive."

TWENTY-ONE

After supper, Rufus took Dolly down Main Street pulling a buggy, rather than the nimble cart he used for daytime errands. With the sun gone down, the temperature dropped, and the buggy was warmer and dryer. Rufus wanted Annalise to be comfortable, even though the ride to the elementary school was only a mile from her home.

He turned left off Main Street a block early, made two right turns, and pulled up in front of Annalise's narrow house aimed back toward Main Street. Her head bobbed in the front window just before she pulled the curtain closed and put out the light. A moment later, she locked the front door behind her and followed the path of concrete stepping-stones, hardly more than rubble, that led to the street. More than once Rufus had offered to clear the crumbling steps and pour Annalise a new walkway. So far she refused. She had fallen once

over the winter, but even then she insisted that a new walkway would ice over just as easily as the old one.

Rufus dropped from the bench at the front of the buggy and offered a hand to Annalise. He was never sure if she would accept his assistance or walk past him to heave herself up into the buggy.

Tonight she accepted, and he squeezed her hand slightly in the process. Her dress was not Amish, but she wore a modest dark skirt and sweater rather than jeans. She had gotten pretty good at braiding her hair and pinning it close to her head. He liked her hair down, but of course he would not tell her that.

"I was surprised to find you with Joel," Rufus said once they were moving.

"He was there on the path when I came along on my bicycle."

She flashed him a smile, yet it disappointed him. He knew her smiles. This one said, *I'm not going to talk about that.*

"He should have been at home." Rufus let the sway of the buggy nudge his shoulder into Annalise's.

"So I gathered." Annalise was watching the road, turning her head in both directions at the corner.

She still had the instincts of an automobile

221

driver, Rufus thought. He did not suppose anyone ever unlearned how to drive. She had not said anything for weeks now about learning to drive a buggy. He waited for three cars to pass before giving Dolly rein to turn left onto Main Street and follow the way to the school.

"*Daed* is becoming impatient with Joel," Rufus said. "My brother Daniel used to do the same thing — disappear for hours and see no wrong in it as long as his work was done."

"Daniel straightened out, didn't he?"

"Only because Martha Glick came along. Daniel was smitten hard, and she does not put up with nonsense."

Annalise laughed. Something at the center of Rufus melted every time a lilt escaped her lips. Daniel was not the only Beiler brother to be smitten. But Martha was Amish. The solution had been simple. Daniel and Martha shared a faith and a community that included their families. Annalise's choice would be more complicated.

"I am afraid *Daed* will not be so patient this time," Rufus said. "Joel needs to think about his choices more seriously."

She did not answer. He wondered again what she knew.

They reached the school. Rufus steered

222

Dolly to the edge of the parking lot where she would be out of the way.

"Looks like a good turnout for the meeting." Annalise accepted his assistance down from the buggy.

His was the only buggy, though. Not many Amish men would leave their farms and families for a town meeting, especially in the evening. His own father did not. Still, Rufus had hoped some would come.

Inside the school gym, a few rows of plastic chairs beckoned. Rufus and Annalise sat together. It was an odd sensation to be next to her in a group of people. In church, the most he could hope for was a glimpse of her among the women, across the wide rooms of hosts' homes. Rufus estimated about forty *English* had come — and thirty-five of them were speaking into cell phones, reading cell phone screens, closing cell phones, putting away cell phones.

Annalise used to be like that. He doubted she even had her cell phone with her tonight. People could change. Rufus liked to think so, at least in Annalise's case.

Tom Reynolds stood behind a table at the front of a group of chairs and cleared his throat heavily.

"Thank you all for coming," Tom said as the thin crowd settled. "As you know, this is

223

not an official town meeting. It's just a conversation. A few of us have had some ideas for a project, and it seemed wise to invite others into the discussion. If you wish to speak, just raise your hand and I will call on you one at a time."

Tom scanned the gathering as heads nodded then recapped the idea for creating a recreation area on acreage the town owned. "The likelihood is the town council will make the project official, provided the community is willing to help. The project is outside the town's budget, though, so funding will be minimal. If the idea does come to fruition, it will be because the community makes it happen."

Rufus glanced at Annalise. She seemed to be listening intently. He wished they had sat farther back. He could not tell who might have come in late and sat down behind him.

Karl Kramer, for instance.

As soon as Tom Reynolds invited comments, Mo was up on her feet and standing in the aisle.

"We must have strong leadership," she said. "Someone who knows what he's doing. Someone who has the right skills for the sort of project we're undertaking. I propose that we ask Rufus Beiler to head it up."

Murmurs rose, and feet shuffled, but Mo held up a settling hand. "I know some of you are still unsure about the Amish in our community, but you all know Rufus Beiler. He does excellent work. You could trust him with your life." She turned to nod at Rufus.

"Why aren't any of the other Amish here?" someone asked. "If they are not going to support this, why should we put one of them in charge?"

Rufus winced.

"Tell them." Annalise elbowed him, whispering. "Explain how the Amish stay home with their families in the evening."

He shook his head.

Mo was still in the aisle. "You can't ask for a more dependable man than Rufus Beiler." She pointed around the gathering. "I know some of you have hired him to build your cabinets and to make furniture. When he accepts a project, he commits to excellence."

"Too bad you're not running for president." Annalise covered her mouth to hide her grin.

"Perhaps we should hear what Rufus has to say," someone suggested.

It was as if a wind blew through the place and turned every head toward Rufus.

He stood slowly, his hands on the back of

the empty chair in front of him. "I suspected something like this might come up." He paused. "I recommend we include Karl Kramer in leading this project."

Annie heard the collective gasp.

"Karl Kramer!" Mo put both her fists on her hips. "You can't be serious. Karl Kramer would be the first person to wish the Amish would disappear from Westcliffe and all of Custer County."

"I did not say it would be without challenge." Rufus's fingers drummed the chair's back.

"He tried to kill you last year," Mo said. "If Tom hadn't found you on that construction site, you might have bled to death."

"We don't know that Karl was responsible for that."

"The police dropped the investigation because you would not press charges."

"The past is the past," Rufus said. "I bear no grudge toward Mr. Kramer. I think we both have seen there is work enough in this valley for the two of us — and others. I have already spoken with Mr. Kramer, and he has agreed to be coleaders."

"You and Karl Kramer?" Tom Reynolds's voice quivered in confusion. "You are proposing that you and Karl would work

together?"

"I am."

Objection welled in Annie. Over the winter, she had tried hard to understand Rufus's refusal to press charges against the man who almost certainly attacked him. But Jesus said to turn the other cheek, as Rufus always reminded her. Instead of revenge, Rufus steered his own livelihood away from projects that would aggravate Karl, even sacrificing jobs that would have turned a good profit.

Keeping peace from a distance seemed to be working. So why would he voluntarily step within reach of Karl's slap?

"Rufus." Annie reached over and touched his hand, which still thumped the chair. He dropped his hands to his sides, away from her touch.

Annie grimaced at the sight around them. Voices erupted, people talking over each other. Mo looked like she was ready to punch someone. Here and there others stood to have their say.

Tom held out both hands to settle the crowd. "Let me suggest that this would be a good time to take a break. There are coffee and cookies in the back. We can reconvene in fifteen minutes."

Mo hurtled toward Rufus. Others

227

swarmed as well. Annie found herself snared under a web of swinging elbows. She scooted over one plastic chair at a time until she came to the end of the row. There she stood up to consider the crowd around Rufus.

These people liked him.

They trusted him.

They clamored for him.

Rufus stood patiently in his black trousers and collarless jacket, his hat on his head. If he were married, he would have a beard. No doubt it would grow long and curly, like his father's, and cover the space of chest where his shirt formed a white V under his chin.

On the surface he had nothing in common with these people.

Nothing in common with *her*. The thought unsettled her.

Annie moved slowly toward the table in the back where refreshments were set up. She never drank coffee this late in the day anymore. That was her old life. She might still be tempted to use her phone and drive in Colorado Springs, but staying up all night drinking coffee and working no longer held allure. Drifting toward the meager refreshments merely gave her a chance to think. Annie picked up a thickly frosted sugar

cookie, which she knew for a fact came from the bakery on Main Street, and retreated to a corner.

Rufus's proposal stunned her. Work with Karl Kramer? Yet she could see the wisdom. If Rufus Beiler and Karl Kramer could work together, the Amish and the *English* might truly find their balance with each other. But without funding, Rufus's effort might come to nothing.

Every problem had an answer. At least one, and probably more. It was just a matter of finding the most efficient one.

It was coming to her, taking shape, finding focus. Just because she no longer owned a high-tech business did not mean she could not sift through solutions. By the time Rufus disentangled himself and stood at her side with a steaming Styrofoam cup, she had manipulated the factors to a pleasing conclusion.

She turned her face up to him. "I want to help, Rufus."

"Everyone is invited to help." He sipped his coffee.

"When I sold my business, I put all that money in a charitable foundation. It's not for my personal use. But this project would be perfect."

As usual, his face did not give him away.

Annie plowed ahead.

"They'll settle this question of who should lead the project, and it will be you and Karl, together. You'll insist on the partnership, and because they want you so much they'll take Karl in the deal."

Rufus raised one eyebrow.

"The next issue will be money," Annie continued. "Tom already said the town doesn't have any. If money were not an issue, this recreation area could be done really well, and everyone would be happy to be part of it. I can do my part by arranging the financial end."

His eyes softened now. "Annalise, you have a kind heart. But it's not that simple."

"Why not? I wouldn't be using the money for personal reasons."

"But you would still be controlling it."

She shook her head. "Not if I set up a special account with the bank for you to access. The money would go there. I would have nothing to do with it." She waved her hands, nearly dropping the cookie. "You and Karl could decide together how to spend it."

"Annalise —"

Tom's voice interrupted him as Tom called the meeting back to order.

"Please don't suggest this," Rufus said,

"not until we have a chance to talk more."

She stared into his violet-blue eyes and knew he would never agree, but for now she nodded. "Excuse me. I need to talk to Tom before he starts again."

"Annalise, please, do not speak to him about money tonight."

Annie ducked past Rufus, pulling a phone from her pocket in the same motion. She flipped it open, thumbed a few buttons, and cleared the Internet search history. By the time she reached Tom across the room, her intentions shifted. She held out the phone.

"Carter must have my phone," she said. "If you don't mind, ask him to bring it by the shop."

Tom tucked the phone in his shirt pocket. "I'm going to have to hang his phone around his neck. Or take it away from him. I'm not sure which."

"He was helping me when he set it down. Anyone could have picked up the wrong phone."

Tom scanned the room. "We'd better get started again."

Annie returned to her seat next to Rufus.

When the meeting reconvened, Mo reluctantly agreed to the arrangement Rufus suggested, and others agreed. Karl and Rufus would run the project — including raising

the needed donations of materials, labor, and money.

The ride home was quiet. Rufus pulled on the reins in front of Annie's house, set the brake, and turned on the bench to face her.

"Thanks for the ride." Annie knew she was muttering but she could not help it. Why was it so hard for Rufus to understand that using the money in her foundation could benefit everyone in Westcliffe? She started to get down from the bench.

He put a hand on her shoulder. "Annalise, why do you think the *English* buy my furniture and cabinets?"

In the dark, she could not see his eyes. What was he really asking? "You do beautiful work. I don't have to be Amish to see that."

"Other people produce their merchandise more quickly, for less money."

"But it's not as good. There is value in your craftsmanship. It will last."

He nodded. "It is the Amish way. We build to last. Furniture, families, communities. There are no shortcuts."

"I don't see why generosity would undermine the Amish way." Heat crawled up the back of her neck.

He picked up one of her hands. "Some-

times the solutions must come from within the problem."

TWENTY-TWO

A week later Beth Stutzman laid another thick slice of pork roast on Rufus's plate. The third one. Fortunately, her father had already scraped the last of the mashed potatoes from the serving bowl.

Rufus smiled blandly into the beam of Beth's face.

She sat on his right. On his left was Johanna, and across the table sat Essie. Their uniform hairstyle accentuated the similarities of their features, differentiated only by different eye colors.

The Stutzmans were living in their own home — and not a minute too soon, which was an opinion Rufus kept to himself. When Beth invited him to dinner as a way to say thank you for his help in readying their home, he assumed his whole family would be there. He came straight from Mo's motel after installing some trim. Even then, he assumed his family would arrive in the second

buggy at any moment. Only when he saw how the dining room table was set did he realize he had been singled out for the invitation.

"Tell us what you've been working on, Rufus." Ike Stutzman tore a corner off a slice of bread and steered it into his mouth. "The girls tell me you make beautiful end tables."

"I do have several orders for custom tables." Rufus politely pushed his fork through the tender pork. "I'll be taking a load to Colorado Springs next week."

"Do you make tables for the *English*?"

Rufus swallowed another bite, unsure of the shading of Ike's question. "Many *English* appreciate our value in both beauty and usefulness. It is not against *Ordnung* to do business with them."

"I suppose not."

Stifling a sigh, Rufus ate yet another bite of pork roast. "You seem to have settled in well here."

"I miss your family already," Beth said.

With her hair pinned perfectly and her posture flawless, Beth exuded competency at everything she put her hand to. Rufus resisted her gaze. "I'm sure we will see each other," he said.

"I have a feeling I will find myself wander-

ing to your place in the afternoons, looking for a way to be helpful."

"I'm sure there will be plenty to do here," Rufus said. "You'll get used to a new routine soon enough."

"But our view is not nearly as lovely as yours."

Rufus nodded politely. It was not possible to have a bad view of the Sangre de Cristos from anywhere around Westcliffe.

"Where are the boys tonight?" he asked.

Edna Stutzman waved one hand. "Oh, you know, *rumschpringe.* They are having their running around time."

"They have made friends with some town boys." Beth seemed eager to share the information. "Your brother introduced them."

Rufus's eyebrows lifted a notch. Joel was introducing Amish boys to town boys?

"The boys have talked about *rumschpringe* for years," Edna said. "They just need to get it out of their system. We're sure they will settle down when the time comes."

Rufus nodded. Mark and Luke struck him as a little young for *rumschpringe,* not even old enough to attend Sunday night singings. Not old enough to consider courting. They were barely out of school. *English* boys their age would still be looking forward

236

to high school. Amish boys should be taking up a man's share of household chores, especially in a family just moving to a new farm.

But Mark and Luke Stutzman were not his sons.

And neither was Joel.

"Were you pleased with the outcome of the meeting last week?" Ike stabbed his fork into the last of the green beans on his plate.

Rufus recognized the seasoning in the green beans. They must have come from his mother's cellar, canned from last year's garden bounty. Franey would have made sure the new family lacked nothing.

Including him, apparently.

He roused to answer Ike's question. "I'm pleased that community support seems to be growing. Even in the last week, more people have come forward and said they want to help."

"Are they *English* or Amish?"

"Both. I am only trying to do what is right."

"Then perhaps it will work out. You are an honorable man."

Ike's look of approval moved from Rufus to Beth. Rufus resisted the urge to squirm.

"I made pie," Beth announced.

All three daughters stood and began to

stack dishes. Rufus saw no way out.

Forty minutes later, after insisting he could not eat a second slice of blackberry pie, Rufus climbed into the buggy and told Dolly to take him home.

If only he and Annalise could have a quiet, uninterrupted meal. They needed to do better than snatch a few minutes at a time.

"The estate did not look too promising. I'm not sure what's in the boxes," Mrs. Weichert told Annie on Friday afternoon. "I made an absurdly low offer for the whole lot, unseen. I did not expect they would accept it."

"Let's hope there's an amazing find in one of them." Standing beside the truck bed full of boxes and crates, Annie wriggled out of her unzipped sweatshirt. Drenched in the sunshine of a May sky, she jumped at the chance to work outside.

"I pulled up next to the trash bin on purpose," Mrs. Weichert said. "Use your own discretion. Feel free to chuck whole boxes if you don't see anything we can use."

"I'll get right to work." Annie hefted herself up on the open tailgate.

"I need coffee."

"Fresh pot ten minutes ago."

Mrs. Weichert disappeared through the shop's back door. Annie went to work. She

estimated at least thirty boxes and crates of various sizes, all of them securely sealed. She pulled a box knife off her belt loop and went to work. Slashing open the first six boxes within reach revealed assorted books, handmade crafts, a porcelain figurine collection, dishes, fabric scraps, and throw pillows. Annie could see already that she would have to go through every box to find the one item that might make it to the shelves. Another batch would make a local thrift store very happy, and the rest was headed for the Dumpster. She immediately set aside the box of fabric scraps, wondering if there might be anything in it that could find its way into an Amish quilt.

Annie lost herself in the work. Two boxes held evidence of a lifetime carving habit and another a colored-glass bottle collection. Annie set aside a box of books for closer inspection later. A box of photographs made her pause long enough to find a place to sit.

There were almost exclusively black and whites, some of them professional portraits, and some reaching back decades. Perhaps even a hundred years.

Annie turned over a stack of photos and flipped through looking at the backs. A few had partially legible notations of names, places, and dates. For the most part, though,

they were unmarked.

Probably the last person who might have known who these stern faces belonged to was gone. Words like "Mother" and "Uncle N after the war" did little to bring these lives into twenty-first-century memory. Someone was giving away an entire family history because no one was left to remember it.

Annie thought of the lists of names that traced her family and Rufus's. Three hundred years ago they shared an ancestor. Now they had an occasional unsubstantiated story, or a rare photo from her family. A year ago she had paid attention to none of it. Now she could not imagine boxing it all up to sell to a stranger willing to haul it away.

She let out the heaviness that had gathered in her chest and wiped an eye with a knuckle.

"Annalise, are you all right?"

She turned at the shoulders to see Elijah Capp standing at the end of the truck, a toolbox hanging from one arm. "Hello," she said. "Yes, I'm fine. Just sorting all this stuff."

"Mrs. Weichert called about a plumbing problem."

Annie nodded. "The sink in the back

room. It's not draining well. I don't think it's anything too troublesome."

"I'll take a look."

"Thank you, Elijah." She raised her eyes to meet his. He seemed to hold words in his throat that he could not bring himself to say. "Is there something else?"

"I don't know if Ruth told you she saw me," he finally said, "when she came down with you a couple weeks ago."

"No, she didn't say anything." Anyone could see Elijah Capp was still twisted in heartbreak.

"I know she's not coming back." Elijah ran his thumb and index finger along the brim of his hat. "But she's not over me."

"Well, Elijah, I think you're right. On both counts."

"She's wrong if she thinks I can't make my own choice. I wish she would make room for happiness."

Annie moistened her lips. She was not sure she understood what he was talking about — and if he were planning something, she was not sure she wanted to know what it was. She sliced open another box. "What are you saying, Elijah?"

He shifted his weight and shrugged one shoulder. "Ruth and I are not any more unlikely than you and Rufus."

241

Annie stopped, midmotion, and turned her whole body toward Elijah. Squatting in the dust in her jeans, picking through the remains of an unknown life with her hair once again tumbling out of its ponytail, she felt about as un-Amish as she had at any moment in her life.

"At least you and Ruth have the past together," she finally said.

"That's not good enough for me." Elijah's jaw set.

"Still, it's something." Annie's legs ached from squatting. She stood up and looked down at Elijah from the truck bed. "Sometimes I think Rufus and I are getting close, but I always manage to disappoint him with what I don't understand about being Amish."

"Is that how you think he feels?"

"Doesn't he?" Annie doubted Rufus talked to anyone about his feelings, so how would Elijah know?

"He's not disappointed. He just doesn't know what to do with you."

"Because I'm *English*? Because he has no business getting involved with me?"

"Because you do the unexpected."

Annie blew out her breath. "That must frustrate him no end."

"I think it pleases him no end."

"I don't know if I can ever follow *Ordnung*. Rufus deserves to be with someone who understands his life."

"He deserves to be with someone who *is* his life."

Air rushed into Annie's throat far too fast, and she turned away.

Elijah shifted his toolbox to the other arm. "I'll go see about that stopped drain."

Annie smoothed out the purple Amish dress on her bed. It had once been Ruth's dress. Ruth, someone who knew how to be Amish.

Annie had done so well over the winter.

She learned to cook. She *would* learn to quilt properly. Her ears throbbed with Pennsylvania Dutch and High German. She learned to pray. Sort of. And she had broken the spine of her Bible with wear.

Then she went home and wore that stupid red dress — still hanging in the closet of her childhood bedroom.

When she put it on, she slid into old skin, where everything fit. Nothing about her life since had fit right.

Annie dropped her T-shirt and jeans to the floor and pulled the purple dress over her head. Her fingers had become nimble with pinning the pieces of the dress in place. She yanked a brush through her hair,

243

pinned up the blond mass, and put on a prayer *kapp.*

She did not have a mirror in her bedroom. The only mirror in the house was the small one in the bathroom. But she still had her imagination, and it served her well in forming a mental picture of herself.

Perhaps her own ancestors had looked not so different from this. Plain dresses. Tamed hair. *Kapps* on their heads as they sought to discern humility and peace as a way of life.

The rap on the door sounded distant, as if it came through the centuries rather than simply up the stairwell. Annie almost did not move, not willing to surrender the moment. But the sound came again, more insistent.

There was no time to change. Besides, it was no secret to anyone in town that she sometimes wore Amish clothing. Annie clutched purple yardage in her fingers and descended the stairs.

She opened the front door. "Rufus!"

"Hello, Annalise." He stood with his hands crossed in front of him at the wrists. "I am more than a week delayed, but I thought perhaps we could have that walk."

Annie smiled and laid her hand in his open palm.

■ ■ ■ ■

"Am I taking you away from something?" Rufus allowed himself to squeeze Annalise's hand as they started down the crumbling sidewalk that she had not allowed him to fix. Yet.

Annalise shook her head. "I was just planning a quiet evening at home."

"I see."

"You're wondering about the dress, aren't you?" Annalise said. "You've seen me wear it plenty of times."

"When you come to supper, or church." Rufus inhaled her scent, her nearness. "But in your own home?"

"It makes me feel peaceful. Helps me think."

"And your thoughts tonight?"

"I haven't felt so peaceful lately. Being Amish . . . well, it's not as easy as people think." Annalise raised brimming eyes. "And I've missed you."

"Things will settle down now," Rufus said. "The Stutzmans are in their own house. Life will go back to normal."

"I hope so."

"You have nothing to worry about, Annalise."

"Don't I?"

"No. No one holds a candle to you." Rufus squeezed her hand again.

"Let's take a very long walk, then." She squeezed back.

"What do you have in the way of garden tools?" he asked as they reached the street and fell into rhythm with each other.

Annalise sucked in a smile. "For my garden? I'm afraid I don't have much to work with."

"Why don't we walk over to Tom's hardware store? Jacob is going to need something that suits his size to break up your soil tomorrow."

"Tomorrow?"

"I thought my brothers and I could do the tilling while you're quilting."

"Oh, no you don't. I want to be there."

Rufus paused his steps, forcing Annalise to stop and look at him. "Let me do this for you, Annalise."

She started to protest further but put a hand to her own mouth. "*Demut.* I don't have to do everything myself."

Twenty-Three

"I saw you out walking in that purple dress." Mrs. Weichert moved a set of figurines and cleaned the glass shelf beneath the small statues.

Annie tilted her head to one side as she ran a thumb along a row of forty-year-old books on Monday. "It was a nice evening for a walk."

"I suppose a lot of people think you're crazy, but I think you look darling in those dresses."

Darling? Not exactly Annie's goal. "I wonder if we should give up on some of these books. They don't seem to be selling."

"It takes time. We'll get a lot more week-enders once summer is in full swing." Mrs. Weichert rearranged figurines. "Everybody wonders if you're really going to become Amish."

Annie's reply caught in her throat. She dislodged it and let it slide down.

"It's wonderful to see a young person willing to make a sacrifice," Mrs. Weichert said.

Annie reached back with both hands and tightened her ponytail. "Maybe I should bring those dishes out of the storeroom. It's a complete set, and only a couple of tiny nicks. You almost can't see them."

The ceramic dishes had been one of the best finds in the truckload of boxes Annie had sorted through the previous week. They dated back to the 1970s, but the earth tones looked surprisingly contemporary. In the storeroom now, Annie turned over one of the bowls to find the manufacturer. A name etched in a brown circle was not quite readable. A signature served as a logo, but she could not decide if the vowel in the center was an *A* or an *E*.

The old impulse surged to reach for her iPhone and get on the Internet. She could not do that any longer, but she could use Mrs. Weichert's computer. The laptop was anachronistic in this shop of vintage and antique items, but it served a needful business purpose. Annie moved to the small desk, opened the laptop, and tapped a thumb on the track pad. At least once a week she used a computer to help in her work. Annie's deft navigation of the Internet had yielded price-setting information

beyond Mrs. Weichert's knowledge on several occasions. Even some of the Amish used computers to run their businesses. But for Annie, the automatic movements her hands made, the sleek keys under her fingers, and the familiar sensation of her eyes on the screen — it all taunted, whispering from shadows.

Annie woke the computer, and a search box appeared. Her fingers hovered over the keyboard. Finally, instead of the craftsman's name, she typed two words. *Randy Sawyer.* A list filled the screen. She narrowed the search with the name of the company her old flame was working for now, and in an instant his smiling professional photo and bio burned through her gray eyes.

She closed the search box and took a deep breath. What was she doing?

Could she really make this sacrifice, as Mrs. Weichert called it?

It should not feel like a sacrifice. Should it? She should not be wondering about Randy Sawyer. Should she?

Her walk with Rufus on Friday was three days old now. Annie had seen him briefly at his home on Saturday, where he insisted that she stay with his mother and quilt while he dug her garden. On Saturday evening, she sat on her back porch and inhaled the

fragrance of turned earth, the fruit of Rufus's labor with Jacob. On Sunday, she looked up twice from the shared meal after the service to catch Rufus watching her. The violet focus of his eyes stirred a creeping warmth in her before he diverted his gaze.

No, *sacrifice* was the wrong word. Whatever choice lay before her would not feature what she left behind, but rather what she took hold of. And Rufus Beiler was the person who made her want to take hold.

Exhaling, Annie opened the search engine again and soon found the dishes on the Internet. Early seventies, a midwestern manufacturer, designed by an artist who found local fame in other mediums. A limited edition. Only five hundred sets had been cast in the particular color combination stacked a few feet away from the desk. A complete set of eight was definitely of value. Mrs. Weichert should hold out for a good price. Annie carried the dishes out to the shop and began wiping them clean and arranging shelf space.

The bell on the shop door jangled. Glancing up, Annie recognized Colton, the young man who worked in the hardware store Tom Reynolds owned.

"You got any of that Amish jam?" Colton asked. "My wife wants some."

Mrs. Weichert pointed to the shelf that supported glass jars both Franey Beiler and Edna Stutzman had canned. The man slid jars around with two fingers. Annie supposed he was looking for a particular fruit his wife had requested. Peach and blackberry were all he would find, though.

"It's all over town that Karl Kramer is on a tear." Colton picked up one jar of peach and one of blackberry and moved toward the counter.

"What is he knotted up about this time?" Mrs. Weichert tapped the electronic cash register.

"Apparently he keeps close count of his fertilizer bags." Colton extracted a wallet from his back pocket. "Three bags are missing from a place where he's been stockpiling supplies. Rumor is it's some sort of commercial grade with higher ammonium nitrate."

Annie's hands stilled.

The cash register beeped. "I don't know why Rufus wants to work with that man," Mrs. Weichert said. "You never can tell what little thing is going to set him off. He probably miscounted."

"Who wants to steal fertilizer, anyway?" Colton asked. "This is ranch country. Everybody has some."

Not everybody, Annie thought. Not teen-age boys who did not want to raise suspicions by inquiring about ammonium nitrate levels in the fertilizer at the hardware store one of their fathers owned.

That morning, before he left his workshop for the home where he was installing cabinets, Rufus checked every hook on the wall the third time. The set of small chisels was not there. Now, in the wide yard beside the new home, he emptied his toolbox in the back of the buggy, though he had done this before as well. If the leather case did not turn up soon, he would have to bear the expense of a new set. For now, he chose a larger chisel and replaced the rest of the tools according to the careful arrangement that characterized his toolbox.

Rufus turned at the sound of a car spewing gravel. He put a calming hand on Dolly's rump. The car screeched to an abrupt halt, bouncing forward with unspent momentum before settling. Karl Kramer leaned out of the driver's side window.

"If we're going to work together, you have to give me a phone number." Karl shook a finger at Rufus.

"What's wrong, Karl?"

"I can't meet this afternoon. Somebody is

stealing fertilizer from me, and I intend to
find out who it is."

"Who would steal fertilizer?"

"If I knew that, would I be chewing the
fat with you now?"

"Tomorrow, then," Rufus said. "I hope
you sort things out soon."

"I intend to. Whoever did this is going to
be sorry."

Karl pulled his arm inside the car and accelerated. With his hand on Dolly's neck,
Rufus watched Karl's car hurl down the
road much faster than it should have. He
hoped Karl would calm down before they
met again. If the project derailed because
Karl could not let go of a couple of bags of
fertilizer, Rufus would have little success
convincing anyone to give Karl another
chance.

"Annie, Rufus is here for you."

Annie stuck her head around the corner
from the desk in the storeroom where she
had been making notes about the newest
inventory. Her ponytail sagged and she was
fairly sure a smudge covered one cheekbone,
but she smiled anyway.

"I thought you had a meeting." Annie
entered the main shop and tucked a per-

253

petually rebellious strand of hair behind her left ear.

"Canceled."

Rufus's lips did not turn up, but Annie caught the hint of dance in his eyes. She looked at Mrs. Weichert.

The shop owner waved a hand. "Yes, you're through for the day. Go on, you two."

"I'll drive you home," Rufus said when they stepped out on the sidewalk.

"It's only four blocks."

"We'll take the long way."

Annie took the hand Rufus offered to help her up to the buggy seat. Outside the bakery across the street, two women watched. Annie felt their stares, and she turned her head to smile at them. Curiosity on the faces of onlookers no longer made her self-conscious.

"I'm not sure Westcliffe has a 'long way,' " Annie said.

"We'll invent one."

Rufus guided Dolly past the turn onto Annie's street, going several blocks and then turning the opposite direction. They zigzagged up and down the streets, past the historic Lutheran church and the old schoolhouse, past the small railroad museum and the newspaper office. Each time he had an opportunity to turn in the direc-

tion of Annie's house, Rufus went the other way.

"I suppose in your *English* world this is not much of a date," Rufus said, his eyes forward.

Is that was this was? "This is better than an *English* date," Annie said. "I'm glad to see you."

"Karl is making a fuss about some missing fertilizer."

Annie let three houses pass before she spoke. "Rufus, suppose someone in the Amish community was involved."

"Why would any of our people be involved? We don't steal and our sources of fertilizer generally are more . . . natural, shall we say?"

She smiled. "Well, then, not directly involved. Just theoretically."

"If theoretically someone knew about this?" He leaned toward her.

"Yes. Theoretically."

"Then theoretically someone ought to speak to the elders. But not theoretical elders. Real ones."

Annie nodded. Thinking of Joel, though, complicated her thoughts. She did not for a minute believe Joel would be involved with theft.

"Do you know something?" Rufus asked.

She squirmed. "Not exactly." A false accusation would do needless harm. She chuckled as they went past the same corner for the fourth time. "People are going to think you've lost your mind if you keep driving in circles."

"Theoretically I would hate for that rumor to get back to my parents."

"Then theoretically, I suppose you should turn left at the next corner and take me home."

In front of her house, Rufus helped Annie down. She stood for a moment to stroke Dolly's neck.

"Thanks for the ride home." Annie drank a deep breath and let it out in contentment. "I could make coffee. We could sit on the step."

And then she saw her.

Beth Stutzman clomping down off Main Street toward them. Annie pressed her lips together.

"There you are!" Beth called to them from half a block away. "I've been trying to catch you all over town. Why were you driving as if you didn't know where you were going?"

"Hello, Beth," Annie said.

"Hello, Annalise." Beth's gaze barely moved in Annie's direction, instead focusing on Rufus. "I was hoping you could give

me a ride home."

Rufus caught Annie's eyes.

"You *are* going home now, aren't you?" Beth asked, looking from Rufus to Annie and back again.

Beth's tone grated even as Annie erased her vision of coffee on the front steps with Rufus. "I'll see you later," Annie said.

She saw the sink in his shoulders as he nodded at Beth. "*Ya,* I'm heading home."

He politely aided Beth's ascent to the buggy seat, climbed up beside her, and picked up the reins.

Theoretically, Rufus did not look very happy with Beth's request. Theoretically, Annie was pleased to know he would rather have sat with her on her front step for a few more minutes.

Annie turned back to the house. The missing fertilizer was not theoretical, and neither was Annie's memory of the Internet history on Carter Reynolds's phone.

If only Joel were not being so evasive. The consequences could be far from theoretical.

TWENTY-FOUR

September 1777

Magdalena chose to walk. One of the Stutzman sisters, who had married a Yoder distantly related to Magdalena, had a new babe. Magdalena had offered to do some mending so the new mother could rest and enjoy the child. She knew her own talent with a needle. The couple's mending had stacked up during the heaviness of pregnancy with an older child to care for. Magdalena's repairs would hold for a good long while.

The couple's farm was four miles away. Calculating both the walking time and the visiting time, Magdalena reckoned she had the better part of three hours away from the house, perhaps even four. Magdalena much preferred setting her body in motion and raising her face in the warmth in the sky to wiping noses and shooing children out of the kitchen. The brutality of summer heat

had eased, but the days still brimmed with sun. She would cut through the paths that joined the back property boundaries and stay off the main road, and she would have hours for uninterrupted thoughts while she carried the mended garments to the Yoders.

Babsi's baby had come as well. A boy. They named him Jacob, for his grandfather. The name had been in the Byler family for several generations already, and of course it made Magdalena think of her *onkel* in Berks County, and his son Jacob Franklin. The miles between Lancaster County and Berks County were far from insurmountable, but the two branches of the Byler family had less and less in common. Magdalena supposed that in another generation they would hardly know each other.

If only one of these little Jacoblis could be hers — hers and Nathanael's. He did not come right out and say he did not plan to marry, but anyone could see he had lost interest. He was content. Too content.

It stabbed her sometimes, that he could lose his love for her.

Magdalena pushed out air and moved the old flour sack filled with mended garments to the other shoulder.

She did not see them until she crested the small hill, hardly more than a mound. And

if she had not turned her head at that angle at that precise moment, she might have missed them altogether. Against the slope, four men sat on the ground, huddled around a patch of something. Leather? Paper? She could not be sure.

Magdalena did not realize her feet had stopped moving until she caught his glance. Eyes large and brown stared at her. No hat restrained his shaggy brown hair. They locked eyes while he jumped to his feet. His motion caused the others to look up as well. She heard the slap as rifles moved to their hands, and she froze. Never before had she seen a gun aimed at her.

"I'm sorry," Magdalena muttered. "I won't disturb you." She took a few steps.

"Halt!"

When she turned again, the first man was moving toward her. "What do you have in the bag?"

Magdalena licked her lips and swallowed. "Mended clothing. For a friend."

"Show me."

Magdalena dropped the bag off her shoulder and spread the top edges. He riffled through a few layers with one hand, his musket at the ready in the other.

Who did they think she was? Magdalena wondered. And who were they? She watched

their movements, curious.

"Do you come through here often?" he asked.

"No, not often." Magdalena twisted the top of her bag closed.

"Why are you here today?"

"I felt like walking. Usually I take a cart on the road." She realized now that two of the men wore jackets in shades of red. Not British uniforms, but nevertheless a suggestion of their sympathies. She took a step back and saw fire in his eyes.

"I should be on my way." Magdalena slung the bag over a shoulder.

The man turned and spoke over his shoulder to the others. "Bring the paper."

A younger man — surely no older than fifteen, her brother Hansli's age — picked up the paper they had huddled around. He took five uphill strides and was beside her.

"You will carry this for us."

She met the first man's gaze and fingered the strings of her *kapp*. "I am Amish."

"I know. That's why you are perfect."

"I do not understand."

He pointed. "On the far side of that ridge is a boulder. It looks a little like a bear cub from a distance."

Magdalena stood still, anticipating. She knew the ridge well. Patriots had been

261

gathering there for more than two years.

Now he folded the paper as he talked. "It's a simple task."

"I am Amish," she repeated.

"No one will look in your bag."

"You did," Magdalena pointed out.

"But not because I suspected you. I saw an opportunity."

"Amish do not take sides in a war." Even as she spoke the words, her belief in them trembled.

"When you get to the rock, look to the south. You will see a small cabin."

Nathan's cabin. Magdalena exhaled and inhaled three times before speaking. "What will happen to the men on the ridge if I do this?"

"What will happen to you if you do not? The battles are spreading. Your General Washington is going to lose Philadelphia any day."

"He is not my General Washington," she said. "The Amish have no generals."

"It will be better for you if you are on our side when Philadelphia falls. It won't be long before the countryside is under British control once again. Your theory of neutrality will not hold up then." Without asking permission, he took the bag from her shoulder and plunged his hand inside, pushing

the letter to the middle. His fingers came out empty. "Inside the cabin you'll see a shelf with jars of preserves on it."

Mrs. Buerki's jars of peaches and beans, long forgotten. Magdalena's heart thundered as she realized the squatters in Nathan's cabin were British sympathizers.

"Put the letter under the third jar from the left."

"That's all?"

"That's all."

She held his brown eyes as she raised her bag to her shoulder. "And if I should happen to pass this way again?"

"Then perhaps we will happen to talk again."

"The Israelites could not make bricks without straw, and I cannot make gunpowder without saltpeter." Jacob pulled his leather apron over his head and flung it against the stone wall of the tannery.

"The French are very close to having a fresh supply of powder at Washington's disposal." David sat hunched forward on a barrel, his hands tucked under his thighs.

"That's not much help now." Jacob pulled a forearm across the sweat on his forehead. "The British are marching toward Philadelphia, and they seem to be getting ample

help from sympathizers in the countryside."

"Our officers need harnesses and saddles as well as powder. You're making those as fast as you can. It's a great help, Jacob."

Jacob exhaled and gazed at his youngest brother. "I couldn't do it without you. But if we lose Philadelphia —"

"That won't be the end of the war. We will keep fighting!"

"Sarah is in Philadelphia. She will refuse to leave, you know."

"I know." David put his hands behind his head and stretched his back.

"Joseph is going to enlist any day," Jacob said.

"I know that, too."

"This is hard on *Mamm*."

"Did you ever tell her you saw Maria?"

Jacob shook his head. "I *might* have seen Maria. Why break *Mamm*'s heart all over again if I was wrong?"

"You're right." David raked his hands through his hair. "I'd better go. This time my wagon really is full of potatoes to feed hungry bellies."

Magdalena slipped out the back door, her prayer *kapp* hanging loose around her neck and a shawl around her shoulders. The midnight sky was clear, the moon bright.

This brought both comfort and anxiety. She could see her way, but she would have to remember to stay in the shadows. It would be easier once she was away from the clearing around the house and barn.

She had lain for hours in her bed, waiting for the settled sounds of sleep to come from every room. The new baby fussed himself and his mother into exhaustion, and Magdalena did not dare leave her room until the shuffling behind Babsi's door stopped.

But she was out now, and she allowed herself one deep breath before turning her feet swiftly toward her goal. Twice before she had done this, her heart pounding as she flung herself through gradations of shadow in darkness. Instead of moving up the lane to the main road, Magdalena crept through the back garden and across one fallow field. Beyond it she found the cover that taller crops, though picked bare, would provide.

She never read the letters, although they were not sealed. She simply carried them from one destination to another according to Patrick's instructions.

Patrick. She'd heard one of the men call out his name, unaware she was near. She had not yet spoken hers to him, and he had not asked.

Soon she was across the second field. Dry corn husks crunched under her feet. Every sound magnified, every step thudding, every sweep of her hemline crackling in the dirt.

She froze.

Her steps were not the only sounds she heard.

Magdalena ducked into what was left of the corn row and dropped flat to the ground. She turned her head toward the sound and saw a boot.

A brown boot. The sort Amish men favored. A second boot came into the frame of her vision. Both feet turned toward her and stopped.

"Magdalena, get up."

She bolted upright. "*Daed!* What are you doing out here?"

"Magdalena, get up out of the dirt."

She took her father's outstretched hand and pulled herself to her feet.

"Maggie, what are you doing?"

"I was going for a walk."

"Do you find the moonlight romantic?"

"No! If you think I'm meeting a man, please put your mind at ease. There is no one."

"Let us walk together back to the house, then."

"Did you follow me?" Magdalena's fingers

wrapped around the folded paper hidden under her shawl.

"Yes, I did."

"But why?"

He puffed air softly. Magdalena knew that sound. Her father would not be distracted, not when he obviously found her actions suspicious.

"Magdalena," he said, "would these midnight forays have anything to do with the British sympathizers?"

"Why would you ask that?"

"I would not be the first farmer to suspect they have been camping on my land. Please answer my question."

Magdalena could not tell a full-blown lie to her father. "It is only a few letters. I do not even know what they say."

She winced when her father took her elbow, not because it hurt but because she knew she had pushed his tolerance too far. When he turned her toward home, she did not resist.

"Maria, we are Amish."

"Maria?" She blanched. Her *daed* never mixed up names. "I am Magdalena."

"I'm sorry. Sometimes you remind me of my sister." He relaxed his touch on her elbow. "We are Amish. We do not get involved in these affairs. Force is not our way."

"I am not forcing anyone," she said. "It is just letters."

"And how do you know one of these letters will not change the war?"

The thought made her heart quicken. If she could in some small way contribute to bringing an end to the Patriot uprising, she would feel she had done well. She pushed regret for pride out of her mind.

They walked home without talking. Magdalena gripped the letter, already scheming how she might break away in the morning while her father worked in the field they now traversed. He would watch her closely, but he could not keep her in sight every moment of the day and night.

Philadelphia fell before the end of the month. The day the news reached him, Jacob sat up alone in the middle of the night pondering its implications. British troops, with ample gunpowder, marched the streets where his parents had met and where his sister now lived.

Jacob tapped the table with one finger. He was not going to give up. He had what he needed for a small batch of powder in the iron kettle behind the tannery. In the morning he would carry coals from his own kitchen to light the fire and heat the saltpe-

ter to crystals. He had plenty of lye for boiling the brimstone in linen rags, and red cedar was stacked up outside the tannery for burning. Pounding the mixture into dust would take days.

Jacob rubbed a thumb against the edge of the table, remembering the feel of the silky fine powder that would result from his labors. Perhaps he would use the saltpeter to make a smaller but more powerful batch. He might not have as much as he wished, but General Washington was welcome to whatever he did have. Jacob liked to imagine his gunpowder causing the explosion that would shoot off a cannon.

And he would have to get a message to Sarah and Emerson. David might have some ideas how. If he could get the message through, his sister would offer reliable details about events in Philadelphia.

TWENTY-FIVE

Whether she wanted to admit it or not, Annie half listened to the traffic outside the shop the next morning hoping to hear Dolly's clip-clop. Rufus worked more and more often doing custom work in the subdivision springing up north of town. He created cabinets in his workshop on the Beiler property, which meant he could go days — or even weeks — at a time without needing to come into town. Eventually he had to install his handiwork, though, and Annie liked to think he would look for a reason to meander down Main Street.

When the clip-clop came, however, it was not Dolly but Brownie, and the buggy carried not Rufus but Joel and the Stutzman brothers. From her position at the cash register, Annie saw all three teens drop from the buggy's bench and walk around to the back to unload several crates.

"Did you tell Mrs. Stutzman you wanted

more of her jams and handmade goods?" With no customers in the shop, Annie spoke freely to Mrs. Weichert.

"I don't see any harm in keeping a few of her things. Franey Beiler doesn't do blackberry jam, and it seems to be popular."

"This looks like more than a few jars of jam."

Joel held the shop door open now, while Mark and Luke carried crates. Mrs. Weichert's eyes widened slightly and Annie stifled a smirk.

"Our *mamm* sent in a wide selection," Mark said. "She said you may choose what you would like to keep and we will pick up the rest the next time we are in town."

"My goodness, your mother has been busy. This is quite a bit more than I was expecting," Mrs. Weichert said. Mark moved toward the counter with two crates. Luke had two more.

"We'll get the rest, then," Mark said.

"There's more?"

Behind the crates, Annie snorted then generated a cover-up cough as the brothers stepped out to the buggy.

Mrs. Weichert brushed her thumbs across a quilted pillow sham. "Joel, perhaps you could help Annie take these to the back room. We'll have more space there to go

271

through everything."

Annie was not so sure. The back room was strewn with assorted finds from three separate estate sales, all awaiting cleaning and pricing. But when Joel complied with Mrs. Weichert's request, Annie did the same.

In the back room, Annie set down the crate she carried and slid it up against a wall. "I suppose Carter and Duncan are in school."

"Yes, I suppose they are." Joel nudged two more crates snug up against the first.

"Seems like the bunch of you have been spending a lot of time together."

Joel met her gaze. "Not all that much."

Annie peered at a wooden birdhouse with a single hole in the front. "I wonder if one of the boys made that."

"Might have."

"I guess everybody has heard about Karl Kramer."

"I don't pay much attention to him," Joel said. "His fuse is too quick."

Now why would Joel be talking about a fuse? Annie heard the bell on the door jangle and Mark's soft voice, his words indistinguishable.

"I'll get the rest," Joel said.

As he turned away, Annie wondered how it was he had time for mundane errands for

the Stutzmans when undoubtedly he had chores of his own. It was the middle of the morning, at the height of spring. On a farm. Annie found it hard to believe he did not have work waiting for him at his father's side. Surely the Stutzman boys could have brought their own buggy into town.

Joel returned, his arms full.

Annie smiled, daring him to keep looking so glum. "I'll make more room." She pushed a mostly empty oversized box out of the way.

"This is the last of it."

"I hope Mrs. Stutzman appreciates your help. I'm sure you have a lot of other things you could be doing."

"My morning was fairly clear." Joel brushed his palms against each other, spewing dust. "It is our way to be helpful."

"Yes, of course. I of all people understand Beiler hospitality."

He looked at her, and the corners of his mouth went up, but the gesture did not convince Annie.

"Is everything all right, Joel?" She spoke before she meant to, laying a hand on his forearm.

"Of course. Why should it not be?" He moved out of her touch.

Was that irritation in his tone? Defensiveness? Simple fatigue? Slow and subtle was

273

not going to work. Annie changed tactics.

"What do you know about Karl Kramer's missing fertilizer? Or what do your friends have to do with it?"

"I'd better go."

Joel touched the brim of his hat in a way that made clear Annie would get no further reaction from him.

"Joel, if the boys are getting themselves into trouble —"

"Good-bye, Annalise."

Rufus stood at the end of Annalise's short front walk and tipped his head back far enough that even the brim of his hat did not filter the streaming sun. Annalise sat on her front stoop, her legs stretched out, eyes closed, face raised. Her hair, hanging loose today, draped her shoulders. He was certain that she had not cut it since the day he met her.

And the thought of what that meant made him smile.

She opened her eyes just then, and he saw the joy chase through them before she composed herself.

"I couldn't remember if you were working only half a day," he said.

"I'm off until Thursday. Where's Dolly? I didn't hear you coming."

"I left her grazing. I'm working nearby."

"Are you sure it's safe to leave her unattended?"

"Karl Kramer and I have come to an understanding, if that's what you mean," Rufus said. "But my crew is there."

"Just in case. Okay." Annalise scooted to one side of the step and reached for a plastic container behind her. "I have sandwiches. Ham and cheese?"

Rufus lowered himself to the stoop beside her and accepted a hefty half sandwich. He could not ask for a much more public place than her front yard. Tongues might wag about how much time they spent together, but no one could accuse them of being secretive.

"Tom and I are going to Colorado Springs tomorrow." Rufus rotated the sandwich in his hands, planning his assault on its girth. "I think you should come."

"Really?"

Rufus nodded. "You should see your mother more often."

"Oh."

The sag of her shoulders told him he had said the wrong thing. "Annalise, she is still very anxious about what you are doing here. She needs to know you are not turning your back on her."

"Of course I'm not." Annalise picked at the crust of her own sandwich, the other half of his. "I just don't know what else I can say to explain things to her."

"Just be with her. Let her see that she raised a wonderful, capable woman with strong values. That she isn't losing you."

He heard the edge of hesitation in her breath.

"I'm going to shop for tools, and Tom is going to visit his mother in the nursing home," he said. "We would be back by suppertime."

"How about seeing Ruth?"

"Your mother, Annalise. You need to see your mother. Call her from the shop."

She took a big bite, purposely occupying her mouth, he thought. When she swallowed hard, he knew he had persuaded her.

Lauren was there on the sofa when Ruth entered the suite. Ruth dropped her backpack beside Lauren and plopped into the chair opposite the sofa.

"You should have let me pick you up from work." Lauren peered over the top of her laptop and her glasses at Ruth.

"It seemed like a lot of trouble. You're in the middle of a paper."

Lauren scoffed. "I suspect my professor is

a closet pacifist. No offense. I know you're the real thing."

"No offense taken."

"My professor keeps making me tweak my subject, thesis, sources — the whole thing. He won't admit he just doesn't want to read a paper about incendiary devices and military munitions."

Ruth laughed. "He doesn't want to admit that you know more about it than he does."

"You got that right."

Ruth put her head back, closed her eyes, and breathed out her fatigue. Finding Lauren in the suite always heartened her. Their other suitemates, rarely there, kept to their own rooms. Without Lauren's encouragement, Ruth would do the same. More than once, though, as she lay alone in her bed she grinned at the unlikely friendship between an Amish girl and a self-taught munitions specialist. Ruth understood most of what Lauren talked about now. An entire new vocabulary sorted itself out in Ruth's mind, finding categories and relationships in a peculiar grammar. Weapon numbers and abbreviated names and schematics inserted themselves into conversations about study groups and coins for the laundry. Ruth still was reluctant to believe she would ever have much use for this particular

set of words.

"We should do a driving lesson," Lauren said. "No point in having a car and letting it sit in the parking lot."

"Whenever you're ready."

"Admit it, you like driving." Lauren snapped her laptop shut. "Let's go now."

Ruth did not stifle her laugh. She had been lonely for so long after leaving the valley of her family's home. It was good to once again be with someone who knew her well.

"I'll get the key."

Tom Reynolds was cranky.

His mood rarely faltered this much, but Annie almost wished she were riding in the open bed of his truck instead of wedged between him and Rufus. Before they left Westcliffe, Annie toyed with seeking counsel from both men while the three of them were captive to the road. What if something were going on with the boys? Tom and Rufus could sort it out. In only minutes, though, Tom's disposition clamped her mouth shut.

Tom twisted the steering wheel in a sharp turn. "Carter has too much unsupervised time. When summer vacation comes, he'll have way too much free time."

"He's a good boy, Tom," Rufus said.

"When he was little, Trish and I could not leave him alone for a minute or he'd get into trouble." Tom accelerated. "Can't you keep him occupied on your crew, Rufus? You wouldn't even have to pay him."

Annie blocked out most of Tom's tirade, unwilling to offer Carter up for sacrifice at the moment. She gripped the seat when he took turns a little too fast. She glanced at Rufus every few minutes, admiring his calm responses.

But, no, this did not seem like the time to mention to Tom that his son might be building a bomb and that his Amish friends — including Rufus's brother — might be helping him. She could not be sure, and maybe she was wrong, and she did not want to make false accusations, so never mind. *How do you know?* he would ask. *Because I'm nosy and jump to conclusions and I have no proof,* she would have to say. She did not want the Amish to dub her Nosy Annalise.

They pulled up — finally — in front of Annie's parents' home. With Mrs. Weichert's permission, Annie had used the phone in the shop to alert her mother that she was coming and to make sure she would be home. When Annie got out of the truck, Myra Friesen was already standing in the front door frame.

"I'm not so sure about this," Annie muttered in that moment when she was wedged between the truck and Rufus standing at the open door.

"It's the right thing."

Visions of the red dress flashed through Annie's mind. She would only be home a few hours this time. Surely she could not get into trouble in one afternoon.

No. She wouldn't. She just wouldn't. In fact, she would put that dress in the trash herself.

Her arm brushed Rufus's as she moved past him, and his fingers fluttered for hers.

A rare gesture. He knew how much she needed it.

"When I come back, I will come in and say hello to your mother." As he spoke, Rufus waved at Myra, who returned the gesture with the delay of reluctance.

Twenty-Six

"I only wish you were staying longer." Annie's mother squeezed her tight. "I made brunch."

"Quiche Lorraine?" Just the thought triggered Annie's salivary glands. Her mother's quiche, a family weekend staple during Annie's childhood, was a dish she would like to learn to make now that she was determined to cook properly.

"With a fresh spinach-cranberry salad I still have to put together." Myra turned toward the kitchen.

"Almonds?" Annie followed her mother.

"Of course."

"I took all this for granted growing up." Annie perched on a stool at the breakfast bar, where she could smell the baking quiche and imagine it rimmed by a perfectly golden crust. Her mother would know precisely the moment to remove it from the oven. "The next time I come, maybe you

can teach me to make your quiche."

"I'm glad to hear there will be a next time." Myra opened the refrigerator and rapidly transferred an array of ingredients to the counter.

"Of course there will be a next time, Mom. You're being dramatic."

"I might argue that you're the one with the flair for drama of late, but let's not quibble." Myra dumped a bag of spinach in a colander. "Oh, before I forget, there's some mail for you on the sideboard in the dining room. Some of it looks important."

Annie doubted important mail would be coming to her parents' home. She had been living in Westcliffe for eight months now, and mail came to her house. "Probably junk."

"I don't think so. You'd better look at it." Myra brushed her hands on a dish towel. "I'll get it."

"Mom —" Before Annie voiced her protest that she could fetch her own mail, Myra whizzed past her into the dining room and quickly returned.

"This does not look like junk." Myra tapped the envelope that sat atop a clothing catalog and a bank advertisement. "Isn't that the company you sold to?"

Annie picked up the flat manila envelope,

imprinted with the logo of Liam-Ryder Industries. "Yes. It's probably some formality, a notification the government requires."

"I may not be a corporate executive, but that doesn't look like a form letter to me. Open it." Myra picked up a knife and let it drop through a cucumber in six quick taps.

Annie tore the envelope open. "Are you making dessert?"

"I have some Bosc pears. I was going to do something fancy, but I ran out of time."

"We can just eat them fresh." Annie slid a letter out of the envelope.

"I have caramel sauce."

"That would be good, too." Annie scanned the embossed page in her hand. How in the world had Liam-Ryder Industries tracked her down to her parents' address? And why? The sale of her software company, including its intellectual property assets, was final months ago. She let her breath out slowly as she read more carefully.

"What do they want?"

"I'm not sure."

Continued partnership with L-R Industries.

Two years of exclusive creative work.

Operate from the location of her choice.

A financial package that made Annie look twice.

Liam-Ryder Industries had bought her company and her innovative software to track and analyze shopping habits for individuals according to several variables. Now they wanted her, too.

Her next creative challenge could be the next software advance to transform the service industry. Annie turned the letter, the envelope, and the junk mail facedown on the breakfast bar.

"I don't know why they're sending me mail here. Can I help you with the salad?"

"Would you rather have raisins instead of cranberries?" Myra opened a cabinet and pulled out a box. "I have the golden kind you always liked."

"Cranberries are fine." Annie slid off her stool. "Let me make the salad."

The home phone rang, and Myra answered. From her mother's end of the conversation, Annie could tell Myra had launched into another community fundraiser project. Myra's promise to track down a catering list took her out of the room. Annie picked up the knife her mother had abandoned and cut a few more slices of cucumber and considered beginning on the water chestnuts.

She glanced back at the letter from Liam-Ryder. The amount of money they were of-

fering approached obscene levels for only two years of work. The president of L-R Industries had not said exactly what they wanted her to do — that would have been risky to put in writing, she supposed — but Annie knew he would not have approached her if the challenge were not stimulating.

The chase.

The hunt.

The conquest.

That tempted her more than the money. Curiosity made Annie's brain click through its gears. She laid the knife down and picked up the letter again then read it for the third time at a pace that allowed her to speculate on between-the-lines innuendos. Temptation crept through her, as seductive as the red dress had been. Abruptly she opened the door to the cabinet beneath the sink and dropped the whole pile of mail into the trash. She was chopping water chestnuts when Myra returned.

"Sometimes I think it would be easier to skip the chicken. We all just pretend it doesn't taste like rubber," Myra said. "Why don't we just ask people for money and save everybody a lot of time and fuss? It seems like we're always feeding someone's ego with these dinner events."

Annie pinched her shoulders up and held

them there. "Maybe you don't have to plan them anymore."

"Believe me, I'm tempted. Your father insists the social contacts are good for his business." Annie was afraid that if she sliced any faster, her bounty would include a fingertip.

With the swiftness of long habit, Myra tore off a paper towel and wiped up the widening puddle beneath the colander of spinach on the counter. She opened the cabinet door to toss the soggy towel into the trash.

Myra picked up the letter. "Throwing away your mail so quickly?"

"It's nothing I'm interested in." Annie reached for the letter, intending to crumple it this time.

Myra raised her arm and stepped back, keeping the letter out of Annie's reach and already reading. "Annie! This is an amazing opportunity!"

"Under other circumstances, yes, it would be." Annie resumed chopping.

"But two years, Annie. Then you could be comfortable and never have to worry about money again."

"I already don't worry about money."

"Surely you're allowed to make a living. After all, you haven't actually joined the

Amish. It's not too late to back out."

Annie swallowed and laid the knife down carefully before turning to her mother. "Mom, I don't want to back out. That's the last thing I want."

Color evaporated from Myra's face. "I thought you were just thinking about things."

"Well, I've been thinking for quite a while now. It might be time for me to do something more definite."

Myra moistened her lips and twitched her chin. "I read somewhere that the Amish are allowed to use computers as part of their businesses. That's all you'd be doing."

Annie shook her head. "You know it would be much more than that for me. My relationship with computers is a different life, a different set of values than anything the Amish could ever imagine or justify."

Annie felt it when she used Mrs. Weichert's computer at the shop for more than a quick search for information. She felt it when she picked up Carter's phone and looked at his Internet search history. Months of disciplining herself not to depend on the gratification of instantaneous information would melt into a river of slime running through her life if she considered L-R Industry's offer.

"I can't, Mom," she said.

"You could if you wanted to."

"But I don't want to. And I don't want to want to."

"Are you and Rufus getting serious? Is that it?"

"Honestly, I'm not sure what we are, Mom. That's not the point. I want to live more simply, with deeper values."

"There's nothing wrong with the values your father and I taught you."

"I didn't say there was, Mom. Maybe I need to understand them better. Maybe I'm just choosing something more overt. More definite."

"Then it's his family. His mother."

"Franey? What do you mean?"

"You're closer to her than you are to me."

"Oh, Mom."

"Don't deny it. You didn't want to come home while Penny was here because you didn't want to miss your quilt lesson with Franey Beiler. You're replacing me. How can I have a place in your life if you go Amish?"

" 'Go Amish'?"

"You have a family, Annie. Why are you turning your back on us?"

Annie dug the heels of her hands into her eyes.

"You've done that since you were a toddler," Myra said. "It's as if you made up
your mind not to cry and so you just won't.
I bet Franey Beiler doesn't know that about
you."

"It's not a contest, Mom."

Myra gasped and lurched toward the
oven, slamming the door down and reaching in with a dish towel as her hot pad. She
set the quiche on the stovetop.

"Look at that. I've never burned a quiche
before in my life. This crust is ruined."

They ate without saying much. The crust
was darker than usual but far from ruined.
After wedges of fresh pear, they agreed they
would take a walk around the neighborhood. It did not escape Annie's notice that
her mother chose a route that took her past
her old elementary school, past her childhood best friend's house — though her
friend had moved away years ago — and
past her middle school. Annie felt every
tortuous tick of the afternoon's minutes
until it was time for Rufus and Tom to
return.

When the red truck pulled up, Annie was
already waiting outside in one of the two
chairs her mother left year-round on a
flagstone patio. She had said good-bye to
her mother a few minutes earlier. Now she

jumped up and crossed the driveway before Rufus could get out of the truck.

"Let's go home," she said through the open window.

"I was going to greet your mother." Rufus gestured toward the house.

"It's not a good time." Annie lurched into the cab.

TWENTY-SEVEN

On Saturday, Annie parked her bicycle at the bottom of the steps leading up to the Beilers' front porch. The front door creaked, and Jacob Beiler pushed the screen door open wide.

"*Mamm* said you would be here soon."

"Well, here I am."

Annie never could manage to suppress a smile at the sight of the little boy who had attached himself to her nearly a year ago. While Rufus's feelings toward her mystified her at times, Jacob never gave her a moment's doubt. She straightened the fullness of her dress and reached up to make sure her prayer *kapp* had not escaped her head during the ride from town.

Jacob let the screen door slam behind him. "*Mamm* said to tell you she would be right back. Sophie is supposed to be in charge of me. I keep telling *Mamm* I don't need anyone to be in charge of me."

Annie climbed the porch steps and gave Jacob's shoulder a quick squeeze. "So your *mamm* is not here?"

"You're supposed to get everything out and get started." Jacob turned and led Annie into the living room and toward the chest he knew held her quilt-in-progress.

They both turned at the sound of steps coming through the dining room.

"Good morning, Annalise." Sophie nodded with her greeting. "I'm sorry I must steal Jacob back from you. He has not finished his work in the kitchen."

"Of course." Annie put a hand on Jacob's back and nudged him toward his sister.

"Make yourself at home," Sophie said. "You know you are always welcome here."

His shoulders slumped, Jacob trudged after Sophie into the kitchen. Annie lifted the lid on the cedar chest, savoring the touch of Rufus's workmanship in her fingers. Saturday morning quilting sessions illumined her weeks. Annie had missed too many of them recently. Franey Beiler was a skillful, patient teacher. Perhaps she found more to commend in Annie's work than it deserved, but her kindness crafted hope in Annie. As she lifted the quilt out of its safekeeping, Annie listened for the familiar cadence of Franey's steps across the hand-

scrubbed, broad-planked flooring.

Her mother's words from three days ago oozed through Annie's mind now. Was there any truth in them? Annie certainly had not set out to replace her mother with a relationship with Franey Beiler. But did Franey somehow see Annie as a replacement for the daughter who had fled her own baptism rather than join the Amish congregation? Franey taught Annie skills she had taught her own daughters — including Ruth. Annie could bake a decent loaf of bread without a recipe and a tasty apple schnitzel if she paid close attention to the steps of the process. She was in Franey's kitchen often enough at mealtimes to learn more about cooking than she had ever tried to absorb from her own mother. She knew Franey liked her. Loved her, even. So did Eli. If she decided to formally join the Amish, they would welcome her as part of their family regardless of what became of her relationship with Rufus. But would she be a consolation prize? A peculiar comfort to offset Ruth's decision?

Annie shook the thought out of her head. The quilt was in her arms now, and she also snared the small basket that held threads and scissors and templates. She moved to the sofa to take her usual seat, remember-

ing the block she was working on two weeks ago. A hoop still held it taut, as smooth on the bottom as it was on the top.

It took only seconds for Annie to see something was not right. Someone had been working on her quilt.

Someone who used fine, even stitches.

The block was finished — and flawless. Her own stitches, which she had wrestled with for four hours last week, had been picked out with a delicate touch that left the cotton fabric unblemished. Meticulous stitches replaced her work. Each length of thread was exactly the same measurement, equal distance apart, and pulled through with faultless tension. Annie flipped the quilt over and ran her fingertips over the back of the square. She found no knots visible to the eye or available to touch, only the same perfection on the underside that the quilt top boasted.

Fury roiled, then grief. If she quilted every day for a year, she could never replicate that precision.

But perfect as they were, the stitches spoiled her quilt. It was *her* quilt.

Moving off the sofa, Annie spread the quilt open on the floor, squatted, and crept around all four sides, lifting the unbound edges at intervals. Many of the squares were

still basted in place to keep them from moving during the quilting process, but even an unpracticed eye could see the difference between the work she had done under Franey's supervision and the expert stitching that now shone from the block in the quilt hoop.

Annie looked more closely. The thread was not hers. The color match was closer than her choice had been. How was that possible?

She would have to give up. Abandon the violated project. Forget she ever tried to learn to quilt.

Certainly she would never be able to look Beth Stutzman in the eye — she was sure the work was Beth's. Even though everyone knew that Annie's amateur stitching did not measure up to the standards of the rest of the quilts in the Beiler home, no one else would have suggested undoing her efforts. How Beth found the time during the last two weeks, Annie did not know. The Stutzmans were not even living in the Beiler home anymore.

Annie grabbed the quilt with both hands, hurled it at the open cedar chest, taking no effort to be tidy, and stomped out the front door.

Rufus heard the screen door slam from

across the yard and through the open workshop window. He set down his plane and stepped outside in time to see the burst of a rust-colored dress flashing across the yard, past the garden, and into the barn.

He found Annalise there a few minutes later.

On her knees in the end stall with her back to the door, she tore at the pins holding her hair in place. Her *kapp* was already in the straw. He watched, his breath fading, as her blond hair escaped the braids and shook loose. Her shoulders rose with the sudden, noisy intake of air of one caught up in weeping and forgetting to breathe.

"Annalise."

Instantly she was on her feet. She spun toward him, her hair settling around her face and draping across her chest. Both hands now tried to eradicate the evidence of her tears, but Rufus had never seen her eyes so full.

Annalise Friesen did not cry. She solved problems.

"Annalise, tell me what happened." He took a step toward her.

Standing in a shaft of light shed by the window above her, she opened her mouth but closed it without speaking. Again her shoulders heaved.

Rufus lightly touched her shoulder. "Talk to me, Annalise."

She blew out air and breathed in three more times before she could form words.

"Everything is a mess, and I don't know how to clean it up."

"What are you talking about?"

Annalise rolled her eyes, a gesture Rufus had seen a few occasions before.

"You name it," she said, "and it's a mess."

"You'll have to be more specific."

He wanted to take her in his arms and still her quaking. To feel her racing heart — surely it was racing — and count the moments until it quieted. To stroke her forbidden hair.

"My mother, for starters," she said. "I didn't tell you half of what happened on Wednesday. She's petrified I'll become Amish." She clenched the fabric of her skirt. "And look at me, standing here in this dress. What am I supposed to do?"

"I'll speak to her, if you like."

"And say what?" Her gray eyes dared him. "Will you tell her that you don't care for me and I should not become Amish on your account?"

"You shouldn't," he said quietly, knowing that he was ducking her arrow.

"See, I've made a mess with you, too.

What am I doing here, Rufus?"

"You wanted to live a simpler life."

"You have to know it's more than that."

Slowly, he nodded. "I do know. And it is more."

Her tears glistened, welling again. Rufus wanted to wipe them away with his own fingertips. But he did not move. "It's Saturday. You came to quilt, I'm sure. So why are you out here?"

"Because I can't quilt, and everyone knows it."

"You are learning. *Mamm* says you are doing well."

"Clearly someone else has another opinion."

"What are you talking about, Annalise?"

She gestured toward the house. "Go look for yourself. Someone's been working on my quilt and doing a far better job than I could ever hope to do."

"Why would someone work on your quilt?"

"You tell me! Is this an Amish tradition I haven't heard of yet? Is it some secret of *Ordnung* that no one has written down for me? Maybe I should just quit the whole business."

Rufus closed the short distance between them and gripped her elbows, demanding

her eyes meet his.

"You don't mean that," he said.

"Don't tell me what I mean."

"You've come too far, worked too hard, to let this spew out of you."

"So now you're judging me, too. Great."

"I am not judging you, Annalise. But I am going to kiss you."

Her shoulders relaxed as a gasp parted her lips. As he leaned in to take her mouth, one hand moved up her arm and found the back of her neck, under the hair he loved to see hanging loose. His fingers traced her hairline then strayed into the thick waves. The other arm went to the back of her waist to pull her closer, and he felt no protest. Lips soft and yielding responded to the searching pressure he offered.

Rufus broke the kiss at last but stood with his forehead against hers. "Better?"

Her breath came out slow and long. "I'm sorry. I guess I've been more confused than I realized."

"I know we need more time to be together. To talk."

Annalise nodded. "There is something else I need to talk to you about."

"Of course."

"It's about Joel. And Carter. I'm messing that up, too. I'm not sure, but —"

When he heard the noise of the door opening behind him, Rufus straightened, stepped away, and turned. Joel stood in the gap of daylight, leaning his weight into the side of the barn door to slide it open all the way.

"I need Dolly," Joel said, "if you're not planning to take her out."

Rufus turned his palms up. "I'm not going anywhere."

Joel pushed up the latch on Dolly's stall and stepped in. "*Daed* was looking for you a few minutes ago."

"Do you know what he wanted?"

"No." Joel reached for Dolly's bridle on its hook.

Rufus licked his lips and glanced at Annalise. "I suppose I'd better find out what he wants."

She nodded.

He reached a hand out a few inches, but she made no move to take it, leaving him no option but to go without her.

Annie moved out of the empty stall and toward Joel.

"It's not what you think," she said, restraining her wild hair and wishing she had picked up the prayer *kapp*. Why were Ru-

fus's kisses always pilfered from disappointment?

"It's not my business." Joel busied himself
checking the leather of the reins.

"I've had a bad day."

"That happens to all of us. I'm sure you
will sort it out."

"Rufus was . . . well, you know, trying to
help."

"I told you it's not my business."

Annie pressed her lips together, considering her next words. "I've been wanting to
talk to you about Carter. The Stutzman
boys, too."

Now he turned his head toward her, lifting an eyebrow. "It's my turn to say that it's
not what you think."

"Is that my cue to say that it's not my
business?"

Joel gave no answer.

"If someone gets hurt," Annie said, "I will
regret saying it's not my business."

"The last thing I want is for anyone to get
hurt." Finally he stilled his hands and
turned to face her. "Do you trust me, Annalise?"

"Of course, but —"

"No buts. Yes or no."

It was Annie's turn to hold her answer as

Joel led Dolly out of her stall and into the daylight.

TWENTY-EIGHT

A year ago, in Colorado Springs, on a Sunday afternoon, Annie would have pulled on shorts and a T-shirt, hoping for sun in late May. Here in the mountains, even the afternoon cradled cool night air. Over the deep rust dress, Annie wore her thick navy blue cardigan.

Annie locked up the house, going out the back door to where she had left her bicycle leaning against the sagging back porch. She tied her *kapp* in place and hiked up her skirt as far as she dared to keep the hem out of the path of the bike's chain. All afternoon she practiced smiling and speaking polite Pennsylvania Dutch sentences. This time at least she had advance warning that the Stutzmans were coming for Sunday dinner at the Beilers'. When she closed her eyes and remembered the scene from the day before, Beth's unblemished stitches in *her* quilt still rankled. But Annie loved Franey.

She loved all the Beilers. She loved being in their home. She was not going to let Beth Stutzman take that away from her.

Thirty minutes later Annie coasted to a stop in the Beiler driveway and assessed the scene. The Stutzman buggy had not yet arrived. All three of the Beiler horses were in the pasture.

She moved across the yard then paused on the porch, her shoulders lifting and falling as her breath recovered from the mountain ride. Surely by now one of the Beilers had put her quilt away properly in the cedar chest.

"Annalise, is that you? Come here."

Franey's tone carried a note of anxiety that Annie did not often hear from this calm Amish woman. Annie opened the door and stepped into the house. Franey was in the living room, holding her quilt out. She gripped the finished block in her hands.

"What happened?" Franey's perplexed eyes squinted.

Annie did not answer. Franey had to know how the quilt square had come to be perfect.

"This is what made you disappear before our lesson yesterday." Franey expelled air. "I knew Beth was spending too much time here. She came in the afternoons, while I was in the garden, even after her family

moved."

"I should have told you." Annie stepped across the room and took the quilt from Franey's arms. "I was stunned when I found it and thought about quitting. But I am not a quitter."

Annie met Franey's eyes. She saw the slight smile begin in one corner of her mouth.

"No, Annalise Friesen, you are not a quitter."

"I am not going to give up quilting, but I am not going to look at those stitches every time I pick up that quilt for the next twenty years." Annie jabbed at the center of the hoop. "Those stitches are coming out."

"Demut," Franey said.

"What are you saying?" Annie's voice rose with indignation. "Do you mean that humility requires me to let Beth Stutzman ruin my first quilt?"

"Is it pride that makes you want to pull out the stitches?"

"There's a difference between being humble and being humiliated." Annie's retort came low and firm. Surely even the Amish could see the distinction. "I'm going to pull it all out if it takes me the next six Saturdays."

They stared at each other. Annie heard

Jacob humming to himself in the other room.

"It won't take that long," Franey finally said, "because I am going to help you."

Annie grinned. "Thank you."

"First, I am going to have a word with Beth when she gets here tonight."

Annie reached out and put a hand on Franey's arm. "Don't do that. We'll work on the stitching next time, but making a scene tonight will just spoil everyone's evening."

"I would have a private word."

"Still, it is the Sabbath, after all."

"Of course." Franey blew out her breath and folded the quilt properly. "Let her be surprised when she sees the quilt finished."

Annie giggled. "I am trying to practice *demut*, but you are making it hard!"

Franey grinned and squeezed Annie's hand. They turned at the sound of a buggy. The Stutzmans had arrived.

Rufus glanced several times toward the end of the table where Joel sat between Mark and Luke at the Beiler supper table. That all three teenage boys were present surprised Rufus. He had heard enough mumbling from Ike Stutzman over the last few weeks to know that Mark and Luke were missing

as many family meals as Joel. Tonight Eli presided over the table that united Stutzmans and Beilers with great satisfaction. The older boys sat at one end with Ike and Edna, then Stutzman and Beiler girls were around the middle of the table. At the far end, Rufus, Jacob, and Annalise sat near Franey and Eli.

The older boys whispered among themselves, heads together. Joel shook his head. More than once, Rufus saw.

Franey picked up an empty dish. "Let me get some more potatoes."

Across the table, next to Annalise as usual, Jacob leaned forward toward Rufus. "Is the rock really going to be in the way?"

"In the way of what?" Rufus asked.

"The new trail." Jacob glanced down the table. "That's what they're talking about, isn't it?"

Rufus smiled. "Why did God give you such good hearing?"

"He just did." Jacob grinned. "They say you'll have to take the rock out."

"No, I don't think the boulder will be a problem."

Jacob laid his fork down and kicked the legs of his chair. "Is it true *English* have better schools than we do?" Jacob asked.

"Not better," Rufus answered, "just dif-

ferent. Our people learn what they need for a satisfying life."

"But is it better?"

"Why all the questions?" Annalise said, patting Jacob's back.

"I just wondered."

"Well, you'd better eat, or your *mamm* won't be happy with you."

Franey returned with more potatoes and fresh basket of rolls.

As the little boy picked up his fork, both Rufus and Annalise glanced at the older boys. In between passing dishes around the table, the boys huddled with low voices. Something about their demeanor discomfited Rufus, and he looked from one father to the other expecting at least gentle chastisement. None came. Instead, smiles abounded for the Stutzman girls, who had each contributed a dish to the evening's meal.

Ten years ago it would have meant nothing more than friendship for the Stutzmans and Beilers to share a meal in the home of one family or the other. Now Rufus knew better. The girls had grown up in those ten years. Marriage prospects were considerably slimmer for them here in Colorado, as they were for Rufus himself. Every time Rufus had a meal with the Stutzmans, all three

daughters paraded their homemaking skills. Rufus suspected that since he had not made any overtures toward Beth, Johanna now thought there was hope she could attract him. She smiled at him with a new expression tonight — several times.

Rufus turned his gaze away, offering no encouragement. Annalise sat across the table. Yesterday's kiss still lingered on his lips. She deserved better than to have to sit quietly and watch him find the fine line between discouraging the Stutzman girls and sinking to rudeness himself.

By the time his mother was offering coffee with Beth's blackberry pie, Rufus had made up his mind.

"I could use a walk after that fine meal," Rufus said. "Ike, perhaps you'd like to stretch your legs with me." Annalise's brow furrowed, and he saw her catch herself and make her face placid again even as she watched his movements. It was time he set things right.

The older man dipped his head as he glanced to his wife. "Of course."

They walked toward the Beilers' alfalfa fields. "We got here too late to prepare for the spring seeding," Ike said. "Just barely. But we have the early fall seeding to look forward to. We could still have a nice crop

this year."

Rufus nodded. He locked his hands behind his waist. "I wanted to have a word in private, Ike."

"Oh?"

Rufus saw the hope in Ike's eyes. He shook his head. "I'm sorry, Ike, but I must tell you I don't lean toward the attentions of your daughters."

"You are just getting to know them," Ike protested. "We've only been here a few weeks. They are not the little girls you left behind six years ago."

"Clearly. But still, I would not like to think that any of them might mistake my intentions, for I have none. We are old family friends. I mean no harm to anyone, but your fine daughters would do well to turn their attention elsewhere."

Ike's thumb and forefinger stroked his beard. "I see."

"I hope you do, Ike. Your girls respect you. They will listen if you provide guidance."

"Of course they would. There can be no question of that. But I am sorry to hear you feel this is necessary."

"It's best for everyone, I believe."

"It's because of that outsider."

Rufus squelched a sigh. Though it still irked, Ike's response was no surprise. "This

has only to do with me, I assure you. Please do not blame Annalise."

"You defend her quite quickly, I notice."

"Annalise needs no defending."

"I understand your reluctance about the younger girls, but Beth is mature enough to be a wife."

"I'm sure she is, and I hope she will meet someone soon."

Ike huffed. "Well, then. I suppose you are no more particular than you have ever been, or you would have married before you left Pennsylvania."

Rufus put his hands out, palms up. "I felt I should tell you. If you like, I will speak to Beth."

"She is still my daughter and under my care. I will speak to her."

Rufus turned his steps back toward the house. "Perhaps we should have a last cup of coffee."

Rufus discovered the boys had left to take a walk as well. In the living room, sitting among the Stutzman sisters, Annalise looked desperate for rescuing. At least he would get to drive her home.

On Monday afternoon, Annie tooled around town on her bicycle with a list of errands. Mrs. Weichert had decided to run an ad for

a 20 percent off sale in the newspaper. She insisted on delivering the ad the same way she always had — an old-fashioned piece of original art, which her daughter had created with careful lettering. Annie tried to explain that the newspaper would likely scan and digitize the ad anyway, but Mrs. Weichert was not interested in the conversation. She seemed to prefer living in the century in which most of her shop's goods had originated.

Once that was delivered, Annie crossed the street and went down a couple of blocks to the narrow storefront library. The sturdy but kind librarian had called the shop earlier in the day to let Annie know her interlibrary loan book had arrived from a university in Indiana. Annie had found a notation referencing this book in a footnote of another equally obscure title that had come through the shop serendipitously more than six weeks ago. The deeper she got into Beiler — or Byler — genealogy, the stronger its vortex churned. Who knew what the new title would reveal?

Last, Annie had promised Mrs. Weichert she would return before closing time with a three-cheese grilled sandwich from the coffee shop to serve as Mrs. Weichert's dinner before she spent the evening doing inven-

tory, for which she had refused Annie's offer of help.

In Annie's experience, the coffee shop catered to the morning crowd with a burst at lunchtime before an afternoon lull. To her surprise, the coffee shop was bustling at ten minutes to five. She placed an order and paid for it — adding a sandwich for herself — and sank into a brown leather love seat as she waited. At least four orders were ahead of hers, and while friendly enough, the staff did not specialize in speed. The waiting time would allow her to explore the genealogy book and determine if it would yield information about her ancestors.

Annie had done enough reading in coffee shops to block out the voices clattering around her. She turned the library book in her hands, drawing in its age on her breath. Carefully she opened the front cover. After scanning the table of contents, Annie flipped to a chapter in the middle of the book and traced her finger down the center of several pages. Finally she came to a list of names, descendants of Christian Byler. *Magdalena. What a pretty name,* Annie thought, refreshing after generations of Barbaras and Elizabeths and all the variations of those names. She did not know where her own name had come from — she would have to ask her

mother — but *Annalise* made her feel connected to the *Annas* that seemed to turn up in every generation of Bylers.

Annie glanced up at the counter, just to be sure the sandwiches were not ready, as the conversation behind her compelled her attention.

"Carter, your dad has been looking for you all afternoon."

The voice belonged to Colton, the man who worked for Tom Reynolds at the hardware store.

"Um, I had something to do after school." Carter Reynolds.

Annie did not move her head, but she stopped seeing words on the page as she listened to the exchange.

"He's pretty annoyed that you didn't call," Colton said.

"I guess I should skip the latte and go home." Resignation rang through Carter's tone. Nervous resignation.

Annie touched the look-alike phone in her back pocket that Carter had returned to the shop.

"If I were you, I'd call him now," Colton said.

"Um, I guess."

"Don't you have your phone?"

"Actually, no."

"He's not going to like it if you lost your phone again."

"I know where it is. I just don't have it with me."

"The only reason he lets you have a phone is so he can stay in touch with you."

"I know. I just had to use it for something today and . . . left it there."

Annie nearly turned her head to look at Carter. Why the vagary?

"Maybe you should go get it," Colton said.

"Um, I can't really. Besides . . . it might not still be there."

"Why not?"

"Um . . . a friend needed it. For a science experiment."

Annie raised her head out of the book.

"You're not talking sense." Colton sighed. "Here. Use mine."

"Thanks."

"Oh, just a minute. Let me turn off the alarm. It's about to go off."

A cell phone alarm. Missing fertilizer. Boys playing with science. This was not good.

Annie smacked the library book shut and maneuvered out of the love seat as quickly as she could. How fast could she pedal out to the rock where Elijah Capp and Ruth Beiler used to meet?

315

Breathless when she arrived, she was not the first one there. When Annie saw Karl Kramer's car, she pedaled faster, supposing she could get closer on the bike than he could get with his car. She could not make herself believe the boys had a target in mind. Karl was climbing the path that was meant to be a trail soon, a path that would take him straight to the rock with its broad flat surface perfect for stargazing.

When she was within twenty yards of him, she let the bike fall away from under her and threw off her helmet.

"Stop!"

Karl stopped, but only for a moment. "I'm looking for something." He took three more long strides.

"I know. But you have to stop."

"Don't tell me what to do."

"Why did you come here, Karl?"

"I'm working with Rufus to make this into a park. You know that." His face contorted in aggravation.

Annie moved cautiously forward, her eyes scanning for small clues, her heart thudding. She hoped she was wrong.

"Yes, I know," she said, "but why now? Why did you come now?"

"If you must know, I got an anonymous tip about my missing fertilizer."

316

"It's only a few bags, Karl."

"I'm inclined to slap the next person who says that. The principle of the thing is at stake — someone took what belonged to me. I won't stand for that."

"It was probably just some kids seeing what they could get away with." She took a few steps forward and to one side, where she could get a better view of the boulder.

"I can see that. This place is loaded with fresh footprints." He gestured to the ground.

The boys. How many of them? Had Joel been here?

Still Annie searched, wondering if a group of teenage boys would have the math and science skills required for what she suspected. She doubted Carter and Duncan could have done this on their own, but she had heard the Amish claim that their eighth-grade education was comparable to a conventional high school diploma. Did they teach chemistry? Circuitry? Physics? Perhaps. Elijah Capp astounded her with what he understood about circuitry and ignition, and he had never used electricity in his life.

Mark and Luke Stutzman had once blasted rock in a Pennsylvania meadow.

And Joel. How had he dared to ask her to trust him if he knew this was going on?

She guessed that Duncan Spangler would

do anything on a dare.

Carter Reynolds was naive enough to be talked out of his cell phone. In the intrigue of the moment, he would not think about how he would explain its absence to his parents later.

"Karl," Annie pleaded. "Please. You have to stop."

"I am not going to be the butt of somebody's practical joke." Karl kept moving.

Annie saw it then. The fertilizer. The wire. The cell phone with a network of wires taped in place.

"Karl!"

Annie was too far away to see the first vibration of the cell phone. The flash made her cover her eyes.

TWENTY-NINE

October 1777

"Is he gone?"

Jacob turned to see his mother standing at the entrance to the tannery. Elizabeth seldom came to see where he worked, though he had labored side by side at the lime-filled vats with his father since he was a child. No one was with her. She must have walked all the way down from the big house unaccompanied.

Jacob sighed heavily and put down the blade he was using to trim excess leather off a bridle. "Yes, Joseph left."

Though he was sure his mother knew the truth before she asked, Jacob's heart pinched when her face fell.

"He tried to say good-bye," she said, "but I wouldn't let him."

"Joseph will come back, *Mamm,*" Jacob said.

"Do not make promises that are not yours

to keep, Jacobli."

He had no response.

"Losing Philadelphia was the last straw, I suppose." Elizabeth rubbed her palms against her skirt.

"He thought he could be more help at General Washington's side than here. David will finish Joseph's harvest. John will take his animals for the winter."

She stiffened. "I see, then. You boys have it all worked out."

"He was going to join the militia in any event, *Mamm*. We're just trying to make sure his family does not suffer."

"Of course. Perhaps I'll invite Hannah and the children to come stay at the big house, at least for the winter."

"I think they'd like that."

"I would be glad to have the *kinner* around. I can help with the little ones." Her hands moved up and down her thighs. "What will Washington do next?"

"I don't imagine he will walk away from Philadelphia without a fight."

"So there will be another battle. Soon."

Jacob stepped tentatively toward his mother. "I don't see how he can avoid it."

"Where?"

"Perhaps Germantown."

"And this is what Joseph wanted to do."

320

He saw the shudder in her shoulders. "Yes, *Mamm.* This is what Joseph chose. We've lived with danger all our lives. He is not afraid."

"That is what worries me. Because he is not afraid, he will take greater risks."

Jacob wrapped his arms around his mother. "*Mamm,* he has to do this."

"I suppose if you were not making gunpowder, you would follow."

Jacob was silent, feeling for the first time how thin his mother had become in the last year. Why did he not embrace her more often? He would have noticed sooner. "There is no point in imagining *if,*" he said. "I am here. David and I are working together on something that matters to the Revolution."

"Then perhaps it is John I should worry about." Elizabeth pulled away from him. "And Sarah! She's as bad as you boys. Now she's trapped in Philadelphia, and it's too dangerous for any of us to go see her."

"It's an important cause, *Mamm.*"

She covered her nose with one hand. "I have never liked the way this place smelled."

Elizabeth pivoted. Jacob let her walk away, but he followed for a few steps into the sunlight outside the dark tannery. He almost called out to her to go visit Katie for some

321

lunch, but Elizabeth had already chosen the path that would take her back up to the big house.

Magdalena let the old gelding pull the cart at his own speed. She needed time to think. The farms were clear of soldiers now. Both Patriots and British sympathizers had abandoned their local rivalries in favor of the armies amassed around Philadelphia. General Washington's attempt to take back Germantown, five miles north of the city, tightened the British grip on the capital. The untrained American soldiers lost themselves in the fog around the quiet hamlet. They stumbled into defeat rather than marching to victory.

Now it was the middle of October, and many speculated that the warfront would be quiet through the winter. Unpredictable weather made a march of any distance unlikely. Magdalena had been to the cabin twice since the Battle of Germantown and found nothing there but the dusty jars of preserves. She would never know if any of the letters she delivered had any bearing on the skirmishes around Berks County, much less Germantown or Philadelphia. No doubt by now Patrick and the others were serving in a British regiment with proper uniforms

and exulting in the vice strangling the colonies' capital. The Patriots would be forced to give up and the whole matter would be done with.

The gelding slowed a little too much, so Magdalena clicked for him to pick up his pace. She did have legitimate errands at three other farms this afternoon. The Bylers were well known for their apple cider, and Babsi was sending a jug to every family that had helped feed this year's apples into the press. As always, Magdalena would stop in at the Buerkis' before heading home. She wavered between hope and relief every day. She always hoped Nathan would be at the house and she could once again search his face for signs that he loved her. When he was not there, though, at least for one more day she savored the reprieve of not seeing the answer she refused to accept.

She knew that the girls she had gone to school with whispered behind her back. They were married and producing children. Magdalena could have been married, too, they thought, if she would accept the truth that Nathanael was never coming back to her. The war around them had no bearing on the availability of Amish men. A half a dozen would have been interested in Mag-

dalena with even slight encouragement from her.

But none of the men was Nathanael, and they knew not to invite Magdalena to ride with them to a singing or apple schnitzing.

If Magdalena ever married one of them, it would not be for love.

"Come on, Old Amos," Magdalena said to the horse who was slowing down yet again. "We can't sit here in the middle of the fields all day." She nudged the horse, but he took only a half dozen steps before stopping.

Old Amos deserved his name. *Daed* paid little for the animal four years ago because the horse was already ancient. Hardly worth what it cost to feed him, he was no use for anything more than drawing the lightest cart on the simplest errands. Magdalena tried again to get him to move forward, but Old Amos neighed and stayed put. Magdalena would have to get out and lead him. Perhaps with her weight out of the cart he would be willing to pull the jugs of apple cider. Grabbing the halter on both sides of the animal's face, Magdalena leaned away from him.

And then she saw what had made him stop.

The red coat was ripped in at least three places, and the white breeches were ground

brown with mud. She supposed his hat was lost in battle, and he carried no weapon. He lay on the ground, unmoving.

A true British soldier. He must have come from the battle at Germantown, but that had been days ago and miles away.

Magdalena let go of the horse's halter and took three steps toward the side of the road, where the ground sloped and pebbles skittered under her feet. When she saw the unkempt dark hair, she thought for a moment it was Patrick finally in the uniform he dreamed of. But it was not him.

The soldier's eyes were closed, but his chest seemed to lift slightly. Or at least she thought it did. She would have to get closer to be sure. She scratched her way down the hill about twenty feet then stopped once more to watch his chest.

Yes, he was breathing.

And bleeding.

When his eyes popped open, Magdalena gasped. They stared at each other for a frozen moment.

"Can you speak?" Magdalena finally asked. She knelt at his side and gingerly began to inspect him.

"Yes," he said.

In that one word, she could tell he had come from England and not one of the

other colonies.

"Where is the wound?"

"My belly. Are you a Patriot?"

She met his eyes then shook her head.

"A sympathizer, then," he said. "I suppose that is good, though I don't care anymore."

He did not recognize the meaning of her Amish prayer *kapp* and she did not correct him. She had never called herself a sympathizer, but perhaps she was one.

Magdalena undid the last remaining button on his coat and gently separated the shredded red wool from his bloodied shirt. Pushing up the once-white shirt, she exposed the wound — and nearly had to turn away as the contents of her stomach rose to her throat. The hole in his side had been bandaged hastily with cotton strips that nearly fell apart at the touch of her fingers. Fresh blood oozed. Magdalena pulled her shawl off her shoulders and grimaced as she pressed it against the wound.

"I have a horse and cart up on the road. Do you think you can stand?"

"I've come all the way from Germantown, haven't I?"

"I'm astounded you've managed to come so far." She helped him sit up and tried to determine the best way to support his weight. It seemed unfeasible that he had

been roaming the Pennsylvania countryside in this condition, yet here he was. Gray skinned and prone, but alive.

"I'm not going back," the man croaked.

"No one here will ask you to. Let's try to stand."

"War is a hideous thing. I am not going back."

"Don't worry about that now." Magdalena glanced up the hill at Old Amos and the cart. She put one of the soldier's arms around her shoulder, gripped his dangling wrist, and sucked in a deep breath. She stood, pulling him upright alongside her.

Magdalena had never heard such a scream as the one that roared from his lungs now. By the time she managed to get him up the hill and draped him across the cart, he was unconscious.

Magdalena turned the horse and cart in the narrow road and headed toward home. The apple cider deliveries would have to wait for another day. By the time she pulled the cart up as close to the front porch of her family's home as she could get, assorted family members had gathered. She caught her father's eyes as they carried the soldier inside the house and laid him on the table. Babsi went to work cleaning the ragged wound. Magdalena's younger sisters scur-

ried from the water barrel with clean rags, while her brother Hansli stoked the fire that warmed the room.

"Magdalena?"

She turned toward her father's voice.

"Do you know this man?"

"No, *Daed*. I only found him and wanted to help."

He nodded slowly. "You did the right thing to bring him."

"I was not sure you would welcome a soldier in the house," Magdalena said.

"He is not a soldier now, only a man who has lost a great deal of blood."

Magdalena exhaled abruptly and heavily. She had not realized she was rationing her own breath.

"I thought you wanted to be neutral," she said.

"I am neutral. Today I will help this British soldier, and if tomorrow a Patriot turns up on our porch in need, I will help him also. Neutrality does not mean we turn our backs on humanity."

"Thank you, *Daed*."

"You are pale," he said. "His blood is all over you. Go clean up."

"I should help take care of him," she said.

"You have done your part."

Magdalena nodded but could not tear her

eyes off the soldier. She wanted to believe that had he been a bleeding Patriot foot soldier, she would have done the same thing.

But she was not sure.

THIRTY

Rufus was in the small cart. He almost had not come.

The message that summoned him was vague, cryptic, unsigned. It sounded like some sort of mistake. A note had turned up in his toolbox that afternoon. It could have been for anyone. But something about it made him think he would regret disregarding it. He twisted his torso to look at the open toolbox behind him. The note fluttered loose and escaped the buggy on the breeze. Rufus reached for it and missed. Dolly continued to trot forward. It was probably nothing, but he cared about the rock and wanted to be sure he would see nothing unusual there.

Instead, wide tire tracks rutted through the grass — fresh tracks, prompting Rufus to signal Dolly to speed up. He passed a bicycle tumbled in the weeds. Annalise's bicycle.

Rufus had never heard a bomb, but he imagined it would sound just like the blast that split the air

"Annalise!"

Annie fumbled with her phone as she charged the last few yards up the incline. By the time she squatted next to Karl, splayed on his back, she had it open, but her thumb slid off the power button three times before the device began cycling on. For a few seconds, she was terrified it would not find a signal.

"Karl!"

No response.

"Karl, can you hear me?"

Finally her trembling finger pushed the buttons for 911. With her free hand, Annie thumped Karl's shoulder, trying to rouse him. Her eyes scanned for blood — which seemed minimal. What she saw were burns. And beyond Karl, weeds smoldered and flared. Annie dropped the open phone, leaped over Karl, and stomped on flames. They spurted up in new spots as fast as she could kick dirt on them. A more heavily grassed area might already have been out of control. The wind was calm, though, and loose dirt abounded. Both factors worked in her favor. Annie shed her jacket and used

it to smother bouncing sparks.

"Karl!"

Still no response.

Rufus spotted Karl's car, and terror welled. He thought he had made progress with Karl. Why would the man lure Annalise up here? Whatever story he had concocted had to have been good.

Unless there was no story.

Unless Karl had not lured Annalise at all.

Unless Karl got the same sort of ambiguous, handwritten message that had drawn Rufus to this moment.

Annie was far from certain the ground cover would not spark again when she turned back to Karl, who lay silent and still. Once upon a time, Annie had been certified in first aid. A for airway. B for breathing. C for . . . C for. Cardiac something. No. Circulation.

"You have dialed 911." A crackly distant voice bore into Annie's awareness. "Do you have an emergency? We are unable to fix your location."

The phone! Annie snatched it up to her ear. "Don't hang up!"

"What is the location of your emergency?" the 911 dispatcher asked.

Annie glanced around. "I don't know the address. I'm out behind the Beiler farm, where they're thinking about making the new recreation area."

"What is the nature of the emergency?"

"An explosion. I think somebody tried to blow up the big rock." Annie leaned over Karl and turned her ear to his mouth. "Karl Kramer is injured. He's breathing, but he's unconscious."

Annie pressed fingers into Karl's neck to look for a pulse.

"Help is already on the way," the dispatcher said. "Do you have any reason to believe drugs or alcohol may have played a role in this incident?"

"No. I mean, I don't think so."

"Are any weapons involved?"

"You mean other than the bomb?!" Annie's heart galloped in her chest.

"Please remain calm, ma'am. I have already dispatched an emergency team. The information you give me now will assist them when they arrive. Tell me about the victim and the injuries."

Annie took a deep breath. "Fortyish. White male, five ten, 180 pounds."

"Very good. Is he conscious yet?"

Karl moaned again. Annie put a hand against the side of his face, and his eyes

opened. Anger flared in them.

"Yes," she said into her phone. "He's coming around."

"How long was he unconscious?"

"From as soon as the bomb went off, I guess. Till now." Had it been two minutes or ten? Annie had no idea.

"Can he speak?"

"Karl, can you hear me?"

He groaned. "Whoever did this is going to pay."

Rufus threw down the reins and sprinted the final distance. Annalise was hunched over Karl Kramer. He squatted beside her and automatically put a hand on her shoulder. He expected trembling, but she was steady and strong.

"Help is coming." Annalise laid her hand on Karl's chest.

The burn marks on Karl's arms made Rufus flinch. Who could have done this?

Karl breathed heavily. "They blew me up with my own fertilizer."

"Shh. Don't upset yourself." Annalise's hand moved in a soothing circle on Karl's chest.

"It's too late." Karl rolled his eyes.

"What is he talking about?" Rufus asked.

"It's complicated," Annalise answered. "I

tried to stop him."

"You knew about this?"

"Of course not. I just figured it out a little too late. I had no idea he would be here."

"Are you all right?"

"I'm fine. Karl is what matters. We have to keep him awake."

"I am awake." Karl punctuated his words with hostility. "My arms are on fire. Somebody is going to pay."

Karl shifted his knees, as if to roll over and try to rise.

"Don't move," Annalise said, the pressure of her hand deepening against Karl's chest. "They said you shouldn't move."

"Nobody tells me what to do."

Annalise glanced at Rufus. "They said he might have a concussion. He was unconscious for several minutes."

"They aren't doctors," Karl said. "They just answer the phone."

"They're trained for emergencies. We have to follow their advice."

"They're taking their sweet time."

A siren wailed in approach.

"Karl, you listen to Annalise." Rufus spoke more sharply than he had in years. He stood up. "I'll run up to the road and flag them down."

Rufus moved through trampled weeds,

dodging trees and small boulders and holes that could reach up and twist an ankle. He saw only what the future might have been if Annalise had been a few steps closer to Karl Kramer just moments ago, and its vacant blackness sliced through him.

THIRTY-ONE

The next morning, Rufus walked out to the big rock. When his family first came to the valley and purchased hopeful acreage with a stunning view, it was not long before they discovered the big rock. They used to come for Sunday afternoon picnics. His brother Jacob was only a year old at the time of the move. One of the toddler's first recognizable utterances indicated the rock, big as half a room and flat. The field below was low-lying vegetation for which they had not known the names. His sister Ruth found a book at the library, and gradually they learned to identify the strange plants distinct from anything they had known in Pennsylvania.

Now Rufus stood on the rock and looked down on the scene. Yellow plastic tape cordoned off the space where he found Annalise with Karl Kramer yesterday.

CRIME SCENE. DO NOT CROSS.

A crime scene practically on Beiler land. Annalise was as close to being a Beiler as anyone else in the valley, and she seemed to be at the heart of whatever happened.

No one was sure what transpired. The fire department had drenched the smoldering brush to ensure a gust of spring air could not revive the flames. And though officials would not issue their written report for several days, it was clear that an explosion caused the brush fire that left a black scar below the rock.

Now everyone knew where Karl Kramer's missing fertilizer had been. But why?

And why was Annalise there?

Rufus heard a truck motor and glanced up to see Tom maneuvering his red pickup as close as he could before getting out and taking the final stretch on foot. Tom stopped at the yellow tape. Rufus waved a greeting.

"I suppose you're here with the same questions I have." Tom shielded his eyes as he looked up at Rufus.

Rufus nodded. "The area has been carefully combed."

Tom asked, "Have they questioned Annie yet?"

"I don't know. I haven't seen her today." Last night had not seemed like the time to press her for details.

"She's not going to work at the shop today, is she?"

Rufus shrugged. "You know Annalise."

Tom exhaled. "Sometimes I wonder. How about you? Have they questioned you?"

"Not officially. It's not unusual for me to go past here. I promised to give a statement today, but I know nothing especially helpful." Rufus was climbing down the side of the rock. "Do you see anything from down there?"

"I heard they found remains of a cell phone. Bits of wire." Tom kicked up dirt.

Rufus maneuvered down to the ground and began circling to where Tom stood.

Tom crossed his arms on his chest. "Someone planned this."

"But did they mean to hurt anyone? Maybe they got more than they bargained for." Rufus ran his thumb and forefinger around the brim of his hat. "Karl's being the victim — well, it is not good news for the project."

"Some would say he deserved it."

"And they would be wrong. No one deserves stepping into a bomb."

"Well, it's a good thing for Karl that whoever made this bomb didn't have a better idea what they were doing." Tom put both hands on his hips, a familiar gesture.

"Rufus, I know how much you hate getting involved in legal matters, but I don't see how you're going to dodge this one. Annie was here when it happened, and you were here moments later. The sheriff's office is not finished with either of you."

"One step at a time," Rufus said. "I'd like to see how Karl is and what he remembers. Can you drive me to Cañon City?"

Annie sat at her dining room table with a cup of strong coffee, a pad of paper, and a pen. She alternated sipping the coffee and chewing the top of the pen as she considered what she had jotted on the pad.

Carter lost his phone. More than once. So what?

What she overheard yesterday in the coffee shop was not incriminating without reading something into it.

Someone sent a message to Karl, but she did not know who.

Joel asked her to trust him. Several times. Why did she feel like she had made a mistake in doing so?

But what action could she have taken? She had no proof of anything — especially after she deleted Carter's Internet history before returning his phone.

Annie dropped the pen on the pad. She

could talk to Joel. She could talk to Carter. She could talk to Tom. She could seek out an Amish elder. She could talk to the sheriff.

"Friesen, you've lost your edge," Annie said aloud. "If you were capable of making a decision, you would have done it by now."

The knock on her front door provoked a gasp and spilled coffee. Annie scampered to the kitchen for a towel. "Coming!"

Before opening the door, she looked out the front window. Sophie Beiler stood on her front stoop, a basket in her arms. Annie opened the door.

"*Mamm* is so worried about you." Sophie offered the basket. "She's afraid you're not eating."

Annie peeked under the edge of a towel. "So she made cookies?"

"And blueberry muffins," Sophie said. "She just wants you to be okay."

"Come on in."

Sophie set the basket on the coffee table. "*Mamm* also wants to know if you called your mother. She said to tell you that this qualifies as an emergency."

"Um, no." Annie gestured that Sophie should sit down. "I'm not hurt. There's not really anything to tell."

"That's what *Mamm* said you would say. I'm supposed to insist. Where's your

phone?"

Annie patted her jeans pocket. No cell phone bulge. "I'm not sure." She glanced at an end table, then into the dining room. "I must have left it upstairs."

"Shall I get it for you?"

"No. I'll look later."

Sophie tilted her head and lifted her eyebrows.

"Okay," Annie said. "I'll look now."

Searching the small rooms upstairs did not take much time. Annie returned empty-handed.

"I lost my cell phone. That may be the first time in my life I've spoken that sentence."

"Maybe you left it at the hospital. Or in Tom's truck."

"Yes. I'll have to check around." Annie sat on the sofa across from Sophie and lifted the lid on a small box at the end of the coffee table. She extracted a note card. "I think I will just write my mother. It will be less dramatic that way, less for her to worry over."

"You know your own mother best."

Annie's hand gripped a pen and hovered over the card. "So what is everyone saying? I can imagine the buzz."

"Oh, we don't have to talk about that."

"I want to know." Sophie's hesitation made Annie more determined.

"Well, no one knows what happened. The *English* say it was the work of Amish, which is ridiculous. The Amish say it was obviously the work of the *English*. Amish are nonviolent, after all."

"But they do occasionally have to remove an obstacle in a field by force, don't they? So they can plow and harvest easily?"

"Yes, that is true."

"Amish can understand explosives without being violent toward other people."

Sophie said nothing.

"You're holding something back," Annie said. "What is it?"

Sophie raised her shoulders. "A couple of people may suspect you."

"Me!"

"You were there. You understand these things. You could have made the call that . . . that . . ."

Annie rescued Sophie from having to finish that sentence. "I was an expert in a lot of things before I came to Westcliffe, but I promise you explosives was not on the list."

"I don't believe it, of course. No one at our house does."

"I should hope not. Do you know what happened to my bicycle?"

Sophie grimaced. "Joel looked for it when he went for Dolly and the cart, but the police said it was evidence."

"Evidence of what?"

"Well, maybe not evidence. But something to investigate."

Annie slapped her torso against the back of the sofa. "Great. Now I have no transportation. I suppose they have my book, too."

"Your book?"

"I picked up a genealogy book at the library yesterday before everything happened. It came all the way from a university in Indiana. I'm sure it was in the basket."

Sophie removed the towel and nudged the basket toward Annie. "I do have one more question from *Mamm.*"

Annie reached forward and pinched a wedge out of a large chocolate cookie. "Yes?"

"Please come home with me. Lydia is shopping for a few things, so we have the buggy. *Mamm* wants to see for herself that you are all right." Sophie paused for a breath. "She thinks of you as her own daughter, you know."

Annie's throat thickened. She would be sure not to repeat Franey's sentiment in her letter to her mother.

"Please?" Sophie said. "We all want you

to come. You can stay the night."

Annie shook her head. "No, I want to sleep in my own bed."

"Supper, then." Sophie cocked her head. "Rufus should be there."

Ruth twisted her backpack around. Even though her phone was set on vibrate and tucked in a side pocket of the bag, she heard its distinct insistent tone above the rhythm of the bus pulling out of the stop. She did not have to look at the caller ID. It was Elijah Capp. This was the fifth time he had called in the last three hours.

She pulled the phone from the pocket and wrapped her fingers around it, waiting for it to stop buzzing. Elijah deserved a face-to-face conversation, but so far she had not even been able to answer his last several letters. In her mind, she crafted phrases but was dissatisfied with every version. When she found the right words, perhaps she would have the courage to put them on paper. A letter he could hold on to might encourage him more to find his own path. Or hurt him more.

The bus lumbered to the next stop. Ruth stood and slung the backpack over one shoulder, awaiting the sucking *whoosh* of the doors parting at the bottom of the

rubber-coated stairwell. The bus driver, who had been letting her off at this stop for two years, nodded a good-bye into his enormous rearview mirror. Ruth took the steps lightly, as she always did, and the doors suctioned closed behind her.

She could easily imagine what Elijah had to say. He had said everything before, after all. Perhaps she did not have anything new to say, either.

Ruth put her key in the lock of her suite and leaned into the door with one shoulder, a motion of habit. Inside, as she slid a key into the door to her room, she listened for activity in any of the other three rooms. She tossed the backpack and the keys onto her bed, with a fleeting thought that Elijah might be surprised at how thoroughly she was acclimated to the assumption that someone would try to steal her belongings.

"Boo!"

Ruth spun around and grinned. "Hi, Lauren. How is your Tuesday going?"

"I'm ready to blow this joint."

Ruth rolled her eyes and shook her head. "Do people really say that?"

"I'm people. I say it."

"What's the munitions report for the day?"

"My dad Skyped my brother today, then

called me. He hasn't blown up anything even for practice in more than three weeks. He's getting antsy."

What would Elijah think about this conversation? The peaceful plain people hardly had use for a word like *munitions,* but it tripped off Ruth's tongue almost daily now.

Lauren punched the air. "You said you were going to do this. Are you ready?"

"Well, maybe —"

"Oh, no, no, no. There will be no withdrawal tactics now. Bring your identification documents and cash for the fee. They don't take plastic."

"All right," Ruth said. "Just give me a couple minutes to freshen up."

Lauren closed the door on her way out. Ruth went to the dresser, unpinned her hair, brushed it, and pinned it up again in a matter of seconds. From her bottom desk drawer she took the required documents then fished in her backpack for her small wallet.

She flinched when her phone buzzed yet again, but she ignored it. A moment later, though, she heard the notification that someone had left a message.

Elijah would no sooner leave a message on a phone than he would drive a car.

But he had. Something was wrong. She

just knew it. She lifted the phone to look at the screen. Four unanswered calls. A rock formed in the pit of her stomach.

Finally Ruth accessed her voice mail. The rock turned hot. "Lauren!"

Joel was not there for supper. Annie heard the sigh in Eli's voice after the silent prayer at the beginning of the meal.

"He'll come around," Franey said softly in Pennsylvania Dutch. "He must."

Eli scowled into the bowl of peas and carrots.

Rufus was missing as well. As much as she loved Franey — and the whole Beiler family — Annie could not help but be disappointed.

"He went with Tom to see Karl." Franey seemed to read Annie's mind as she passed the mashed potatoes. "They've been gone most of the day."

Annie nodded and held the bowl of potatoes while Jacob served himself.

"Don't take more than you'll eat," Franey cautioned her youngest.

After supper, Sophie and Lydia were clearing the table, having refused Annie's offer of help, so Annie took her unfinished note card to the living room. Determined to tell her parents the truth about what hap-

pened, she did not want to be dramatic. Just the facts. She was still chewing on the top of her pen with the note in her lap when she heard Tom's truck. With a glance toward the empty dining room, Annie crossed to the front door and met Rufus on the porch.

On Saturday he kissed her, after months of holding back. On Sunday he drove her home with murmurs of assurance that Beth Stutzman meant nothing to him. Yesterday he held her hand in the ambulance and all the way home in Tom's truck. It all felt so long ago. She wished she could run into his arms now, feel his heartbeat, his hand at the back of her neck. Perhaps he would take her home again. He could let Dolly slow her pace, as he held the reins with one hand and her fingers with the other.

He gave her a tired smile. "Hi."

"Hi," Annie said. "How is Karl?"

"Okay. It won't be long till he's released. The burns looked worse than they are." Rufus leaned against the house, next to the door. The porch light spilled over him. "At least that's what the nurse said when she came in to change the dressings. I doubt she was supposed to tell us even that much."

"Did he say what happened? Why he was there?"

Rufus shook his head. "The nurse said

someone from the sheriff's office had been there, but Karl was asleep from the pain medication."

"He sounded really angry yesterday," Annie said.

Rufus nodded. "He still is, when he's awake. He's not going to let go of this."

"Can you blame him? Somebody put him in the hospital. He has a right to know what happened."

Her words hung in the air, and she regretted them. This was Rufus. Last year somebody put Rufus in the hospital — probably Karl Kramer — and Rufus had let it go. Only pride, *hochmut*, demanded rights. Humility, *demut*, did not.

Annie stifled a groan. She was never going to learn to be Amish at this rate.

Rufus closed a hand over the fist that held her pen. "What are you writing?"

"A note to my parents. I have to tell them, but I am not ready for a phone call."

"I understand. Just be sure to sign the note."

She tilted her head, questioning.

"I suppose I will have to tell the police about the note I received." Rufus scratched the back of one ear.

Annie's pulse pounded. "What note?"

He squeezed her fingers. "One that I

suspect is very similar to the one that prompted Karl to go out to the rock."

"Rufus! Why didn't you say something last night?"

"Too much was going on. And I don't have the note. It blew out of the buggy on my way out to the rock — before I realized it could be important."

"Who would want to hurt both Karl and you?" Not Joel. Certainly not Joel. Holes like Joel made swiss cheese of Annie's flimsy theory.

She savored the sensation of his hand around hers. If someone was trying to hurt Rufus, her investigation was far from over.

Thirty-Two

March 1778

"We never clear this part of *Grossmuder*'s garden. Why are we doing it this year?"

Jacob looked at his son. At thirteen, the boy had recently announced he no longer wanted to be Jacob Franklin, but simply Franklin. The decision amused Jacob and Katie, but they made the transition with surprising ease. Franklin hoarded pamphlets published by Benjamin Franklin no matter what the topic. Over the winter he seemed to grow four inches in his arms and legs and now was almost as tall as Jacob.

Jacob reached down with a broad hand and pulled out a tangle of withered bindweed from summers past. "It's too overgrown. We should have done this years ago." He filled both arms with weeds and heaped them on a pile he would burn later.

"Are we going to plant this part?" Franklin wanted to know.

"Maybe. When I was a boy we used to grow beets in this section." Maria's beets. That was what it had been. Jacob made no effort to hide from his children that he had a sister who disappeared decades ago, but rarely did anyone speak her name.

"I don't much like beets." Franklin yanked on a vine that was as long as he was tall.

"We don't have to plant beets. It's up to *Grossmuder.* Even if she does not want to plant anything, we should clean it up."

Franklin straightened and gestured down the hill. "Were you really born in that old cabin?"

"Yes, I was. My parents felt fortunate to have that shelter in the homesteading days." Jacob used the structure to store assorted farm tools now.

"And now we're a new country!" Franklin wrapped a thick, thorny, knee-high weed with a rag then gripped it with both hands and pulled. The weed surrendered its existence. He held it up. "I got the whole root." Franklin tossed it on the burn pile.

Jacob smiled and nodded.

"That's what we have to do with the British," Franklin said. "We have to get rid of the whole lot of them. As soon as I'm old enough, I'm going to fight."

Jacob sincerely hoped the fighting would

be over long before Franklin could enlist, though he had heard of boys as young as fifteen finding a place in the militia. Franklin's voice had already deepened, and he had the height of a man.

"Do not glamorize war," Jacob said. "It is ugly business."

"But it's your business, isn't it?" Franklin yanked another weed. "It seems to me, it's the business of all red-blooded American men some way or another."

"Men," Jacob said, "not boys. You are thirteen and needed on the farm."

"I won't always be thirteen."

"And I hope there won't always be a war."

"We have to win, *Daed*. We can't stop until we win."

Jacob knelt and raked his fingers through the earth of a square yard cleared of weeds. Enough talk of war. "It's warm enough and the soil is soft enough. We should turn the earth once we get it cleared."

"Today?"

Jacob heard the implicit moan in his son's question, but he ignored it. "Go on down to the old cabin and get rakes and shovels."

"Yes, sir." As reluctant as he sounded, Franklin did as he was told.

Jacob let dirt sift through the fingers of both hands. The weeds were coming out

easily enough. Whether or not he had really seen Maria on that rainy afternoon nearly four years ago, it was time to reclaim the plot of land where she talked to her beets whenever she felt anxious.

"Daed!"

The cry startled Jacob to his feet. This was not the timbre of a boy calling information to his father over a field. Jacob sprinted across the clearing and crashed down the hill to the cabin. Jacob saw what had caused his son to halt about ten yards short of the cabin. Wrapped in a man's wool coat and beaver fur hat, a form slumped against the door.

"We'd better see who it is," Jacob said.

The form moved and slowly stood. The hat dropped away in the process, and the coat fell open.

She was thin and pale and thirty years older, but her black curls tumbled as they always had. Her visage lacked the fullness of the image in Jacob's memory. If her face looked this thin, he hated to think how lean the rest of her must be. The baggy men's breeches made it hard to tell.

"Maria!"

Her eyes widened in surprise. "Jacobli, is that you?"

He folded her into his arms, breath to

speak gone from him.

"Daed?" she whispered in his ear.

"Gone."

He felt her shoulders drop, even under the heavy coat.

"How long ago?" she asked.

"Nearly seven years."

She pulled back from him, shaking her head slowly, her curls jostling. "I never heard."

How could she have known? No one in the family knew where to find her — or whether she wanted to be found. Relief at seeing her alive flushed through him, but why had she come now?

"The boy is yours?" Maria said.

"My eldest. Jacob Franklin."

"Just Franklin." The boy's voice bore an irritated edge.

"Franklin," Jacob said, "meet your *aunti* Maria."

Maria laughed. "I like your name."

Jacob had always relished Maria's laugh above all his siblings'. He grinned broadly.

Franklin eyed the visitor cautiously. "She's one of the Amish aunts, right?"

Jacob looked toward Maria. "I guess not anymore."

"Not for a long time." Maria's eyes moved from Jacob to Franklin. "Someday I will

introduce you to Mr. Benjamin Franklin, if you like."

Franklin gawked, making his father chuckle briefly. Jacob squinted as if to focus on the details of his sister's presence.

"Are you injured?" Jacob asked.

She shook her head, curls floating free. "Just weary."

"Franklin," Jacob said, "go up to the big house and get your *grossmuder*."

"Yes, sir." Franklin turned and started up the hill.

Maria's face was a question.

"Yes," Jacob said. "Elizabeth still lives. You must see her."

Maria sucked in a breath. "After all this time, why would she want to see me?"

"Because she loves you."

"I would understand if she never forgave me."

"If you think that, you have forgotten who she is."

"I thought I would find Christian here," Maria said.

"Ah. Forgiveness may not be as forthcoming from him."

"Where is he?"

"He moved to the Conestoga Valley years ago. Many of the Amish did. Their land here in Berks County was worth a considerable

amount after they made real farms of the wilderness. They made enough money to start again in Lancaster County, farther from the frontier."

"Bar-bar and Anna? And Lisbetli?"

"Barbara and Anna also have gone to Lancaster County with their husbands," Jacob said. "As far as I know they are well. The names of their grandchildren make a long list. Even a few great-grandchildren have come along."

Jacob reached for Maria's hand, and she gave it to him. He breathed several times as he gathered his words. "Lisbetli went on to eternity. She is buried beside your mother. And *Daed.*"

"But she was the youngest!" Maria keened, sinking slowly to her knees as her wail let loose.

Jacob weighted her shoulder with both of his hands, feeling the pulse of her sobs.

Finally she looked up. "What happened?"

"She birthed a child and did not recover."

"And the babe?"

Jacob hated to dishearten Maria's hope. He shook his head. "She fell ill when she was very young. She lies beside Lisbetli."

Maria stood up and wiped tears with the back of one hand, wandering a few paces from Jacob. "I've missed so much."

Jacob's heart swelled in his chest in the midst of this stunning conversation. Maria was the lost piece in the Byler family. He had to ask the obvious question. "Why have you come now?"

Maria met his gaze. Her voice, when it came, was small. "I am exhausted. I wanted to come home."

"And you have." Jacob closed the few steps between them and wrapped his arms around Maria again. She had not gotten much taller than he remembered — though he had grown from a little boy. The top of her head against his chest did not even reach his chin.

Footsteps disturbed their embrace. Jacob stepped back and turned his sister around. Elizabeth stood at the base of the hill, breathless with disbelieving eyes.

THIRTY-THREE

"Are we almost finished?" Annie set her jaw and glared at the officer on Wednesday morning. "I have to work today."

"Just a few more questions." The officer consulted his notes. "Did you see the note you say Karl Kramer received?"

"I didn't say he got a note. He says he got a note. No, I did not see it."

"And the one Mr. Beiler received? Did you see that one?"

Annie straightened in her chair. "No."

"But you were aware he received one?"

"He told me last night. I didn't know on Monday."

The officer twisted both lips to one side. "Do you have any knowledge of who wrote the notes?"

"No, I do not." Annie slumped. He was fishing. She was itching to get out of the sheriff's office and do some fishing of her own. If she turned up any proof, she would

360

be back.

The officer tapped his pen on his note-pad.

Annie opened her arms, palms up. "May I please have my bicycle? I'd like to be on my way."

"I'm afraid that's not possible."

"Why not?"

"We're not finished with it. That's why." He barely looked up from his paperwork.

"What exactly do you need the bike for?"

"We found assorted tire tracks on the scene."

"The hill was too steep. I left the bike at the bottom. I told you all this." Frustration brewed in her gut.

"When we're finished with the bicycle, you'll be the first to know."

Annie spied the interlibrary loan volume in between a notepad and a file folder. "May I at least have my library book back? Do you have any idea what the fine is for losing an interlibrary loan? Surely you don't think an old history book is complicit in the explosion."

"Sarcasm will get you nowhere, Ms. Friesen."

She scowled and met his gaze. Without taking his eyes off her, the officer reached to one side and extracted the book from the

stack of paperwork.

"We'll be in touch," he said.

Annie grabbed the book before he could change his mind. "Find out who hurt Karl Kramer. It wasn't me."

She pulled the note to her parents from her back pocket and marched down Main Street to the post office. With a groan she realized she had just missed the daily mail pickup.

Annie shoved the note through the letter opening, scowled, and set her course for the shop.

"You can't let this go on, Rufus."

Rufus tapped the cabinet hinge with the rubber mallet. "Mo, I know the explosion rattled everyone. I cannot control the way people feel. Perhaps they just need time."

"Don't be silly. People listen to you."

"I'm a simple Amish cabinetmaker." He nudged the hinge once more.

"Marv Hatfield said he wants to drop out. If we lose Marv, we lose both his sons."

Rufus dropped his mallet into his toolbox and wiped his hands on a rag. He was installing cabinets in a newly constructed home. Mo was not even supposed to be on the premises. Rufus glanced around, relieved that the general contractor was

nowhere in sight.

"Alicia Paxton is the environmental guru of the whole town," Mo said, "and she thinks it's dangerous to proceed."

"I'm sorry to hear that."

"So do something before we lose every cent of funding along with all the donated labor."

"It only happened the day before yesterday," Rufus said. "We have to wait for things to settle down. The sheriff will find whoever was behind it. Perhaps people will reconsider then."

"They think it's because of the Amish, that they set the bomb."

Rufus raised an eyebrow under the brim of his hat. "It is not our way to make bombs out of fertilizer and a cell phone."

"People are saying it was a bad idea to join forces, that it's better if the Amish and the *English* live separately."

"That is the Amish way, after all," Rufus said.

"How can you say that? You've been behind this joint project all along."

"I still am. But it is true that it has been our way to live separately for hundreds of years."

"Are you dropping out, too?" Mo widened her stance, a hand on her hip.

"I promise to talk to them." Rufus set aside the thought of Ike Stutzman's vehement opposition. "But I am not going to move forward without Karl."

Mo groaned. "Oh, Rufus, why can't you let that go? If we hadn't involved Karl, maybe the explosion would not have happened in the first place."

"The man has burns all over his arms and neck."

"I know. And I feel bad for him, as rotten as he is. But we can't risk the project for him."

"We have time," Rufus said. "While Karl is healing, we'll keep talking."

Mo sucked in her lips. "You don't think Tom Reynolds will back out, do you?"

Rufus adjusted the tilt of his hat. "I couldn't say."

By Wednesday afternoon Annie's cell phone had been missing for two days. She picked up the telephone in the shop and dialed Tom's number. No, he had not seen her phone in his truck.

She hung up and pulled a phone book from beneath the counter, found the number, and dialed the hospital in Cañon City. Following a system of automated prompts, she finally reached a nurse in the emergency

room who left her on hold so long Annie was about to hang up and start over again. In the end, though, the lost and found box did not yield Annie's phone, either.

The shop door jangled, and Annie switched to customer alert mode. But rather than customers, Mark and Luke Stutzman entered.

"Our *mamm* asked us to see what you've decided to keep in the shop," Mark said.

Annie gestured to the shelf Mrs. Weichert had arranged. "The blackberry jam does well, and the embroidered pillowcases."

"I'll tell Beth. She is the one who makes the pillowcases."

Of course she was. Miss Perfect Stitches. Annie forced a smile. "Well, if she has more, I'm sure Mrs. Weichert would like to have them. They've been popular."

"We can take anything that is in your way," Mark said.

"Mrs. Weichert is not here, but I'll look in the back room."

Annie crossed the store, vaguely aware that the boys were following at their own pace. In the storeroom, she riffled through Edna Stutzman's crates.

Well, Edna's work and Beth's. Maybe the other girls had contributed something, but Annie suspected the superior stitchery that

customers had been admiring was Beth's. A full-sized quilt had lasted barely two days on display, despite a price even Annie thought was outrageous.

Some pot holders and small wooden toys had not sold, and Mrs. Weichert had returned them to the back room. Annie placed them in a crate and applied her own discretion to finish filling it. The sound of shuffling just beyond the door told her the boys had finally come to the back of the shop, where she knew they would wait politely. She picked up the crate, pausing to gain a firm grip.

The boys were speaking rapid Pennsylvania Dutch to each other. Annie strained to understand something. She had been hearing this language in the Beiler home and around tables after church services for eight months, and if pressed, she was capable of bits of polite conversation with speakers who indulged her with a reduced speed. But the words spewed too swiftly from the boys. Annie understood only fragments that did not seem to connect logically.

But one word was unmistakable, and she heard it four times.

Joel.

And another. *Phone.*

Behind Annie, the building's back door

opened to a rush of spring air.

"I saw the buggy," Mrs. Weichert said. "I figured the boys were here."

"I was just gathering some things that aren't selling."

Mrs. Weichert ran a hand over the contents of the crate. "You've chosen well. I'll talk to them." She took the crate from Annie's arms.

At the back of the shop, the boys switched to polite English.

The shop's phone rang, and Annie moved to the counter to answer it.

"Come get your bike," the caller said. "We're finished with it."

THIRTY-FOUR

Annie lowered her bicycle to the ground in the same spot where she had left it two days ago. She took the hill faster this time, curious to see what the spot looked like now that the crime scene tape was gone. Finding her lost phone among the singed brush seemed unlikely, but she had nothing to lose by looking.

She stood on the hill, staring at the rock, and wondering what the boys could have thought they were accomplishing by trying to blast out a chunk of the hillside with a homemade bomb.

Unless they accomplished exactly what they intended.

She hated to think any of them were capable of hurting Karl — and certainly not Joel. It just did not make sense.

Annie kicked around in the dirt. Rain the previous evening had wiped out footprints and washed blackened brush into stripes

down the incline. She set her feet squarely in the place where Karl Kramer had lain, and memory sparked. Her hand had still clenched the phone when she boarded the ambulance. She had it when she answered questions in the emergency room. After that, she was unsure.

Wandering back toward her bike, Annie wondered if the sheriff's officers had found anything useful among the footprints and tire tracks that had crowded the ground. Sophie's revelation that Annie was under suspicion for the explosion simmered in her mind. When Annie reached her bike, she yanked it up with fresh determination. If Joel had something to do with this, she was going to find out. And for Carter's sake, Annie hoped that what she suspected was not true.

Securing her helmet, Annie put the bike in motion and let gravity pull her down the slope and back on the main road. Hours of daylight remained at this time of year, plenty of time to pedal to the storage site and look for anything that might have changed since the last time she was there. Grateful to be on pavement again rather than in the uneven brush of the hillside, Annie pedaled harder.

Lost in her thoughts, she did not hear the

car approach from behind. She felt its wind as it whizzed by — a little too close for comfort — and she gripped her handlebars more firmly.

It was a blue Prius, just like the one she used to own. The vehicle slowed ahead of her, and in watching it, Annie lost her concentration. She strayed off the pavement onto the gravel shoulder, where she lost her balance. Putting out one foot, Annie managed to avoid toppling, but it was not a gracious moment. She got off the bike and pushed out her breath. Ahead of her, the blue Prius stopped abruptly on the side of the road.

The driver's door opened. Ruth Beiler got out. Annie grinned.

"Whatever you were thinking about the crazy driver, you can keep to yourself." Ruth beamed and dangled the car key. "It's all true, but just don't say it."

"You're driving!" Annie laid the bike down to embrace her friend with both arms. "I assume you're doing it the legal way."

Ruth laughed. "Of course." She pulled her wallet out of her skirt pocket and extracted a long rectangle of paper. "The State of Colorado made it official yesterday."

Annie glanced at the car. "Yesterday? And

you drove all the way down here by your-self?"

"When I heard what happened, I knew I had to."

Ruth bent her head in toward Annalise, admiring the sheet of paper that gave her the freedom to stand on this road at this time.

"My friend Lauren gave me driving les-sons," she said. "I was nervous about taking the road test, but she said I was ready."

"And she was right!" Annalise leaned against Ruth's shoulder. "I'm so glad to see you. Does your mother know you're com-ing?"

Ruth shook her head. "Only Elijah knows."

"Elijah?"

"He called and told me what happened to Karl, and that you and Rufus were there."

"It wasn't really an emergency. Rufus and I are fine."

"Elijah didn't know that when he called. He just knew you were at the hospital. I think it rattled him that it happened at . . . our rock."

"I didn't know you were speaking to Elijah these days."

Ruth looked away. "I'm not. Not exactly."

"What does 'not exactly' mean?"

A car rumbled past, and Ruth step farther off the side of the road. "Elijah writes, and I don't answer. I did for a while, but it's wrong, so I stopped."

"Why is it wrong?"

Ruth shook her head. "It can't be anything. I was not fair to him when I left on our baptism day. He only got baptized because he thought I was going to do it, and then I left. Now he's baptized, and we can't be together."

"Are you sure?"

"I'm going tell him once and for all."

Annalise tilted her head to one side. "You've said that before."

Ruth kicked a rock. "I know. But it's wrong. I have to stop it before we do something Elijah would have to confess to the elders."

"You're trying to protect him?"

Ruth nodded.

"Because you care for him?"

Reluctantly, Ruth nodded again. She hoped Annalise would not comment on the blush that that warmed her face and neck.

"Elijah is a grown man," Annalise said. "He can make his own choices."

"I don't want him to choose to leave because of me any more than Rufus wants

you to choose to become Amish because of him."

"This sounds like a conversation that shouldn't be happening on the side of the road."

"Why are you here, anyway?" Ruth asked, pointing down the lonely highway.

"I lost my phone."

"And?"

"And I just wanted to go back and see where it happened again. I'm trying to make sense of it. I have pieces, but they don't add up."

"Where are you going now?"

Annalise hesitated, but Ruth waited.

"Well," Annalise said, "since you have your driver's license and a car, maybe you'd like to give me a ride."

"Anywhere," Ruth answered. "What about the bike?"

"I happen to know how to put the backseat down in that car. We'll jam it in somehow."

Ruth followed Annalise toward the Prius, where Annalise swiftly pulled a couple of levers.

"Are you sure about this?"

Annie pushed the car door closed and glanced across the open space ahead of

them. "Sorry to drag you so far off the road, but I knew the Prius could handle it."

"I'm sure you know more about the car than I do," Ruth said, "but what are we looking for?"

"I'm not sure. Clues."

"Clues?"

"Just follow me."

"Why did we have to park in the trees?"

"You'll see."

Annie led the way, hearing the hesitancy in Ruth's steps.

"I don't think I've ever been here before," Ruth said. "How can that be?"

"I think that's what they're counting on."

"Who's 'they'?"

"I hope I'm wrong, but I have to be sure."

After a couple of minutes, the fenced area came into view, still covered in thick plastic sheeting. "I think Karl Kramer uses this place for storage," Annie said.

"It doesn't seem very convenient," Ruth observed.

"That's one of the pieces I haven't figured out." Annie scanned the area for guys in hard hats. "The coast is clear."

They circled around, while Annie tried to remember where the loose flap was that had given her access the last time.

"Annalise, I'm not sure about this," Ruth

whispered.

"Here." Annie punched a hand through a slit, pushed aside thick plastic, and ducked through the fence. "Coming, Ruth?"

Ruth's head appeared. "What is this place?"

"Hurry up." Annie reached out and tugged on Ruth's wrist.

"Ow!"

"Shh."

"What are we doing here, Annalise?"

"There has to be something here."

"Like what?"

"Just look for something that doesn't belong."

Annie dragged her fingers along a pile of flooring underlayment and a carton of four nail guns. Next were two rolls of plush gray carpet and neat upright row of windows in three sizes, and beyond that a half dozen enormous rolls of black roof sheeting. A skid of concrete blocks seemed especially out of place. Ruth had taken her own path through the maze of construction supplies. Annie could see the top of her head as she moved along a makeshift aisle.

"Ruth? Are you finding anything?"

No answer.

"Ruth?"

"You'd better come here."

THIRTY-FIVE

Annie hustled around a stack of two-by-fours to kneel beside Ruth. "What is it?"

Ruth's arm was wedged between piles of three-inch PVC pipes banded in sets of six. When she pulled it out, her hand gripped a neatly folded cloth. When Ruth unfolded it on the ground, Annie saw that it was a shirt — an Amish shirt. Between its layers was a small case holding four small chisels.

"Joel's shirt!" Ruth said softly.

"Are you sure?"

Ruth nodded. "I remember the fabric. It was the only time *Mamm* tried dyeing cloth herself. She wasn't happy with the irregular color. She just made the one shirt. The rest went into quilts."

Annie fingered the fabric between thumb and forefinger. "The quilt on your bed has some of this."

"Right. Jacob's quilt, too."

"I think these tools belong to Rufus." An-

nie put the thought out of her mind that Beth Stutzman knew more about chisels than she did.

Ruth nodded. "He uses them for fine work."

"He replaced the set the last time he went to the Springs because he couldn't find it." Annie put her hand under the shirt so she could take the tools without touching them, wondering if fingerprints could be lifted from steel. She was not taking any chances. She folded the shirt around the set again. "We can go now."

"What are you going to do?"

"I have to talk to Joel."

"But Joel wouldn't have anything to do with the explosion."

Annie saw the protest in her friend's eyes, even in the dimness of the plastic shelter. "I'm afraid that remains to be seen."

Annie asked Ruth to drop her off at the end of the field where Joel was supposed to be working. Together they lifted the bicycle out of the Prius.

"Shouldn't I come with you?" Ruth said.

"I think it's less complicated if I go alone."

"Well, if you're sure . . ."

"Go on to the house," Annie urged. "Your *mamm* will be glad to see you."

Ruth winced. "Not if I show up in a car."

"I told her I gave you my car."

"That's different from seeing me actually driving it."

"You have to tell her eventually."

Ruth nodded. "Right now, though, I want to go find Elijah. Don't tell anyone you saw me."

"Okay." Annie reached out and squeezed Ruth's hand. "Find a way to tell me how your talk goes."

Annie watched Ruth strap herself into the car and navigate carefully back to the road. Then she put the bundle in the basket on her bicycle and began to pedal across the field.

She found Joel right where he was supposed to be, kneeling to inspect a row of alfalfa that would be ready for harvest in a few more weeks. He stood as she approached. Annie took the shirt from the basket and laid her bike down.

Joel reached for the garment, and Annie moved it out of his grasp. "I'll be curious to hear what you have to say about this."

"It's an old shirt that *Mamm* gave to Edna for her boys," Joel said. "I have nothing to say anything about it."

Annie opened the shirt and revealed the

378

tools. "How can you not say anything about this?"

"I am not accountable to you, Annalise." His eyes hardened.

"Would you rather explain this to the elders?" It was the worst threat Annie could think of at the moment.

Joel was unflapped. "I asked you to trust me, Annalise. I thought you did."

"That was before a bomb went off, and before I found your brother's missing tools."

"Why were you looking?"

Annie pressed her lips together and blew her breath out her nose. "I was there, remember? I was the one who saw what happened to Karl Kramer. I was the one checking to see if he was breathing. That gives me some rights."

"Rights. Not very Amish of you."

"A man has been injured, Joel. Give me a reason not to go straight to the police with what I suspect." Annie wrapped the shirt around the tools and used the sleeves to tie a vicious knot.

"Suspicions are all you have. What you need is a confession." Joel put one hand on the bundle. "I will fix this. I just need a little more time." He spread his fingers to take the shirt from her.

She snatched it back. "How much time?"

Joel looked up and swallowed hard. "Three days."

"Everyone hopes the police will get to the bottom of things before then. Including me."

Joel spread his hands. "I might not need three days."

"I don't know if ultimatums are very Amish, either, but here's the deal." She untied the sleeve knot, opened the case, and removed the smallest chisel. "You get the shirt and the case. And three days. If you don't fix this by Saturday, then I will."

The moment Ruth pulled off the highway onto Main Street, she regretted the decision to drive into town. Old habits tugged. In fine weather, she and Elijah used to walk into town on any errand they could scrounge up in exchange for the miles of conversation. In chill or damp, they took a buggy and often Jacob. Periodically they would turn their heads toward each other in shy smiles. Their mothers seemed not to mind the hours they spent together. And why should they? Ruth and Elijah were sixteen when they found the wideness of their common ground — old enough to think of marriage. If their mothers had known how often they spoke of life beyond

Amish bonds, they might have been less generous in assigning errands in town.

Ruth was startled by how much it pleased her to have a car. And a driver's license. These possessions made this trip into town inaugural. Until Annalise's gift of the Prius, Ruth never entertained car ownership. She still thought of herself as living plain. But now she would save hours every week by not having to arrange her life according to bus schedules, and she could go wherever she decided to go.

And that was the very thing that made owning a car objectionable to her own people. Independence of will. Pride of ownership. Ruth gripped the steering wheel, determined that driving a car would enrich her life, rather than subsume it.

She drove the length of Westcliffe's primary street, turning around only when she reached the sign that welcomed her to the adjoining community of Silver Cliff. Even before she glanced at the dashboard clock, Ruth knew she had most of an hour before she was supposed to meet Elijah. She could not bring herself to get out of the car, though. If she spoke to anyone, the conversation would drive straight to awkward and complicated. The *English* shopkeepers would assume she was more like them now

than she actually was. Amish neighbors would say nothing impolite, but their lips would press together in disapproval.

Ruth made a series of left turns that took her to the short street Annalise lived on. She parked and turned off the engine in front of the narrow green house. She was not sorry she had come to see for herself that Annalise was all right. She had been calling Annalise's phone for two days and getting no answer, so finding Annalise on her bicycle on the side of the highway liberated her from what she had let herself imagine. A lost phone was all that kept Annalise from quelling Ruth's fears herself. And it was right to speak to Elijah face-to-face and impress upon him that he must stop contacting her. She only hoped she would be strong enough when she sat beside him on the rock.

And then there was Joel. Annalise had refused to allow Ruth to stay with her to confront Joel together. Ruth's imagination could not conjure a believable explanation for the tools wrapped in Joel's shirt. And Joel certainly had no business amid the stored construction supplies.

Ruth pushed the button that lowered the driver's side window a couple of inches. Fresh air blew across her face. Closing her

eyes, she leaned her head back, imagining being with Elijah in just a few minutes with the words in her mind still too unformed to speak.

A rap on the window startled her.

Ruth sat up straight, straining against the seat belt, and saw her little brother's face pressed against the glass.

"Jacob!"

"See, *Mamm,*" Jacob said, "it is Ruth."

Ruth released the seat belt and got out of the car. She knelt and let Jacob wrap his arms around her neck.

"He insisted he saw Annalise's car on Main Street," Franey said. "He was halfway down the block before I caught him. Then he said it was you in the car, not Annalise."

Ruth stood, stifling regret. "Hello, *Mamm.*" She stepped forward to kiss her mother's cheek.

"So you are driving." Franey shifted a shopping bag to one hip.

"Yes."

"When I heard that Annalise gave you the car, I was not sure you would accept it."

"It was a gift. I would not want to be ungracious." Ruth scratched a temple.

"You know I am very fond of Annalise, but I am afraid she does not understand that she is complicating your life with such

a gift, rather than simplifying it."

"I am already finding it to be a practical gift."

"You have always said you would remain plain at heart even though you want to live and work outside our community." Franey's shoulders dropped as she moved her head slowly from side to side.

"I still feel that way."

"But driving a car, Ruth. I don't understand." Franey wrapped both arms around the sack.

Jacob tugged at the back door. "Can I have a ride?"

"Jacob, no." Franey put a firm hand on her son's shoulder and pulled him away from the car. "Ruth may have her reasons, but this has nothing to do with you."

"Maybe another time," Ruth said.

"Please don't encourage him," Franey said.

"Maybe Ruth can drive us home," Jacob said. "Then we won't have to wait for *Daed.* He's taking a long time."

"Jacob, be patient. We should wait for your father to finish at the hardware store." Franey glanced back toward Main Street. "The house is open, of course. Ruth can go on ahead and we'll see her for supper."

Ruth winced. "I'm sorry, *Mamm.* I can't

stay. I only came to be sure Annalise was all right. Elijah told me what happened. I'll speak with him, and then I have to go home. I have to be at work at six in the morning."

Ruth appreciated her mother's effort to smile through her disappointment.

"I'll come again soon, *Mamm*. The car will make it so much easier to come back more often."

"Next time I want a ride!" Jacob said.

Ruth stroked the back of his head. "We'll see what *Mamm* says."

"Let's go, Jacob," Franey said. "Maybe your *daed* has something for you to carry."

" 'Bye, Ruth!" Jacob waved and started trotting up the street. Franey followed.

Ruth sank back into the driver's seat. Every choice she made seemed to dishearten her mother. Her thoughts turned to Elijah. She had to face him and disappoint him as well.

He was waiting for her on the rock. He sat at the front ledge with his legs dangling, and she approached from behind. His stocky frame tilted back, his weight on his hands a few inches behind his shoulders. Suspenders striped his white shirt, and the black hat on his head was slightly off tilt, as it usually was.

She loved him.

But he deserved a better love, one that did not tear his life apart.

As she hoisted herself up the final incline and onto the rock's flatness, he heard her. He dropped one shoulder, turned his head, and grinned.

"Hello." Ruth stood on the rock, looking at the scar on the ground below them. "Were they really trying to blow up our rock?"

"No one knows for sure, since no one knows who was behind the explosion."

"It's been three days." Ruth moved toward the center of the boulder. "What's taking so long?"

"It's a small town. You cannot go around making accusations until you are sure. That kind of damage can never be undone."

"I suppose not." Ruth did not like to think of anyone accusing Joel of anything — and certainly not this.

Elijah pushed up to his feet and stood beside her. "I'm glad you came."

Ruth slid a step away from him. "Elijah, I don't want to hurt you."

"Then don't. Don't say it."

"We can't keep going around this circle pretending that there will be a happy ending."

"We can have a happy ending if we want it."

"You know it's not that simple. If we're not careful, we'll be the ones causing damage that cannot be undone. I should know. I seem to be pretty good at it already."

"Don't chastise yourself." Elijah reached out and touched her elbow.

"Elijah, please."

He moved closer, wrapping his arms around her. She buried her face in his neck and let the tears come. The security of him. The warmth of him. The scent of him. The sureness of him. When he put his thumb under her chin to tilt it up, she did not resist. Could not resist.

The kiss lasted a long time. Finally Ruth pushed away.

"We should not be doing this."

"I love you, Ruth. There's never going to be anyone else."

"Yes, there will — but not as long as we have anything to do with each other. It's not fair to think we can be friends. And it's outrageous to think we can be anything more. If you can get me out of your mind, you would have a chance to find the kind of love you can build a life on."

"How do you know what I want, Ruth? How do you know what I'm willing to do?

387

Do you think you are the only strong one?"

"I'm not sure that what I did was strong, Elijah. If I were strong, would I be here now? Would I have wanted you to kiss me?"

"Ruth, you've punished yourself enough over the last two years. You can stop."

"I'm not punishing myself," she insisted. "I only want the best for you. I don't want you to go through what I've been through, and I can't come back. I'm not coming back. You have to accept that."

"I do accept it."

She met his eyes, dark and probing. "No," she said. "I will not be the reason. Please don't write to me, Elijah. Don't call. It's best this way."

THIRTY-SIX

March 1778

"Mamm," Jacob said, "Maria has come home."

When she did not answer immediately, apprehension flashed like lightning. Jacob felt it, and then it was gone. Whatever questions roiled in his mother, she would not turn her back on Maria.

He glanced at his half sister, who seemed less certain of Elizabeth's forgiveness.

Elizabeth's face contorted its way from blanched to flushed. "I remember the day you came in the bookshop with your father and Lisbetli. You were five years old."

Maria laughed nervously. "More than forty years ago. Lisbetli chose you before the rest of us did."

"Both of you were beautiful little girls, and I wanted nothing more than to stand alongside your father and watch you grow into women."

Jacob heard the breath go out of Maria. "I told *Daed* we would see you again," she said.

"I waited for you to come back to the shop then, and I've waited again all this time."

When his mother and sister were in each other's arms — sobbing — Jacob breathed his own sigh of relief. He turned to his son, who had watched the interchange with his mouth hanging half-open.

"Franklin, go get your mother. Use the wagon to bring everybody up here quickly."

"Everybody?" Maria echoed. "How many are there?"

"Four boys, two girls," Jacob answered. In another situation, he might have mirrored the polite inquiry with one of his own. But he would have to save his curiosity about Maria's family for another time. "Go, Franklin."

The boy turned and scuttled down the hill.

"Come, Maria," Elizabeth said, "let's go to the house."

An hour later, Jacob confined himself to the main room of his mother's house, savoring the comforting presence of his children. He sat in the chair nearest the fire to be sure none of the little ones came too near the grate. Catherine nestled in his lap, and the baby dozed in the same cradle Jacob

himself had slept in so long ago. Joseph's two children squabbled at his feet, but Jacob paid no mind. He was listening to the sounds coming from the kitchen, where Elizabeth heated water over the small hearth for the tub and Maria gasped with delight at the luxury of a hot, unhurried bath. Jacob's wife, Katie, and Joseph's wife, Hannah, huddled in the kitchen looking for ways to be helpful.

Katie came out of the kitchen and glanced around. "Where's Franklin?"

"I sent him to ride out to John's and find David in the north field." Jacob paused to plant a kiss on top of Catherine's head. "Getting a message to Sarah is more complicated. And Joseph? I don't know where he is."

"We haven't had a letter since before Valley Forge," Katie said. She wiped her hands on her apron. "Hannah tries not to show it, but she's frantic."

"How's Maria?"

Katie laughed, the sound that cracked Jacob's heart open every time.

"Underneath all those clothes was a layer of dirt thick as window glass," she said. "But it's coming off little by little."

"I hope she'll tell us her story."

"Don't rush her, Jacob. She's been gone

thirty years. She will need time."

Her counsel was wise as always, and Jacob nodded.

"I'm on my way upstairs to find her a dress," Katie said. "Your *mamm* says Sarah leaves a couple of work dresses here. Maria is too short for Elizabeth's clothes."

Another thirty minutes passed before Maria appeared in the main room, shyly tugging at a faded calico dress that hid her thinness. A girlish ribbon at the base of her neck temporarily tamed her long black hair. Behind her, Katie, Hannah, and Elizabeth stood like ladies in waiting. Jacob rose to greet the entourage.

"I have not worn a dress like this in a long time," she said. "I hardly know how to walk."

What had she been wearing? Jacob wanted to know. He swallowed the question and smiled.

"Ethan would be pleased, I think," Maria said.

"Ethan?"

"Her husband," Katie supplied.

Apparently more had transpired in the kitchen than a thorough scrubbing.

"I've been in one disguise or another for years," Maria said. "A wagon driver, a farm wife, a dairy farmer on milk runs. Usually

in drab colors and fabrics that no one would notice."

Jacob tilted his head. "Perhaps a brown tweed jacket and breeches, and a hat pulled down low over your face behind the State House? The sort of thing no one would notice in a steady rain?"

He watched Maria's eyes widen.

"Yes, I was there in the State House yard that day," he said. "With so many people there, I couldn't move quickly enough to follow you."

She gasped. "I cannot believe it. You knew I was in Philadelphia?"

"I was not sure I could trust my eyes," he said, "and Sarah did not see you at all."

Elizabeth stepped forward and gripped Jacob's arm. "You never told me!"

"I did not want you to be disappointed."

"Knowing she was alive — that's all I would have needed."

"I'm here now," Maria said, "and I'm ready to tell you where I've been."

Jacob gestured for everyone to sit. Katie and Hannah shared the settee, each one first bending to pick up a toddler. Elizabeth sat in the rocker Jacob's father had made. Maria stood at the stone fireplace, one hand on the black oak mantel with fingers tenuously exploring its familiarity.

"I remember when *Daed* found this piece of wood," Maria said. "He knew it would be perfect here."

Jacob had been too young to remember. At the moment, he wanted to hear a piece of more recent history. She let her fingers trace over a few of the ridges of stone rising from floor to ceiling then turned to face her expectant listeners.

"Ethan came to Irish Creek when I was sixteen. He was only here a few weeks. An *English*. He hired himself out for odd jobs. I met him one day when I was visiting at the Stutzman farm and he rode through looking for work."

"They would never have hired him," Elizabeth said. "Not the Stutzmans."

Maria smiled. "You are right. But it was all the introduction we needed. I followed him, and we walked along the creek. It was love. I was *in lieb.*" She raised her eyes to Elizabeth. "Suddenly I understood why *Daed* would consider leaving the Amish to marry. But I was Amish. Barbara and Anna and Christian were Amish. I was next. I was supposed to be baptized."

"We all thought you wanted to join the church," Elizabeth said.

"I suppose I would have, if I had not met Ethan. Then it did not seem as if keeping

the family happy was a good reason to take such a step. I wanted to explain to Christian. I knew he was the one who would be most hurt. We could have worked it out in time, I think. But Ethan wanted to keep moving, and he wanted me to come with him. He did not propose anything unseemly. He said we could go to Reading and be properly married. Then we would go west."

"I do not understand all the disguises," Jacob said.

"That came later." Maria turned and held her hands out to the fire's warmth. "We did go west. Ethan did not take me anywhere I did not want to go. I knew adventure was waiting for us, and we found it."

"Where did you end up?"

Maria laughed. "We did not end up anywhere. We moved around western Pennsylvania and into Ohio. Trapping. Selling furs. Helping people outfit to go even farther west. God did not bless us with children, and perhaps it is just as well. That left us free for our new work when the time came."

"New work?"

"We did not hear about the citizens of Boston dumping tea into the harbor for a long time. But as soon as we learned of it, we wanted to be part of forging this new country. By the time we got to Boston, fight-

ing had broken out. Boston was not the only place in trouble."

"New York?" Jacob asked, trying to recall the early turning points in the war. "And, of course, Philadelphia."

"And many places in between," Maria said. "Our experience in the wilderness suited us well for moving behind enemy lines, posing in all sorts of roles." Her voice thickened. "But we often worked separately, with a common base. When Philadelphia fell to the British, Ethan got trapped in the city, and I was beyond the British line. I haven't seen him in months, and none of my connections has heard anything about him. I was at Valley Forge all winter, on the fringes of Washington's camp."

"Valley Forge?" Elizabeth sat up straight. "The last we heard, Joseph was at Valley Forge."

Maria shook her head. "I didn't know. Who knows if we would recognize each other if we were face-to-face."

"He should have come home." Elizabeth sank back into her chair. "Washington has done nothing but try to survive the elements."

"Joseph is an officer, *Mamm,*" Jacob said. "He cannot leave his post simply because he would be warmer at home."

"It's brutal," Maria said. "Not enough food for the soldiers, much less all the people following the camp hoping to find work. Clothing is in short supply, illness in long supply." She turned her gaze to Elizabeth. "I finally had enough. If I could not be with Ethan, or do some good for the cause, then the suffering is pointless."

"So you came home," Elizabeth murmured.

"The siege can't last forever," Jacob said. "General Washington has not given up. Abandoning Philadelphia would be tantamount to abandoning the United States."

Maria sighed heavily. "I know. But it's hard not knowing what happened to Ethan. Before now, I never realized how hard it must have been on all of you when I left."

Jacob watched Maria's eyes drift around the room, then back to Elizabeth's and settle there.

"I would have tried to sneak past the British lines," Maria said, "but I'm fairly certain someone betrayed me. The British were warned to watch for me. And I was so tired. I *am* so tired. A hot bath — do you have any idea how long it has been? Years! I'm weary of not eating. I'm weary of sleeping on the ground in the cold."

Elizabeth stood up and wrapped Maria in

her arms. Jacob met his mother's pleading eyes over his sister's shoulder.

"I cannot promise anything," Jacob said, "but we have some connections of our own. When David gets here, I will talk to him. Perhaps we can get word to Sarah. She might know somebody who knows Ethan."

Maria laughed nervously. "What a rebellious bunch we all turned out to be. Christian must be scandalized."

Jacob watched his mother blossom in Maria's company. On the first morning, they walked to Lisbetli's grave, where they shared a long cry. Elizabeth cooked meat as fast as Jacob could hunt it and pulled potatoes and vegetables from the cellar at rates reminiscent of the days she was feeding ten children. She insisted Maria sleep late in the mornings and drop off for a nap whenever she wished. Often when Jacob climbed the hill to the big house in the late afternoons, Maria slept on a mat in front of the fire, and Elizabeth watched over her, stitching a new dress for Maria or making over an old dress of Sarah's. Maria seemed to fatten up by the day and moved with increasing energy. She took long walks with her nieces and nephews, surprising Jacob with visits to the fields or the tannery.

Jacob measured Maria's return to health carefully and with pleasure. However, he did not forget that she had come to Irish Creek expecting to find Christian, her only full-blooded brother.

"It is time, you know," Jacob said one day when Maria sat at the kitchen table in the home he shared with Katie.

"Time for what?"

Her eyes told him she knew the answer. "I will take you to Christian," he said. "You will enjoy meeting his daughter Magdalena. She looks just like you."

Maria looked away. "They probably think I am dead. Considering what I have been doing, perhaps it is better that way."

"No, Maria." Jacob spoke softly. "Bar-bar. Anna. Christian. They all deserve to know what became of you."

"If I never saw them, how would that change the way things are now?" Maria said. She stood up and began to pace the kitchen.

"Because now I know," Jacob said. "David knows. John knows. *Mamm* knows. Our *children* know. You can't ask us to conspire to deceive the rest of the family. And besides, that is not the point."

"What do you mean?"

"You came here to find Christian. It is time you did."

THIRTY-SEVEN

Annie had plenty to keep her busy while she waited for Joel to prove his word. However, Rufus's chisel would remain within reach every minute. Rufus would believe her account of how she came to have it. If Joel was smart, he would not take three days.

On Thursday, she prepared for her first sewing lesson. Annie had never been to the home of Betsy Yoder before, but the house seemed especially suited to the task of hosting a group of women with their sewing projects. By the time Annie pedaled to the Yoders', several buggies stood outside the home, horses hitched to split-rail fencing. Annie's fabric was folded neatly and laid into the basket hanging from her handlebars. By the end of the day, she hoped, the fabric would be cut according to Franey's pattern and Annie would have some notion of how the pieces would go

ether to form a dress.

Inside, the Amish women greeted her politely, offered refreshments, and suggested a table Annie could use to lay out her fabric. Franey soon appeared with her pattern and hovered while Annie flipped and turned pieces, looking for the most efficient way to lay them out. The process was not entirely foreign to her. Myra Friesen knew her way around a pattern, and Annie had witnessed her going through the basics of ironing the fabric flat, arranging pattern pieces, pinning them down, and carefully cutting. In her software-creating career, Annie had often mentally rotated three-dimensional objects and looked for how the pieces fit together. She did not imagine fitting together sleeves and bodice front and bodice back and skirt and waistband fitting was so different. The women watching her cut remembered aloud the first dresses they had made — some with fondness and some with frustration.

Edna and Beth Stutzman arrived just before lunch and seemed to take over the room with both conversation and their own projects. When she decided to participate in this day, Annie had steeled herself to expect the Stutzmans. If she was seriously considering becoming Amish, she would have to find a way to be gracious toward the Beil-

ers' old friends, no matter what Beth had done to her quilt.

Beth crossed the room where Annie stood at the cutting table. Annie raised her head and looked Beth in the eye with a smile. Beth smoothed her skirt and looked the other direction. Annie managed not to roll her eyes.

Sandwiches and salads appeared on a long narrow side table in the Yoder dining room. Annie set aside the puzzle of fabric, leaving Franey at work while she left to fix a plate. She sat off to one side, where she could quietly marvel at her own involvement in an event such as this one. A year ago she had not even heard of Westcliffe, Colorado. Her own family history was a blur that did not interest her. She was wealthy and likely to become more wealthy. Her life was a string of conveniences and serial immediate gratification.

On the outside, Annie hardly recognized her life now. The inside was another matter. When familiar impulses welled, the challenge of forming new responses loomed. *Humility, humility, humility,* Annie reminded herself, even as she followed Beth's movements around the open, connected rooms.

Beth filled a plate. Annie watched her situate a chair where she could see clearly

around the ragged circle.

"It's terrible what happened to that man Karl Kramer." Beth rearranged the pickles on her plate. "I've heard he's not a nice man at all, but it's awful that someone would want to hurt him."

Murmurs of agreement rose around the room.

"The *English* don't understand our peaceful ways, I suppose." Beth paused to take a delicate bite out of a turkey sandwich. "Certainly I will never understand why they feel the need to blow each other up." She shifted her head toward Annie and raised one eyebrow.

Annie forced food into her mouth to keep herself from speaking. Someone had put too much mustard on the ham sandwich. The spicy kind. It stung her tongue, and her eyes watered.

"The *English* police will sort it out," someone said.

"It does seem to be taking a long time," someone else observed. "I'm not sure I understand why. It's been three days."

"Many people would have a motive against Mr. Kramer."

"They have several suspects, I heard," Beth said. She gave Annie a colorless smile. "But I believe one in particular is coming

to the forefront. At a time like this, I take comfort in belonging to people of peace."

Annie nearly choked on the bread she was stuffing in her mouth.

"I understand you are very technical, Annalise." Beth had both eyebrows raised now. "What kinds of explosions have you been involved with?"

Annie licked her lips and turned to Mrs. Yoder. "The sandwiches are delicious." She chewed harder.

"If it were an Amish matter," someone said, "we could take it to the bishop. I'm sure he could get to the bottom of it."

"But of course this is not an Amish matter." Beth took another bite and glared again at Annie. "Annalise, even as an outsider to our ways, you can see that it is plain silly to think our people had anything to do with this unfortunate incident."

Annie filled her mouth again.

Beth picked up a pickle slice. "The bishop's time would be better spent reminding our men of their duty to the community."

Chew. Chew. Chew.

"Rufus Beiler, for instance," Beth said. "Why would he wait as long as he has to obey God's will and marry?"

A couple of young women giggled. Annie drew in a long, slow, spicy mustard breath.

Edna Stutzman spoke up. "You are right as usual, Beth. I will speak to your father myself, and he will speak to the bishop. Rufus Beiler is a dear young man, and we should not sit by idly while his faith weakens."

Annie's chewing slowed. Picking on her was one thing. But picking on Rufus? No amount of *demut* would allow her to listen to any more of this drivel.

The bishop. She swallowed. Yes, Bishop Troyer.

Annie took her plate to the kitchen, gathered up her dress pieces, expressed her gratitude to the hostess, promised Franey she would talk to her soon, and looked Beth in the eye one last time.

This was the first time Annie ever pedaled to the Troyers' farm, and she misjudged the miles. By the time she arrived, wind had stung her face red and dirt streaked the hem of her dress. Even under a helmet — which she had come to realize was not a very Amish device — her *kapp* was hanging behind her head, hair straggling out of its pins. Annie paused at the gate that marked the bishop's yard and tried to put herself back together before knocking on the front door.

The bishop was a minister, right? She could talk to him confidentially and make him aware that certain members were using the sewing day to spread gossip. Maybe she would not even need to name names. Just raise a concern. She was not a complete snitch, after all.

Mrs. Troyer welcomed her, and Annie gratefully accepted the offer of a glass of water. Sipping it, she sat alone in an unadorned parlor while the bishop's wife went to fetch her husband. Annie used the time to catch her breath as well as collect her thoughts. She would not have to accuse anyone of anything directly. A few plain facts would reveal whether he leaned toward any particular conclusion — on both gossip and explosions.

A few minutes later, bearded and attired in a black suit, the bishop greeted Annie with a smile.

"Annalise, I am so glad you've come."

Had he been expecting her? she wondered. Maybe he knew more than she realized.

"I thought you would be the right person to talk to about all this," she said.

"Of course. I did not realize you knew about the classes yet. I did not want to presume you were ready until you came forward."

Classes?

"Baptism classes will begin in four weeks," the bishop said as he took a seat across from her. "We usually meet while the rest of the congregation is worshipping."

Baptism classes?

"Well, of course, I've been thinking about it," Annie said. The bishop seemed so delighted to see her. How could she tell him she thought some Amish boys were not living up to the peaceful reputation of their people? Or that the women of his flock were gossiping?

"Your case is unusual, of course." The bishop planted his hands on his knees and leaned forward. "The other baptism candidates are all younger and have grown up in Amish homes, so I hope you will feel free to ask any questions at all. I'm happy to answer them."

"Thank you. That's good to know." Annie squirmed in her chair.

"Baptism is an important step in our church. If you feel you need extra sessions to understand our faith, I'm sure we can arrange them."

"Thank you. I know your time is valuable." Her repeated gratitude encouraged his smile. Annie's brain fumbled for a way to change the subject.

"I want you to feel fully convinced of our ways of humility and submission before you're baptized."

The door from the kitchen opened, and the bishop's wife appeared. "I am sorry to interrupt," she said, "but the bishop is already late for a previous appointment."

The bishop stood. "Annalise and I have had a good talk. She is going to join our new baptism class."

THIRTY-EIGHT

Annie waited.

She heard nothing from Joel on Thursday. In her mind, the conversation with Bishop Troyer replayed, and she kept hitting the STOP and REWIND buttons to listen again. Baptism had been the last thing on her mind when she showed up at the bishop's house. Was it *Gottes wille,* God's will, that the discussion had taken such a turn and she had not regained control?

Mrs. Weichert had scheduled her to work Friday morning. Annie opened the shop earlier than scheduled. If Joel was looking for her and did not find her at home, he would come to the shop. At the very least, she hoped he would give her some clue that evening when she joined the Beilers for the evening meal.

Annie was not sure if the ticking she heard was from a clock at the back of the shop or her own brain measuring out Joel's delay.

By 11:00, no one else had come into the shop all morning. She sat on a stool behind the counter, hunched over her interlibrary loan genealogy book.

Pioneer Jakob Beyeler, immigrant from Switzerland in 1737, spawned two family lines. Rufus and Ruth descended from Christian, Amish leader of the eighteenth century. Annie descended from Jacob II, as he was known in the genealogy books — not Amish. The original Amish settlements in Pennsylvania surely were seeking a reprieve from the persecution of Europe. But July 4, 1776, must have changed the North American climate for the Amish. War. The notion of the decisions Pioneer Jakob's sons must have faced during the Revolutionary War intrigued Annie, propelling her search through the book for any mention, any scrap of a mention, suggesting the political affiliations of her ancestors.

The distraction was successful. Another hour and a half passed in silence. When the shop's bell finally announced a customer, Annie startled and nearly fell off her stool.

Rufus nodded at the three *English* men standing in the middle of the aisle at Tom's hardware store and stepped past them as politely as he could. He had only come in

for some sandpaper. He took five packages, in three different grits, off the racks and moved toward the front of the store. Tom was at the counter dumping change into one of the two cash register drawers.

"I'm not used to seeing you in here." Rufus laid the sandpaper on the counter.

"It's still my store," Tom said. "I lost Colton to the lure of the big city. He gave me barely three days' notice and moved to Pueblo."

"Sorry to hear that. I liked him."

Tom picked up the sandpaper. "Are you putting this on account?"

"If you don't mind."

The trio from the aisle migrated forward.

"You're Rufus Beiler, aren't you?" one of them asked.

Rufus turned. "Yes, that's right."

The man extended a hand. "Hayes Demming."

Rufus shook his hand. "Nice to meet you."

"We've been wondering when you're going to get that community project moving."

Rufus glanced from one face to another. "No doubt you heard Karl Kramer was injured. He needs time to heal."

"We were all set to help. Still want to."

"I appreciate that. I'm sure Karl will as well."

"I've been talking to businesses around town," Hayes said. "Every day more people are on the fence. If you wait much longer, you won't have the help you need."

"We must wait for Karl," Rufus said firmly. "I gave him my word we would work together."

"That was before the explosion. Do you really think he expects the entire town to wait for him?"

"I don't presume to know what he expects," Rufus said. "I only know what I promised."

"The window is going to slam shut," Hayes said. "I'd hate for the whole project to go bust after all the hard work that has gone into it already."

"I hope that does not happen." Rufus picked up his sandpaper.

"Rufus," Tom said, "perhaps you should reconsider. There's a lot at stake."

"Talk to Karl," Hayes suggested. "It's your project more than it is his. Maybe he'll understand."

Rufus tilted his head. "I don't think we should be bothering Karl right now — certainly not to ask him to back out."

"He wouldn't be backing out so much as stepping aside. If he really cares about the project, he'll want it to move forward."

"When the time is right, it will move forward."

Hayes shook his head. "Okay, but don't be surprised if it's you and Kramer carrying the whole load."

"Thank you for the conversation, gentlemen." Rufus touched the brim of his hat.

The men drifted back down the aisle.

Tom pushed the cash register drawer closed. "Are you sure, Rufus? This is no time to be stubborn."

"Gottes wille," Rufus said softly. God's will. He picked up his sandpaper and stepped out into the sunlight.

A flash of Amish black caught his eye, and he blinked in the direction of the moving form.

Joel.

Rufus made up his mind in that moment. Joel was not his son, but someone had to talk to him.

Rufus moved quickly down the sidewalk. Only when he was close enough that Joel could not claim not to have heard him did Rufus call out his brother's name.

Joel stopped and turned.

"I did not know you were planning to come into town," Rufus said. "I would have asked you to make a few purchases and spared myself the trip."

"I didn't plan," Joel said. "Something came up."

"Oh?" Rufus wrinkled his forehead. "Is everything all right in the fields?"

"The fields are fine." Joel shifted his weight.

"Is everything all right between you and *Daed*?" Rufus nudged Joel a few steps down a side street.

"Of course."

"*Daed* has been very patient with you." Rufus crossed his arms over his chest. "Perhaps even to the point of indulgence."

"I get my work done." Joel moved his brown eyes to scan the street in both directions.

"What are you looking for, Joel?" Rufus did not waver.

Now Joel's eyes fastened on Rufus. "It's nothing."

Annie left the shop mumbling, *Demut, demut, demut.* She had finally convinced Mrs. Weichert to send her weekly ad to the newspaper in electronic format, and now the editor claimed the file had corrupted and insisted Annie must come to the publication's office and straighten things out. She tucked a printed copy of the ad in a folder just in case and set out down the block.

Two black hats, brims nearly touching to form a single platform, made her stop. She took two steps back and pressed herself against the brick wall of a shop to listen.

"It's nothing," Joel said.

"It does not seem like nothing, Joel," Rufus said. "You miss a lot of meals. You go into town without telling anyone. You don't seem interested in the farm. I see the looks *Daed* and *Mamm* give each other at dinner."

"It's nothing," Joel repeated. "Everything is under control."

"What is it that you have to control?"

Annie inched closer. Rufus had asked the question that haunted her. She felt the outside of her jeans pocket for the shape of Rufus's tiny chisel.

"I'm sure you have things to do." Joel was made of rock. He was giving his brother nothing to speculate about.

Now Annie's hand slid into her pocket, where her fingers gripped the chisel's handle.

"You're right. I do have things to do," Rufus said. "But we will finish this conversation later."

Annie had never heard Rufus be so firm with Joel. As she saw Rufus's shoulders turn, Annie ducked into the shop whose wall she had been holding up. She turned

her back to the front window, busied herself looking at a row of mismatched teacups, and waited for the brothers to walk their separate way on the street. When she stepped back onto Main Street again, she headed to the newspaper office with the ad.

Then she would find Joel.

As she expected, she solved the technology glitch at the newspaper in a matter of seconds. She left the print copy of the ad as a backup. The whole transaction took no more than four minutes. Joel could not have gotten far.

In jeans and sneakers, it was simple enough to power walk a few blocks, detouring down a side street to avoid passing Mrs. Weichert's shop for the time being. She caught up with Joel as he ducked into the coffee shop.

This was the place where the puzzle pieces had fallen into place just a few minutes too late only four days ago. Annie tugged on the glass door and followed Joel in. A moment later she touched his elbow.

Down the block, Rufus set the packets of sandpaper under the seat of the small buggy. Only then did he remember his promise to his mother to bring home coffee beans. He glanced toward the coffee shop, smiling at

the notion of taking his mother the gourmet beans she would never buy for herself.

Outside the plate glass window a few minutes later, Rufus paused. Shielding his eyes from the sun's glare, he peered through — and saw Joel.

And Annalise. They stood close together, their faces somber.

And Annalise was holding the tiny chisel from the set he had lost weeks ago.

Slowly, Rufus opened the door and stepped into the coffee shop. He approached Joel and Annalise.

"Tomorrow." Annalise thrust the chisel toward Joel. "Period. No discussion. Or I use this."

Joel turned, met Rufus's eyes, and strode out of the shop. Rufus did not try to stop him. It was Annalise he wanted to talk to now.

She looked shocked to see him and shoved the chisel into her pocket.

"That looked like a serious conversation."

"Yes, it was."

Rufus sucked in his bottom lip then pushed it out. If Annalise had been wearing an Amish dress, she would not have been able to hide anything from him. Did she understand the isolation that came with keeping a secret?

"Annalise, why do you have one of my lost chisels?"

She puffed her cheeks as she blew out her breath. "Rufus, can you trust me for one day?"

"And my chisel?"

"I promise you will have the whole set back tomorrow. Just trust me."

He did trust her. He was less sure about Joel. The two of them were up to something.

"Tomorrow, then."

At four o'clock on Saturday afternoon, Annie shoved a rake into the garden soil Rufus had tilled for her two weeks earlier. Nothing was planted yet. She was not accomplishing anything in particular, other than keeping herself distracted.

Four o'clock. If Joel thought she was going to wait until the stroke of midnight before taking action, she would not hesitate to straighten him out. She pounded the points of the rake into the ground three times with particular fierceness.

Two more hours. That was the absolute outside limit.

Annie did not hear the car pull into her driveway in front of the house, but she did hear the doors slamming. Joel would have a lot of gall to show up in a car. She let the

418

rake drop and stormed around the side of the house. Her parents' silver Toyota was parked in the driveway.

"Mom! Dad!"

"You scared us half to death with that note." Myra charged toward Annie and gripped her around the shoulders. "We came as soon as we got your letter."

"I'm sorry. I was trying not to scare you." Annie stepped out of her mother's grasp and lifted a cheek to her father's kiss.

"You used to be familiar with an invention called the telephone." Myra inspected her daughter from head to toe. "Surely getting caught in an explosion qualifies as an emergency."

"I know. I'm sorry. I should have found a phone." Annie wiped her hands on her jeans.

"You should *carry* a phone."

"Daddy, isn't this your golf day?"

"I was headed to the golf course when your mother showed me the note."

"I ruined your golf game. I'm a crummy daughter."

Brad Friesen shook his head. "No, you're not. Puzzling, perhaps. We're just grateful to see that you're all right."

Myra held out an envelope. "Liam-Ryder Industries is still after you."

Annie propped her rake up against the green shingle siding, brushed her gloved hands together, and took the envelope. She would open it later. At some point she would have to tell them with finality that she was not interested.

"Come on inside," Annie said. "Let me clean up and I'll tell you what happened — though I told you most of it in my letter."

While Annie washed up, her mother brewed a pot of coffee. Annie found a box of crackers in the cabinet and sliced up some cheddar cheese and an apple she had meant to eat two days ago and arranged everything on a platter. Then starting at the beginning, she told her parents about the day of the explosion. The task was more difficult than she imagined, since she decided to leave out information about her own suspicions or her deal with Joel.

"It's entirely unfair for anyone to accuse you." Myra was adamant.

Of course Annie agreed.

"Brad, perhaps we ought to drop in at the sheriff's office. Where do you suppose that would be?"

"Mom, please don't. The police don't seriously suspect me. It's just rumor, and it will blow over."

"You can still come home for a while,"

Myra suggested.

"Mom," Annie said quietly, "I am home."

Mother and daughter locked eyes. Only a rap on the front door pulled Annie's gaze away. She got up to answer the knock.

"Franey!" Annie glanced over her shoulder at her parents sitting on her sofa. It would be rude not to invite Franey in. With an inward wince, Annie stepped aside. "Mom, Dad, you remember Franey Beiler."

Brad was on his feet and extended his hand, which Franey shook.

"I only just heard," Franey said, turning to Annie. "You never said a word, you sneaky thing."

"About what?" Annie asked.

"The baptism classes, of course." Franey pressed Annie against her chest. "I'm so pleased. I'm sure Rufus will be delighted, too."

Annie stepped out of Franey's embrace and smoothed her hair with both hands.

Myra cleared her throat. "Annie, perhaps we should offer Franey some refreshment. I'll be happy to help you in the kitchen."

"Please sit down," Annie said, gesturing to the chair she had vacated. "We'll be right back."

"Baptism classes?" Myra hissed in the

kitchen. "When were you going to mention that?"

"I can explain, Mom. I went to see the bishop about something else, and everything got mixed up. I didn't know it was going to happen."

"You seem to have agreed to join the classes." Myra composed herself, swallowing hard. "I know enough about the Amish to know that baptism means you are joining the church."

Annie straightened her shoulders. "Yes, that is what it means."

"You could be baptized in our church at home, you know. You don't have to join the Amish to be baptized."

"I know. But to join the Amish church it is required."

"But this is what you want?"

Annie nodded slowly.

The door opened, and Brad stuck his head into the kitchen. "Franey has just invited us all for supper. I said yes."

THIRTY-NINE

April 1778

The rhythm of a team pulling a wagon gathered in the distance, eventually disturbing Christian Byler's prayer thread and causing him to open his eyes as he sat in his favorite outdoor chair. Amish clatter, Patriot clatter, British clatter — it all sounded the same at this stage. Over the years his wife's suggestion that he cut down the tree at the end of their lane became more insistent, but so far Christian resisted. Whatever came down the road would come whether they could see it or not, and their response would be the same. So why sacrifice a tree whose wood they did not need?

The ruckus slowed enough that Christian knew the wagon would turn into his lane. A moment later, he recognized Jacob in the raised seat. The woman beside him was not Katie, though. Christian had not seen Jacob's wife in years, but a woman did not

change her frame and coloring.

Christian stood and waited for the wagon. Jacob pulled the team to a stop, set the wagon's brake, and jumped down. Christian's eyes never left the woman, who was slower to descend. Jacob said nothing but simply stepped aside.

Christian had seen those black curls on only one woman's head. "Maria," he murmured.

She smiled awkwardly.

The dress she wore was not Amish, but he had long ago given up that hope. Was she alive? That had been the specter question, and now he had his answer.

"You certainly took the long way back from the creek," Christian said, a smile forming at one end of his mouth.

"In the end, though, I came home." Maria moved slowly toward him.

All the moments Maria missed crashed through Christian. His entire marriage to Lizzie. The death of Lizzie. His wedding to Babsi. The births of all his children. The baptisms of his older children, all of whom honored him when they chose the Amish way for themselves. The close community of families who understood their old ways. The young men who might have courted her.

Christian swallowed hard. She was here

now. Maria was here.

"You must come inside," he said. "Babsi — my wife — will want to meet you."

Within an hour the house was full. A couple of the children went running to find the others in gardens and fields and barns. Christian's married children rolled into the farm in wagons of their own, with their offspring raising the noise level in the yard. To them, Christian knew, Maria was more folklore than family. She was the mysterious sister who disappeared and was never found. She was the one about whom everyone wondered but few spoke.

Christian watched Maria's every move — the sweep of a hand familiar from childhood, a laugh matured but as easily provoked as in years gone by, the hair that refused taming, the violet-blue eyes of their mother.

Magdalena was on foot, as usual. She preferred the simplicity of walking where she wanted to go. Walking alone for miles every day pressed her anxieties out through her extremities. And if she took a little longer than usual for an errand, no one remarked. If occasionally a loaf of bread or a jar of preserves or a jug of cider did not make it to its intended recipient, so be it. It

425

went to good use.

With the British army garrisoned in Philadelphia, demand for food and basic supplies multiplied. At first, Magdalena diverted the occasional bag of flour or corn. At the harvesttime last fall, this was easy enough to do. Over the winter, she watched Nathanael's empty cabin. His family still tried to farm some of his acreage, but no one paid attention to the structure. When Magdalena offered to dust the place from time to time in case Nathanael should decide to move into it, no one objected.

No one believed Nathanael would move into the cabin. Not after three and a half years. If he did not marry, he would not move from his parents' home.

So Magdalena gathered foodstuffs there. Brazenly, she carried hot coals from her own family's hearth and built a fire in Nathan's cabin, where she cooked three dozen loaves of bread and four cakes before passing them to a farmer whose name she did not know. He took a wagon of goods to the outskirts of Philadelphia, where British troops were eager to have them.

To Magdalena, the ease of it all was flabbergasting. Did her Amish dress and prayer *kapp* truly provide such unsuspecting protection? Or was her safety confirmation she

was doing God's will?

The injured British soldier from last fall had disappeared long ago. He was not ungrateful for the care the Bylers offered, but he wanted only to be safe well away from the war. Magdalena always supposed he had gone farther west. He seemed not to care that he might never see his country or family again.

Her steps took Magdalena into the family's lane now. The wagons were familiar — her own siblings and aunts were here. But why? Why all at once? She had been gone only a few hours. Surely this gathering was unplanned.

Daed. Panic propelled her into a run.

She burst through the front door into a swarm of cousins and nieces and nephews. Laughter. Food. Children's games. These were not signs of sorrow or concern. Magdalena let out a long breath.

"Magdalena!" her father's voice boomed. "Come and meet your *aunti* Maria."

Aunti Maria? The lost aunt? Magdalena swallowed air and followed her smiling father into the kitchen, where the chatter and clatter of women at work oozed familiarity. Several pots hung in the hearth.

"Maria," Christian said, "Magdalena is here."

Magdalena watched the woman at the hearth turn, a large wooden spoon in one hand. She smiled.

"She looks just like you, Maria," Christian said. "Don't you think so?"

"I have not seen myself in a proper glass in many years," Maria said, "but you flatter me to think I was ever as beautiful as this young creature."

Magdalena flushed. The Amish did not talk this way. She never saw her own reflection in anything but a clear pond, and it would have been prideful to think herself beautiful.

She met the glowing eyes of her aunt with hesitancy behind her own smile.

Jacob settled into a chair on the porch. Christian had done well for himself in Lancaster County. Several real estate transactions yielded good profit for him. The spacious home sheltered his large family with ease, and the land around it prospered in provision year after year. Most of the farms that bordered his land were also Amish, which seemed to deepen Christian's contentment.

Christian silently occupied the chair next to Jacob. Most of the visitors had left. Maria was still in the kitchen showing Babsi

and Magdalena how she cooked in her years on the frontier. The two brothers looked out on the remains of the setting sun.

"I suppose I will head home at first light," Jacob said.

"Thank you for bringing Maria to visit."

The finality in Christian's tone made Jacob squirm. He leaned forward, his elbows on his knees, and his hands dangling. "Visit?"

"I love my sister," Christian said. "Seeing her again has filled an empty spot in my heart. But she cannot stay here."

"So you've made up your mind after one long afternoon together?"

"She honored me with honesty. If she had come straight from the frontier with no political opinions, it would be different."

Jacob exhaled. "She's your sister, Christian. Your full-blood sister."

"And she's a Patriot zealot."

"You might say the same of me."

"You do not seek shelter in my house," Christian said.

"I'm here tonight. I've been here before."

"You go home to your gunpowder every time. When you drive past the farms, no one wonders what is under the canvas in your wagon. But Maria. A zealot is not something she does. It is something she is."

"And that compromises you?"

"We live apart, Jacob. We are neutral. I will not put my family at risk for Maria's cause."

Magdalena tired of watching Babsi and Maria cook after everyone had left. What was so unusual about roasting squirrel? Magdalena abandoned the household's best spoon in a basin of gray water and went out the back door to the stables. She wanted to check on the old gelding. They asked little work of the beast anymore. Magdalena wondered how much longer her father would tolerate sustaining an animal that did not earn its keep.

She stroked the gelding's neck. She would have to stay away from the kitchen for a long time to avoid making small talk with a stranger late into the night.

The door creaked open, and her father and aunt entered the stables. The tone arising from their mingled approaching voices sent Magdalena ducking into the hay. Revealing herself now would prove awkward. Instead, she squatted out of sight.

"Christian, try to understand," Maria's soft voice pleaded.

Magdalena heard the supple slap of leather against the wall, the familiar sound of her

father rearranging bridles hanging on hooks inside the door. He always did that when he had to say something that he did not wish to say.

"It would only be trouble for all of us," her father said, "including you."

"It's been so long," Maria said. "I did not expect you to send me away as soon as I got here."

"Maria, I cannot put my family at risk."

"What about God's will?" Maria challenged.

"What about it?"

"If it is *Gottes wille* to keep your family safe, I doubt I have the power to endanger them."

Magdalena choked on the thought of the danger she might have brought to her family.

Christian exhaled heavily. "You haven't changed in all these years. You always were a vexing child."

"Don't make light, Christian," Maria said. "I'm alone. I want my family."

"You have Jacob. He shares your sympathies."

"I had hoped you and I had a bond that transcended wartime sympathies."

Magdalena listened to feet shuffling in the hay.

431

"You can't stay, Maria. That is my final word. You have admitted your history with the Patriots."

"And if I were supporting the British?"

"It would make no difference."

Magdalena pressed a fist against her lips. Her aunt was the enemy. There was no more gentle way to put it.

Her father, of course, had no enemies. The war had nothing to do with him.

But it had plenty to do with Magdalena.

And it had plenty to do with Maria.

Magdalena wished her aunt no harm. But she could never be on the side of people who had stolen her future with Nathanael. She was glad to hear her *daed* be so firm that Maria must leave.

Magdalena had lived her whole life without knowing her *aunti* Maria. She saw no reason to change course now.

FORTY

Franey rode with the Friesens in their car, leaving Lydia, Sophie, and Jacob to take the buggy home. Annie sat in the backseat beside Franey. Every effort her mother made at polite conversation stabbed. Franey reached over and squeezed Annie's hand. Annie appreciated the gesture but withdrew her hand quickly, lest her mother turn her head and see.

Brad turned off the highway into the Beilers' long driveway and parked the car close to the house. As the foursome went up the steps to the front porch, Franey chattered about what she planned for supper and how pleased she was the Friesens were joining them. Franey pushed open the front door. Annie saw the split-second halt before Franey continued into the house and held the door open for the others.

"It looks like we'll have a roomful of guests," Franey said, motioning to the

young men in the living room. "I would like you to meet the sons of our dear friends, the Stutzmans. This is Mark and Luke, with my son Joel."

Annie swallowed hard. Joel. Sitting between Mark and Luke on the sofa, the brims of their three identical black felt hats forming a stiff line. Joel held a bundle in his hands, and Mark and Luke looked far from pleased to be sitting in the Beilers' living room.

"Ike and Edna are on their way over," Joel said. He glanced at Annie, who transferred the glance to her parents.

"Is something wrong, Joel?" Franey asked.

Annie nudged her mother's elbow. "Why don't you sit over here?" She gestured to two comfortable chairs positioned apart from the main seating area and breathed relief when her parents complied. Annie watched Franey's face, her heart racing in anticipation of Joel's revelation.

"Mark and Luke have something they need to say." Joel measured his words. "Let's wait for Ike and Edna."

"We have guests," Franey said. "Annalise's parents. I wonder if Ike and Edna might come another time."

"It can't wait," Joel answered.

Annie perched on the arm of the chair her

mother occupied and wondered if the tremble of her veins would pulse through the furniture.

She wanted Rufus to be there. If the boys were going to confess, she wanted him to hear for himself. And she wanted his strength in the room when the explosion came — when truth collided with expectations.

What had Rufus heard about her baptism classes? she wondered. Would he be pleased, as his mother was, or would he wonder why she had not told him herself?

Sitting beside and slightly behind her mother, Annie could not see Myra's face. But she recognized the posture, the tightness of concentration in the way Myra leaned her neck forward a few inches and held her head straight up. She did not intend to miss anything.

Rufus, where are you?

Annie heard the back door open, and she turned her head to listen for steps coming through the kitchen. Eli appeared in the dining room and stilled his steps to take in the scene in his living room. Annie heard another set of footsteps — the right ones now. Rufus entered and stood beside his father. She breathed a measure of relief.

Eli and Rufus roused at the same moment

and moved across the rooms to greet Annie's parents with warm handshakes and kind greetings. Rufus glanced across the room at Annie again. He started to move toward her, and her breath caught.

A vehicle roared to a stop outside. At the sound of slamming car doors, Rufus detoured to the front door and pulled it open. Tom Reynolds stomped up the porch steps. Behind him, Carter Reynolds was less enthusiastic about this visit to the Beilers'. Annie watched the boy carefully. When he stepped inside the house and saw the Stutzman brothers, his eyes widened and his shoulders tensed.

"Good," Tom said. "All the perpetrators are here."

"Perpetrators?" Eli said. "That's a strong word, Tom. Come in and sit down, please."

"You'll understand in a minute, Eli." Tom sat in Eli's favorite armchair and pointed for Carter to sit in its twin. They faced the sofa, where Mark and Luke both began tapping their feet in jerking rhythms.

"What is it, Tom?" Franey asked. She stood behind the sofa, facing Tom.

Rufus, at last, moved to stand beside Annie.

"I looked at my cell phone account online," Tom said. "I always look over the

lines my kids are using just to be sure no one is abusing the privilege of having a phone. Usually I'm flabbergasted at how many texts Carter sends or how much data he uses. This time there was practically nothing. Carter's line hasn't been used all week."

Tom reached into a pocket and pulled out a phone, a simple old-fashioned phone that flipped closed.

"Carter," he said, "why don't you tell everyone what you told me about this phone."

Carter looked at his lap. "It's Annie's. I found it in my dad's truck. She left it there when he brought her home from the hospital the day of the explosion."

Tom waved the phone in the air. "This is the phone I've seen lying around the house. I thought Carter was being forgetful about carrying it."

At the sound of a buggy clattering to a stop outside, Annie dipped her head to look out the window. "It's the Stutzmans."

"Perfect timing." Tom crossed his arms across his chest. "Perhaps we'll wait for them before we continue."

Franey opened the door. As soon as Ike stepped inside, with Edna right behind him, he demanded, "What is going on here? An

English drove up to our house in his car and said he was your neighbor. He handed me a message practically ordering us to come."

"I sent that," Joel said from the sofa.

Annie leaned forward and whispered to her parents, "Maybe we should move to the dining room, out of the way."

"What is that boy doing with your phone?" Myra wanted to know, but she surrendered her chair to Edna Stutzman and moved with her husband to the dining room table. Annie leaned against the partial wall that separated the dining room from the living room. Once again, she met Rufus's gaze across the room.

Tom Reynolds continued his inquest. "Some of you know that Carter and Annie Friesen have the same model phone. They got them confused once before. I'm going to let Carter tell you what happened to his phone and why he tried to pass Annie's off as his."

Every set of eyes in the room fixed on Carter Reynolds. He worked his lips in and out for a good twenty seconds before he formed any words.

"We used mine as the alarm for the bomb."

The gasp that went up did not include An-

438

nie. Her shoulders sagged with the truth that she had been right.

"Joel tried to tell me not to get involved," Carter said, "but I wouldn't listen."

"Get involved with what?" Eli Beiler asked.

Carter pointed limply at the boys on the sofa. "They wanted to blast out the rock. They said they knew how to do it, that they'd done it before in Pennsylvania."

"We *have* done it before," Mark Stutzman said.

Ike's fingers were working his beard. "We once blew a boulder out of a wheat field. Is that what you are referring to?"

Mark nodded. "We watched carefully."

"It was Duncan's idea," Luke said. "He dared us. He didn't think Amish boys would be smart enough."

"Duncan Spangler?" Tom said. "Carter, you didn't mention Duncan earlier."

"He always says mean things about the Amish."

"He dared us," Luke repeated.

"I didn't want to do it," Mark said. "Luke is the one who stole the tools. And the fertilizer."

Annie let her breath out as Joel unwrapped Rufus's missing tools.

"Luke!" Ike barked. "Explain yourself!"

Luke picked at a worn spot in his trousers. "I just wanted to look at the tools. I was going to put them back. Then I realized I could use them to attach wires to the phone."

"Where did you get the wires?" Ike asked.

Mark glanced at Tom.

"From my hardware store," Tom said. "They didn't need very many feet. It would be easy enough to snip a length off the roll in the back of the store."

Luke nodded.

Annie straightened up and faced the boys on the sofa. "So you did steal Karl Kramer's fertilizer?"

"It was the easiest way," Luke said. "We wouldn't have to answer any questions about what we needed it for, and his storage was already halfway out to the rock."

"Annalise," Rufus said, "the small chisel?"

She swallowed, moistened her lips, and nodded. "Yes, I have it. I found the whole set in Karl Kramer's storage area. I told Joel . . . well, the truth had to come out."

Myra Friesen cleared her throat. "Annie, what is this all about?"

Annie met her mother's eyes then moved her glance to Rufus before continuing.

"When Carter and I mixed up our phones a few weeks ago, I saw his Internet history.

He was looking at ways to make bombs. I know it was wrong of me to look at his phone, and maybe I should have said something, but just looking at the Internet didn't mean he was going to do anything."

"It wasn't me!" Carter slid forward in his chair. "They took my phone. They said they were allowed to use the Internet because they haven't joined the church. I didn't know what they looked up."

Annie believed Carter — almost. "But you knew about the fertilizer, and you knew they wanted to use your phone to set off the explosion."

Carter nodded.

"So why didn't you get your phone back?" Tom wanted to know.

"I didn't realize they meant the phone would be part of the explosion. Then I didn't know how to get it back. I was afraid I would accidentally do something to set off the bomb."

"We should never have let you run around with these *English* boys," Edna Stutzman said. "We never dreamed they would influence you this way."

Annie rolled her eyes. "Somebody got hurt," she said. "Karl Kramer is recovering from burns."

Rufus cleared his throat. "And the mes-

sages to Karl and me?"

"We wanted witnesses that it worked. That's all." Luke's voice had flattened. "You and Karl are in charge of the project. We figured you were going to take the rock out anyway."

"We had made no such decision," Rufus said quietly.

"And why does Kramer keep those supplies out in the middle of nowhere, anyway?" Luke asked, his voice finding its edge again. "I wouldn't be surprised if they were all illegal. Stolen."

"Contractors always have leftover supplies. And that is not the subject of this conversation," Tom said with surprising calm. He turned to Annie. "Perhaps you should continue, Annie."

Around the room, faces crunched in puzzlement.

"I knew something was wrong, but I didn't have all the pieces," Annie said. "I couldn't tie anyone to the fertilizer, for instance. And you can't accuse someone based only on Internet search history. I used to look up all kinds of crazy stuff. It didn't mean I was a terrible person. But people were saying I had something to do with the accident, so I went to Karl's storage site looking for clues to find the truth. Ruth and

I discovered the tools wrapped in Joel's old shirt."

"Ruth has something to do with this?" Franey burst out.

"No." Annie's answer was immediate and final. "She knew nothing about it. I just asked her for a ride that day, and to help me look for clues. She recognized the fabric as Joel's shirt. Otherwise, I would not have known who to go to. I confronted Joel, and he asked me to trust him."

"We'll have to call the sheriff's office, of course." Tom was not leaving room for discussion. "If no one had been hurt, that might be different, but even Karl Kramer deserves justice."

"It's only a *rumschpringe* prank," Edna Stutzman said, though she glared at her sons.

Tom's expression did not bend. "It's a crime."

Outside, another car squealed to a stop and a car door slammed.

FORTY-ONE

This time it was Franey who went to the window. "It's Mo."

She pulled open the front door once again, and the innkeeper stomped in.

"Where's Rufus?" Mo's progress stopped as she swept the room with her eyes. "Well, this is an odd bunch to find together in the Beiler house."

Ike Stutzman stood up. "Our visit is concluded." His wife and two sons rose and followed him, wordless, out to their buggy.

Annie glanced at her stunned parents, still sitting at the dining room table, before she crossed to the window at the front of the house. "I think he's angry, but it's hard to tell."

"Ike Stutzman would never let anyone be sure of the answer to that question," Rufus said.

"What does he have to be angry about?" Mo asked.

Annie glanced at Rufus.

"Let's not concern ourselves with that at the moment," Rufus said. "Why have you come all the way out here, Mo?"

Mo pointed a finger at Rufus. "Because of you! And I warn you, I am probably not as skilled as Ike Stutzman at disguising my anger."

"Why don't you have a seat?" Rufus suggested.

"No. I'll do a better job of staying mad if I stand up!" Mo's hands went to her hips. "You've got to get off your high horse and get this project moving."

Rufus calmly took a seat next to Joel on the sofa. Annie watched him from the window.

"I plan to go visit Karl soon and see what his progress is," Rufus said. "Perhaps his doctor has said when he will be well enough to work."

"That could still be weeks. We can't wait that long." Mo gestured toward Tom. "Speak up, Tom. I know you agree with me."

Tom cleared his throat. "I do agree with you, Mo. But it's Rufus's decision to make."

"Oh, come on, Tom, you can be more persuasive than that!"

Silent, Tom held his palms up.

"The police will figure out who is behind

445

that explosion," Mo said. "The important thing is that we don't let an unfortunate event stop our momentum. I've heard nothing to suggest it would be dangerous to keep moving, but of course we can be more vigilant if that will make people feel better."

Annie saw the glances being exchanged around the room. Some of them were aimed at her.

"I want some answers, Rufus Beiler," Mo said. "I'm not leaving until I get them."

Annie grimaced and caught her mother's eye. Crossing back to the dining room, she leaned in and whispered to her parents, "Let's go into the kitchen."

"Perhaps we should just be on our way," her father suggested once they were behind the closed kitchen door. "It hasn't turned out to be a good time to visit."

"I'm so sorry about all this," Annie said. "I had no idea it would all come to a head this way. I'm sure this is not what Franey had in mind when she invited you to supper."

"It's all right," Brad said, "but we are in the way, and I would not want to hold Franey to her invitation under these circumstances. Another time."

Annie nodded. "I'm sure she would understand. I'll speak to her after everything

calms down."

Myra drew her spine straight. "You two have lost your minds if you think I'm leaving now."

"But, Myra —"

Myra cut off her husband's thought. "I am not expecting supper, of course. But look what our daughter has been in the middle of. How can we just walk out before we know the outcome?"

"I'll call you," Annie said, "later tonight."

"And where is your phone?"

"I'll get it from Tom. I'll tell you everything."

Myra calmly pulled a chair out from under the kitchen table, sat down, and scooted the chair in.

Annie swallowed. "Okay, then. I'll start some coffee."

Annie found the pieces of the stainless steel stovetop drip coffeemaker in the dish rack and assembled it, placing it on the stove. She reached into a cupboard for the coffee.

"You seem to know your way around another woman's kitchen," Myra observed.

Annie opened the coffee. "They always tell me to make myself at home." *I'm one of the family,* she wanted to say but had the good sense not to.

The back door opened and Lydia, Sophie, and Jacob tumbled in.

"What's going on?" Sophie asked. "We just saw the Stutzmans leaving. Ike was driving a little fast, I thought."

"There are three *English* cars in front of the house," Jacob pointed out. He looked at Myra and Brad with wide eyes. "And two *English* people at the table."

"These are my parents, Jacob," Annie said. "Mr. and Mrs. Friesen. You've met them before."

"Oh. Nice to see you again."

"Mom, Dad, you remember Rufus's sisters, Sophie and Lydia. Jacob is their littlest brother."

Myra smiled pleasantly, and Brad offered a handshake to Jacob, who returned it with manly enthusiasm.

"Annalise," Sophie said, "what is all this commotion about?"

"There's no short answer," Annie said softly. "I'm sure you'll get the whole story."

"We've never had three *English* cars here before," Jacob observed. "Maybe it's a new world record for an Amish family. But it would be against *Ordnung* to be proud of it." He slid into a seat across from Myra and asked her, "Is one of those cars yours?"

"Yes," Myra said, "the silver sedan."

"Mr. Reynolds drives the red truck, right?" Jacob kicked a table leg in rhythmic repetition.

Sophie put a hand on his shoulder — a little tightly, Annie thought.

"Don't ask so many questions, Jacob," Sophie said. "And stop kicking the table."

"Sophie," Annie said, "would you mind making this pot of coffee for my parents? I'll take Jacob out to check on the chickens and see if we can get the wigglies out."

"Certainly." Sophie moved swiftly to the stove and lit it.

"I'll be back in a few minutes," Annie assured her parents.

Out on the back porch, Annie gulped air. Too much was happening that she could not control.

Rufus listened patiently and managed to mollify Mo with the promise that they would speak again after he had been to visit Karl. With that assurance, she got behind the wheel of her dated green Chevy sedan and negotiated her way back to the road.

That left Rufus looking at Eli, Franey, Joel, Tom, and Carter.

"I smell coffee," he said. "Perhaps we should all have some."

"Good idea," Franey said. "I'll get it."

"I'll do it, *Mamm.* Just sit and relax."

He believed Carter's naiveté. Giving him a cell phone was meant to make his parents feel more secure while they gave him more independence. Rufus doubted Carter would have thought to research bomb making if not prodded by someone else.

In the kitchen, he found Sophie sitting quietly with Myra and Brad Friesen, who were both drinking coffee.

"Where has Annalise gone?" he asked after greeting them.

"Out with Jacob," Sophie supplied. "He was not going to quit asking questions. I suppose she could see I'd had my fill of him for one afternoon. Mr. and Mrs. Friesen have told me a little of what has been going on here."

"It's been quite an afternoon," Rufus said. "Sophie, if I could prevail on you to take the coffeepot out to the living room, I'd like to talk to Annalise's parents."

Rufus invited the Friesens to walk with him away from the house, away from the commotion. They walked across the open yard behind the Beiler home, and he led them on the wide path that meandered from the house and would eventually come out at the big rock. He did not plan to take them that far, though. There was no need

to heighten their anxiety by taking them to the place where they all might have lost Annalise.

"I'm grateful to have a few minutes to spend with you," Rufus said. "I wanted to speak to you about Annalise."

"Yes?" Myra's response was guarded, perhaps even suspicious.

"I know her choices have seemed odd to you." Rufus chuckled. "They seem odd to me, too."

"I hope you are not pressuring her in any way." Myra batted at a dangling branch.

"I assure you I am not."

"She seems fond of you," Brad observed.

"I hope so. I am fond of her." Genuinely. Deeply.

"If she changes her whole life for you, and you reject her, how will she ever get over that?" Myra's tone splintered.

"I don't want to hurt Annalise." Rufus stopped on the path and turned to Brad and Myra. "I don't want her to change for me. I haven't asked her to do that. Please believe me."

"So you are going to reject her!"

"No, I —" Rufus began to respond, but Brad interrupted him.

"No, Myra, you've got it wrong." Brad fixed his gaze on Rufus. "This young man

loves our daughter enough to stay out of the way of her choice. It's the only way she can be sure. Have I got that right?"

Rufus nodded.

"So she's not getting baptized because of you?" Myra asked.

Rufus swallowed hard. "I had not heard that she was getting baptized at all."

"We just found out ourselves," Brad said softly. "She's going to start the classes."

Annalise was planning for baptism? Rufus's heart beat faster as he smoothly turned the trio around and headed back toward the house. "The classes will be an opportunity to ask questions. It will be good for Annalise to listen to the answers."

"I don't want her to feel pressured," Myra said.

"Myra," Brad said, "have you ever known our daughter to do something she did not willingly set her mind to?"

Myra grunted. "No. She has always been headstrong."

Brad extended a hand, and Rufus shook it. "Rufus, I'm beginning to understand what Annalise sees in you. There is much to admire. If you two decide you have a future, I know you will have her best interest at heart."

■ ■ ■ ■

Annie stood outside the chicken coop while Jacob sprinkled feed around and giggled at the hens that pecked the ground in response to his gift.

She blinked twice when she saw her parents and Rufus emerge from the path in the back. Her stomach clenched at the thought of the three of them together without her.

"Will I get to talk to your *mamm* and *daed*?" Jacob threw another handful of feed.

"I hope so. I know they would like you."

Annie looked again at Rufus and her parents. This time, she saw peace in her father's face, and the weight of anxiety was gone from her mother's posture.

"Jacob," she said. "How would you like to talk to my parents right now?"

FORTY-TWO

Only once had Rufus been to Karl Kramer's office in the construction trailer that had been at the same location for at least five years. Twice Rufus visited Karl in the hospital. And now, after a quiet observance of the Sabbath the day before, he was on Karl's personal property for the first time in a rural area outside of Westcliffe. Rufus did not know Karl kept horses. When he saw them on Monday morning, he made Tom stop the truck so he could get out for a closer look. At least a dozen nosed around in the field before him, and he supposed more grazed in the pasture beyond his view.

"I wonder if Karl has ever thought about selling horses to the Amish." Rufus leaned on the top rail of the fence.

"It's a hobby, I think." Tom sat in his truck with the door open.

"I had no idea. It could be a profitable hobby. If Karl weren't so busy resenting us,

he would see the opportunity under his own nose." Rufus paused. "I'm sorry. That was unkind."

"You're certainly doing your part to close the gap. Come on. Let's get this over with."

Inside the house a few minutes later, Karl was alone. After admitting them reluctantly, he moved with some care, but Rufus was encouraged to find him mobile and using his hands. They sat in a large central room, and Rufus told the story that had unfolded on Saturday.

"You're telling me we know exactly who is responsible for this?" Karl's face reddened under the healing burns. The set of his jaw made Rufus's stomach sink.

"We are telling you what the boys said," Rufus said.

Karl jammed a finger in the air toward Tom. "And your boy was in the middle of this?"

Rufus put his elbows on his knees and leaned toward Karl. "Carter did not understand everything that was happening."

Karl thrust his finger toward Rufus now. "If you're telling the truth, it's the Amish boys who knew what they were doing."

"Although they failed in their goal, yes, they seemed to have the best understanding of the science and math necessary." Rufus

paused. "We're here today to ask your forgiveness."

"Forgiveness!"

Rufus nodded and glanced at Tom. "I'm sure the parents will want the boys to make their own apologies as well."

"Forgive this?" Karl held his arms out in front of him, burns still healing under dressings. "You can't be serious."

Annie twisted her lips to one side in thought. On a sheet of notebook paper on her dining room table, she wrote down all the facts that had emerged from two days before. Then she numbered them and rewrote the list in a way that accounted for events in the order in which they must have occurred. Next to each event, she jotted the initials of the boys involved at each stage.

In all the commotion, Luke Stutzman had raised a curious question. Why did Karl Kramer store construction and landscaping supplies so far from his office or the areas where he was actively building? Annie's experience with construction was limited, but it seemed to her that the collection was more systematic than left over.

Annie chewed on the top of her pen now. On another sheet of paper, she began to sketch what she remembered from her sur-

reptitious visits. Neat rows of fence posts, cement bricks, carpet rolls, unopened five-gallon paint cans, tubs of grout, a stainless steel double kitchen sink, pallets of bricks, bags of cement, landscape edging.

Black market? she wrote. But that made no sense, given what was there.

Skimmed? Quite possibly.

Stolen? Annie circled this word. It would be just like Karl Kramer to steal from other contractors if he thought they were cutting in on his business. After all, last summer Karl arranged for someone to knock Rufus unconscious and then mutilated brand-new cabinetry Rufus was about to install.

"He's still up to his old tricks," she said aloud as she threw down her pen.

The sympathy she had been feeling for Karl Kramer over the last week dissipated in an instant. Maybe he got what he deserved after all. But what would happen to all the stolen goods now? Karl Kramer could still get away with his shenanigans.

Annie went upstairs and put on running shoes. What would she do for exercise, she wondered, when she adopted Amish dress all the time and could no longer wear running shorts and tennis shoes?

Rufus doubted it could be good for Karl to

457

be this worked up. Perhaps they should have made sure a visiting nurse would be in the house when they brought this news to Karl. Rufus had heard that someone came every other day to check on Karl, and that his ex-wife even stopped by to help change dressings.

Karl winced in pain as he spread his fingers in haste. "I want the names of all those boys. Don't even think about trying to protect any of them."

"We don't seek protection," Rufus said. "The boys know what they did was wrong."

"Even Carter understands he got mixed up in something he shouldn't have," Tom added.

"Write down their names, and the names of their parents. This will be a matter for the sheriff's office. I intend to pursue the case to the fullest extent of the law."

"Of course that is your prerogative," Tom said. "We have not hidden this from the sheriff. Rufus and I spoke to him Saturday night and again this morning."

"Then why hasn't he arrested the whole lot?" Karl demanded.

"The boys say they never meant to hurt anyone. That part was accidental, and frightened them into silence. The real point is that the sheriff has very little physical

evidence."

"He has their confessions!"

"He is making a point to talk to all the boys today to take their statements," Tom said. "But he told us this morning that his officers did not get any useful footprints or tire tracks from the scene. Of course there are no fingerprints."

"Get to the point, Tom," Karl barked.

Tom raised a shoulder and squeezed it against his neck. "He's not sure he could make a case."

"That's up to the district attorney's office."

"Of course it is. But the court will appoint a separate attorney for each boy," Tom said. "The lawyers will jump on the lack of physical evidence and the contradictory statements from the boys about who was doing what. The confessions likely will be thrown out as coerced."

"Since when did you take up the practice of law?"

"I'm just telling you what the sheriff said."

"The sheriff is not the district attorney." Karl glowered across the room. "Why are you really here?"

Rufus glanced at Tom. "For just what we said — forgiveness."

■ ■ ■ ■

Annie's run took her to the edge of a field where a tent of plastic sheeting sheltered assorted contractor supplies. From the cover of trees, Annie watched a pickup truck back up to the shelter. The driver got out, released the tailgate, and began unloading.

Annie crept closer while he had his back turned, ducking behind a set of boulders. The man wore a hard hat, and Annie recognized his bulk. He was the same man she encountered the day she discovered this stash. She had gotten past him that day, and she would get past him again.

Better yet, she would not even try to get past him. No doubt he was a wealth of valuable information if she could pry it out of him. Annie retraced her steps into the trees, mussed her hair a bit more, and set off at a controlled jog. She cut right across the field and came to a stop at the back of the truck. Her breathing sounded heavier than it really was.

"Hello!" she called to the man. Close up, she could see he was transferring one-hundred-pound bags of sand as easily as if they were paper plates stacked and ready for the trash.

He paused and examined her. "I told you before to stay away from here."

"I know. But when I run past here I can't help being curious about what it is. Kind of a strange place to stockpile supplies, if you ask me."

"Who asked you?"

"Well, no one. Good point. I guess I just have natural curiosity."

"Curiosity killed the cat." He resumed moving sandbags.

Annie determined to smile. "I hear all this stuff belongs to Kramer Construction."

"Not exactly." The man's rhythm of moving sandbags remained steady.

Aha! It *was* stolen! "That's just what people say," she said.

"People should mind their own business."

"Still, it's a curious thing."

"Lady, do you have a direct question you're festering to ask?"

"Would you answer a direct question?"

"Don't think that counts as direct."

Annie pressed her lips together. She would only have one chance to ask the right question.

Her phone sang a song, making her jump. She had promised her mother she would leave it on for a few days so her parents could reach her. This was a local number,

though. She turned her back to Hard Hat Guy to answer.

"Hello?"

"Annie, it's Tom Reynolds. I just wanted to apologize one more time for what Carter did. He should never have kept your phone."

"I know. And I think he knows. Apology accepted." She glanced over her shoulder at Hard Hat Guy. The truck bed was empty, and he slammed the tailgate closed.

"I'll make sure he makes restitution."

"Thanks, Tom. I believe Carter got in over his head. I'm sure I can work through it with him." Hard Hat Guy disappeared within the plastic sheeting, taking one sandbag with him.

"Still, he needs to learn that his bad judgment has consequences. Karl is not about to let him off the hook."

"Are you out at Karl's now?"

"In my truck. Rufus is still inside. I think he hoped to make one last plea for mercy."

"I'd like to talk more later, Tom, if that's all right."

"Sure. We'll be talking a lot, I suppose."

Annie clicked the phone closed and turned around. Hard Hat Guy was nowhere in sight. She stepped toward the opening where he must have gone in. With her hand pushing back the plastic sheeting, she

glanced back over her shoulder. Whatever she did, she would have to explain her choice to Rufus. She was pretty sure she knew what he would say. And it would not be good.

"They are young boys," Rufus said.

"Young men," Karl countered. "Among your people, practically grown, as I understand it."

"Among our people we seek forgiveness whenever we can. And our way is not to withhold it. Our *Ordnung* commands us to forgive."

"Don't try to convert me, Rufus."

"Of course not. But your forgiveness would free the boys to make honest restitution, rather than merely be punished."

When Karl did not retort immediately, Rufus held his breath.

"What do you have in mind?" Karl finally asked.

"They will apologize to you, of course. In person. Then they can work extra hours on the project. We can teach them something of what it means to be a man by owning up to their responsibilities."

Karl grunted. Rufus waited.

"So you still want to move forward?" Karl

asked. "Together?"

"Of course. Are you willing?"

FORTY-THREE

June 1778

David burst into the barn. "It's over!"

Maria jumped from the stool where she was milking a cow. In the hayloft above her, Jacob pitched down a load then stilled his movement.

"When did you get back?" Jacob asked his brother.

"Just now." David drew his arm across his forehead, wiping a stripe through the grime that darkened his complexion.

"How close did you get to the city limits?"

"I was practically across. But I had delivered the last of my load. It would have looked odd to go in with an empty wagon. The merchants in the city have nothing to sell me."

"Could you really have gone in?" Maria asked.

"The Brits don't seem to care. General Howe resigned his command. Clinton's in

charge and has his eye on New York. No one cares about Philadelphia."

Maria knocked over the stool in her hurry to get out of the stall. The cow mooed.

"You can't leave the cow half-milked," Jacob said. "Finish what you're doing, Maria."

"I have to go to Philadelphia." Maria righted the stool but did not sit down.

"Are you sure it's not a ruse?" Jacob jammed his pitchfork into the hay and threw down another load. "They could be trying to catch the Patriots off guard and trap them in Philadelphia."

David shook his head. "The British are packing up. Moving by sea to New York."

Jacob leaned on the pitchfork. "If Washington follows, we'll be right back where we were two years ago."

"We'll see Sarah again," David said. "We can put *Mamm*'s mind at ease."

"Ethan was there." Maria squatted and yanked on a teat. The cow's mooing intensified. "He had to be."

"Don't take your frustration out on the poor cow," Jacob told Maria. "We'll go to Philadelphia soon enough."

"It's already too late to be soon enough." Maria's hands found their rhythm again.

"The British are settled in well. They can't

clear out in an afternoon. A couple of days won't make a difference at this point."

"What if it were Katie?" Maria said. "Would you still want to wait a couple of days? Ethan could be anywhere."

"Exactly. And it will be easier to look for him when the glut of troops thins out." Jacob stood the pitchfork upright in the hay. "I'll help you finish the milking."

Jacob waited three more days. He made sure the horses he and Maria would ride had fresh shoes for the rugged terrain. Maria and Katie packed saddlebags so full it took both of them to tighten the straps. David rode to surrounding farms asking about fresh news from Philadelphia. Jacob resisted Franklin's pleas that he be allowed to ride to the city, pointing out instead how much work there was for the boy to do in his father's absence.

On the fourth day, Jacob and Maria rode to Philadelphia, unencumbered by a wagon. At the outskirts of the city, they pulled the reins to take cover in a grove of black oak while they assessed the scene before them for themselves.

The armed patrol of soldiers in red coats was gone. Instead, British troops moved about as if under orders, briskly and efficiently, but paying little attention to

Americans wandering in and out of their paths. Weapons hung slack at their sides while they nailed crates shut and loaded wagons headed for British ships sprawling around the harbor across the city.

"We can go in," Maria urged. "Nothing is stopping us."

Jacob nodded. "I'll show you the way to Sarah's house."

They threaded through the streets, one behind the other. Soldiers carried goods out of private homes where officers had taken up residence, with or without the consent of owners. Some shops were boarded up, while others were open with few wares to offer.

"Looks to me like the British helped themselves to everything Philadelphia had to offer," Maria muttered.

"Now they'll go and do the same injustice in New York."

"I have half a mind to divert a wagon or two of food to people who deserve it."

"Let's find Sarah and Ethan first." Jacob nudged his horse to the right, making a turn onto a wide avenue.

Sarah's house looked untended even from down the street. Spring bushes grew wild and unshaped. Flower beds sprouted knee-high weeds. A window on the front of the

house was broken and boarded over.

"We'll go around to the back," Jacob said.

There they found the door to the carriage house wide open, and the only animals within were snarling raccoons.

"She's gone, Jacobli," Maria said.

"Wait here." Jacob dismounted and handed the reins of his horse to Maria. He took his rifle with him as he walked through the covered outdoor summer kitchen and pushed open the back door of Sarah's house. Downstairs, soiled dishes dotted the tables. Upstairs, the beds looked used but in disarray. The walls were cleared of art. Even the knickknacks looked displaced.

What had they done with Sarah?

When Magdalena heard that the British were evacuating Philadelphia, her first thought was whether Patrick, the British sympathizer, might come back.

Her second thought was what might happen if he did.

Nothing, of course. She had done his bidding at sporadic intervals for a few months, captured by his good looks, but she had been *in lieb* with Nathanael in those days. What she did for Patrick was revenge Nathan would never take for himself.

Patrick could be anywhere. Philadelphia.

New York. Dead in an unmarked grave. And it did not matter because Magdalena had no thought to leave the Amish families she had known all her life. She might be restless from time to time, but she belonged with her people.

"Maggie, you're not listening." Her father's voice bore through her reverie.

"I'm sorry, *Daed.*" Magdalena exhaled and focused on her father's face, straining to keep track of the instructions he fired off.

"Jonas will be waiting."

"Jonas?"

Christian tilted his head. "What is wrong with you today, Magdalena?"

"Nothing." Magdalena took the reins from her father's hands and let him help her up to the seat at the front of the buggy. She remembered now. Jonas broke the axle on his buggy three days ago. The blacksmith had not repaired it yet. His only horse was limping as a result of the incident. He needed to borrow the wagon and team, and Magdalena was to deliver them. If Jonas offered to drive her home, she should accept.

Jonas Glick. His wife had died the previous year giving birth. The child perished as well. Magdalena was surprised he had not remarried already. What was he waiting for?

Her own father had married again within weeks after her mother's death, and her parents had been married far longer than the Glicks had been.

Some of Magdalena's friends asked her the same question. What was she waiting for?

In a few minutes, the farm came into view. Jonas Glick leaned against the fence marking his property line. Magdalena liked the relaxed slope of his shoulders. In spite of his loss, he had none of the intensity bottled up in Nathan or the strident passion of Patrick. When he saw her coming and waved, curiosity struck.

They found Sarah, several hours later, in a narrow shop on Market Street. Jacob recognized the plain calico pattern of her dress. His mother had edged a quilt for Katie with the same fabric. Jacob remembered because Katie made a joyous fuss about having brand-new fabric in the quilt, something that had not happened again in the ten years since. Jacob did not care for the shade of green, but he did not dare tell Katie.

It had taken him too long to think of this place. Now Sarah stood in the dim light at the far end, surrounded by boxes, her hair

long ago fallen from its pins in several places.

"Jacob!" Sarah dropped a handful of loose items and hurried across the shop to embrace him.

Then he stepped aside and once again Jacob witnessed the wide eyes of recognition when Sarah saw Maria for the first time in almost three decades.

The sisters locked arms around each other and swayed in tearful embrace.

"Thirty years!" Sarah murmured. "I never stopped wondering about you. We have so much to catch up on."

"We will. I promise." Maria looked up at the hammered tin ceiling. "I remember this place. It was a bookshop. Elizabeth worked here. This is where we first found her."

Jacob smiled. "The family she worked for stayed in touch over the years. Sarah lived with them for a while when she first came to Philadelphia." He gestured around. "They used to sell inks and papers. What happened?"

Sarah shifted a crate. "The British write a lot of documents. They used every drop of ink and every scrap of paper in the place. When I heard the shop had been abandoned I knew we could put it to good use."

Maria plunged a hand in a box and came

up with assorted vials and corks. "Medical and surgical supplies."

"Dearer than gold these days." Sarah took from another box a thick roll of bandages. "Women are tearing their bedding into strips to send to the military hospitals."

"I used to divert goods like this," Maria said, "from British hospitals to ours."

Sarah glanced at Jacob. "As it turns out, a number of boxes have gone missing from British shipments as of late."

Maria grinned.

"What happened to your house, Sarah?" Jacob peeked in another box. "Where is Emerson?"

"The British instituted mandatory quartering for their officers. Emerson and I chose to stay with friends rather than wait on them. They hired their own Loyalist maid."

"I don't think they paid her enough. It appears she has not been there in some time."

"Sarah," Maria said, "I have a husband. He's missing. Jacob says you may know people who could track down my husband."

"Emerson knows a lot of people. We'll start looking as soon as he gets back."

The muscles in her face stretched in an

unfamiliar curve. Magdalena had not done much smiling in the last few years.

But Jonas Glick made her smile.

After the Sunday night singing, he offered to take her home in a small open cart pulled by his half-lame horse. When he spoke, his eyes lit with shy wit that peppered his conversation. Magdalena wondered why she never saw his sense of humor before.

She thought he was a shy farmer, and he was.

She thought he was a grieving widower, and he was.

But he was quick-witted and resourceful and thoughtful. He looked her in the eye when they spoke. Making conversation was never hard. When he brushed her arm in the process of guiding the reins, Magdalena wondered what his embrace would feel like. If he wanted to kiss her, she would let him. Magdalena touched two fingers to her lips just at the thought.

"We've searched for four days and found nothing!" Tears welled in Maria's eyes. "Even my old network has fallen apart."

"We'll find Ethan." Jacob hoped his voice sounded certain. "Just not on this trip."

Maria paused on her horse beside Jacob and looked back at Philadelphia. "It breaks

my heart to leave without him. He's here somewhere!"

"You heard what Emerson said. Many of the young men in town have joined an organized militia unit. He is fairly sure Ethan is marching to New York."

"But he is not certain. What if Emerson is wrong? What if I am giving up too early?"

"Sarah and Emerson will be in touch if they find any clues at all."

"I could go to New York and look for him there."

"And you might be wasting your time. You wrote a message. Emerson will do his best to get it to Ethan when he has reason to believe it will reach him."

"I should stay and help with the war effort. I have a lot of experience sneaking behind the British lines. No one pays attention to a woman. They'll say anything in my presence."

"It's been so good for *Mamm* to have you there. . . ."

"I know. But Ethan is my husband."

"It's time for you to be safe, Maria."

"If Ethan is not safe, I am never safe."

FORTY-FOUR

"Rufus, how long is this board supposed to be?" Luke Stutzman called from twenty feet away, where he stood ready with a measuring tape and handsaw.

Rufus pointed past Luke. "You have to ask Karl."

He watched as the teenager hesitated, turned around, and approached Karl. Across the outdoor space, Rufus could not hear what Karl said, but he saw Luke's head bobbing in understanding. The young man moved to a spot clear of congestion, measured the board, took the pencil from behind his ear to mark it, and got ready to saw off a few inches. Luke was doing well. Amish and *English* had arrived together at this day after all.

Rufus studied the drawings in his hands, pleased with the turnout from the town on a Saturday morning in late June. This was their first workday. Crews were digging

holes for posts that would mark the trail, while others cleared rocks along the route and cut back limbs. Karl's injuries limited his ability to handle tools himself, but he was capable of giving clear instructions. Luke and a few other Amish boys worked under Karl's supervision constructing a small shelter in the open area where hikers might take refuge from rain or get out of the sun. Three picnic tables were under construction, also under Karl's eye.

The work would not be done in one day. Later volunteers would spread pea gravel along the trail to keep mud at bay on the mile and a half loop. The large boulder — Ruth's rock, in Rufus's mind — would stay right where it was. Rufus had two park benches in his workshop awaiting final sanding and staining. Eventually thick boards would frame a children's play area. Steps carved out of the earth at regular intervals would make it easy and safe for people to climb to the top of the rock and enjoy the view. That had been Rufus's intention all along. He and Joel would build a discreet fence to signal where the Beiler land started behind the rock, but they would make no real effort to keep out anyone who wandered across the boundary.

Rufus turned at the sound of a truck and

found Tom and Carter getting out.

"Sorry we're late," Tom said.

"There is still much to do," Rufus said.

"Carter," Tom said, "grab a rake from the back and see if you can help along the trail."

As Carter walked away, Rufus asked, "How is he doing?"

Tom pursed his lips and nodded slowly. "Apologizing to Karl was no piece of cake. Carter was relieved when that was over. Talking to the sheriff scared him half to death. He'll be a lot less naive going forward, I'm sure. But he's not giving me a pile of excuses or pointing the finger elsewhere. He's owned up."

"They all have," Rufus said, "even Joel. He was trying to protect Carter and talk some sense into the Stutzman boys, but apparently Duncan wouldn't let up with his dares. Joel thought it was all talk, but it escalated over a weekend. He realizes he should have spoken up sooner and gotten help. This was not the way to prove he was a man."

Tom nodded in agreement.

"The sheriff told me Duncan tried to deny his involvement."

"Not for very long," Tom said. "He knew he was cornered. His father tells me Duncan won't be leaving the house on his own

for a long time."

Rufus nodded. "But he promised they would both be here later today."

"And Annie?" Tom asked.

"She had a long talk with the bishop about how the Amish handle these things," Rufus said. "She's not quite satisfied on the question of why Karl keeps that stockpile where he does, but she has backed off of trying to prove anything malicious."

"The sheriff's office knows it's there. If there's foul play, they'll find it."

"I hope all they find is goodwill."

"Ha! Rufus Beiler, you do have a way of thinking the best of people." Tom gestured toward Karl and the Amish boys working on the shelter. "I don't know what you said to Karl to get him to agree to this, but it seems to be working."

"We cannot ask others to do what we are not willing to do ourselves. We are building more than a trail together."

Ruth Beiler's blue Prius was parked alongside her parents' barn. She had walked down to the work site along the path she had tamped down with her own steps over the four years she had lived in the family's home outside Westcliffe. Now she was on her knees, with hands gloved, digging out

rocks that could cause someone to stumble and leaving them in a line along the side of the trail. Beside her, Elijah Capp was doing the same thing.

Elijah had not spoken much this morning, but when she knelt to begin working, he chose his place beside her.

"Shouldn't you be doing something more important?" Ruth asked. "You know how to build things."

"I am where I want to be." Elijah gripped the rock Ruth had been digging around and pulled it out of the earth.

She had broken his heart over and over in the last two years, and he kept bringing it back and offering it to her again. Ruth could not help but smile at Elijah now.

As soon as the date was set to begin work, Ruth knew she wanted to help. Lauren had come with her, claiming she had nothing better to do with her weekend, though Ruth knew perfectly well that Lauren had a term paper due on Monday for her summer semester sociology class.

"Your friend works hard," Elijah observed.

"Lauren does not have a slow speed about anything."

Lauren wore her camouflage pants and army boots tied halfway up her shins. She had gravitated toward a task that would al-

low her to hold a power tool, and now she gripped a cordless drill in the middle of one of the groups making picnic tables.

"I like her." Elijah spoke simply without looking up.

Ruth raised her brow. She liked Lauren quite well, too, despite their differences. But her stomach had clenched slightly at the thought of Lauren meeting her parents and Amish neighbors. Lauren did not change anything about herself to try to fit in — she did not soften her military wardrobe, she did not feminize her haircut, she did not seek out the company of women awaiting instructions from men.

Lauren was herself, no matter the setting. That was all Ruth sought for herself as well.

By now Ruth and Elijah had developed a rhythm. With a garden shovel, she loosened the dirt around rocks, and with his muscled hands, Elijah pulled them out. Ruth glanced at their mothers, who had set up a portable table together and made sure the workers had water and snacks. Franey Beiler leaned her head in toward Mrs. Capp in a way that Ruth regarded as conspiratorial.

Ruth went back to digging. She always wanted to be able to come home to visit her family, but even two determined Amish mothers could not change the realities of

Ordnung.

"I will wait, you know," Elijah said.

Ruth had no words.

She only knew that, in this moment, she loved clearing rocks beside Elijah Capp.

Annie unloaded lumber from the back of a pickup and strapped it on a sturdy dolly with wide wheels. With a heave, she shoved the dolly toward the trailhead, where others waited to take the load to locations along the path. Stacks of beams would become stretches of protective railings to guide walkers in safety. She was already sweating through her T-shirt with the effort of the first four trips. When she felt the load lighten in the middle of her fifth trip, she knew it was Rufus whose hands captured the handles of the dolly. Annie stepped aside.

"Thank you," she said.

"You're welcome. They should have tried to get the trucks in closer."

"Too late now. We're almost finished unloading."

"You look overheated. Take a break."

Self-conscious, Annie tugged on her T-shirt to pull it away from her sticky skin. "I'm all right."

"I'll walk you back to the table to make

482

sure you get some water."

Together, they transferred custody of the cart to someone who would drag it along the roughed-out trail.

A new confidence had settled between them in the last few weeks. The interlude Annie witnessed — but did not hear — between her parents and Rufus had wrought transformation. Annie no longer looked at every young Amish woman she met as someone more suited for Rufus than she was. Rather than fear she and Rufus could never have a future together, she began to feel that they would.

She had to complete the baptism classes first. And she had to have one more candid conversation with him to say something he might not want to hear. She did not want to say it, but she had to be complete to be honest.

But today was not that day.

At the Amish worship gathering the next morning, exhaustion was evident, but so was enthusiasm. In a few more weeks, the recreation area would open officially, and neither the Amish nor the *English* would feel they were intruding in each other's space. They would have brought the dream to reality together.

Annie hummed to a hymn that had become familiar to her over the last year, though she still struggled with the High German words. She held the *Ausbund,* seeking the meaning in the words, even if she could not pronounce them smoothly. Rufus had translated this one for her once.

Love will never come to nothing. Everything has an end but love.

Love alone shall stand.

Love clothes us for the wedding feast because God is love and love is God.

Oh love! Oh love! Lead us with your hand and bind us together.

Annie leaned her head to one side, catching Rufus's eye as he sat among the unmarried men across from the women. Though she held her lips captive in their solemn pose, she let her eyes smile.

At the bishop's subtle signal, three teenagers stood to follow him out for the rest of the worship time. Annie stood as well, her stomach fluttering. They stepped quietly together to a rear room in the home of the family hosting worship that Sunday.

Two and a half hours later, Annie emerged from the house into the sunlight. As she expected, men and boys busied themselves with setting up tables, both inside and outside. The smells of baked ham and

potato casseroles and apple pies mingled in the fragrance of June asters and columbine.

Rufus was waiting for her at the end of the driveway. She approached him and let out a nervous breath.

"You did it," he said.

"I did."

"How do you feel?"

"Overwhelmed. I've learned so much about the Amish in the last year, but baptism classes are deep!"

"It's a serious commitment in our church. Everyone wants you to be sure."

"I can tell." Annie put her fingers to her temples. "It's so much to take in."

When Rufus did not speak right away, she raised her gray eyes to the violet blue of his.

"Of course you can change your mind right up until the baptism day," he said, "but most people are sure when they start the classes."

"Don't you think I can be sure about this?"

He let another moment of time beat. "My parents think of you as a daughter, you know."

She nodded.

Another beat. "They've been through a lot."

"I'm not Ruth."

"I know."

"I wouldn't put my own parents through what they must be feeling if I weren't serious."

"Serious is not the same as sure."

"I'm sure."

He nodded and produced a smile. "Then I'm glad. Very glad."

"You'd better get used to seeing me in Amish dresses, because I'm finished with jeans and sweatshirts."

"The wardrobe change might be troublesome for your investigations."

Annie waved her hands in front of her. "I'm finished with all that, too. I don't have to have the answer to every question that crosses my brain. And I can ask for help. You'll see."

She stifled a giggle as he quickly bent and kissed her lips.

A wave passed through her, a quiver of unfinished business. Maybe he had already guessed what she needed to voice. Would that make it any easier to speak it aloud?

Rufus took her hand and led her behind a pine tree. His lips sought hers again, and she gave herself to the kiss.

FORTY-FIVE

October 1778

"I hope you are not trifling with Jonas's affection." Christian sat in the comfortable chair by the fire. Outside the window, he watched the last sliver of light slide down behind his west pasture. "He's a worthy man."

Across the room, Magdalena turned a page of her book. Christian was fairly certain she had been going through the motions of reading all evening. The lamp burned low now, but she made no effort to raise the wick.

"Magdalena." Christian spoke in a tone he normally reserved for his younger children.

She looked up. "I heard what you said, *Daed.*"

"Don't play with him. He's tender enough."

"I'm not playing with Jonas." Magdalena

closed her book firmly and tucked it into the rocker beside her. "I recognize that he has many fine qualities."

"You could do worse."

"I know, *Daed.*"

"He came and spoke to me today. His intentions seem clear."

"He spoke to you?"

Did she really not know the man's feelings? "There is yet time in this wedding season."

Magdalena was silent. Christian supposed she was calculating the weeks. Couples sometimes married even in early December. Was she also thinking of Nathanael? She had not spoken of him in a long time.

Christian liked Nathanael well enough. He seemed to make Magdalena happy — four years ago — and Christian would have been glad to take him into the family. Magdalena's devotion was admirable. For years, she believed Nathan would come to himself, and they would resume planning their life together. But she was twenty-one now.

"Magdalena?" he said softly.

"Yes, *Daed.* I know. It's been four months since Jonas first asked me to ride home after a singing."

Christian nodded. "Well, then, we will see what he says when he sees you next."

He read nothing in his daughter's face as she fingered the ties to her prayer *kapp.*

"I'm ready to turn in," she said. "Good night, *Daed.*"

When she kissed his cheek, he felt habit more than affection.

Jacob looked up and smiled at his wife. She did not often venture into the tannery or the powder mill behind it. With his long polished stick, he stirred the mixture in the kettle hanging over the fire, wondering if he dared add more saltpeter. Bigger explosions in rifles would shoot bullets faster, and this might be a great help in the war effort.

"I hope you're being careful." Katie stretched her neck to inspect the contents of the pot without coming close to it.

Jacob lifted an eyebrow.

"I know," she said, "you're always careful."

He fixed his eyes on hers. "You don't like the tannery any more than my mother does. You must have come down here for something. What's on your mind?"

Katie nodded. "Maria is so discouraged. Maybe you should talk to her."

"I can't think what else to say." Jacob slowed his stirring. "I can't imagine what

she is going through waiting to hear news of Ethan."

"I don't want to imagine what it would be like if you were missing. But I'm worried about her."

"I'll try talking to her again."

"I am afraid she is going to do something rash. You might control your explosions, but I am not as sure about Maria."

Ignoring the chaos of the kitchen on the weekly baking day, Magdalena left her stepmother and her half sisters to the task. The younger ones would grumble about why Magdalena did not have to help, but Babsi would shush them and help them learn the balance of ingredients that kept the family in bread.

Her father's admonition was clear. Because Jonas had spoken to him, Magdalena had to prepare. The next time she saw Jonas could be the conversation that changed her life.

She passed the stables and the old gelding, passed the idle cart she easily could have taken, passed the fence that framed the west pasture. She would walk ten miles today if it took that long to clear her mind. At the end of the lane, Magdalena looked in both directions, considering her options.

Then she turned toward Nathan's land. She wanted to see the cabin one last time.

The miles disappeared under her feet. The cabin was in view, and then she was at the door, and then inside gazing at abandonment. Nathanael's mother had retrieved his bedding years ago, and the bare mattress was rolled to one end of the grid of rope that once supported it. Pots still hung from hooks over the dry, cold hearth, but thick dust turned their color from black to gray. One chipped plate sat in the corner of the trestle table with its rough-hewn planks. Magdalena had once imagined a happy life in this room. Then it had housed her rebellion, her outcry at the war that stole her future.

Suddenly seeing the cabin was not enough. She had to see Nathanael.

She found him in the wheat field on his own land, which he had continued to farm with his father's help. The harvest was in, but Nathanael carried a rake to tidy whatever disturbed him as he paced the rows.

Magdalena waited for him at the end of one row. Halfway down the row he lifted his eyes and saw her, but he did not speed his steps as he once would have.

"Hello, Nathan." When she reached him, Magdalena spoke softly, searching his eyes.

491

"I hear you had a bountiful harvest."

"A very good harvest, yes, considering the war." Nathanael stood the rake upright and leaned on it slightly. "God has shown mercy."

Magdalena twirled the loose string of her *kapp* and swallowed with decision. "We haven't had a talk in a long time."

He met her gaze. "I suppose we have moved past those days."

"Have we?" Magdalena held her breath.

"I want you to be happy, Maggie." Nathanael busied himself with the rake, breaking up clots of earth.

Did he? Then why had he abandoned her all those years ago?

"I know about Jonas," Nathan said.

Magdalena waited. She had not tried to hide Jonas from anyone.

"He will be a fine husband to you."

"You could still be a fine husband to me." Magdalena barely heard her own words.

"You would be a fool to want me."

His words stung.

Nathanael slammed the rake into a tangle of dirt, weeds, and dry remains of wheat. The ground split, shooting chunks in several directions. Magdalena instinctively stepped back.

"Nathan," she said. But he did not look up.

And he probably never would.

Jacob judged it was time to clean up and go in for dinner. The mixture in the kettle was distilled to crystals. The brimstone, tied in a linen rag and soaking in weak lye for the last hour, was ready as well. Over the next two days, he would pound the ingredients into a fine powder. Out of curiosity, he wanted to test the mixture and see for himself how much the greater measure of saltpeter increased the power of a shot. For the time being, he would carefully store the components separately.

Maria stormed into his view. "I have to leave," she said bluntly.

Jacob pressed his lips together and turned his eyes to his sister.

"I cannot sit around the farm any longer." Maria paced toward the tannery then pivoted and returned to the kettle hanging in the makeshift powder mill.

"Be careful," Jacob said. "Don't touch anything until I get the mess cleaned up."

Maria halted. "You're keeping me here against my better judgment, and now you're speaking to me like a child."

"Gunpowder is dangerous at any age."

"Yet you continue to make it."

"Maria, you don't know where Ethan is."

"I'm not going to find him sitting in Berks County."

"Give Sarah more time. She will not give up."

"I could go back to what I used to do, moving behind the British lines."

"You arrived here exhausted and malnourished."

"I am recovered. I could be still useful to the Revolution."

"You are useful here. Since John and David joined the militia, I have three farms and four families to look after, plus the tannery and the mill. I'm sending as much leather and gunpowder to the troops as I can. It's hard to find anyone to hire for the field work. A few Amish men are willing, but I can barely pay them. I need your help to keep everything running or we may have soldiers with no gunpowder."

"That's not enough for me, Jacob. The British have New York. George Washington is worn out. Maybe I could do something to bring this war to an end. It might take only one intercepted message to gain the decisive victory."

"And maybe you could get yourself killed. Where would that leave Ethan?"

"Our three brothers have all taken that risk. You take it every day in your own way with this powder." Maria swiped her fingers in frustration through the fine dust on top of a barrel.

"Maria, don't —" Jacob's warning was too late. The slight gray particles drifted to the fire.

The explosion was small, but it was enough to throw Maria off balance.

Magdalena waited for Jonas to find his words. For a well-spoken man of wit — who had already broached the subject with her father — he was breathing long and hard between phrases.

But he held her hand, and she liked the feel of his calloused palm against hers. The warmth of him. Eyes that gladly met hers. Sitting with him rather than alone.

"Will you have me?" he said at last.

Magdalena took a deep breath. She had practiced the words in her head many times. "If we ask the minister to read the banns at the next service, we can marry before the end of November."

"I do care for you, Magdalena."

She smiled. "I know."

He laid a hand against her cheek, guiding her face toward his. When his lips pressed

against hers, the firmness of his kiss surprised her. Even more surprising was her response — free of hesitation, full of eagerness. Sensation flushed through her, and the years to come flashed through her mind.

Years of being married to Jonas Glick.

Their children filling the house.

Growing old together.

Jonas deepened his kiss. Magdalena welcomed it.

FORTY-SIX

Carter Reynolds stuck his pinky fingers into the corners of his mouth and whistled.

Immediately, the crowd hushed and heads turned toward the open tailgate where Rufus Beiler and Karl Kramer stood side by side in the back of a pickup commandeered for a makeshift platform.

Rufus looked out on the crowd. He guessed that almost half the town's population had made their way out to the recreation site on the Saturday morning in the middle of July — two hundred *English* in one place. Amish families from surrounding parts of Custer County turned out in greater numbers than Rufus anticipated. In their white shirts, black jackets, and rich, dark dresses, they bobbed in and out of clusters of *English*. Everyone was curious to see the finished work, even those who had not participated in building it.

Tom Reynolds knocked his knuckles on

the side of the truck. "You have to say something, Rufus. Now or never. And speak up, for Pete's sake."

Rufus cleared his throat. "Welcome, and thank you for coming. I ask you to pay close attention to Karl Kramer now. He has a few things he'd like to say to get our celebration started."

With that, Rufus jumped down from the truck and drifted to one side of the crowd as Karl shuffled, removed his bright yellow hard hat, and expelled a sigh. Rufus took his place beside Annalise just as Karl began to speak.

He looked down at Annalise, whose eyes were forward. Her hair was the most tidy he had ever seen it, controlled by pins and captured under her white prayer *kapp.* He missed her ponytail and the days when she used to let her hair hang free. But perhaps he would one day again see her thick hay-toned blond hair shaking loose, this time for his pleasure.

Annalise looked up at him and whispered, "Has he got a long speech?"

Rufus raised an eyebrow. "I'm not sure how long it is, but you'll like it."

Her shrug held the shoulders of a new green dress against her neck. A dress she had made herself. "He's certainly surprising

a lot of people lately."

Karl held his hat in front of him with both hands, his injured arms hidden under long sleeves. "I haven't always been the easiest person to get along with. That's the truth, and I know it."

Annalise grimaced and looked around. Rufus nudged her with his elbow, never breaking his somber pose.

Karl cleared his throat — twice. "A lot of you thought this day would never come. Me, working with the Amish. But it's pretty clear what we can accomplish together when we decide to."

Applause broke out, and Karl had to wait for it to subside before continuing.

"Today we're celebrating Phase 1 of turning this area into a place everyone can enjoy."

"Phase 1?" Annalise looked up at Rufus. "I thought the project was finished."

"Just listen," Rufus whispered.

"We have a beautiful nature trail," Karl said, "and a picnic spot, and benches for enjoying the view of the mountains. We even have a stargazing rock, thanks to a few young men who did not quite know what they were doing."

Nervous laughter rippled through the crowd. Karl shifted his stance.

"We framed in a playground, but many of you have heard that we ran out of funds and don't have anything to put there. That's not quite accurate."

"What is he talking about?" Annalise asked.

Rufus covered her hand with his. "Shh. Keep listening."

"Let me show you what Phase 2 is going to be." Karl reached behind him and picked up a roll of blueprints then unfurled it in one hand. "We're going to build the best children's playground in Custer County. I invite you all to come and look closely at the plans. Now, I realize you may still be wondering about the supplies we need. Some of you have wondered about a supply center I have not far from here."

"Is he looking at me?" Annalise whispered.

"Might be." Rufus twisted his lips. "Just listen."

"I have rented that land from the county. I needed a place to keep certain supplies separate from the houses I've been building. 'Why?' you might be asking."

"I certainly am," Annalise muttered.

Karl continued, "I confess my motives were not admirable in the beginning. I figured if I quoted a few dollars high and ended up with extra materials, maybe

someday I could cut some serious corners on a project and increase my profit. After all, nobody makes a perfect estimate every time. Contractors always have extra supplies."

"What is this, true confessions?" Annalise asked.

"Patience, Annalise," Rufus said.

"I have decided these extra supplies will have a more noble purpose," Karl said. "We'll build a playhouse like you wouldn't believe out of the lumber and shingles. The PVC pipes will make a great jungle gym. And get ready for the biggest and best sandbox you've ever seen. Of course we'll have swings and a slide."

Rufus grinned now and looked at Annalise. Her jaw hung slack.

"Did you do this?" she asked.

"I read him the story of Zacchaeus from the Bible," Rufus said. "The rest was up to God."

"How long have you known?" Annalise asked.

"Not long. You were asking questions. Luke was asking questions. But every contractor has leftover supplies at one point or another, and it's a good guess customers don't want that stuff lying around their

brand-new houses, even if they did pay for it."

"But this idea for the playground?" Annalise asked.

"That came from Karl."

Annalise looked down at her hands laced together. "And that might never have happened if I had written a blank check for the project."

"Many things require much patience."

"Thank you for being patient with me."

She lifted her face again, and it looked perfect under the *kapp.*

Annie pressed her lips together. Around her, the crowd was shifting as some moved closer to see Karl's plans for the playground and others returned to enjoying the features of the recreation area.

"Rufus," she said, "can we go for a walk?"

"Do you want to try out the trail?" he asked.

Annie shook her head. "No. I want to talk. Privately."

"All right," Rufus said, "let's walk down toward the road."

Annie turned to follow him, catching her foot on the hem of her dress. She would have to turn up the hem on this dress to wear it regularly. A year ago she never would

have thought of doing that herself. She would have taken the garment to a dressmaker or, at the very least, her mother. Or, more likely, she simply would have stopped wearing it and bought something new. Much had changed in a year.

Once they were free of the crowd, Rufus let Annalise step in front of him as they made their way down the hill toward the road. Her form, even under the drape of an Amish dress, enchanted him. The way she held her shoulders. Her slender neck rising from the collarless garment. Her certain steps that made her skirt swish more than she realized. From a step or two behind her, he could feast without making her self-conscious.

How beautiful she is, he thought. How easily he could let himself imagine a future together. She would let down her hair and he could freely revel in the wonder of her loveliness. Someday their own children could romp on the playground that Karl proposed to erect, while he and Annalise sat on a bench he had crafted.

He reached for her hand, squeezing it as he fell in step beside her.

At the road, Annie inhaled heavily and let it out in controlled measures. This would not

be an easy conversation. She hoped she could form her words more smoothly if they were walking and not looking at each other.

"Rufus," she said, "I made some assumptions about Karl Kramer that were not accurate."

"Many people did." His answer was mild, and she knew he had no sense of what she proposed to talk about.

"He did some bad things in the past. Last year, when he hurt you and you ended up in the hospital —"

"We don't know for sure that was Karl."

"Well, he scared the living daylights out of me one time." Annie pressed on. "All this spring, ever since I discovered that stash of supplies, I've thought the worst of Karl Kramer. I confess even I had my doubts when you said you wanted to work with him."

"Annalise," Rufus said, "I sense you are working up to something. What is it you feel you must say?"

Annie kicked the dirt. "Karl Kramer is the last person I would think could ever make me examine myself. But all this business has made me realize I've been judging him based on his past, and now it looks like he wants to be something different in the future."

"We all have pasts," Rufus said. "We carry

them with us into the future."

Annie swallowed. "I don't want to carry my past into the future . . . into *our* future. I don't want to have secrets that might disappoint you later, when you find out."

Rufus paused in the road and turned her to look at him — just what she had hoped to avoid. "We are plain people, Annalise. You can speak plainly to me."

"I love you, Rufus," she said.

"I know. I love you, too."

She lowered her eyes to the ground. "If we marry, I want our marriage to be everything you've ever dreamed of, everything you've been waiting for."

"Annalise, what is on your heart?"

"I've . . . not been pure." She could not look at him as she said these things. "I wasn't going to church much in those days. I suppose I put my faith in a box off to the side. Jesus didn't have much to do with certain choices. I had a boyfriend in college, and we . . . we should not have, but we did."

"I see," Rufus said quietly.

Annie swallowed hard again and blew out her breath. "That's not all. I went to a technology convention once and had what the *English* would call a one-night stand. I don't think I ever even knew his last name.

I have never been proud of that. I've hated myself for it." She tensed her arms and balled her fists. "Even now, I hate remembering it."

"Annalise —"

"Please, let me finish." She moistened her lips. "Last summer, when we met, I was running from my intellectual property attorney because he betrayed me and was trying to steal my business."

"I remember."

"He was also my boyfriend, and he often stayed the night. At some level, I knew it was wrong, but everybody was doing it. The box my faith was in was up on a shelf by then."

Rufus was silent, and Annie lifted her eyes to his at last.

"I don't know what assumptions you've had about my past," she added. "But I wanted you to know the truth. My faith is off the shelf now. I want to follow Jesus and be a new creation. But I can't change the past."

Those violet-blue eyes bore into her.

"If you'd rather find an Amish woman who has always had strong faith," Annie said, "I understand. You probably want someone who hasn't . . . I don't want to be in your way." Annie laughed nervously. "In

case you haven't noticed, you're what the *English* would call a great catch. You could have any Amish woman you wanted."

Say you want me. Say you want me. Say you want me.

Rufus turned his head at the sound of his name, and Annie startled. Karl Kramer appeared from around a clump of bushes at the side of the road. How long had he been there? Annie wondered.

"Rufus, we can't have this party without you," Karl said. "People are asking for you."

"I'll be right there."

"You'd better be." Karl turned and began to climb the hill.

Voices and children's squeals wafted down. Annie realized she was holding her breath.

"Annalise," Rufus said, glancing up the hill.

She could see in his eyes that he wanted to say more. Dread rose up. "You'd better go," she said softly.

On the way up the hill he did not hold her hand. A thickness came over her chest, squeezing her throat.

Forty-Seven

June 1780

Jacob climbed the hill in the afternoon sun hoping he would not regret leaving his horse behind. At a brisk clip, the familiar walk from his home to the big house took barely twenty minutes.

While Maria was staying at the big house, Jacob felt less pressure to check on his mother frequently. After the gunpowder explosion threw Maria against the tannery six months ago she had no choice but to remain in Berks County while she waited for the leg to heal. Jacob had heard the bone snap. A slight limp now reminded Maria of one careless gesture, but her determination was undeterred. But Maria was gone now, and Jacob was never sure what he would find when he arrived at the clearing his parents had carved out forty years ago. His mother had not been on a horse in years, but he kept one stabled near her house just

in case someone else might need it.

Maria agreed to stay with Sarah in Philadelphia, rather than chase the front lines of battle. At least there she could seek out the remnants of her own old network of subterfuge and perhaps uncover word of her missing husband.

No encouraging information had come through yet, but Jacob understood why Maria held on to hope. He had not heard from any of his brothers in almost a year. The most he could do was follow news of the battles and suppose that Joseph, John, and David were enmeshed in the fighting or working the supply lines. Jacob still manufactured gunpowder when he could find the saltpeter to keep the mill going. If he could get a load to Philadelphia, Sarah seemed to be able to feed it into channels effectively and sometimes even produce a fair price for it. He found comfort in imagining his own brothers loading their muskets with powder from his mill.

His mother was in the garden. He and Franklin helped her with the planting eight weeks ago. No doubt she was inspecting the shoots that carried the promise of bushels of vegetables. She looked unsteady to Jacob — more unsteady every day. She stumbled, and his heart lurched. He was

509

still yards away.

Elizabeth fell. Jacob broke into a sprint.

"Mamm!" Jacob had his arms under her before she could sink into the soft soil.

Hours later, while his mother rested in her own bed, Jacob and Katie murmured in the kitchen.

"She should not be on her own. She should come stay with us." Katie put her hand on top of Jacob's as they sat at the table where he had eaten the meals of his boyhood.

"She has lived in this clearing since she married. She will not have it any other way."

Katie nodded. "I'll talk to Joseph's wife, and John's as well. We can all drop by more often. Some of the grandchildren are old enough to help, too."

Jacob exhaled. "I wish my brothers could make it home, even for a visit. She has not been the same since David and John decided to enlist."

"Age and heartbreak are not a productive combination."

Jacob disentangled his fingers from Katie's. "I can at least send a message to Christian, and we should let Sarah and Maria know."

Katie straightened. "What are you saying?"

"She's weaker all the time. We cannot deceive ourselves about what is coming."

"What does it say, *Daed*?"

Christian handed the letter to Magdalena, who scanned it quickly.

Magdalena held the page with thumb and forefinger on each side. "Elizabeth is failing. Jacob says she hardly gets out of bed anymore." Elizabeth was the one who gave Magdalena her first reading lesson using an old primer of Maria's.

Anxiety filled Christian's chest, the pressure building until he lifted his shoulders in three quick breaths.

"Daed?"

"I'm all right," he said. He could not manage more words at that moment.

Elizabeth Kallen had come into their lives through the will of his widowed father. She was not Amish and had no thought to become Amish. For years, Christian held that against her. But Christian could not imagine his boyhood without her. She had opened her heart to five motherless children. Never had she suggested he try the ways of the *English*. Except for not being baptized and joining the church — and the colorful fabrics she dressed Sarah in — Elizabeth

lived as plain as any of their Amish neighbors.

Christian was only eight when his own mother died. The truth was he had far more memories of Elizabeth caring for him in maternal ways than he did of Verona Yoder Byler. He was not yet prepared to mourn Elizabeth Kallen Byler, but if Jacob's note was an accurate assessment, he had little time to ready himself for the coming reality.

"Are you going to go see her?" Magdalena asked.

"I suspect I will be sorry if I do not." Christian lowered himself into a chair. "She was always so kind."

"May I come with you?"

Christian was at a loss to know what to do with this stubborn daughter. Magdalena should have been married six months or more by now. She ought to have been busy on Jonas Glick's farm, making the place her home, perhaps waiting for a child to quicken within her.

Instead she had called off her engagement. If she could not be wife to Nathanael Buerki, she said, she would be no wife at all. Christian could barely bring himself to look Jonas Glick in the face. What was he supposed to do with a daughter unwilling to become a wife?

When Christian spoke to Babsi later that evening, she confessed she suspected she was with child again. A wagon ride over through the countryside with a passel of children had no appeal. The next day he rode out to the farms where his older sisters thrived. Although they burst into tears at the news of Elizabeth's decline, both had family pressures that would make the trip with him impossible.

"All right," Christian said that night to Magdalena, "if you still want to go, we'll leave in the morning."

They took a small wagon and a team, rather than just two mounts. Her father had seemed to want to fill the wagon with gifts but in the end settled for a dozen jugs of apple cider. He said he remembered that Elizabeth had always liked cider. *Daed* would not let Magdalena drive, however. So she opted to spend part of the journey drowsing in sun-drenched hay in the wagon's bed with the jugs.

When they crested the final hill before the Irish Creek settlement, *Daed* halted the team. Magdalena peered at the view, searching her mind for the memories of the little girl she had been on Irish Creek. She watched her father now as his face creased

513

in longing and memory as well. He finally raised the reins again, and the team lumbered down the soft slope.

At the back door, her father knocked softly, and a moment later, Katie opened the door. Behind her, Maria and Sarah stood up from the table.

Jacob was out in the barn. Magdalena followed her *daed* into Elizabeth's bedroom and stood quietly while he watched her labored breathing.

"I need to go find Jacob," he said softly. "Will you stay with her? If she wakes, she should not be alone."

Magdalena nodded and settled into a rocker where she could watch Elizabeth. A few minutes later, Maria slipped into the room.

Magdalena stifled a sigh at the sight of the Patriot spy. Why had she even wanted to come on this trip? Her *onkel* made gunpowder, and her aunts spied on the British. She should have realized she was walking into a den of the enemy.

She bit her lip. She was not supposed to have enemies. No one knew what she had done for Patrick. And she was not sorry.

"I heard you were getting married," Maria said, her voice low and even and soothing. "Then I heard that you did not."

"He was a good man, but not the right man." Magdalena made no effort to explain that Nathanael was the right man but she could never have him.

"Then you made the right decision," Maria said.

Magdalena lifted her eyebrows slightly. No one at home thought she made the right decision.

"My family would not have understood the husband I chose," Maria said, "but I have no regret. I'm only sorry that we have been separated for two years because of this war."

Magdalena said nothing, but her throat thickened.

"Is there someone else who is the right man?" Maria asked.

Magdalena nodded. "The war has taken him away from me as well."

Maria nodded. "Then you know my heart."

They settled into silence, Magdalena considering her aunt's words. Oddly, Maria was the one who understood her best.

Elizabeth's breath grew jagged, and Maria and Magdalena leaned forward in tandem.

"Does she do that often?" Magdalena asked.

Maria shook her head. "This is different. I

think you should go get your father and Jacob."

"*Daed* hoped to see her awake."

Maria pulled her lips back in a grimace. "Go get them, Magdalena. Look in the barn or the stables."

"Someone has to be with her all the time," Jacob told Christian. "Ever since she fell in the garden, we've been watching her, but every day she grew weaker."

"You've cared for her well all these years, Jacob."

"I could never approach how well she cared for all of us." Jacob rubbed his temples with both hands.

"I hope to tell her how grateful I am for the early years. I should have done it long ago instead of harboring judgment. I was a grown man with a family of my own before I could see what *Daed* saw when he married her. She never spoke against the Amish and always let me be the man I was destined to be."

A knock made them both turn to look behind them at the stable door. Magdalena stepped in. Jacob was struck afresh with how much she resembled Maria.

"Maria says you should come," Magdalena said softly.

"Elizabeth?" Christian said. Jacob watched the color drain from his brother's face.

"Just come."

FORTY-EIGHT

October 1781

"Will you give up gunpowder now?"

Jacob looked at the upturned face of his wife as she reclined in their bed. Her hands rested on the familiar swell of her midsection.

"The war will end soon," Katie said. "Cornwallis surrendered. It's only a matter of time before the British come to terms with their defeat."

"That's all true." Jacob sat on the side of the bed and yanked off one boot. "But soldiers are not the only ones who need gunpowder. Farmers need it for blasting rock out of new fields. Hunters need ammunition for their rifles. It may still be a profitable business."

"At least you can sell it freely instead of sneaking around."

Jacob removed his other boot then sprawled across the bed in his clothes.

Squalling from the loft above them made him sigh.

"It's Lisbetli," Katie said. "She's been fussy all day. She will settle down on her own."

"But if she wakes up the others, we'll have a riot on our hands." He put his hand on her belly. "Where are we going to put this babe once he doesn't need to be with you all night?"

"We always seem to manage."

"Maybe we should move to the big house." The house at the top of the hill stood empty since Elizabeth's death. But it had once housed ten children. Jacob well remembered the spacious upstairs bedrooms.

"Or," Katie said in a tone that made Jacob catch her eyes, "we could move to North Carolina."

"North Carolina?"

"We've talked about it since before we were married. David wants to do it. Then your father died and we did not want to leave your mother. Then the war started. . . ."

"And now the war is over and *Mamm* is gone," Jacob said.

At fifty-two years of age, Christian Byler was content to leave the work of converting

519

church benches into tables for a meal to younger men. In another month, he and Babsi would host worship and the meal that followed. Today, he stayed out of the way, huddling with a group of older men at one end of the Stutzmans' wide porch. When their conversation drifted to news of the war's end, though, Christian scowled.

"It makes no difference to us," he said. "You know this. We live apart and do not concern ourselves with matters of the *English.*"

Christian saw no purpose in speculating on what changes a new American government might bring, but the faces of his friends told him they were not finished with the topic.

"They might well enact new laws and impose them on us," Joseph Stehnli said.

"There are bound to be taxes," Levi Lapp said. "The new government already owes huge sums to private investors who funded the war."

"So we'll pay our taxes but have nothing to do with it." Christian threw up his hands and left the group.

He crossed the porch and descended the stairs. On the ground, he balanced himself on the railing and closed his eyes briefly. He should not have let his hunger cause him to

speak cross words. Turning, he looked up the stairs and into the house. The young men were nearly finished. Women were already putting food on some of the tables.

Christian cocked his head at the sight of Nathanael Buerki laying a board to form the last of the tables.

Nathanael was laughing. He had never stopped coming to church, but Christian had not seen Nathan smile or laugh in years.

Christian collected his plate of food and sat on the men's side of the room. He expected other family heads would gather around him, as they often did, but Nathanael was the first to take his seat across from Christian. He spoke little, which did not surprise Christian, but Christian did catch Nathanael smiling at some of the banter around him.

But more than anything, Christian saw where Nathan's eyes drifted.

To the women's side of the room.

To Magdalena.

He seemed to follow her every movement, causing Christian to do the same. She had become a lovely woman, even if she had refused to marry.

Nathanael's bass voice startled Christian. "Brother Byler, I wonder if Magdalena is going to the singing tonight."

Christian broke a piece of bread before answering. "She seldom goes. She is mindful of her age, I think." Since she had decided not to marry, she saw little purpose in the singings.

The light in Nathanael's eyes flickered. Before it sputtered out, Christian said, "Perhaps if she had an invitation . . ."

Nathanael nodded and turned his eyes again to Magdalena.

Jacob stood at the top of the hill on the fine Sunday afternoon. He was born on this land. All his children were born on this land — so far. As soon as Katie said the words aloud, they both knew they wanted to go. The new babe could be born in North Carolina.

The land was rich with much to offer. Irish Creek ran right through it. Over the years more than a hundred acres were cleared for farming, and dozens more awaited the ambitious effort of taming forest. His tannery was well-positioned, and the vats were large. Houses, barns, stables, gardens, outbuildings. Yes, the land would find appeal to many prospective buyers. But this land had been the dream his father carried from Europe close to half a century ago. Jacob's dream was North Carolina.

If the land sold quickly, they might yet move to North Carolina before the year was out. As long as they could begin the journey before a blinding snow, they could creep south away from the threat of severe weather that might bind them for the winter.

He would find land on the coast and they could drink in the ocean's beauty whenever they wished, with its spray misting across their faces. Or he would find land with saltpeter hidden under its undulating beauty and have a sure supply of the key ingredient for his powder.

First, Jacob had to wait and see if any of his brothers would straggle home from the still dismantling war. David might still want to move to North Carolina with them. But Jacob could not abandon the families of Joseph and John before their return. Joseph had made captain not long ago, so he might yet have responsibilities to discharge. Their wives had received no official notifications. If the brothers were at the final battle at Yorktown, though, painful news might still come.

With a deep breath, Jacob braced himself for the choices all the Byler brothers might make in the coming weeks.

Magdalena felt his eyes on her. Seven years

ago he followed her movements in the same way, making her stomach quiver with giddiness. When he first spoke to her, at a singing, she thought she would melt into a puddle.

She was a young woman then, believing in a future. Now she was a spinster. No one had actually used the word yet, but it was not far off. Jonas Glick had been her last chance.

But now Nathan was watching her. When she drifted to one end of the porch with a group of women — all young mothers except her — he drifted to the other end of the porch with a group of men. When she went inside to help clean up after the meal, suddenly he was there to move benches out to the waiting wagon that would take them to their next destination. When she took her little sisters for a walk up the lane to look at the horses in the pasture, Nathanael drifted along behind them.

Finally Magdalena let the little ones run ahead of her. She adjusted her pace to keep them in view but also to let Nathanael close the gap. She paused and leaned against a fence. Though not boasting the blazing heat of the summer, the October sun spilled its brilliance across the pasture. Hues of green flickered under the hooves of dozens of

horses. Magdalena liked to think the beasts offered their own form of worship of their Creator while their owners were in the house singing the solemn songs of the *Ausbund.*

She kept her eyes forward, squinting into brightness. He moved into her peripheral vision, and her breath caught. He stood for a long moment, and Magdalena thought she was going to have to expel her breath in an undignified way.

Finally he spoke. "Hello, Maggie."

The weight lifted off her chest as she turned to face him. "Hello, Nathan."

They had not spoken since before she disgraced herself by breaking her engagement to Jonas Glick after the banns had been read, just days before the scheduled wedding.

"I wonder if I might pick you up for the singing tonight."

Magdalena laughed nervously and put both hands on the fence in front of her. "Will the others think we are too old?"

"Does it matter?"

He looked so earnest. He had aged since the last time she had looked at him so carefully. But surely so had she.

"I suppose not," she said.

"Gut." He laid a hand on hers at the fence

and lifted his eyes to the horizon. "We don't have to stay long. Perhaps after a song or two we'll leave the younger crowd to themselves and take the long way home."

Magdalena wriggled one hand so that she could hook a finger through his. "I would like that. Very much."

They stood there, side by side, silent. Magdalena labored for even breath. She had prayed so long, for so many years. He had been lost to her, a shell housing what had once been her Nathan. No matter how many times she waited patiently for him to explain what he felt, why he could not love her still, he said nothing. And then she had given up.

And now he might be coming back.

It was only one singing, but he would not have bothered if that were all that was on his heart.

And she might never know why. She did not care why. She cared only that Nathan was coming back to her.

Jacob sorted the stack of envelopes. They did not collect their mail often, but today the Kauffmans dropped it off. He let one envelope after the other fall to the kitchen table, looking for news of family members.

Sarah's handwriting jumped out at last.

"News?" Katie came into the room with one little girl on her hip and another gripping her skirt.

Nodding, Jacob tore open the letter. He scanned it then made himself slow down and read carefully.

"Maria has set out on her own," he said. "With the war ending, she would not wait another day for word of Ethan."

"He could be lost," Katie said quietly. "If he was not mustered into a unit, there might be no record of what happened."

With their two youngest children present, Katie would not speak of death directly. But every contact Maria had, every contact Sarah and Emerson had — the inquiries had led to nothing. The more months that elapsed, the more Jacob thought Ethan must have met his end. The outskirts of a battle. A British unit collecting prisoners. The slip of a horse's foot at the side of a ravine.

Jacob expelled a breath. "I would have liked to meet the man who persuaded Maria to leave us all those years ago."

"You might yet." Katie's eyes grew brighter with tears brimming in them.

"Perhaps. No doubt Maria will persist where others have given up."

"At least she waited until the fighting

ended. It's safer now. She might come back to us again."

Jacob wanted to believe Katie's hope.

FORTY-NINE

The weekend passed. Annie did not see Rufus alone. She had supper Sunday night with the Beilers, and Rufus took her home — with Jacob on the seat between them, prattling about a speckled egg he had found that morning.

On Monday, Rufus stopped in the shop to say he would be busy for a few days preparing to take some furniture to the Amish store in Colorado Springs.

On Tuesday, Annie did not hear from Rufus at all.

On Wednesday morning, she put on her purple dress and pedaled to the Beilers', determined to track him down. If he had decided they could not have a future, she just wanted him to tell her straight to her face. When she reached the farm, though, Sophie greeted her on the front porch with the news that Rufus and Tom had loaded three hope chests and two rockers in the

back of Tom's truck to take to the furniture store in Colorado Springs. They left twenty minutes before Annie arrived.

"Come inside anyway," Sophie said. "I am just polishing tables and trying to straighten up. I would love your company."

Annie forced a smile. "Put me to work." She would rather be busy, and Mrs. Weichert was not expecting her in the shop.

"Jacob pulled a drawer out," Sophie said, waving a rag in the direction of a small desk in the corner of the dining room. "Everything fell out. The papers are a jumbled mess. Maybe you can sort them out."

"I'll certainly try." Annie sat at one end of the table with the drawer in front of her. Sophie polished at the other end.

"Looks like letters from Pennsylvania." Annie quickly stacked seven letter-sized envelopes written with the same even hand.

Sophie nodded. "Daniel writes at least once a month. Matthew sometimes sticks a note in too."

Annie had sat at the Beiler table on countless nights while Franey read news from Pennsylvania with smiles leaking out of the creases of her face. Annie found two more letters and added them to the stack. She put the envelopes in chronological order according to the postmark date and fished out

a rubber band to wrap around them. She had fantasized about someday meeting Daniel and Matthew and their wives. Perhaps they would travel to Colorado for Rufus's wedding.

Annie inhaled and let her breath out through her nose. The Beiler brothers might indeed come to see Rufus get married, but she would not be the bride. Rufus's distance over the last four days made that perfectly plain. Still, she would like to hear him say it. He owed her that much.

Demut. Humility. Annie reminded herself that if she were going to be Amish, she could not proudly demand that anyone owed her anything.

The rest of the drawer's contents were assorted pads of writing paper, envelopes, stamps, black pens, and cards. Annie picked up a card made of stiff white paper, a half sheet folded once. The handwriting, in Pennsylvania Dutch, looked feminine.

Rufus's name leaped off the paper.

Rufus pushed the button that lowered the window on the passenger side of Tom's truck and let his right arm dangle outside.

"Can I tell you a secret?" Rufus said.

Tom turned toward him and raised an eyebrow.

"I hardly ever rode in a car when I was little, but I remember one time when we had to go to Philadelphia. I stuck my head out the window, straight out into the wind. My hat blew off and my mother was . . . well, annoyed. But I remember loving that sensation of the air rushing into my face."

Tom laughed softly. "I suppose a buggy doesn't kick up much of a wind."

"No, sir."

"Go ahead," Tom said, "stick your face out."

Rufus shook his head and pulled his arm inside. "Child's play." He put the window up.

"You never let your guard down, do you?" With one hand, Tom pulled the steering wheel left to navigate a turn.

"I'm not sure what you mean. It's ridiculous for a grown man to stick his face out the window."

"Ridiculous," Tom echoed. "As ridiculous as falling for an *English* woman?"

Rufus did not speak. He felt the flush rise in his neck.

"Annie wants you," Tom said. "Tell me you know that."

"Yes, I know that."

"She's changing her life for you."

"No, she's changing for herself."

"Hmm." Tom put both hands on the wheel and straightened himself in the seat. "For a while there, you two seemed to be an item. What happened to change that?"

Rufus turned his gaze to the colorful whir of brush and small trees outside the window.

"You and I have known each other for almost six years," Tom said. "You don't have to tell me for me to know when your mood is changing. You have something on your mind that you're not talking about."

Annalise had told him the truth. She had not been out of his thoughts for the last four days. She was a woman of strength and determination. Telling him the truth had only confirmed that in his mind.

Tom tapped the steering wheel. "I'll stop pestering you with personal questions."

"You challenge me, Tom. Today I needed it."

"Good. Now let's get back to business. Maybe I'll use the interstate this time."

Rufus grinned. "The wind in my face will be stronger that way."

Annalise deserved the truth in return. Rufus resolved to give it to her before the sun set.

"So that's what happened to that card." Sophie put down her polishing rag and took

the card from Annie's hand. "Rufus was looking for this a while back. He's usually so careful with his own things, but somehow this ended up in *Mamm*'s drawer."

"What is it?"

"I don't really know. Somebody Rufus used to know, I think." Sophie pressed the card flat between her palms. "I'm curious, too, but it would be wrong to read it."

"Of course." A woman. A new letter from a woman Rufus used to know. Annie swallowed the jealousy that burned upward from her stomach. They had come so far that she almost believed it could be true. If her honesty made Rufus hesitate, she was glad to find out now.

She still had the rest of the Beilers. And she was not about to give them up. Jacob delighted her with his inquisitiveness. Franey had taken Annie to her heart. Eli's firm gentleness inspired Annie, and Lydia and Sophie received her as a sister.

"I was little," Sophie said idly. "Younger than Jacob. I think it happened right after I turned five."

"What happened right after you turned five?" Annie set aside a couple of pencil stubs to throw away.

"That's just it. I don't know what happened. I only remember that my parents

534

were disappointed with Rufus, which hardly ever happened."

Annie straightened, attentive.

"After that," Sophie said, "Rufus stopped going to the singings."

"And he never married," Annie said softly.

"Well, not yet." One side of Sophie's mouth twisted in a smile as she glanced at Annie. "Now there's you."

Annie stacked three writing pads with the largest on the bottom. It would be up to Rufus to decide what to tell his family when the wedding they had come to expect did not happen. "I'm so glad to know your family, Sophie. You all teach me so much. I hope we'll always be friends."

"Of course we will. Why wouldn't we?" Sophie set the white card down and dipped her rag in furniture polish and scrubbed again. "You're going to be baptized. After you join the church, you and Rufus will be together, and no one can object."

"One thing at a time," Annie said. "I have a feeling the bishop would like my German to be better."

"I'll help you. We can study any afternoon you like."

"Thank you, Sophie."

"We can even start today, if you like."

Annie traced her fingers over the drawer's

neatness. Sophie laid the folded white card on top of the other papers before picking up the drawer.

"Whatever happened in the past doesn't matter," Sophie said. "I judge Rufus by the man he is now, and I'm proud to call him my brother." She put her fingers to her lips. "Oops. *Hochmut.* But it's true. I only hope I find a man like Rufus some day."

"You will," Annie said. "And he'd better deserve you."

"I wouldn't have it any other way." Sophie slid the drawer into its proper space. "And don't you pay any attention to Beth Stutzman."

"What do you mean?"

"She acts like she knows something about Rufus."

"Really?"

"I don't think she does, though. She's just out of sorts because Rufus chose you."

Had he chosen her?

FIFTY

May 1804

"Step back, Johann." Jacob gestured away from the rifle barrel held in place by the vise.

"*Daed,* that's too much gunpowder."

"You sound like your mother," Jacob said. "She's been telling me to be careful for thirty years."

"You should be careful."

Jacob shook his head. Johann, the only Byler child to be born in North Carolina, was twenty-two. He had a solid understanding of gunpowder manufacturing. He had been helping Jacob for years. But he was his mother's son.

Jacob stuffed the barrel, tied a string to the trigger, and stepped back into his son's caution zone. He pulled the string, and the rifle splintered the air.

Jacob laughed heartily as he moved in to reload. "It's getting faster. It's almost ready."

"Almost ready?" Johann challenged. "*Daed,* you're using more saltpeter in the mix, and stuffing more mix into the barrel."

"That's the point. A faster shot will take down a deer that much more quickly, and at greater range."

"Your customers will like that."

Katie appeared behind them, pausing to lean against the stone structure Jacob used for a workshop.

"I'm sorry to bother the two of you," she said, "but I could use some help moving crates of preserves from the cellar up to the kitchen."

"I'll help you."

Johann kissed his mother's cheek, a gesture that always made Jacob smile.

"I'm sorry you had to come all the way down here to ask for help," Jacob said. "I've kept Johann too long."

"It's no problem. The day calls for a walk."

"It's a fine day," Jacob agreed.

Katie turned to go. "Be careful."

Jacob smiled and said, "I love you, too, Katie Byler."

Jacob watched mother and son traverse the gentle slope between his workshop and the house and garden. The years in North Carolina had brought them adventure and prosperity. Johann was born in their new

state — just barely. The older children grew to adulthood, married, and embraced their own adventures, some of them moving west to Tennessee and Missouri. Katie was gray haired, as was he, and less nimble than in their youth. Nevertheless her beauty startled him in ordinary moments. Now she raised one hand and laid it on their tall son's back as she bent her head in to attend his words.

Jacob sifted silky gunpowder through his fingers. This was perhaps the smoothest batch he had ever ground. The saltpeter had crystallized perfectly, the brimstone softened in the lye flawlessly. Perhaps he could stuff in a few more granules than he had only moments ago.

The sound that preceded the blast told him a fraction of a second too late that he had pressed his ambition too far.

Magdalena cradled the babe in her arms. As long as she kept moving, the child slept.

Magdalena's daughter Sally, her firstborn, slept in the house, exhausted from caring for a colicky babe who was happy only while in motion. Constant indulgence would not teach the *boppli* to sleep, but Magdalena claimed a grandmother's privilege. She had walked the miles of Lancaster County since she was young, and now in her midforties,

she did not complain. She still covered miles every day. It was no trouble to carry the tiny girl as she roamed through the brisk afternoon air.

The now contented child molded to Magdalena's chest. This was her first grandchild. Seven years of waiting for Nathan had found fulfillment in seven children and more than two decades together. Magdalena gave thanks every day for the life she had lost hope for.

She expected many more *kinner* would follow, and she intended to savor every moment with each one.

The years with Nathanael were not always bright. When his mind muddled, she kept the children quiet and prayed for patience. As the house filled with *kinner*, though, his heart filled with joy. He never spoke of the years they lost, and Magdalena long ago ceased wondering about them.

On this day, in this place, she held her joy in her arms and watched the child sleep. And that was enough.

Magdalena turned her steps toward her father's farm, where her daughter napped. She did not want to surrender her grandchild any sooner than she must, but the afternoon waned, and the task of preparing a meal at her own hearth awaited.

■ ■ ■ ■

Christian heard the gentle steps on the porch and knew Magdalena had returned from her afternoon walk. He looked up from his book beside the fire as she padded into the room.

"Is Sally still sleeping?" Magdalena's voice was a low coo. The baby waved an arm once but did not wake.

"Soundly." Christian had raised enough children to know how to manage his voice in the presence of a sleeping infant.

"I hate to wake her."

"Let her sleep a few more minutes." Christian gestured to the chair across from him and was glad to see Magdalena settle into it without protest. The marvel she held in her arms was his great-grandchild, and he would not soon tire of watching tiny gestures and the shifting faces of sleep.

"I've brought your mail." Magdalena reached under her shawl and pulled out a bundle of envelopes.

"Anything interesting?" Christian took the packet and began flipping through it.

"I did not peruse. It is your mail."

The child squeaked, and both Christian and Magdalena startled slightly. Christian

lowered his voice further.

"Here's something from your *aunti* Katie."

"*Aunti* Katie? Doesn't *Onkel* Jacob usually write?"

"I haven't heard from him in almost five years." Christian stiffened and slit the envelope. He pulled a single sheath, unfolded it, and read quickly. He gasped. He had not known this particular grief would sit so heavily on his chest, making it impossible to breathe.

"He's gone."

"Gone?"

"Six weeks ago. An accident at his gunpowder mill."

"I'm sorry, *Daed*," Magdalena said softly.

"I am, too." Christian's fingers lost their grip on the sheet of coarse paper, and it fell to the floor. His spine softened, and he slumped in his chair. "Oh, Jacobli."

FIFTY-ONE

Annie pedaled home well before supper-time. She could have stayed — she required neither invitation nor reason to be at the Beilers'. At any moment, Rufus could enter the family home and she would feel the pressure building in her chest while she waited to see if he would speak to her. The vigilance of expecting the worst wore her down, and she wanted to go home.

Annie did not pedal especially hard. When the incline challenged her balance at such a slow speed, she got off and walked the bike up the hill, taking the seat again only when she knew she could coast the rest of the way home as long as she circled the pedals a couple of times every thirty seconds.

Home — her narrow, green-shingled house with irises and daylilies, cornflowers and primroses splashed across the front. Annie leaned the bike against the side of the house, as she always did. Rufus was always

after her to use the kickstand, but it was such a beat-up old bicycle to begin with that she did not see the point of worrying about scratching it. She gently kicked a pedal and watched the mechanism spin, supposing that now that Rufus was keeping his distance she would not have to concern herself with his opinions on her bicycle.

She followed the path of dilapidated concrete steps around to the front of the house and knelt to inspect the flowers. In them she saw the hope she craved. Her bulbs and flowers came from neighbors and Amish friends dividing their bounty. It was too soon to know whether they would survive the winter and burst out of the ground again next spring — green bubbles struggling to burst through earth and un-bend themselves, nascent stems of promised beauty. The billowy hem of her skirt settled in the dirt as she examined bits of green and pink and violet for reassurance of her hope.

Sighing, Annie rose and circled around the house to the vegetable plot in the back. Rufus, Joel, and Jacob had dug the plot and transferred seeds from the starter plants Sophie had grown in the Beiler kitchen. Soon she would have summer squash and swiss chard and green beans. In the fall she

would have sweet corn, potatoes, pumpkin, and winter squash.

And she would be proud of what she had accomplished.

No, not proud. *Demut.*

She would not be ashamed. Perhaps, she thought, that was not the same as being proud. A peaceful, simple life that helped her understand God's ways more clearly was all she wanted. If only she could learn to regard people with kindness and dignity, rather than competition and suspicion.

It was because of Rufus. Even if she did not become his wife, he had left his mark on her, and she would always be grateful for that. He was the one who challenged her to see the world — and her own life — from a new angle. Because of Rufus Beiler, she could not simply go back to Colorado Springs, accept a lucrative offer from Liam-Ryder Industries, and resume a life of determined winning.

Annie swallowed the lump in her throat and looked at her garage. Could it be made over into a small stable for a horse and small buggy? Perhaps it could be fortified, or perhaps it should be torn down and she should start over. She should have asked Rufus's opinion long ago. She still could, Annie reminded herself. Rufus Beiler had

not died; he simply was not choosing her. He could still be her carpenter of choice, starting with building a back porch that did not threaten to collapse every time she stepped on it.

Annie pushed open the back door and went into her house. In the kitchen she pulled open a drawer and pulled out two items, the latest letter from Liam-Ryder Industries with a twenty percent increase in the financial offer, and a business card bearing Randy Sawyer's contact information. She ripped them both to shreds. No matter what Rufus decided, these documents had nothing to do with anything anymore. She would not continue her baptism classes with these temptations hidden in her kitchen.

The knock startled Annie. On her sofa, she roused from dozing and pushed off the light afghan. Licking her lips, she tested her coiled hair to be sure it held its form. The knock came again, sounding insistent this time. Annie leaned forward enough to see out the front window.

Dolly was there, with the buggy. Rufus's buggy.

In two seconds, she was at the door, pulling it open.

"Hello, Rufus."

"Hello, Annalise." He seemed not to know what to do with his hands and finally settled on clasping them together in front of him. "I thought we should talk."

Annie squelched the instinct to ask if he would like to come in. He would decline, as he always did when they were alone. Instead, she closed the door behind her, smoothed her skirt, and sat on the top step. When Rufus lowered his lanky form to sit beside her, her heart lurched into overdrive and she had to force herself to breathe. At least sitting side by side, he could not see the color seeping out of her face.

"I've been thinking about what you told me the other day." Rufus leaned forward, elbows on his knees.

Annie waited. Even if she had wanted to speak, she could not have.

"That took courage," he said. "I've always admired that trait in you."

He had? All this time Annie had thought Rufus regarded her as impetuous and out of control.

"You did not have to say anything. I don't think I ever would have asked."

Annie held her breath.

"There was a young woman," he began, nerves rattling in his timbre, "in Pennsylvania. I was about Joel's age. Everyone

thought we would be the perfect couple. We became adept at finding ways to be alone." He shifted his weight to one foot and then the other. "I am not as pure as you think me to be, either."

"Rufus —"

He held up a hand. "I need to say more."

She nodded, stunned.

"After we had . . . well, we realized we had let our curiosity get the better of us, and that's all it was. My parents were devastated when we told them. Her parents insisted we had to marry. I felt guilty enough that I would have done it, but she refused."

In the silence that engulfed them, Annie found her voice. "Did you care for her at all?"

Slowly he shook his head. "I learned the hard way to be circumspect in all things. To avoid temptation and gossip, I even stopped going to singings."

Annie did the mental math. "But that must have been more than twelve years ago."

He nodded.

"And since then? No one?"

"No one. Ike Stutzman is not the first man with daughters to get ideas, but I did not want to make that mistake again."

"You wouldn't, Rufus," Annie said. "You

understand second chances — you give other people a second chance all the time."

"I had a letter from her a few months ago," Rufus said quietly, looking away. "She never married, either."

The white card. The feminine writing. The way Sophie tactfully took the card from Annie and reminded her she should not read it.

The question blurted out before Annie could stop it. "Does she want to marry you now? After all this time?"

Rufus shook his head. "She just wanted me to know she is happy, just the way she is. She heard that I never married and hoped it was not because of her."

"And was it?"

He shook his head. "I've been waiting to feel about someone the way I feel about you. When I finally felt something . . ."

Annie giggled. "I turned out to be *English*." She tilted her head, and her prayer *kapp* slid off.

Rufus snatched the *kapp* before it hit the sidewalk. "If you had any idea how often I've wanted to kiss you . . ."

Annie chuckled. "Not nearly as many times as I've wanted you to kiss me."

"I don't think of you as *English* anymore." Rufus shuffled his feet. He turned to look

at her. "You are just Annalise, with the sharp mind God gave you and the earnest heart God has been shaping in you this last year."

"You have been the one to show me that heart, Rufus."

"You are beautiful, Annalise Friesen, inside and out. If you'll still have me, I hope and pray we can have many years together."

Annie's face split into a grin. "I still have to be baptized."

He nodded.

"I promise not to run out on my baptism. I *am* going to do this."

"I have no doubt. And then we'll marry. I will do my best to make your parents know this is the best thing for you."

Annie glanced around the quiet street. Dolly nickered and shook a fetlock. Otherwise the neighborhood was clear of observers.

"Do you want to kiss me now?" Annie asked. "Because I really want you to."

"Without regret?"

"Without regret."

She put a hand on his chest and leaned in to him. His arms went around her as his mouth found her lips.

Annie moaned. Now this was the kind of kiss she had been waiting for.

AUTHOR'S NOTE

When I started the Valley of Choice series, I began the journey of imagining the lives of my own ancestors. I have bits and pieces of information about where they lived, what property they owned, when or how they died. On these hooks I hang my story. Jacob Byler, son of pioneer Jakob Beyeler, is my ancestor. When I learned that he died in 1804 in a gunpowder mill explosion, it made all the sense in the world to me that he should be absorbed in making gunpowder for the Revolutionary War. His son Abraham was my grandfather's grandfather.

I find myself taking liberties with the real town of Westcliffe, Colorado, and for that I ask the indulgence of the people of Custer County. The setting of the series has taken on a personality of its own, but that does not mean that the true town is populated by people who are any less fine.

I find the mysterious blend of an imagined

past, a possible present, and a place of so many prospects to be the perfect wrapping to hold my story of people who stand on a line that can change their futures and dare to step over it.

ABOUT THE AUTHOR

Olivia Newport's novels twist through time to find where faith and passions meet. Her husband and two twenty-something children provide welcome distraction from the people stomping through her head on their way into her books. She chases joy in stunning Colorado at the foot of the Rockies, where daylilies grow as tall as she is.

The employees of Thorndike Press hope you have enjoyed this Large Print book. All our Thorndike, Wheeler, and Kennebec Large Print titles are designed for easy reading, and all our books are made to last. Other Thorndike Press Large Print books are available at your library, through selected bookstores, or directly from us.

For information about titles, please call:
  (800) 223-1244

or visit our Web site at:
  http://gale.cengage.com/thorndike

To share your comments, please write:
  Publisher
  Thorndike Press
  10 Water St., Suite 310
  Waterville, ME 04901

11/13

DATE DUE

DEC 2 6 2013	
MAR 1 1 2014	
MAY 0 2 2014	
SEP 1 8 2014	
SEP 2 5 2014	
JUL 1 3 2015	
DEC 3 1 2015	
MAY 1 2 2017	
FEB 2 2 2018	
1-11-20	
	PRINTED IN U.S.A.

In Plain View